EVERGREEN
FALLS

KIMBERLEY FREEMAN

Touchstone
New York   London   Toronto   Sydney   New Delhi

Touchstone
An Imprint of Simon & Schuster, Inc.
1230 Avenue of the Americas
New York, NY 10020

First Touchstone trade paperback edition August 2015

TOUCHSTONE and colophon are registered trademarks of Simon & Schuster, Inc.

For information about special discounts for bulk purchases, please contact Simon & Schuster Special Sales at 1-866-506-1949 or business@simonandschuster.com.

The Simon & Schuster Speakers Bureau can bring authors to your live event. For more information or to book an event, contact the Simon & Schuster Speakers Bureau at 1-866-248-3049 or visit our website at www.simonspeakers.com.

Interior design by Jill Putorti

Manufactured in the United States of America

10   9   8   7   6   5   4   3   2   1

Library of Congress Cataloging-in-Publication Data

Freeman, Kimberley, 1970-
 Evergreen falls : a novel / Kimberly Freeman.—First Touchstone trade paperback edition.
   pages cm
 I. Title.
 PR9619.4.F75E94 2015
 823'.92—dc23

                                                    2015004263

ISBN 978-1-4767-9990-2
ISBN 978-1-4767-9993-3 (ebook)

In memory of Stella Vera
Star of Truth

EVERGREEN FALLS

PROLOGUE

1926

They keep saying "the body" and Flora thinks this might make her scream and never stop. Speaking in whispers that are not quiet enough, as men do, they say it over and over. "We can't have *the body* simply lying in a room here." "If we put *the body* in the bathing pool, then it might appear to be a drowning." "But when they examine *the body* they'll find no water in the lungs." And so on. All the while Flora, locked in the grim prison of her mind, unable to comprehend anything since she discovered the poor, pale remains, shivers against the icy breeze that licks through the open door and stalks the tall eucalypts that line the dark valley.

"If the old man gets wind of this," Tony says, punctuating his observation with a short puff of his cigarette, "he'll slam that bank vault shut and Flora here won't get a thing."

She wants to say she doesn't care about the money, that death has never seemed so vast and present and final than in this moment, standing by the remains of a real person who only yesterday breathed and cried. Her lips move, but no sound emerges.

"What do you want to do, Florrie?" Sweetie asks her.

"No point speaking to her," Tony says, shaking his head in the low light of the hurricane lamp. "She's going to need a few belts of whiskey to snap her out of it. Look, the only thing we're certain about is that people can't know. It must seem to have been an accident. A fall while out walking the bush track."

"In the snow? Will anybody believe that?"

"Ask yourself what this person's reputation has been," he says, and—oh, dear God—he pushes the toe of his patent-leather wing tip gently against the body so that it lifts then sags back onto the floor. "Not really a solid citizen." Tony seems to realize Flora is listening and checks himself. "Apologies, Florrie. I'm just being practical. You have to trust us."

Flora nods, in shock, unable to make sense of the situation.

"How far shall we take it, then?" Sweetie asks.

"As close as we can get to the Falls."

Sweetie nods and reaches down to lift the limp legs in his meaty hands. Flora moves to help, but Tony pushes her away, gently but firmly.

"You wait here. You're no use to us as you are, and it's murderously cold. I don't want two bodies on my hands." He flicks his cigarette butt out the door ahead of him, and it arcs into the snow, a brief ember soon extinguished.

Flora watches them go. They lumber into the dark and the cold, until they become small figures at the boundary of the garden, then disappear down the stone steps that lead into the valley. Rain has begun to fall, fat drops from the swirling night sky landing silently on the snow. She stands at the door, her fingers turning numb, and watches for their return.

The rain will wash their heavy footprints out of the snow, along with the possible track of limp, dead arms that drag between them. But the rain will also wash over the body, a wet shroud, a sodden burial. Flora puts her head in her hands and weeps, for her shock and her disappointment and her loss and for the horrors that are no doubt to come. *Poor Violet*, she says over and over in her mind. *Poor, poor Violet.*

CHAPTER ONE

2014

If I'd had any experience with men, if I wasn't a thirty-year-old virgin working in my first job, I might have known how to speak to Tomas Lindegaard without sounding like a babbling fool.

"The usual?" I said as he approached the counter. "You know, you can sit down and wait for table service. If you like. Or not. I mean, I don't want to boss you."

Tomas smiled, his bright blue eyes crinkling at the corners. "I might surprise you today and order something different," he said.

I laughed, then realized I was laughing too loudly and stopped abruptly.

"Short black," he said.

"But that's what you always . . . oh."

He was smiling again, and I smiled back, intoxicated a moment by him as I always was. Then I saw Mrs. Tait arrive and hurried off to help her. As independent as she wanted to be, she needed help to get herself into a chair with her walking stick and her stiff joints.

"Thank you, my dear," she said as she settled in her seat. "A double-shot latte and a cigarette, please."

It was the same joke she always made. Mrs. Tait had given up smoking thirty years ago, but maintained that she missed it every day, no time more so than while drinking coffee.

"Got it," I said, and made my way back to the counter where Penny had fired up the coffee machine. The sound of steam drowned out the clattering noise of the café and the dull pulse of the music. Tomas had taken his regular table, right in the middle of the room.

Penny looked at me and inclined her head slightly in Tomas's direction, giving me a meaningful smile.

I shrugged. I had no idea whether Tomas was as interested in me as I was in him, despite our daily interactions. He was one of a team of architects working on the refurbishment of the historic Evergreen Spa Hotel, especially flown in from Denmark to design rooms and break my heart. Penny owned the café, a sparkling glass-and-chrome nook at the end of the freshly renovated east wing of the Evergreen Spa. I was certain Tomas would be more interested in her, with her gym-toned body and Spanish genes on her mother's side. Surely a skinny blonde with pale eyebrows couldn't compete.

Penny shoved two saucers at me: one holding Mrs. Tait's latte, the other with Tomas's short black. "Take Mrs. T's first," she advised in a low voice, "then linger, okay? You know how to linger?"

I nodded, delivered Mrs. Tait's latte and then took Tomas his coffee.

"Thanks, Lauren," he said, shaking two sugar packs between thumb and forefinger before dumping the contents in his coffee. "Quiet this morning?"

This was my opportunity to linger. "Yes, though I quite like it when it's busy. You get into a rhythm."

Small talk. Here I was making small talk. Not as hard as I'd thought it would be.

"Would you like to join me for a moment?" Tomas said with a lovely smile.

A prickle of excitement. I glanced back at Penny, who motioned I should. I heard my mobile phone start to ring in my bag under the counter, but I ignored it. Back and forth we went, light topics, slightly deeper topics—he was divorced, no children—eye contact, laughing. Flirting. We were flirting. The thought caught me with a warm rush. I heard my phone again.

Then Penny was at my shoulder. "Sorry, Lauren." She held out my phone, which had just started to ring again. "It says it's your mum and she keeps calling. Might be an emergency."

The three letters MUM flashed on the phone's screen. "I'm sorry," I said to Tomas. "I'd better take this."

"Of course," he said, draining his coffee. "I'd best get going anyway."

I took the phone from Penny and hurried to the corner behind the magazine stand. "Mum?"

"Where were you? I called three times!"

"I'm at work. I can't just drop everything . . ." Then I told myself not to be so harsh with her. "It's hard when I'm at work, that's all. I was serving a customer." I glanced over my shoulder. Tomas was gone. But he'd left something on the table. I made my way over.

"I got worried when you didn't answer. Why are you there so early?"

"The early shift. For people on their way to work." It was a key, attached to a plastic key tag. Written in the window on one side was *Tomas Lindegaard*. I flipped it over and on the other was *Old West Wing*. I went to the door and pushed it open. The street was lined with workmen's vehicles and tall pines. In the distance, a man on a ride-on mower was tidying the footpath. No slow-moving tourist cars crawled for parking spaces near the Falls walk yet. No sign of Tomas.

"I'm sorry. You know how I worry," Mum said.

"Yes, I know how you worry." I pocketed the key in my little black apron and let the door close behind me. Penny was clearing Mrs. Tait's coffee and chatting to her, but otherwise, the café was empty. "Is it urgent?" I said to Mum.

"Not really. It's just . . . Adam's books . . ." The catch in her throat.

"I'll take them," I said, decisively. "Ship them up here."

"You're going to stay, then?"

"Yes, of course." I took a breath, preparing myself for what I knew would come next.

"It's a long way from home."

"It *is* home now."

"I worry, is all . . ."

Worry. That word again.

"I'm fine up here." More than fine. Better than I'd ever been. I was away from my hometown on the coast of Tasmania, living in the Blue Mountains behind Sydney, by myself. Learning how to do things other people discovered as teenagers: pay rent, manage my own laundry, budget for groceries. So much later than I should have.

"It seems wrong for you to be that far away. The house is so empty and . . . are you sure you're okay? I don't want something to . . . go wrong."

Two to three times a day Mum phoned me, and two to three times a day she raised the specter of something "going wrong." It frustrated me so much that my teeth ached, but it also made my heart ache. We weren't an ordinary family. I wasn't an ordinary daughter. Nothing about our circumstances was ordinary.

"I promise you," I said, for the hundredth time, "you don't need to worry about me."

She sighed. "Nobody can promise that."

"I'm going to lose my job if I spend any longer on the phone," I lied. "We're so busy this morning. Send up those books. I could use something to occupy me in the evenings." The evenings were long and empty. The television reception was patchy, Penny was my only friend so far, and I couldn't rely on her to entertain me every night. I'd taken to going to bed early with a cup of tea and a slice of fruitcake, and reading out-of-date celebrity magazines from the back of the rack.

"All right, I will, but—"

"Bye, Mum."

Penny watched as I slid my phone into my bag and got back to work.

"Everything okay?" she asked.

"Always is," I said.

It was only later, much later, that I remembered Tomas's key. I had slung my apron on the bed when I got home, and headed straight for the bath. My granny flat in Evergreen Falls, behind Mrs. Tait's house and five minutes' walk from the café, had a bathroom barely wide enough for me to spread my arms in, but the bath was deep and the window beside it opened onto the enclosed and private courtyard garden. I luxuriated in bubbles for a while, but when I put on a load of laundry I heard something clunk against the inside of the washing machine. As I pulled the key out of my dirty apron, I felt faintly guilty.

I left the key on the kitchen bench while I ate dinner—another frozen microwave meal for one: beef stroganoff this time—and considered it under the overhead light. *Tomas Lindegaard*. Such a lovely surname. Outside the windows, dusk was deepening. The construction site would be deserted now. Even Penny would have flipped the CLOSED sign in the café window. I knew where Tomas was staying while working on this project: I'd seen his rental car outside a cottage with a long, oak-lined driveway four blocks away. My heart thudded a little harder at the thought of knocking on his door.

I changed out of my bathrobe and into a clean T-shirt and jeans, pulled on my shoes, and left the flat.

The evening was warm and soft, the air thick with the smell of pine and eucalypt. I'd moved here at the start of the summer, and three months later, in March, I hadn't suffered through a hot day. The breeze was up and the sky was pale amber streaked with pink clouds. I took the hill up towards the main road, my feet crunching over dropped branches and pine needles.

No car outside Tomas's house. The disappointment gripped me keenly. What had I hoped for? Events of the past meant I had no chance of forming any kind of normal relationship. Though I longed for one with all my heart.

I sighed, turned, and headed home.

But I didn't want to go home. Perhaps he was still at the site, I told myself. I set a course for the Evergreen Spa Hotel.

She was a rambling beauty, sunset colors staining her lichen-spotted stone walls. The grounds stretched a kilometer across, perched on the edge of an escarpment and gazing down over valleys and hills as far as the eye could see. Two towering, century-old pine trees flanked the front entrance, each encircled by a meter-high garden bed that overflowed with weeds and yellow flowers. The hotel had been built in the 1880s, enjoyed its heyday in the early twentieth century, and then fell into disrepair after World War Two, when it was used as a dispatch center for the military. A halfhearted attempt to renovate it in the 1960s had seen the east wing restored sufficiently for weddings and functions. Then that, too, had been boarded up. Last year, the developers had moved in. Tomas had come. Penny had leased the café. I had fled my parents in Tasmania and begged her for a job, serving locals and tourists but mostly site

workers. The east wing of the Evergreen Spa was on track to open later in the year.

But the west wing, the original two-story stone structure with its ornate Italianate arched windows and bracketed cornices: well, hardly anyone had been in there for decades.

And I had the key.

My life to this point had been spent avoiding spontaneous things, all to save my mother's nerves. I'd never climbed trees, I'd never gone around in cars with boys, I'd never flitted off to the beach if friends asked me (when I had friends, which was rarely, because I was no fun to be around). I'd grown up considering everything through the prism of my mother's perspective. She would have hated me inserting the key into the lock and turning it until it snicked. She would have hated me taking that one last look around the deserted site, serenaded by trees that rustled softly and distant traffic on the highway. She would have hated me stepping inside and closing the door behind me, to find myself in darkness. Because she would have hated it, I did it.

The windows had all been boarded over in some dim, distant past, and of course the electricity was not connected, so I pulled my phone out of my back pocket and switched on the torch. It was a narrow, short beam, but it would stop me from tripping over anything. Shining it around, I realized I was in some kind of foyer, with swollen parquetry, high ceilings and peeling cornices, flocked wallpaper whose corners sagged unhappily from stained walls, as well as a dusty broken chandelier that picked up the light from my torch beam and refracted it into a thousand crystalline sparks across the walls. I caught my breath, and in doing so inhaled a lungful of dust that made me cough for thirty seconds without stopping.

I stood there for a long time, in the middle of the foyer, trying to imagine what it had looked like in its prime; what it might look like in a few years when Tomas and his team had refurbished it. I felt a strange sense of privilege, seeing it like this. Raw, untouched, the layers of years still thick around me.

I shone my light about. On one side, a hallway branched off in front of me, on the other, a set of stairs. I didn't trust the stairs to hold me, so I headed down the hallway, past a few empty rooms, and found myself in a large scullery. The floor was lined with uneven tiles, and a giant cast-iron oven dominated one wall. The big square sinks were full of silt. One of the boards was missing, and through the grimy window I saw the underside of an outdoor staircase, across which hung a DANGER, KEEP OUT sign. I felt a distinctly guilty prickle. I knew I should leave.

I made my way back down the hallway and across the foyer to the door, only to find that it wouldn't open. There was no hole for the key on this side, and the handle was missing, leaving only a protruding stalk of metal. I put my phone between my teeth where it could illuminate my guilty feet, and twisted my hands around the stalk with all my might. My hands slipped off red and sore and smelling like old metal.

My heart fluttered as I realized I was locked in and nobody knew I was here. I could call Penny or Mrs. Tait. Or my mother—that idea made me laugh out loud, dispelling my initial alarm. I switched off the torch in my phone to preserve the battery while I thought it through.

But of course, this building was so vast, there would be other ways out. I headed back down the hallway and checked for exits in the empty rooms. The scullery door was boarded shut. Right at the end of the hallway were two doors: one with clear access, the second under the long slope of a staircase. I tried the first, but the

handle wouldn't budge. I inserted the key, and it gave a millimeter and then gave no more. So I tried the second door, and that was my big mistake.

The key slotted in and turned with a wrench, I pushed the door in and met with resistance. So, I pushed harder and—*crash!*

My pulse shot up. The initial crash was followed by a second, and a third, and then thud after thud as whatever I'd shoved the door into collapsed onto the floor. I gingerly switched on my torch and looked into what appeared to be a storeroom, the ceiling only just above head height. Judging by the mess, when I'd pushed the door in, I'd inadvertently knocked a heavy ceramic urn against the leg of an old table. The table leg had given way, and all of the things on it—suitcases, boxes of bric-a-brac, books, lamps, other items I had no hope of identifying—had slid to the floor in a jumble. The urn had survived, but an entire tea set had not.

I was faced with a dilemma: use the rest of my phone battery in lighting the scene of the crime sufficiently to clean up and hide the evidence, or call Penny and tell her what I'd done and suffer the humiliation.

I settled on a third option: clean up quickly, then find Tomas and confess all, and offer to pay for the tea set. Maybe the table. He would think me an idiot, and that would be that. It was a relief, in a way; no more longing for what I couldn't have.

I set my phone against the wall on the floor, to give me enough light to work. The table was beyond redemption, the leg cracked. I gathered the tea-set parts and put them just outside the door. I righted boxes, stacked suitcases, picked up shoehorns, and collected old light fittings and spare doorknobs and jumbled them all away as neatly as I could.

Then I lifted an overturned box and found myself looking at an old gramophone. Corroded clips on three sides and a broken handle told me it had once been portable. As I carefully picked it up I saw that the side had cracked open in the fall. As I set it down on the floor near my phone, the light caught on something white, half hidden in the exposed crack. I poked inside, and pulled out a sheaf of envelopes tied with a discolored velvet ribbon.

I untied the ribbon and leafed through them. None was addressed, but there were clearly contents in all of them. I lifted the flap on the first, and slid out crackling, yellow pages. Handwriting in ink had been made sepia by time.

My darling, what torture it is that I cannot come to you tonight . . .

Love letters. Old love letters. Suddenly my heart swelled. I had stolen a key, broken into a deserted building, and found old love letters. I felt wonderful, heady, alive. *Take that, Mum.* This was just the kind of excitement I had missed in life by being too cautious. *Take that, Dad.* I retied the ribbon. *Take that, Adam.* A sudden barb of guilt cooled my joy. How could I think that? None of what happened had been Adam's fault. He had never wanted to cast such a shadow: nobody on earth would have wanted to cast such a shadow.

I put the bundle of letters by my phone, and did my best to reorganize the storeroom, including propping the broken table against the wall. Then I pocketed the letters in my jacket and left, closing the door behind me. My torch helped me find my way back to the scullery, to the single unboarded window. I leaned across the sink and tried to push up the sash. It gave a little. I climbed onto the bench and stood in the sink, an inch deep in mud, and pushed up with all my might. With a groan the sash rose, the window opened, and I could smell the fresh evening air. I climbed out and closed the window behind me, then headed around the back of the building and through the car park to the street. Night had fallen while I'd been inside, and under the streetlight, kicking mud off my shoes,

I could see that my clothes were covered with dust. As I patted at it ineffectually a car beeped at me from behind, and I turned to see headlights approaching. I stepped off the road onto the damp grass, and the car pulled up beside me. It was Tomas.

"Need a lift?" he said, in his faint accent.

I felt so ashamed I could barely speak. "I . . . look, I need to talk to you about something."

He raised his eyebrows with a hint of a smile. "Hop in, then. We'll go back to my place. I live close by."

Back to his place. I sighed. "Okay." Then I was in his car, the love letters in my pocket, and we didn't talk for the short drive to his cottage.

A security light switched on as we approached the porch. I expected him to ask me what I'd been doing at the Evergreen Spa, but instead he said something about the lovely night, about how much he liked it here in the Blue Mountains, about how different it was to living in Copenhagen; I'm sure I answered, but my brain was racing, trying to figure out how I was going to confess to him what I'd done.

He slung his keys on a sideboard and led me to the kitchen. I slipped off my shoes in case there was still mud on them, and tried to brush off more dust.

"Can I make you something? Tea? Cocoa? I wouldn't dream of making you coffee: you usually make it for me."

"No, I'm fine."

"I'm going to make cocoa. I make it the way my mother did. It's very nice."

I forced a smile. "Okay, then, you've twisted my arm."

"You sit down and tell me what it is you have to talk to me about."

I sat at the kitchen table and watched as he searched for a cast-iron pot, which he put on the stove. While he turned to take milk from the fridge and I couldn't see his face, I said, "You left your key to the west wing at the café today."

"Ah, so that's where it went. I searched my office for it twice."

"I'm really sorry. I put it in my apron and then my mother called and . . . she's very . . . high maintenance."

"It's no matter."

"Do you . . . go into the west wing often?"

He poured the milk into the pot and then came to sit with me while it warmed. "Not often. We're not scheduled to work in there for another six to twelve months."

"I went in." My heartbeat thundered past my ears as I said this. I remembered a time I'd woken Adam from a deep sleep and Mum had roared at me and I felt just like this. In serious trouble.

He smiled. "Naughty girl."

"It gets worse. I couldn't get out. I opened another door and it turned out it was a storeroom and I . . . knocked some things down."

"What things?"

"A lot of things. I broke an old tea set. God, I hope it wasn't an antique."

He was still smiling, which gave me a little comfort.

"I'm so sorry. I'm not usually like this, I promise you. I have led such a straitlaced life. You can't even imagine how straight I've been. I don't know what got into me."

"Curiosity, perhaps?" he said, rising and returning to the stove to stir the milk. "It's all right. No harm done."

"But I broke things."

"The west wing was cleared out long ago. It's probably old bric-a-brac of no value. Certainly nothing irreplaceable. Put it out of your mind."

Relief flooded through me. "You're very kind."

"Did you think I'd wag my finger at you?"

"I wasn't sure."

"I'm just glad you're not hurt. I don't know if you would have been covered by our insurance."

"I stayed away from the stairs."

He busied himself with cocoa, honey, and two enormous cups. "How did you get out?"

"One of the windows in the scullery was unboarded."

"Resourceful girl." He brought the cups and sat down again.

I sipped my cocoa. It was silky and sweet. "Oh, my," I said. "This is wonderful."

"I'll tell Mama you like it next time I talk to her."

I smiled at him, then remembered the letters. "Look," I said, pulling them from my jacket and sliding them across the table. "I found them inside an old portable gramophone."

"What are they?" He carefully untied the ribbon and opened one of the letters. After a moment his eyes met mine with a smile. "Love letters?"

"I think so. I only looked at one."

He cleared his throat. "*My beloved. Today I lay in the sunshine behind the tennis court and in my mind I was with you again as we were last night, and my mouth was filled with the sweet dew of your—*" Tomas laughed. "I can't read this aloud. Too sexy."

My face flushed warmly as he refolded the letter and passed the bundle back to me. "You keep them. But I'd better get my key back from you."

"Are you sure I can keep them?"

"I insist. Read them all and give me a summary of the best ones. See if you can find out who they were from and to. If they were hidden, perhaps the love affair was hidden, too. You may have happened upon a secret."

The thought made me glow a little with excitement. Or perhaps the excitement was from sitting with Tomas at his kitchen table, drinking his mama's cocoa. Happiness.

We chatted. He told me about his mother and I told him—a little—about mine. I wasn't ready to give him my whole life story. Not because it would take too long—I could have written it on the head of a pin—but because I wanted him to get to know the real me first.

Whoever the real me was. I still didn't know.

He offered me another hot cocoa. I dearly wanted to stay, but my mother was due to call at any moment, and I didn't want to talk to her in Tomas's presence, or ignore the call and have her panic again.

"I'd best get away," I said. "But thank you."

"Do you need a lift?"

"No, I don't live far away. I have a flat behind Mrs. Tait's house. You know, the elderly lady who's always at the café?"

"Yes, I do know her. She had me over for tea one afternoon when I first moved to town."

We were at the porch now. Moths banged themselves against the light.

"Well, good night," I said.

"Friday," he blurted suddenly. "Can I take you to dinner?"

My brain took a moment to catch up with my heart, which was already singing *yes* in a grand opera voice. "Friday evening? Yes. Yes, I'd love that."

"Good." He looked relieved. His smile was wide. For me. I found it impossible to believe. "I'll pick you up at six?"

"Yes. That would be . . . well, I'll see you tomorrow morning in the café, won't I?"

"I'll be in Sydney for the next few days. So . . ."

"So . . ." I grinned stupidly. "See you Friday night."

Then I was making my way home in the dark, buzzing with excitement. When my phone rang and I knew it was Mum, I didn't even groan.

CHAPTER TWO

There were eleven love letters in the bundle, each full of a passion so scorching that I had to fan myself to cool down after reading them. Dark clouds had closed in outside, and the steady beat of rain on the tin roof drowned out the music I had put on. One by one, I pored over them, looking for names, dates—anything that would help me place them. All I knew by the time I'd finished was that they were written by a man whose initials were SHB; that the man had a sister who was never named (she was "Sissy" throughout); that they were written in or shortly after 1926 (a quick Internet search for the first "Miss Sydney" winner told me that: apparently she was staying at the hotel at the same time); and that their love affair was definitely forbidden. Oh, and that SHB was borderline obsessed with his lover's "rosy nipples," which received a mention at least once per letter.

I tied the letters with the ribbon and put them on my bedside table, then switched off my lamp and snuggled down. Being in bed on a rainy night was one of my favorite pastimes, which tells you a lot about how few pastimes I'd had.

I lay awake a long time, thinking about Tomas. I closed my eyes and tried to imagine him doing some of the things that SHB had done to his lover. I was not completely without sexual experience: I'd had a few fumbling relationships that didn't get past a second date, and a one-night encounter with a much older man who had taught me things about my body I didn't know it could feel. But no long-term boyfriend, no going "all the way," no getting swept away. How could I? I'd lived with my parents, and if that didn't stop men asking me out, it certainly stopped me saying yes. Every time a relationship became possible I would tell myself, *Just one more year; it can't go on much longer, surely.* Then I'd hate myself for thinking it.

Of course, when I was finally released I barely knew what to do with myself, and grief and guilt weighed me down.

But I liked Tomas. When he was around, I felt shiny, as though something bright beckoned me from just around the corner. I suspected he might make happiness possible.

I went to sleep wondering whether SHB and his lover had been happy, back in 1926.

I arrived home from work the following afternoon to a note pinned on my door. *Boxes delivered to my place for you. Come for them when you can. LT.*

It took me a moment to figure out. Mrs. Tait. I had no idea what her first name was, but now I knew it started with L. She had introduced herself as Mrs. Tait and that's what everybody called her.

I changed out of my work uniform and made my way down the side of the house to Mrs. Tait's front door, and rang the bell.

"Oh, hello, dear," she said, fumbling with the door. "Come on in. You've got some packages."

"They're books, I think," I said, seeing the boxes stacked neatly inside the doorway. "My mum sent them up. She's, ah, clearing out my brother's room." I found myself standing inside an immaculately kept, restored 1930s cottage, painted in pale blue and cream, with sun streaming through the windows. "Wow, your house is beautiful."

"Not really my house. I inherited it from my mother. I came to it by good fortune, not hard work. Would you like tea? I've just boiled the kettle."

"Yes, that would be lovely."

"Is a tea bag all right? I'm afraid I don't stand much on ceremony."

"Perfectly fine. I'm white with one."

"Sit down, I'll be right back."

I sat in a plush lounge chair, and sank into it deeply.

After a few minutes she returned with two mugs, placing one on the side table next to me, then settling on her sofa. Her steel-gray hair was pulled back in a tight bun, and she wore a plain navy shift dress, which made her pale skin seem almost translucent, and her eyes very bright blue.

"That's a lovely color on you," I said.

"I did always love navy," she said. "Not many can wear it."

I smiled. "You wear it very well."

"You should do something about those eyebrows."

"Do you think?"

"Just because they're pale doesn't mean you can't tame them. Go and see Vana on the high street. She'll find them for you." She raised her own eyebrows. I had to admit they were beautifully shaped.

"My mother had no eyebrows at all," she continued, sipping her tea. "Plucked them out completely in 1928 so she could draw them back in. It was the style at the time. Had to draw them in for the rest of her life, and as her hands became less steady . . ." She laughed. "God rest her soul."

"How long ago did she die?" I asked.

"Fifteen years ago."

"She lived here?"

"Oh, no. She never lived here. It was one of her investments. My mother had quite a lot of money, and she worked very hard for it." She shook her head. "I never worked hard enough for her taste. I disappointed her, I think."

In that moment, she seemed not a woman in her eighties but a sad child, and I felt a twinge in my chest for her. "I'm sure that's not the case. She must have loved you."

"Oh, she loved me. But I think she wanted me to be a doctor or lawyer or something special, but I didn't have the brains for it, you see. Ah, well. All in the past now." She smiled, brightly. "You said these books were your brother's? Is he moving up here with you?"

I hesitated over what to say next. Why did I always feel as though it were a secret, something that we couldn't talk about? Perhaps it was the way my mother had kept the world away that had made our lives seem somehow furtive. "He's dead," I said finally. "He died about four months ago."

"I'm so sorry. How old was he?"

"Thirty-five."

She clicked her tongue. "Such a shame at such a young age. An accident?"

"No, he was sick for a long time. It was . . . not unexpected." I sipped my tea, hoping to close down the discussion. "Tell me more about your mother," I said, forcing a smile. "She sounds formidable."

"Yes, that's a good word," she said, glancing over her shoulder at a set of framed photographs on the sideboard. Smiling people in old-fashioned clothes. "When I came along, she decided she wanted me to have a better life than she'd had. Dad was often unwell, so he stayed home with me, and Mum went out to work in a perfumery in Sydney, and worked her way up, then when the business was in trouble she convinced a bank to loan her enough to buy it. I barely saw her: she was at work from dawn until late in the evening. She was a real career woman at a time when women didn't have careers. Made her own fortune."

"Wow. What a wonderful life she had."

"Yes. You'd think so. That's the official version." Her voice was wistful.

"Official version?"

"There was a lot she didn't tell me. There's a lot I still don't know."

"Like what?"

She shrugged off my question. "Dad raised me, and we were very close. She often traveled and we got on without her. I always remember how she smelled when she came home, as though the perfumes she worked with had all seeped a little into her pores. She'd lean over me and press cool lips to my sleeping cheek, and I'd wake just enough to smell her and hear her say she loved me . . . Oh, dear. I'm getting quite teary. It happens these days. I find myself remembering things from so long ago. So long ago."

"It's all right. Cry away."

"Such happy memories, all bright and sharp at the edges. They'll all disappear when I die." She trailed off. "I've said far too much and you must be bored."

"I'm not bored. You should write it all down."

"For whom to read, my dear?"

"Your children?" I suggested, then hoped that she had children and wasn't alone in the world.

She sniffed dismissively. "They wouldn't be interested. They're off living their lives. One in London, one in New York, one in Vancouver. A bunch of high achievers. Not a single grandchild for me between the three of them." She frowned, looking into the bottom of her teacup. "One cup is never enough."

"You need a pot, and some bigger cups."

"Yes, I suppose I do."

I rose, and made to clear away our cups.

"No, no," she said, "don't bother. It will give me something to do. Do you need a hand with those boxes?"

"I can manage them."

"Good," she said. "I was only being polite." Then she laughed at my expression, and her face creased into a thousand lines.

"Come and see me again," she said.

"I certainly will, Mrs. Tait," I replied.

"It's Lizzie," she said, her eyes sparkling.

"I certainly will, Lizzie," I repeated, and I felt as though I had been bestowed with a special honor. Even Penny and Tomas didn't know her first name.

I wasn't the kind of girl to change my outfit seven times before a date, because I had already decided—possibly within seconds of Tomas asking me out—what I would wear. My only nice dress. It was knee length, black, sleeveless, gathered at the waist with a diamanté star. I lived my life in jeans and T-shirts, and this was the one thing I had that made me look like a woman, rather than an asexual teenage slacker. I had no idea what to do with makeup, but Vana at the beauty salon had indeed "found" my eyebrows and tinted my lashes as well. I studied my face as I brushed my hair in the mirror, and decided this was the closest I'd ever been to pretty.

I was, however, ready far too early and perched on my couch for a very long twenty minutes, waiting for Tomas to arrive. My flat was a long way back from the street, so I strained to hear his car's engine or the crunch of his footsteps on the gravel at the side of the house. Poised like a cat. Anxious, running over scenarios in my head, each of them ending in disaster and mortification. In the end, my warning that he was nearby was the *ting-ting* of a text message. *Out front talking to Mrs. T.*

I grabbed my handbag and smoothed my dress down, then headed out of the flat.

Mrs. Tait—Lizzie—was watering her front garden, deep in conversation with Tomas. He wore a dark gray sports jacket over a blue shirt and jeans. He had that wonderful Scandinavian coloring: golden hair, olive skin, blue eyes. But it was more than his looks that had attracted me. There was a kindness about him, a softness around his mouth.

"Hello," I called as I approached.

Lizzie turned and gave me a broad smile. "I hear Tomas is taking you on a date."

I could feel my cheeks grow warm. "Yes, well . . ."

"Good on you both. What glorious children you'd have. Tall and fair-haired and kind-eyed." Then she was laughing at our shuffling discomfort, and I couldn't help but feel fond of her for having such a wicked sense of humor.

"Shall we?" Tomas asked, indicating his car.

"Bye, Lizzie," I said, kissing her powdery cheek.

"Lovely eyebrows," she whispered, before releasing me.

As Tomas and I drove into the long dusk of summer we were quiet a few moments, then he said, "How come you get to call her Lizzie?"

"I spent some time over there yesterday, listening to her tell stories about her mother."

"She must like you."

"I hope so; I like her. There's something about her, isn't there?"

"Yes, as though age hasn't mellowed her at all."

"I think she's quite lonely. She told me her children are all overseas. She's proud of them but misses them, too." I watched the landscape drift by. "I think I'll try to spend more time with her. It's not like I have that much to do."

More quiet. I shifted in my car seat, turned my hands over in front of me, studying them.

"You look nice," he said.

I glanced his way. His eyes were straight ahead on the road, but he was smiling.

"Thanks," I replied. Then, "So do you." My heart was in my mouth. I was *so* inexperienced at this. "Where are we off to?"

"I have reservations at L'Espalier."

"Wow. That's fancy. French food, right?"

"Yes. I hope that's all right."

"Of course." It wasn't all right. I had a delicate stomach. Rich things didn't agree with me. My French was hopeless, so I wouldn't have a clue what I was ordering. My anxiety wound up a notch.

We pulled into a car park a few minutes later and walked up the hill to the restaurant. I was having trouble in my wedge heels, trying not to stomp. *Concentrate. Breathe.* The main street of Evergreen Falls was quiet and dark except for the occasional burst of laughter and light from the eateries that lined the way. I looked longingly at Vintage Star, an unpretentious eatery in the front of an antique shop where I knew I could read the menu and order a good ungarnished steak. But we walked past it and were soon finding our table at L'Espalier.

"Wine?" the waiter asked as he laid my napkin across my lap.

"I'm driving, so I won't drink," Tomas said.

"Yes," I blurted, almost desperately. "Wine, please."

The waiter brandished the wine list and I scanned it, trying to hide my horror at the prices. Was Tomas paying?

"A glass of that one," I said, stabbing at the cheapest white.

"We don't sell that one by the glass."

"We'll have the bottle," Tomas said smoothly. "I might have half a glass with you." He smiled at me across the table, his skin smooth in the candlelight. I smiled back, but it may have been a grimace. I heard my phone ring in my handbag and knew it was Mum, and realized I had forgotten to tell her I wouldn't be home to take her regular call. Well, not forgotten so much as avoided telling her, because she would ask questions and I would either have to lie or tell her I was going on a date with a man, which would prompt her to lecture me again about the dangers of men.

"You're miles away," Tomas said to me.

"Not in a good way, I'm afraid," I said. The phone started to ring again.

"Do you need to answer that?"

"I . . . It's my mother."

"You know that for certain?"

"This is when she always calls me."

"Every Friday?"

Every day. I wasn't going to tell him that. I wasn't going to tell him she also called at least twice—random times—throughout the day.

"Perhaps you'd better take it, then," he said. "I don't mind."

I opened my bag, removed my phone, and switched it off. Tonight, I was going to be an adult. "She'll live," I said, sounding more flippant than I felt.

The waiter returned with a basket of bread and our wine, which I gulped a little too fast. Tomas didn't seem to notice. He asked me questions about my mother and my father; I answered him honestly if not thoroughly. Dad was a science illustrator who ran his own business from home, Mum was a retired social worker who had devoted many years to caring for my sick brother, who had died recently.

"I'm sorry to hear that," he said.

"Yes, it's . . ." I refilled my glass. My head swam a little as I tried to focus on my menu. "I can't read French."

"The dishes are translated in English underneath, see?"

Still the waiter didn't come. The restaurant was busy, noisy, a little hot. We picked at the bread, smiling at each other awkwardly until finally the waiter came for our order. Tomas ordered in perfect French, making me feel even more inadequate.

"How many languages do you speak?" I asked.

"Just English and French."

"And Danish."

"Of course. I'm from Denmark." He shrugged. "I want to hear more about your brother. You must miss him."

Another gulp of wine. "I do, but . . . you know . . ."

"Go on."

I took a deep breath. "When I described my family to you just now . . . well, it probably sounded completely normal, if a little sad. But we kind of aren't normal. Or weren't. Because of Adam."

He smiled gently. "You'd better explain."

Fortified by wine, I tried to get at the nuance of the situation. My brother's illness had lasted sixteen years. From first signs at nineteen, to a lung transplant at twenty-one, to the endless panicked trips to emergency with colds that ordinary people could recover from in a day but could be a death sentence for him, to the various diagnoses of other horrors that the medications wrought upon his body and the related surgeries, to the slow tortured wait for the transplanted lungs to give out. Some people get a good ten years, they told us. Adam got fourteen. All the while we waited, held together by his awful sentence, afraid to go out in the world lest we bring back a germ that would kill him. My mother's brain rewired to see certain death for her offspring everywhere. Her caution was not just for Adam; as the surviving child, I was her only consolation, and she couldn't bear to lose me, too. She kept me in. She begged me to undertake my university degree remotely, and I didn't bother to finish it because I felt so divorced from the experience. She asked me not to go out to work, but instead she employed me to help her with Adam, and he did need a lot of help, a lot of our time. She kept me as close under her watchful eye as she kept her terminally ill son. The four of us, in that house, held close by illness, all hearing the deafening tick of time's passing for sixteen years.

Tomas was a wonderful listener. He knew when to ask questions, when to sit back and let me be silent. His watchful eyes occasionally searched for our waiter, and occasionally alighted on my hand as it went for the wine bottle again. But he didn't stop me and, truly, once I'd started it all came pouring out.

"Wow, I'm really drunk," I said when I was done and Tomas was gazing back at me with empathy. Immediate regret. Why had I told him everything? I was an idiot. "I shouldn't have told you all that," I said.

"I'm glad you did."

"Where is the waiter? I'm really hungry and my stomach feels kind of . . ."

"I think they've forgotten us."

I glanced around the room. It spun a little.

"You don't drink often, I take it?" he asked.

"Hardly ever."

He stood, dropping his napkin on the table. "Come on. I'll take you to my place and make you a sandwich. We need to get something into your stomach, and I don't think anything rich is going to sit well with you."

The waiter dashed after us calling apologies, but Tomas waved dismissively and handed him a fifty-dollar note for the wine.

On the hill down to the car, my body's ability to balance on the wedge heels failed me completely. Tomas caught me, arm around my waist, and guided me to the car. I was aware dimly that the night was going very badly, that I was a drunken mess after four glasses of wine in less than an hour and I had confessed to him that I had lived my adult life like a character out of *Flowers in the Attic*. But all his concern seemed focused on getting me in the car and then on the way home.

"I'm sorry," I said.

"For what?"

"For embarrassing you."

"You haven't embarrassed me."

"For embarrassing me."

He pulled the car to the side of the road and turned to me, reaching for my face with a warm hand. "Lauren, there is no need for anybody to be sorry. Now, I'm taking you to my place, all right? For food. Nothing else."

"Right." *Nothing else?* What did that mean?

The car sped off again. The last blush of sunset on the horizon. Everything seemed to whir and blur around me. I pressed my hands to my forehead.

"Nearly there," he said.

"I'm sorry."

"You're going to have to stop saying that."

Then we were outside his house and he was helping me out of the car. He got me inside. Things got a little woolly for a while, but it seems I had hot tea and a toasted cheese sandwich, and then Tomas was sitting beside me. "Why do you like me?" I said. "You're so wonderful and I'm so . . . me."

"Just drink your tea," he said gently.

"But . . ."

"I like you because there's something very real about you, Lauren. Your heart is in your eyes. I don't know. I'm not good at saying these things."

I finished my tea and sandwich while he watched. He was so gorgeous. I leaned in to try to kiss him, but he backed away and grasped me gently by the shoulders. "No," he said. "Not like this."

He moved to clear away my plate and cup, and I sat alone for a few moments, listening to him in the kitchen.

The next thing I knew I was waking up in grainy morning light, still wearing my dress and heels, under a light blanket on Tomas's couch.

The shame. The horrible, crawling shame. Snatches of the previous night came back to me. Drinking too much, talking too much, falling over too much, trying to kiss Tomas and being rebuffed. I looked at my watch: it was just before five. If I crept out now . . .

But my bladder was too full for a quick escape. I climbed slowly to my feet, head pounding, and glanced around the room. Couch, coffee table, television. No rug, no bookshelves, no paintings. Tomas was renting, which perhaps explained the lack of finishing touches on the place. The cottage was silent. I could hear birdsong from outside.

I spied a likely hallway in the hope of finding a bathroom, slipped off my ridiculous shoes, and made my way quietly down it.

Shortly after, I was halfway out the front door, congratulating myself on having got so far without waking Tomas, when I heard his voice.

"Sneaking out?"

I turned. He stood behind the couch, in blue pajamas, rubbing sleep out of his eyes.

"I'm sorry—"

"I forbade you from using that word last night, remember?"

I shook my head. "I don't really remember much."

"Stay," he said, smiling. "Let me make you some toast and coffee, at least."

The idea of coffee caught my attention. "You don't hate me?"

He shook his head, laughing. "That's the last thing I feel for you."

I closed the door on the cool predawn air. "Thank you," I said. "And thanks for the blanket. And for being . . . you know . . . a gentleman about it all."

"Follow me," he said, and I followed him to his kitchen, where he switched on the light and indicated I should sit at the table.

"So, I take it you're not usually a big drinker?" he said as he fired up his coffee machine.

"Ah, no. Nor a big dater, I'm afraid. I was very anxious."

"I find it impossible to believe I could make anyone anxious." His bright blue eyes were twinkling.

"You don't know the half of it."

"You told me a lot of it last night."

"I didn't tell you I've never had a boyfriend." The word *boyfriend* felt wrong in my mouth, like a word I should have used fifteen years ago, not now.

"Not one?"

I shook my head. He busied himself making coffee, and I sat in my embarrassment until he placed a cup in front of me and joined me at the table.

"Really?" he said, picking up the same conversation. "Not one relationship?"

"I couldn't. For . . . all those reasons I spoke about last night."

"But didn't you want a relationship? Didn't you want a life?"

"Of course. I longed for it. But . . . Adam's life seemed to depend on me not doing anything I wanted. Then his impending death made me feel selfish for even wanting something."

"Did you have dreams? Aspirations?"

"Not really. Beyond maybe getting married one day, having children. When Adam died and I realized I had some freedom, I discovered I didn't know what I wanted to do."

"So you came up here to find yourself?"

I shook my head sadly. "I came up here because Adam always wanted to. I didn't have a dream, so I just picked up his."

Tomas sipped his coffee, wearing that listening expression that had kept me talking so long last night.

"He spent some time up here in the two years before he became ill. He talked a lot about coming back. For a long time, when he was younger, he was quite agitated about it, about not being well enough to travel. As time went by, he stopped talking about it so much. But he had a framed photograph he'd taken on the bush track to the Falls, and he had it enlarged to a meter across and hung on the wall of his room. He spent a lot of time looking at it, I imagine, when he could do nothing else." *Dammit, no.* On top of everything else, my voice shook and I had to blink back tears.

Tomas reached his hand across the table and covered mine with it. "Cry if you need to. It's okay."

"I think women are supposed to be more mysterious than I've been on this date," I said.

"I don't like mysterious. I like you. Maybe all those extra years with your family meant that you didn't learn how to be hard, or cool, or false. Maybe that's exactly why I like you, Lauren."

His kind words made me cry for real, and as I did he sat patiently, stroking my hand with his thumb.

"I need to be honest with you, though," he said, and an ominous chime rang out in my heart. "Knowing what I know about you now, about your . . . inexperience, I suppose you'd say. I'm due to return to Copenhagen in June, and I won't be back until January next year. Then, six months after that, I'll be returning home for good."

"Home? To Denmark?"

"Yes. So, I can't . . . I wouldn't be able to offer you anything . . . you mentioned marriage, children. It's better that I warn you. I'm not here forever."

"That's fine," I said, probably too quickly. "I don't mind. I'd really like to keep seeing you. I'm sure our second date will be better than the first. It can't be worse."

He tapped my hand gently. "Let's have our second date now, then."

"Breakfast date?"

"How about a quick piece of toast, then let's go back into the west wing, and see if we can find any more about our forbidden lovers."

"I'm wearing an evening dress and ridiculous shoes," I said.

"We'll stop by your place and get some sensible ones, then."

I grinned at him. "Okay."

The faint dawn light fell in cracks through the boarded windows, but Tomas had brought a large torch with a long beam, and I got a much better sense of the faded grandeur of the place.

"Will you try to preserve the original look?" I asked as he shone the torch onto the ornate ceiling. "The pressed-metal designs are magnificent." I was much more comfortable now in jeans and a long-sleeved T-shirt.

"It will look very different when I've redesigned it. I haven't drawn up plans yet, but I need to knock through some walls and build others. The developers want to maximize the space. As for what the interior decorators will do: Who knows?" He handed me the torch. "Lead the way."

I led him down the corridor to the storeroom. Old floorboards creaked beneath our feet, and the dust itched my nose.

He fished out the key and unlocked the door, then shone the torch around. "Good grief, what a mess."

"Will they just throw all this out?"

"I'm surprised they haven't already. They must have missed this room."

"Are you going to tell anyone about it?"

He shook his head. "The developer won't care. We can go through these things, if you like. If you're interested in our little historical mystery."

"That would be fun."

He squeezed my hand, then leaned in towards me and kissed me lightly on the lips. My head swam a little.

"Now for our third date," he said. "Coffee at my favorite café."

I smiled, imagining the surprise on Penny's face when we turned up. But then I remembered. "Oh! I'm due at work at six thirty! What time is it now?"

He shone the torch at his watch. "Six fifteen. Good thing we're on site."

"I'll have to dash. Third date. Soon."

"Tonight."

"You're on. I'll make you dinner at my place. Seven o'clock?" I boldly kissed him on the mouth, letting him open my lips with his tongue, then ran off up the corridor while he lit my way, and out into the early-morning light. Smiling like a fool.

CHAPTER THREE

My shift seemed to drag on forever, but I was free at two. I picked up some groceries and went home to marinate steaks and make a pasta bake and salad. A long bath followed, and I finally washed off the grime and stale alcohol smell. I could easily have fallen asleep in the water, but I needed to unpack Adam's books before Tomas arrived. There was no space in my sitting room for unnecessary clutter.

Wrapped in my dressing gown, I sat on the floor and opened the first box. In it was a letter from my mother.

I hope you enjoy these books, and take the time to remember your brother—my darling son—when you read them.

With a pang, I remembered I'd turned off my phone last night at the restaurant. I quickly located it in my handbag, switched it on, and waited as it downloaded seven increasingly desperate voice-mail messages from Mum. With the phone jammed between my shoulder and cheek, I began to unpack the books.

"Hello?" she answered breathlessly.

"It's me."

"Where have you been?"

"Nowhere. I just forgot to turn my phone on."

"Lauren, you must be more careful. It's not fair to me to disappear like that. I've been worried out of my mind. I called the police but they wouldn't do anything."

I took her admonishment with good grace as I moved books from boxes to bookshelves, apologizing, feeling like a teenager, but then when I could finally get a word in, I said, "Mum, I'm a grown woman. You really can't expect to know where I am every second of the day."

The line went quiet, and I knew I'd hurt her feelings. "Sorry, Mum," I said again. "But don't worry about me, okay? I'll be fine." Because I felt guilty, I said too much. "I've met a man."

"A man? As in, a boyfriend?"

"Yes. He's great. He's an architect from Denmark."

"Does he speak English?"

"Yes, Mum." Trying not to sound exasperated.

"You need to be careful, Lauren. You're not good with men."

"Well, I'll never be if I don't spend more time with a few," I said, trying to sound light. "We have our third date tonight." That's what Tomas had called it. It made me smile. I'd never made it to a third date before. "I'm cooking for him."

"That's good. You're a good cook. I'm glad I took the time to teach you."

I could tell she wanted to say more—dire warnings, promises that I would always be welcome back at home if things went wrong, requests for assurance that I was safe—but she didn't, and I recognized the effort that took. "I'd better go," I said. "Trying to tidy the place up before he arrives."

"You invited him to your house? This early in the relationship? What if he gets ideas?"

Ideas. Oh, how I hoped Tomas had ideas. The same ideas I was having.

"Mum. Stop worrying."

She grumbled some more, but eventually said good-bye, with a promise to phone early tomorrow to see how things had gone.

I put aside my phone and turned my attention more fully to the books. Some were dusty and yellowed. Novels and history books and books about space or cars. I blew the dust off them, shelved them. I finished one box, then another. Most of these books I would never read, but it wouldn't feel right to give them away or dump them. A book about the Blue Mountains caught my eye, and I opened it to glance through the pictures. As I did, a photograph fell out.

It was a young Adam and a friend of about the same age. I realized with delight that this photo was taken right here at Evergreen Falls. I recognized the viewing platform on the ridge, where they leaned, shirtless, talking to each other. Their shoulder blades, like the buds of angel wings, hunched up. Adam's fair hair was long. I didn't know his friend, but he was dark-haired with a handsome profile. I flipped the photo over. Written on the back was: *Adam and Frogsy. Love you guys. Drew xxxx.*

I turned back to the picture. Adam was eighteen or nineteen in this photo, right before he'd grown ill. He'd had no idea what was coming. He looked happy and relaxed, talking to a friend in front of the majestic view. Frogsy and Drew. He'd never mentioned friends with those names, and nobody from his time in the Blue Mountains had contacted him down in Tasmania. I went carefully through the book, looking for more photographs. There were none, but I did find an inscription at the start of the book, in blue handwriting: *Happy nineteenth birthday, and here's to many more years of joy. Love from Frogsy.*

Adam didn't get as many years as Frogsy had wished him, and

certainly few were filled with joy. I put the book aside and gazed at the photo a long time. Frogsy was an unusual name. Did he still live around here? But then I realized: Frogsy was a nickname. Maybe it rhymed with something, or maybe he looked like a frog, or wore a lot of green. Unless he still used the nickname, I'd be unlikely to find him. Still, I'd show Penny the photograph and ask her. Or even Lizzie; she had lived here a long time.

These were the thoughts running through my mind when I heard a knock at my door.

"Tomas!" I said as I opened the door, pulling my dressing gown tightly together. Had I completely lost track of time? "I wasn't—"

"I'm sorry," he interrupted. "I have to cancel."

"Cancel?" No third date. There was never a third date.

"Sabrina . . . my ex-wife . . . she's had a car accident. My number was in her mobile phone as her emergency contact. I have to . . . I'm driving down to Sydney right now, getting a flight to Copenhagen."

His ex-wife? Wasn't she . . . ex? Even in my confusion I recognized that it wasn't the right time for me to ask this, so I said instead, "Of course. Is she badly hurt?"

"Very, very badly. She's going into emergency surgery right now. She might not make it." He set his jaw against tears, took a breath. "I know it sounds crazy, Lauren, but she has nobody else. Both her parents are gone and she has no siblings. I need to get back there and take care of everything. I'm her oldest friend."

"I'm so sorry. What a terrible thing to happen. Go. Don't worry about me."

He managed a half smile. "You are extraordinary. Here, I have something for you." He picked up my hand and pressed something into it, closed my fist over it, and pulled me against him. Kissed me on the lips. So hard. "I don't know how long I'll be away. I'll call."

Then he was gone, crunching back down the gravel beside the

house. I heard his car pull away, and then I opened my hand and looked at what he had given me.

It was the key to the west wing.

I obsessed, of course, about Sabrina, his ex-wife, his oldest friend. I would periodically remind myself that poor Sabrina was on death's door and that I was being so uncharitable I would certainly go to hell, but I couldn't help it. Scenarios would play out in which he stayed in Denmark to help her recover and ended up remarrying her. Why shouldn't he? Who was I to make a claim on him? Two dates, which were really one very long date during which I had behaved embarrassingly. Mum was right. I was too inexperienced with men. I was vulnerable.

But on Monday morning at three, my phone tinged loudly. I opened my eyes and picked it up. A text from Tomas. *Safely in Copenhagen. Sabrina serious but stable. Still unconscious. Send me your e-mail address.*

I typed out a reply and waited in the dark, sitting up in my bed. The only sound was the thrum of my pulse.

Ting-ting. *I'll be in touch when I can. Need some sleep. Need to contact Sab's cousin. Solve the mystery while I'm away.* ☺

"I will," I typed, and pressed Send. Then I was alone in the quiet dark.

I promised myself I would start clearing out the storeroom in the west wing on Monday after my shift, but when I left the café and made my way down past the ballroom, I saw a group of men standing near the colonnade. I hung back among the overgrown hedges and watched them. I was fairly certain Tomas hadn't asked the owner's permission for me to go in and poke around, and I didn't want to get him in any trouble. The men were in deep conversation, and I would have been in plain sight if I walked past them to let myself in.

Instead, I doubled back and made my way through a breezeway and then across the old tennis court to the edge of the escarpment. A long stone wall, about hip height, ran the length of the Evergreen Spa's boundary. Its Doric columns were spotted with wear and lichen and in some places were crumbling into rubble. A set of old stone stairs led . . . somewhere. A wire fence had been erected across the entrance to the stairs, with a danger sign attached. I heard voices approaching, and hesitated. The desire to go unnoticed in my prowling around the west wing fought with my desire not to slip on a crumbling stair and go hurtling to my death. What would Mum say if she saw me?

I was over the fence in a moment. The stairs were solid, if a little worn, but they soon ran out and I was standing on an overgrown, stony path that wound down into the valley. The Evergreen Spa had been a health retreat in its day, and perhaps this had been an old walking track. I was charmed by this idea. From the town, many fine bushwalks zigzagged up and down to the Falls, and they were all well maintained, with handrails and stepping-stones. They were also usually busy with tourists. I liked the idea that nobody had trod this path for a long time. The sun was warm on my face, the afternoon breeze up.

The path took me down on a slow curve into the valley. The flora contrasted sharply with the introduced oaks and conifers that lined the streets of the town. Instead, I passed red gums and she-oaks, wattle and banksia. Here and there, old tree branches covered the path and I had to pick my way over them. Years of leaf fall, peeled bark, scratching ferns, and loose rocks sought to pull my feet from under me. I leaned on the rock wall for balance as I made my way down and down. The canopy grew thicker now, coachwood trees and gray myrtles.

I looked up and saw the edge of the escarpment far above me. I'd have to climb all the way back up at some stage, and clouds were moving in. I hesitated, but then I saw something odd about a hundred meters away, so I kept going to get a better look. I soon came across two metal cables, about my thumb's width. One hung slack and curled up on the end, but the other plunged far below. The source of both appeared to be at the top of the escarpment, behind the hotel.

Curious now, I picked my way down farther amid the sharp smell of the forest, the clear call of bell miner birds and the rocks green with mold in the shadows. My feet crunched on until I found the path had crumbled away and I couldn't go any farther.

I knelt down and peered over the ledge, and I could see far below, where the cable ended: a little iron structure had come to rest against the sediment-striped cliff. I had no idea what it was, but clearly it had something to do with the hotel. Would Tomas know?

Sweat was trickling under my T-shirt now, and I sat back on my haunches and wished I didn't have to slog all the way back up. I could hear distant traffic, and thought that if I could get to the bottom of the valley, I might find a road, a bus stop, a town with a taxi. I looked around. Was that another track that wound off into the valley? Or just another dead end?

I picked myself up and followed it. A huge fallen red gum covered the track, so I leaned against the bark and peered over. Definitely a track. I wriggled up onto the tree, then half slid, half fell down the other side. I picked my way between rocks and spiky grass trees, ducking under bulging overhangs. Around the bend I could already see that the track was running out; it sheared into the rock wall and all that was left was a big drop.

But as I drew closer, I saw the cave.

Above me, the clouds had dissolved. Romantic ideas about sheltering in the cave from the coming rain dissolved, too. I accepted that I would have to trudge back up the path, but first I wanted to see how deep the cave was.

The opening was small, and flanked by a slab of granite about chest height. I had to bend almost double to enter, but once inside I could stand up. The cave was about the size of my bathroom, although the ceiling was much lower. A strong, unpleasant smell of animal pervaded the dark and cold. I started to think about spiders, and then I couldn't get out of there quickly enough.

It was as I was coming out that I saw something that looked like a design etched into the back of the rock that half covered the opening. I peered at it closely, then realized I was looking at a love heart carved into the stone. The granite had been too hard for curved lines, though. The heart had sharp corners, and the lettering inside was also sharp, made of lightning bolts. But the letters were clear enough. *SHB.*

I stared. My letter writer, SHB, had carved this. No, that wasn't right—SHB's secret lover had carved this. Who was she? I reached out with tentative fingers to touch the carving, feeling the past and present collide. Only when I touched it did I realize there was something else carved here, but I couldn't see it in the dim light.

I pulled out my phone and lit up the torch. The other carving wasn't letters or love hearts. It was scribble. Violent scribble, not as deep as the letters but carved into the rock nonetheless. With force. Perhaps even with anger. My skin prickled.

I flipped the phone around, turned on the flash, and took a photograph to send to Tomas. I searched the rest of the cave with the torch but did not find any more carvings. I stood for a long while gently running my fingers around the sharp-edged heart. The mystery deepened.

CHAPTER FOUR

1926

Somewhere, far away, up above the water, Violet could hear her name being called.

Her eyes flicked open. Sunshine hit the water and refracted green and blue. She shot up and broke the surface. The late-autumn sun slanted through the willows and she-oaks. Ada stood beside the swimming hole, beckoning wildly.

"Please, Violet. We'll be late."

"We've ages."

"I'm going without you."

"Suit yourself."

Ada stomped off through the grass and Violet rolled onto her back to float. Ada had always been a wet blanket. It was one thing not to own a bathing suit, but quite another for her to raise her eyebrows at Violet's, especially when she was so proud of it: black with an emerald belt and matching emerald bathing cap.

"She's right, you know," Clive said from where he sat on a flat rock with his sketchbook open. Violet wondered if he was drawing her. "You will be late."

Violet and Ada worked together at the Senator Hotel in Sydney's city center, where Violet's shift started in an hour. Plenty of time. "You all worry too much." She rolled over and dived under again, her eyes closed, a curl loosed from her bathing cap tickling her cheek. Then up again, and this time she swam until she felt the stony ground beneath her feet. On the bank, the towel and dry clothes were waiting. The cold hit her hard. This might be her last swim until October, perhaps. Violet loved to swim, loved to disappear into the liquid-crystal water. It took more than a bit of cold to put her off.

"Look at you," she said to Clive, peering over his shoulder to see his picture: she was a little disappointed to see a willow taking shape on the page. "Man of leisure."

"It's temporary. The new job starts in a few days." He turned his face up to her and smiled. "You'll come and see me, won't you, Violet?"

Violet knew that Clive was sweet on her. They had worked together the past two years at the hotel. "Maybe. It's a terribly long way up to the mountains." She pulled her dark hair free from the bathing cap and toweled it vigorously.

"But the hotel is so grand. You'd love it. All the ladies in their fine gowns."

"I'd just be annoyed that I couldn't wear a fine gown myself." Violet had no intention of visiting Clive. He was her summer romance, and summer was long gone. Besides, all they'd shared were a few dances and one brief kiss. "You'll survive without me," she said.

"Maybe I will, maybe I won't," he replied lightly. He said and did everything lightly. Even his hair and eyes were light, as though the sun were caught in them.

Violet pulled her dress on over her wet bathing suit and headed towards the path that led to the train station. Her shoes and stockings were in her bag.

"I'll be leaving on the eight a.m. train from Central Station," he called after her. "If you want to see me off."

"I have an early shift," she called back. It wasn't true, but it was easier than saying she wanted to avoid a farewell scene.

"Good-bye, then," Clive said.

She waved, then picked up her pace.

In the end, they were both right, curse them. Violet ran up the stairs from the room she shared with three other waitresses, still buttoning her uniform, curls damp, exactly ten minutes after her start time. Ada smiled smugly from the dining room, where she distributed white china plates to a table of businessmen.

"You're late," said Mr. Palmer, her mealymouthed young boss.

"Yes, I was unavoidably delayed. I'll work back instead."

"Swimming. You were unavoidably delayed swimming."

"Did Ada tell you that?" Violet would knock her flat for such a betrayal.

"No. Your wet hair told me. You look a disgrace, and I'm certainly not going to allow you in here to serve my best customers." He indicated her blouse, which she saw was misbuttoned, the front gaping, and the world could see clear through to her singlet. "It's over, Violet. You're fired."

"No." Sunshine and swimming and flirting with Clive all evaporated in her mind, and she was left only with the image of her poor mother, sewing with arthritic fingers. "Please. I'll work back, I'll try much harder."

"You've already had two warnings," Mr. Palmer said, and he was telling the truth, but she wanted to argue with him anyway.

"You can't fire me!" she exclaimed, raising her voice until it took on a shrillness that even she couldn't stand. "I'll make a complaint to the hotel owner."

"Go right ahead," he replied in a soft voice, turning away from her. "Be packed and gone by tomorrow at ten. Hand in your uniform as you leave. It's halfway off you already."

Violet clutched at her blouse, desperate to say the very thing that would make him change his mind. Mama would be so disappointed with her. So very, very disappointed.

Violet couldn't face Mama with no job. She simply couldn't. She sat at the back of the tram, in the dark where she couldn't be seen by other passengers, and cried. Wrapped in her misery, she nearly missed her stop but remembered just in time to pull the bell. She alighted two streets from where her mother worked as a laundress and seamstress for a wealthy family, the Ramseys, in Roseville. They had four children who were noisy, and one who was quiet and covered in teething hives and who was compelled to wear white socks over his hands to stop him scratching his sores raw. Mama received only her bed and board for her work, and relied on a little money from Violet to help out.

Violet stopped a few doors away, her small suitcase and portable gramophone suddenly very heavy, and took a deep breath. "Mama, I lost my job," she said under her breath. Mama would look sad, maybe make that tutting sound she made, ask what happened, and find a way to blame Violet. But she wouldn't say, *I rely on you, what will I do without that money?* She was far too proud for that. Violet had to leave the money under the tea tin when her mother wasn't looking. They never spoke of it. In fact, her mother often talked of the importance of being independent, ever since Violet had turned fourteen and Mama had forced her out of school to find work. That was nearly six years ago, and her employment record had been patchy ever since.

Violet glanced up. The lights were on in Mama's room at the side of the house. "Mama, I lost my job," she said again, and she strode with purpose towards the house.

She let herself in to save her mother getting up. Mama's knees grew worse as the months went by. Violet had no idea how she stood by the copper every day, stirring sheets and pillow slips and towels. Violet's mother was not old—only forty-five—but her own mother and grandmother had succumbed early to arthritic pain. Violet wondered if it would come to her one day, too, or if she had inherited her father's joints. Not that she knew where or even who her father was.

Mama looked up from her threadbare chair by the window, gave Violet a puzzled smile and said, "I saw you up the street. Why do you have your trunk with you?"

"Mama, I . . ."

Mama waited, expectant.

"I've got a new job. Up in the mountains."

"Really?"

"The Evergreen Spa Hotel. Much fancier than the Senator."

"Good girl. When do you start?"

"Soon. Can I stay with you until then? I had to give notice at work, and they were beastly about it and kicked me out straightaway. I'll help with the laundry, and I have a spot of money saved, so I can pay for my own food." Violet's heart was hammering in her throat. A lie, a great big lie. Now she had to convince Clive to find her a job, or it would all fall apart.

Violet arrived at Central Station at ten minutes to eight, dressed carefully in a gray silk dress and black wool stockings. She wanted to look appealing, but not too appealing. She made her way across the busy concourse. The train waited at the crowded platform, and Violet feared that he might already be on board and she'd missed him. Would she have to follow him all the way to the Blue Mountains? She pushed through the crowd, searching for his pale hair, but all the men in brown and gray suits wore brown and gray hats, so she started calling, "Clive! Clive!"

In the end, he found her, approaching her from behind and grasping her shoulder so that her heart gave a little jump.

"Violet! You came!" His gray eyes were shining, and it almost hurt to say what she had to say next.

"Clive. I'm in a terrible mess. I've lost my job. I wondered if . . . you could ask about a position for me at the Evergreen Spa?"

The light in his eyes dulled, and for a moment irritation crossed his brow. But the expression was fleeting and he smiled nonetheless. "Not only will I ask, I'll tell them you're the best waitress I've ever worked with."

"Thank you," she said, and released the half breath she didn't realize she'd been holding on to. "I'm so grateful. I'm not proud. I could be a chambermaid just as well as a waitress. I simply . . . I simply can't be out of work for long. Mama's joints are bad and I know she worries she won't be able to work much longer."

"You can rely on me," he said, then hesitated, about to say something else.

"What is it?" she asked.

"Can I rely on you?"

"Rely . . . I'm not sure I know what you mean." Her heart was in her throat. Was he asking her for some kind of favor she wasn't prepared to give? He didn't seem that sort of fellow, but she had to admit she'd led him on terribly.

"If I tell them you're the best waitress I've ever worked with, you won't make a liar of me, will you? You won't turn up late or be rude to the head waiter or flirt with the customers?"

Violet winced. It was a painful but true portrait of her behavior at work. "Clive, I should be so grateful that I will grow up. All the way up. I will not besmirch your good name, I promise."

"Good." His eyes were kind. He tapped her chin with his thumb.

Violet knew he wanted to kiss her, but she dropped her head to discourage him.

"Well, then. I hope to see you very soon."

"Send a telegram to my mother's if they say yes. I'll be on the next train."

He straightened his hat and headed for the train. Violet did the right thing and waited until it pulled away from the platform, waving to Clive and even blowing a kiss to him, though he was turning away from the window and didn't see it. Perhaps it was for the best.

Flora stood in the corridor, bags on the thick rug at her feet, and waited.

Tony tapped his foot impatiently. "Is he coming?"

"He says he is."

She knocked on the door again. "Sam? Do hurry up. We'll miss the train."

"I should have arranged a car to come for us," Tony said.

"Then he'd make the car wait. He knows the train won't wait. It will make him hurry up."

She waited. The silence stretched out. Farther down the corridor, another of the hotel room doors opened and a chambermaid emerged with a ball of dirty sheets. She gave them a curious glance. Flora put her hand to her fair hair, pinned in an elaborate knot at the back of her head, covering her face with her forearm. How she hated people looking at her.

"Sam?" she said again.

"Not coming."

The muffled answer made Tony's eyes roll and his hands fly up in the air, a characteristic gesture. "I give up. Sort him out. I'll tell the others we're probably staying."

Flora helplessly watched him go. She knocked on the door again, dropping her voice. "Sam, let me in. Tony's gone."

She heard movement as he rose from the bed. Then the door opened and he peered out, checking for Tony.

"I told you. He's gone."

"You've lied to me before, sister." His dark, dark eyes were glazed and a familiar sweet, organic smell filled the room. Syrup and geranium.

Flora pushed the door in and Sam let her by, then returned to the bed and his tray of precious things. A lamp. Awls and scissors and tweezers. And, of course, the long, elaborate pipe. She indicated the equipment accusingly. "You promised me."

"It was too hard a promise to keep."

"Then we must go home. We must get back to the farm, where you have family who can help." They had been sent to the Evergreen Spa Hotel by their father in the hope that the fresh air and the spa water—imported from Germany—would improve Sam's health. Flora, five years older, had been put in charge of making her brother better. But it was a task at which she was doomed to fail: the opium had him so strongly in its grip, and she was fairly certain he had found a regular supplier up here. This was the reason he didn't want to leave.

Tony's father, a good friend of her own father, had suggested he join them. They had been engaged for six months now, and were no closer to a wedding date. Both families hoped that an extended holiday together would throw a little fuel on a fire that hadn't kindled as readily as they had expected.

"I think we should stay a little longer," Sam said. "I saw a poster. Christmas in June. Let's just stay for that. It's only five weeks away."

"Five more weeks?"

"Come on, Sissy." He lit another pipe, sitting cross-legged on his bed. "Don't be a grump."

She clamped her teeth tightly to stop herself from screaming. "I'm meant to look after you. I'm not making your life hard because I enjoy doing so."

"The Iti does."

"Don't call Tony that. Besides, he's not Italian. He's American."

"American Italian, though. Oily as a—"

"He's my fiancé," she interjected hotly. "He'll be your brother-in-law soon."

"Where is he now? Making a deal with the mob?"

"Sam, stop."

"Brown eyes and bullets. That's what you're marrying."

"Our father has approved. Your opinion of Tony is irrelevant." Their father had more than approved the marriage. He had arranged it. "Anyway, I love Tony," she added, realizing it sounded defensive. "He's been more than patient with you."

Sam was slipping away into his golden bubble now, his breathing slowing and his eyes half closing.

Frustrated tears welled in Flora's eyes, but she blinked them back. "Sam, you must stop that."

"I can't," he said, in a small voice.

"Then you must see a doctor." Suddenly this seemed the best idea she'd ever had, and she brightened. "Will you see a doctor while we're up here? If you promise to, I'll write to Father and tell him we're going to stay. Until Christmas in June."

He waved her away. "Yes. Yes, if that's what it takes. You arrange it."

A small ray of hope lit her heart. "Consider it done," she said, then left him lying on the bed. As she closed the door behind her she saw that the same chambermaid had moved farther up the hall. Again, she eyed Flora curiously, perhaps wondering what she was doing on the men's floor. Flora raised her chin and refused to make eye contact as she strode past. Now she had to give Tony the news that she was staying five more weeks. He wasn't going to like it.

Flora eventually found Tony at the tennis court, in a leisurely doubles game with Vincent, Harry, and Sweetie (the latter, a hulking thug of a man, was so named for his habit of calling every woman he met "sweetie"). She stood for a while watching. Their white clothes were dazzling against the green tennis court, and they laughed and shouted merrily to each other. Tony and his friends were so different from Sam. They were men who readily understood the world, and made it spin with casual, confident hands. Sam was a cipher in the margins, pale and rose-cheeked, with hair and eyes darker even than Tony's. Sam had ever been a strange boy: fey and somehow bewildered. Since the moment he had come into the world, Flora had been compelled to look after him—both by her parents, who had little time for children, and by her own heart, which loved him immeasurably and fearfully.

By contrast, here was Tony, all gleaming olive skin and well-muscled forearms, banging the tennis ball about with his dark hair flopping forth over his eyes. How her heart had stung when she'd first seen him. Handsome and worldly, the heir to his grandfather's shipping business, Tony was all charm and poise. Flora loved him, loved him madly. It was the idea of marriage she was not enamored of. Not yet.

He still hadn't acknowledged her presence, so she tried a wave; it was Vincent who held his serve and said, "Tony, you can't ignore her forever."

Was that what he was doing? Ignoring her? Well, she could withstand that. Wounded pride was for fussy women.

He turned and she waved again, then called, "I have to speak to you."

"Go," said Vincent, always the kindest of Tony's entourage. "We'll meet you in the coffeehouse later."

Tony handed his racquet to Sweetie and came to take Flora's arm. "Come on, Florrie. Let's take in the view."

The tennis court was on the edge of the escarpment, and they walked across it towards the gleaming white stone fence that lined the boundary of the hotel gardens. When Flora was sure they were out of earshot of his friends, she said, "Sam isn't going."

"Then you and I will leave him here."

"You know we can't. Father was very particular. I'm to take care of him."

"Take care of him? The impossible task. Does your father *know*?"

"About the opium? I . . . I don't know. Maybe he does and he pretends he doesn't. But if he knew . . . It's just . . ." Her eyes darted away.

Tony stopped and turned her to him. "What is it?"

"I can't leave him."

"He's nearly twenty."

"No, I *can't*. I'm to stop him from doing anything foolish if I hope to . . . inherit." She knew she shouldn't talk about money. Tony had plenty, but her family had more. Much, much more. The Honeychurch-Black family owned property and titles the world over, and had for centuries.

"Ah. I see." He tilted his head a little to the right. "That's cruel."

"Father's not cruel. He's sensible. He wants to make sure Samuel is safe."

Tony nodded, then he pulled her close against him and bent his lips to her ear. "You will be all right. Don't you worry."

"How do you know that? You don't know that for sure."

He didn't reply. Instead, he began to croon to her slowly, softly.

She loved it when he sang to her. *La Boheme* or *Tosca* or any other bel canto tune. She closed her eyes and leaned in to him; his tennis whites smelled like lemon and sunshine.

"Do you really think everything will work out?" she breathed after a time, when her heart didn't feel so trapped behind her ribs.

"I promise you it will." Then he gently pushed her away from him. "But I can't stay another day. I'll take the afternoon train down to Sydney."

"You'll be back?"

"As soon as I can. A few days. I have business that won't wait as prettily as you." He grazed her cheek with the back of his hand. "Gorgeous girl."

She couldn't help but smile. "Sam said he'll let me take him to a doctor. That's good, isn't it?"

"It sure is, Florrie. Don't stop hoping."

They walked hand in hand back towards the tearoom. *Don't stop hoping.* She wouldn't. Not as far as Sam was concerned. Not ever.

CHAPTER FIVE

A grumbling gray sky awaited Violet when she stepped off the train at Evergreen Falls station. She pulled the collar of her wool coat up high and tightened her silk scarf: the rust-colored one with hieroglyphics on it that she had bought the day before. It contrasted beautifully with her structured white dress. Scarves and hats were her weakness. And dresses. And also shoes. She needed to slow down and save her money, especially as the Evergreen Spa had only promised her two months of work. They were closed over the winter, and she would be sent back to Sydney then.

But still. She had a job after only a week out of work. Bless Clive. Where was he?

He had promised to meet her. She searched the platform but couldn't see him. She sat on the long painted seat and waited. People arrived, collected loved ones, headed off. Noise and movement. Motorcars and sulkies on the road. Then just Violet, left by herself. A rough wind drove dry leaves skittering up the platform. Cold gray clouds moved in and started to spit.

Of course she didn't have a brolly. Planning ahead was not her forte.

The clock on the station wall told her forty minutes had passed.

She couldn't wait here in the rain forever. Violet pulled her hat down tighter over her ears, grasped her suitcase in one hand and her gramophone in the other, and went to the porter's office for directions to the hotel.

It was raining hard by the time she had walked the half mile to the Evergreen Spa, a cream-colored building of arched windows and colonnades, flanked by a row of pine trees. Her clothes were damp and her shoes were squelching and sodden from deep puddles. Her suitcase seemed to weigh a ton, wearing a deep, purplish groove in her hand. But at last the doorman pulled open the tall front door and ushered her in.

"Thank you," she said to him, water dripping off her nose. "Do you know where Clive Betts is?"

The doorman shook his silvery head. "No, ma'am. I don't know that name. Is he a guest?"

"No, he's a carpenter. A handyman. He started work here recently."

"Sorry, ma'am. There's many of us works here. Nearly a hundred. If he's new, I mightn't know him."

The doors closed behind her and she found herself standing in an ornate foyer, on a gleaming parquetry floor. Dark red wallpaper, flocked with Oriental designs, covered the walls all the way up to the remote ceiling, with its dazzling white plaster and relief pictures. Despite the miserable weather outside, the high windows were designed to catch and reflect light, especially into the glittering chandelier that hung in the center of the room. A long rug ran from the door to an oak desk, where a distinguished-looking woman sat reading through a large, leather-bound register. Something about her presence compelled Violet to walk towards her: she would tell Violet what to do and where to go.

"Hello," Violet said, approaching warily.

The woman looked up. She had the air of aristocracy about her, with her hooked nose and white hair piled high and severe on her head. She wore an elegant blue dress with an equally elegant gray cardigan over it, and ropes of lustrous pearls. "Oh, you poor child. You're wet through!"

"I'm Violet Armstrong. I'm . . . new."

The woman rose, beaming, and held out her hand. "So pleased to have you here, my dear. I'm Miss Zander, the manageress." She made "manageress" sound like an exotic, foreign term. "Clive spoke so highly of you."

"Clive. He was supposed to meet me at the train."

"Tomorrow," Miss Zander said. "We were expecting you tomorrow."

Violet cursed herself. First impression: mix up the days and turn up soaking wet.

"It's of little consequence," Miss Zander continued. "Here, let me find somebody to watch the front desk and I'll take you to your new room." She beckoned a bellboy for Violet's luggage and muttered a room number to him, then summoned a pretty, red-haired girl to mind the reception desk. Violet admired her smart blue uniform and white scarf and wondered if one day she would be able to work the desk. Already her head was full of dreams. Welcoming the wealthy guests, being admired for the nobility of her smile and the set of her pretty chin . . .

"Come along, keep up," Miss Zander said from across the room. "I don't have the whole day to show you about."

Miss Zander marched her down the hall and stopped at a cupboard with a red door. From around her waist she pulled out a long braided rope holding a set of keys. She eyed Violet up and down. "Hm. You're a little slimmer than Clive Betts had me expect. Still . . ." She yanked open the door and pulled out three uniforms for Violet. "These should fit."

Violet took the clothes in her arms: black dresses buttoned at the front with two rows of white buttons, and white bandeau head-bands.

Miss Zander locked the door and marched off again. "It's bed and board, and we'll match your salary at the Senator. Let Alexandria know how much you were being paid. Don't think to lie; she'll call them on the telephone to check."

"Who's Alexandria?"

"The redhead at the front desk. My deputy."

"How do I get her job?"

Miss Zander rounded on her, peered at her for a moment, then laughed loudly. "Dear, you'd get her job by being born a different person from a very different family."

The comment stung, but Violet smiled through it.

"Now, follow me. This corridor is used for storage, works, office administration, and, of course, the kitchen. Upstairs are the guests. You never need to go there. Ever." She paused for dramatic effect. "Downstairs are the staff lodgings and the staff dining room, which is the only place you will ever eat."

"Where do the guests eat?"

"The grand dining room and the ballroom are one and the same space. That's where you'll be serving food. You must, under no circumstances, ever take food from the upstairs dining room. Nor can you smoke. Evergreen Spa is a cigarette-free hotel. We are a health resort, you know."

"It's fine, I don't smoke." This wasn't strictly true. Violet always had a shiny case of cigarettes in her bag, for dances or parties or just for flirting, even though she didn't relish the feel of the smoke scratching her throat.

"Good. It's a filthy habit. For training, I'll put you with Myrtle, who's very experienced, and she'll show you what to do. Down here." They began to descend a staircase. No carpet or rug, just unfinished wood. "Your room is the third on the right. You'll be sharing with Myrtle and Queenie. Don't take advice from Queenie. She's a bit slow."

Miss Zander knocked briskly once, then fetched a key to open the room. Three beds were lined up under a window that was at the level of the grass outside. Her suitcase and gramophone waited on one of the beds, along with some folded linen. Through the gauzy white curtain, Violet could see a pair of men's shoes. She approached the window and peered up. It was Clive.

"Ah, there he is," she said.

Miss Zander furrowed her brow. "Now, I know that you and Mr. Betts are friends, but I expect you to work and not chat. As you aren't rostered on until dinner tomorrow night, I expect you to leave him be to get on with fixing our kitchen shutters."

"Of course."

The older woman then reached across and wiped her thumb hard across Violet's lips.

"Ow," Violet said, cringing away.

"Just making certain your lips are that color naturally. I won't tolerate my girls wearing makeup. You're not ladies of the night."

"Understood, ma'am."

Miss Zander smiled, all high-handedness evaporated. "I do hope you'll be happy working here, dear. You've a sweet face."

"Thank you." Violet glowed a little, and wondered how, on such short acquaintance, she'd decided she very badly wanted Miss Zander to like her.

"Myrtle is on shift. Get yourself dry and changed. Laundry and bathroom are just across the hall. Here's your key. If it fines up, get out for a walk. Fresh air is good for the constitution." She nodded once, then left in a swirling wake of perfume.

Violet went once more to the window. The room was very dim with so little light, and with the dark clouds outside. But when she looked up, she could see Clive working in the rain, sleeves rolled up to his elbow, his body flexed in concentration on the task at hand. She knocked on the glass but he didn't hear, so she simply stood for a while looking at his shoes, dripping on the bare wooden floor.

Myrtle was too young to be described as kindly, and yet that was precisely what she was, with her round body and big bosom and soft white hands. That afternoon and evening she gave Violet a speedy induction to the Evergreen Spa. Fortunately, Violet had worked in hotels long enough not to be intimidated by the various rules and things to remember. She was given a five-day roster, all split shifts: eleven until three, and then five until nine. Even though she wasn't rostered, she worked the earlier shift alongside Myrtle for experience. The lunch tables were all laid out beautifully, with silverware polished to a blaze, and a huge silver platter of seasonal fruit in the center of every one. Violet pinched an orange and hid it up the leg of her bloomers as she was finishing her shift.

Outside, the sun was shining and the sky was blue and white. It was a day to be outside, preferably singing. She hummed to herself as walked around to the back of the building, where she released the orange from its hiding place and began to peel it. That's when she saw Clive, still working on the kitchen shutters.

"Clive!" she called happily, and ran over to him.

He looked up, puzzled. "Aren't I supposed to collect you from the station in an hour?"

"I came a day early. Found my own way. Look, I already have my uniform." Violet twirled for him.

"You look wonderful. I'm so glad you've come." He beamed, then she remembered what Miss Zander said, and how Clive had made her promise not to get him in trouble.

"I'd best not disturb you. Miss Zander said to leave you be while you're working." She pocketed the orange peel.

Clive returned to the shutter, which he was screwing in with a large screwdriver. "Wonders mightn't cease. Violet's doing everything she's told."

She brandished her orange. "Almost everything."

He laughed. "You be careful."

She wandered off, biting into the juicy orange, down towards the escarpment.

Violet stopped under a swaying gum tree and caught her breath. The view that unfolded before her was spectacular. The ancient valley, carved into sedimentary rock faces of gray, red, and brown, bristling with leaves of every shade of green, stretched in front of her for miles and miles and miles. Clouds made dark shape-shifting shadows in the distance, and she could see the flash of sun off the famous Falls. It would be far too cold to swim. Wouldn't it? She had hours before her next shift.

A gentle slope led down into the valley. Myrtle had told her that if she took any path, she would eventually come to a sign that showed which direction to take: to the Falls; to the farms at the bottom of the mountain that sent their fresh produce straight up on a flying fox; or to the next towns along the range.

"You mustn't be late for your first proper shift, Violet," she said to herself as she started down the path.

Because so many guests at the Evergreen Spa came for the health-giving benefits of spa water, fresh air, and physical activity, good money had been spent making the paths clear and wide. She followed the way down until she came to the painted wooden fingerpost that showed her where to go next. As she finished her orange, she studied the sign. Then she wiped her sticky fingers on the grass and headed off towards the Falls.

Violet found herself mostly in the shade, and wished she'd brought a jacket. Under the long sleeves of her dress she could feel goose bumps rising on her arms. She hugged herself and rubbed her upper arms, hoping that the path would turn her into the sun shortly.

The path wound down, up, and around—through eucalypts and ferns—and she was glad she was wearing her low-heeled work shoes. Bellbirds and kookaburras called from the shadowy growth on either side of her. The day grew very quiet, apart from her footfalls. The activity warmed her, and then the path turned into the sun and she could see the Falls in the distance, gleaming.

She stopped, eyes wide. A man was standing very still in the sunshine on a large flat rock beside the Falls and, unless she was very much mistaken, he was completely naked.

Violet hung back in the trees, heart thudding. Was he some kind of madman? Was he dangerous?

She peeked again. He was still a long way away. He looked young but old enough to know better, and, yes, he hadn't a stitch on.

Deciding she was well hidden by trees, she moved forwards, in and around until she came out on the next bend, with a clearer view.

There he was, about three hundred yards away across the valley, arms up above his head. He had very dark hair, pale skin, a well-shaped body, a pleasing symmetry about his face, though she couldn't see any detail in it. She imagined his eyes must be closed, and he was simply enjoying the feel of sun on his bare skin. She envied him his freedom, his lack of care.

But she certainly couldn't go down to the Falls while a naked man stood there, so, with more than a little disappointment, she made her way back to work.

Flora dressed carefully in a cream wool dress and fur stole. She very much wanted the doctor to think well of her. The shame of being related to an opium addict was not something she wore lightly.

She fixed her fair hair in the mirror. So many pins. Flora didn't have a single friend with long hair anymore. They'd all had it cut short, into sharp bobs or chin-length finger waves. Perhaps she was old-fashioned.

Flora laid down her brush and leaned close to the mirror, so close her breath fogged it. *Please let today go well.* She had approached Karl, the Swiss health expert who ran the program here at the Evergreen Spa, and politely inquired as to the whereabouts of a good, discreet doctor in the area. He had recommended Dr. Dalloway, about five minutes away by motorcar, on the other side of the train line, and had duly made her an appointment for today.

Staring into the mirror, Flora frowned, noting how it drew a furrow between her brows. Then she lifted her expression and watched her forehead turn smooth and pale. How like her father she looked, with her straight nose and straight mouth, as if whoever had drawn her had run out of inspiration. Plain. Not a kind way of saying ugly, for she wasn't ugly. She was just . . . plain. It had always seemed unfair to her that her outward appearance gave nothing away about the treasures within: her intellect, her kindness, her sense of duty.

She sniffed, stood up straight. What did it matter? Beauty wouldn't attract more good fortune than she already had. She glanced at the carriage clock by the bed. Five minutes after two. Sam was late. Had he forgotten? The car would be waiting.

Flora pulled on a narrow-brimmed felt hat and picked up her leather purse. Sam was on the next floor down, the men's floor. She didn't like to go there often. Tony's thuggish friend Sweetie was often there, despite Tony being back in Sydney, and he was always far too pleased to see her.

She made her way down the stairs and along, then knocked gently on Sam's door.

No answer.

Louder. Calling, "Samuel Honeychurch-Black. You promised me. You *promised* me."

Still no answer.

She scrabbled in her purse for the spare key to his room, which Tony had managed to charm out of Miss Zander for her. "I'm coming in, Sam," she called, hoping he would be dressed. More than once she had walked in on him half dressed or naked. He seemed to care little who saw him.

No Sam.

His disappearance was as predictable as it was frustrating. His suitcase sat open on the Oriental bedspread, clothes were strewn about over the bed and gilded chair, and his tray of opium smoking paraphernalia lay on the carved wooden desk. Flora hesitated. What if she simply threw it all away? What if she simply took it down to the escarpment and let it all tumble down into the valley among the rocks and leaves?

Yes, what if she did exactly that, and then withdrawal from his addiction made Sam so sick he died? She had watched him try to give up more than once, and the fevers and chills that racked his body had been so alarming she had breathed in relief only once he had smoked a pipe. She knew too little about the drug, about what it was doing to him, about whether he might die. She lived, instead, with a constant, quiet buzz of anxiety.

Flora resolved she would visit Dr. Dalloway anyway. She could use the time to ask him all the questions for which she needed answers, and it would probably be better if Sam wasn't there for some of them.

She locked the room behind her and made her way down the

stairs, checking in the library just in case—Sam often hid in there—then across the parquetry foyer and out into wintry sunshine. The sky was as pale as watercolor, and the sun a long way off. The car was waiting, and she gave the driver the card with Dr. Dalloway's address and sat back on the long leather seat to watch the scenery speed by.

Shortly, they were outside the doctor's surgery. She instructed the driver to wait for her and took a deep breath before heading up the path. The doctor's house was a pretty painted cottage with roses in tidy pots crowded on the patio. There had been a time when Flora had wanted to be a doctor. Her father wouldn't hear of it, of course, but nonetheless she had made inquiries at the universities and built the fond fantasy of a life helping others, unlocking the puzzles of illness, using the sharper edges of her mind. But she was far too rich and well bred a woman to be allowed to study medicine.

She rang the bell, expecting a maid or a wife to answer the door. Instead, a young man greeted her. He was an inch taller than her and stocky, with curling auburn hair, and dressed beautifully in white serge trousers and a striped silk shirt. He wore horn-rimmed glasses, the kind known as Harold Lloyds, after the famous comic actor.

"I'm here for Dr. Dalloway," she said.

"That's me," he replied.

She had to stop herself from saying, "You're very young." She'd expected a crusty father figure, and wondered if she would be able to be honest and plain with a man her own age. Especially one with such a warm smile.

"You must be Miss Honeychurch-Black," he said, extending his hand. "But where is Mr. Honeychurch-Black?"

She shook his hand firmly. "He's . . . ah . . . May I come in?"

"Certainly."

Flora followed him into an entranceway. "I do thank you for making time to see me, Dr. Dalloway," she said.

"Please, call me Will."

The closed door to her left had a PRIVATE sign on it, and she presumed it to be his living quarters. To her right was a small waiting room, through which he led her into a surgery that smelled of lye soap and tea-tree oil. Charts and diagrams of bodies were pinned to the walls. Only once she was sitting down and the door was closed behind him did she finally explain.

"My brother has disappeared. Oh, don't look concerned. He often disappears. He's most in danger when he's in his room . . . I think."

Will cocked his head. "I don't understand."

"No," she said. "I'm explaining all this rather awkwardly, aren't I?"

He smiled. "Take your time."

She was struck again by the warmth of his smile. It reached all the way to his eyes and beyond. Within. Her discomfort edged away a little every time he did it. "All right, then," she said. "My brother is . . . He uses . . ." Her mouth was dry. "He smokes opium."

Will picked up a pen and started to write. "I see."

"Karl, the health director at the spa, he said you would be discreet."

"Absolutely, Miss Honeychurch-Black."

"Flora."

"Can I ask you, Flora, how long he has been smoking opium?"

"At least a year. He went to China with a friend for several months and brought the pipe back with him."

"How much does he smoke?"

"In a day? A week?"

"Let's say a day."

"Well, given I'm not with him all the time . . . I'd say it might be anywhere between ten and twenty pipes."

"How early in the day does he start?"

"I don't know for certain. His mood alters throughout the day. Manic some mornings, maudlin on others. He's often further away in the afternoons, then angry at dinner. I think he smokes himself to sleep." Her voice trailed off to a whisper. The shame. "I should add, he's always been moody. Eccentric. Even before the . . . you know."

Will was still writing. "To your knowledge, has he ever tried to stop?"

"Oh, yes, several times. But it's horrid. He gets fevers and his guts turn to liquid and he moans and shakes. I'm so afraid he's going to die." Her voice dropped low. "Will he die if he stops?" she asked.

He looked up and frowned. "Coming off the drug is awful, it's true, but it won't kill him. No, the far greater danger is that he keeps taking it. Quite apart from the fact that he is much more likely to have an accident, to take too great a dose and stop breathing, to damage his brains and his organs, the addiction uses up the spirit. Many opium addicts grow so unhappy that they eventually self-murder."

A chill ran from Flora's toes to her scalp. Her stomach felt hollow.

"Unfortunately, there is no easy way for him to stop. I suspect, since he isn't here with you, he's not particularly motivated to stop."

"How can I make him stop, then?"

"You can't."

His words were delivered gently, but she felt their cold, cruel edges in her body. Her eyes pricked with tears, and she dropped her head in embarrassment.

"Here," he said, pressing a handkerchief into her fingers.

"Thank you," she managed, balling it into her palm and letting the tears fall as quietly as she could. A minute passed. She gathered herself, dabbed her eyes, and offered him the handkerchief.

"You keep it," he said.

She folded it and slid it away in her purse.

"Flora," he said, "the toll of opium abuse is usually felt very strongly on those closest to the addict. You must take care of yourself."

"Thank you." She stood, determined not to meet his eye again, nor see that warm smile tinged with pity. "If you send the account to me at the Evergreen Spa, I will post you a check."

"Any time I can be of assistance—"

"Thank you," she said more firmly, then hurried outside.

In the car, she took a deep shuddering breath and laid her upper body down on the seat. What a horror, to love somebody so much and be doomed to watch him destroy himself. And by destroying himself, destroy her chances of happiness, too. Because if she couldn't get him off the drug, Father would disinherit them both. Would Tony still marry her without her family connections? She had eyes in her head, and she could see he was handsome as clearly as she could see she was plain.

She opened her purse and pulled out Will's handkerchief, which she pressed to her too-warm face. The car bumped over the rail tracks. Her brain felt crowded. *You can't make him stop.*

No, she wouldn't accept that. Somehow, she would reach him. He was still her darling Sam, her baby brother. She would find his heart, and she would make him see what he was doing to himself. What he was doing to them both.

Violet loved the way the dining hall looked at dinnertime. The chandeliers, which hung dormant all day, were switched on to their full, dazzling brightness. Each table was lit by a wheel of candles, and an orchestra played quiet music as the guests filed in, dressed in their beautiful evening gowns. Violet hated to admit it, but she was starstruck by many of the guests. The newly crowned Miss

Sydney was here, a tiny flat-chested beauty with a heart-melting smile and bright blond curls. Accompanying her was a man Violet assumed was her father until he dropped his hand in full sight and squeezed Miss Sydney's bottom. Also here was the famous opera singer Cordelia Wright, a blinking, mole-like woman with powdery skin and a sharp tongue. At another table sat the curmudgeonly poet Sir Anthony Powell and his novelist wife Lady Powell, who was renowned for writing stories so highbrow nobody could understand them. Violet had read more than a few of Sir Anthony's poems in school, and had found them a little dull. Myrtle told her that these few minor stars were not as spectacular as some of the guests she'd seen over the years, including American film actors and English royalty.

The dinner bell rang, and Violet started to run between the beautifully lit dining room and the harshly noisy kitchen. The kitchen manager and head waiter, Hansel, was an ill-tempered German man and the second in charge an equally ill-tempered Austrian man. They ruled the other waitstaff with a rod of iron, shouting and clanging in the kitchen, but silent and obsequious in the dining room. The two seemed to hate each other, and argued much of the time in hot German. Luckily, the cooks were always friendly, particularly the older gentleman everyone simply called Cook, with his round red face. In the dining room, Violet picked up snatches of conversation between guests.

"It's well past time when I should return to New York."

"So I said, *I won't take a penny less than ten thousand for it.*"

"No, it's a big Studebaker car. I'm not a peasant."

Their voices and sentences whirled past her, and she was more aware than she had ever been of the difference between herself and the very rich. These people made even the guests at the Senator seem humble. They lived a life her imagination could not grasp.

After the main course, things slowed down a little. Guests began to move onto the dance floor, and the orchestra played a lively waltz. Violet longed to dance but had to content herself with tapping her foot as she collected plates. Many of the diners skipped dessert, so she returned to the kitchen with a tray of fruit salads that she knew would end up in the pig bucket. Too difficult, though, to hide a fruit salad up the leg of her bloomers.

Myrtle stood by the big stone basins, running her hand under water.

Violet joined her. "What happened to you?" she asked.

Myrtle turned her round, flushed face to Violet. "I burned my fingers on the coffeepot," she said.

"Let me see." Violet turned Myrtle's hand over. Her fingers were bright red. "You need to see Karl; he'll put something on it."

"Table eight have no dessert!" Hansel shouted at them in heavily accented English.

"That's my table," Myrtle said.

"She's burned her hand," Violet called to him. "Give me a moment." She turned to Myrtle. "Go. Find Karl. I'll cover for you."

"You're a dear."

Violet scooped up her tray of desserts and headed for table eight. She offered the desserts around, looking curiously at a young, dark-haired man at the table. Could it be? He did look rather like the man she'd seen naked a few days ago. He was staring at the ceiling, as though he could see the music collecting there. The fair-haired woman at his side was in conversation with another man, a handsome Italian who Violet thought might be a film actor. The fair-haired woman wore a long string of pearls around her neck and was anxiously twisting them between her fingers. Violet set down her tray just as the woman called out, "Oh, no!"

Violet looked up. The young woman had stressed her necklace

to the point that she had broken it, and the pearls now bounced everywhere.

Quickly, Violet dropped to the floor and began to collect the pearls before they rolled away. As she scooped them up, she was aware that another person was on the floor with her. She reached for a pearl under a chair and found herself accidentally grasping his hand.

"I'm sorry," she said, realizing it was the young man from the Falls. What was the etiquette? Did she mention she had seen him naked? The thought made her laugh inside, and she had to try very hard to keep it in.

But the young man simply looked at her—his gaze burning through her eyes and deeper, deeper—and Violet felt trapped, her heart thudding. The music seemed to quieten, the pearls forgot themselves, and Violet gazed back at him. A slow heat kindled in her legs, crept up her thighs, burned up her ribs.

"Did you find them all?" This was the Italian man, only his accent was American.

Violet was returned to her senses. "I . . . I have these," she said, sitting up and offering the Italian man her handful of pearls.

"Good girl," he said, with a charming smile. Even though he was handsome and pleasant, looking into his face inspired a pale watercolor feeling next to those she had just experienced with the other man.

But that man was gone now, sitting back up at the table, counting pearls into the fair-haired woman's hands. The disaster now resolved, Violet handed out desserts and returned to the kitchen.

Who was he?

She pondered this for the rest of her shift, and tried to hang about at their table to hear them speak or to catch his eye, but the man's gaze had returned to the ceiling. One by one, the other guests at table eight stood up to dance, and Violet realized the fair-haired woman and the Italian were a couple. Eventually, only the dark-haired man remained.

Violet was clearing plates at the neighboring table by this stage, and was surprised when she turned around to see the man standing there, very close.

"Hello," he said, without smiling.

"Hello," she replied, warily.

"Thank you for helping my sister. It was very kind."

What an odd thing he was. She smiled. "You're welcome." Then, even though she knew she shouldn't, she extended her free hand and said, "I'm Violet."

He looked at her hand for a moment as though unsure what it was, then picked it up and pressed it to his lips. Softly, gently, at first, but then fervently and hotly. Violet glanced around, frightened that Hansel would see her and sack her. He felt her pull away and released her, his hands slack at his side as he gazed at her.

"I'd best keep working," she said, as the giddy desire receded.

"The necklace was meant to break," he said, "so that you and I could meet."

Violet didn't know what to say. They stood a few moments in heated silence until he said suddenly, "Samuel Honeychurch-Black. You can call me Sam."

"I'm sorry, Mr. Honeychurch-Black, but I'm not allowed to call guests by their first names."

"And do you always do as you're told?" Was it a challenge? There was no smile, no twinkle in his eye.

She hesitated, then boldly said, "No. No, Sam, I don't."

Then he smiled, and it was like a star blazing into life. Violet experienced it like a physical blow. She may have even gasped.

"I hope to see you again," he said, bowing his head.

Out of the corner of her eye, Violet saw Hansel enter the dining room. She put her head down to clear the table. When she next looked up, Sam was gone.

As Tony whirled her about, Flora watched Sam talking to the waitress.

"That's not good," she said.

"What?" Tony asked, following the direction of her gaze. "Oh, let him flirt."

"He doesn't flirt. He falls in love."

"Then let him fall in love. She's just a waitress. Nothing will come of it."

But Tony hadn't seen it happen before. Back in their hometown, three times now Sam had fallen for a woman who was beyond his reach in some way: a much older woman; a novice visiting the local church; the young wife of the grocer. Each of them disasters, for he loved them like a child loves a duckling. Fascinated, eager, but fatally clumsy. Broken hearts and homes and dreams. For none of them had had the power to resist him in those brief, bright months he had decided he would love them forever.

"Would you like me to have a word with him? Man to man?" Tony asked.

"He won't listen to you."

"That's true."

The music played on, and Flora tried to enjoy the dance. She watched the pretty, dark-haired waitress from afar and, although she didn't know her, felt worried for her nonetheless.

CHAPTER SIX

Violet kept her eyes peeled for Sam at the breakfast shift the next morning. Every time the big double doors swung open she expected to see his dark hair, and every time they swung closed without his appearance she fought disappointment. Many of the guests didn't come to the dining room for breakfast, choosing instead to have a meal brought to their room or to dine in the coffeehouse.

She cursed herself for being such a fool, for thinking that his interest meant anything.

With a mixture of deflation and embarrassment, she returned down the stairs and along the dim corridor to her room. The door was already open, and she found Miss Zander inside.

"Oh, Violet. There you are."

"I was on shift." Violet realized that Miss Zander had pulled back her mattress and was searching underneath. She bristled. "Is there a problem?"

"I will tell you in just a moment."

Violet's eyes darted towards her purse, hung on the back of the door, remembering the cigarette case inside. "Are you searching for something in particular?"

Miss Zander stood, patting her hair. "Pearls."

Violet's stomach went to water. "Pearls? Who's accused me of—"

"Nobody," Miss Zander said, quickly and sternly. "Here, let me check your pockets."

Violet raised her arms and Miss Zander felt in both pockets.

"My purse is behind the door," Violet said, deciding to come clean. "There are cigarettes in it, but they aren't mine."

Miss Zander raised one eyebrow. "Not yours, eh? Luckily, I already found them and disposed of them, though I've left the case in your purse. As for pearls, I've checked the whole room, and you're in the clear."

"Why were you looking for pearls?"

Miss Zander's mouth hardened. "You are very forthright."

"I'm not a thief."

"Oh, I see. Your pride is wounded. Not to worry, dearie. It was only a precaution. No, a Mr. Honeychurch-Black, one of our guests, came to see me this morning."

Violet tried to hide her interest. "Oh?"

"He wanted to commend you to me for being so quick to assist him and Miss Honeychurch-Black last night, when she broke her pearl necklace. I was merely checking to see you hadn't kept one or two, because that would be terribly embarrassing. As I don't know you very well yet, I thought the path of least resistance was to search your room. Now, have this." She reached up the sleeve of her blouse and pulled out a small folded envelope. "Mr. Honeychurch-Black insisted on giving you a thank-you note. I told him there was no need, of course, but . . ." She shrugged.

Violet took the envelope and slid it into her pocket.

Miss Zander narrowed her eyes. "Aren't you going to open it?"

"Later," Violet said, feigning indifference.

"Hm." Miss Zander pursed her lips and watched Violet for a moment before she spoke. "Don't get ideas. About him."

"I know my place," Violet said. She wanted to be alone to open the envelope.

"Good girl. I like you, Violet. Don't tell her, but I'm going to let Queenie go at the end of the week if you say you'll stay on."

"Yes!" Violet exclaimed, too quickly. Then remembered poor, dull, bony Queenie and finished guiltily, "I need the money for my mother. She has terrible arthritis."

"You make a good impression on people, Miss Armstrong. Keep it up."

Violet felt the warm glow of Miss Zander's restored approval.

Miss Zander left, and Violet quietly closed the door behind her, then climbed onto her bed cross-legged in the weak light from the high window. She hadn't the patience to be slow or deliberate, so she ripped the envelope open and shook out a crisp, folded piece of hotel notepaper, and what looked like a button.

She picked it up. It was, indeed, a button—a large one, about an inch across. But on it was glued a dried flower and a pin on the back. The whole thing had been lacquered so it could be worn as a brooch. Had he made this for her? The thought filled her with excitement that heated her cheeks. She unfolded the note.

A precious pretty thing for a precious pretty thing. Gratitude. Your SHB.

"Your Samuel Honeychurch-Black," she said aloud, and lay back on her pillow. Not *Yours, SHB.* Not formal. No: *Your SHB.* As though he belonged to her. Why would he write that? Did he really think she was pretty? And precious? She closed her eyes and held the note to her nose, sniffing it deeply. It smelled of something wild and sweet.

Then she sat up. If Miss Zander could come in here and go through her things whenever she pleased, Violet had to find somewhere to hide this note where it wouldn't readily be found.

She scanned the room. Purse, suitcase, mattress . . . all had been overturned or searched. Then her eyes lit on her portable gramophone. She had bought it at a secondhand shop in Sydney, and it had always had a loose back panel. She rose and went to it, unbuckling the lid and flipping it open. She put aside the three records she kept in there and carefully prised the corner open with her nail, then slid the note inside. The thought that it might lose its sweet smell in there made her sad, but she didn't want to risk Miss Zander finding it and wondering if there was something going on between her and Sam.

Was there something going on between her and Sam?

Violet clipped the lid back on the gramophone and returned to her bed, lying back to daydream about Sam. Confused, but smiling all the same.

She didn't see Sam again that evening, or the next. Thursday came, her day off, and she dragged her feet getting out of bed. Queenie took forever in the bathroom, and by the time Violet was dressed and down at the staff dining room in the basement, most of the other staff had either gone on shift or headed out for the day.

Breakfast in the staff dining room was not skimpy. Every morning a long table was laden with platters of chops, sausages, bacon, and eggs. The men had one side of the dining room and the women the other, but in practice any couple who wanted to chat simply sat near the middle of the room, and turned around to speak to each other. Violet saw Clive on his side of the dining room, and took her bacon and eggs where they could talk.

"Ah, here is the lovely Violet," he said, his light gray eyes crinkling up with warmth.

"You're having a late breakfast, too?"

He indicated the empty plate he had pushed to the side. "No. I'm drawing."

He held up his sketchbook to show her his re-creation of the front of the hotel.

"That's very good, Clive," she said, sitting at the long wooden bench. "Why do you never draw people?"

"I do," he said, head bent over his drawing.

Her vanity got the better of her, and she asked, "How come you never draw me?"

He put down his pencil and looked at her curiously. "Because . . ." He trailed off.

"Because?"

"Because a page is too flat and too small to capture you."

She dropped her eyes, let herself smile even though she knew she shouldn't.

"Now listen, Violet, do you still have that gramophone?"

"Yes, I brought it with me."

"Some of the lads and lasses are meeting at an old abandoned house, other side of the rail line, at three this afternoon. Apparently it's empty and the floors are good for dancing."

This time she did not try to hide her smile. It seemed an age since Violet had danced. Back in Sydney, she would go to a tea dance on Martin Place every Saturday. Two-and-six would buy all the tea and scones she could consume, plus an orchestra that seemed to know any song she could think of to request. "You want me to bring my gramophone?"

"Yes, and your records. Invite Queenie, and whoever you see who isn't working this afternoon. Myrtle knows where it is."

"That sounds like fun," she said, beaming.

"Why don't you meet me out front at half-past two? We can walk together."

She paused. Was he asking her to go with him as a couple? This was tricky. Had he read her questions about his drawings as flirtation? Lord knew men were always misreading her that way.

"Just to share the walk," he added quickly. "I can carry your gramophone for you."

"Yes, why not," she said, relieved. "Lovely."

After breakfast, she took a brisk walk around the grounds, pretending she wasn't glancing up at the windows trying to guess which room was Sam's. She knew that the men's rooms were all on the second floor, but of course she didn't see him. She wondered how hard it would be to find out which room he was in. Then she kicked herself. What would it matter even if she knew? She could hardly go and visit him.

No. She simply *had to* stop thinking about him.

Violet returned to her room and spent the day chatting with Myrtle and Queenie, and tidying up the dress she planned to wear to the dance that afternoon. It was over a year old, but she had paid the princely sum of nine shillings for it and intended to keep wearing it until it dropped off her. It was shell-pink georgette—necessitating two petticoats—with floating side panels and edges of creamy lace that had never been sewn on properly and so lifted and curled at the corners. As she sewed them down, Myrtle dug out a pair of pink satin shoes with diamanté clips that she thought might match the dress. Violet was delighted to find they fit perfectly, even if they were a little stained around the heels. She tied a cream, beaded bandeau in her hair, then pinned the brooch Sam had given her to her dress. By now, it was time to help Queenie and Myrtle dress and arrange their hair. Violet had clever hands for hair. She'd cut her own off just below her ears a few months earlier.

At two thirty, Myrtle declared it time to go. "Shall we all walk together?" she asked, pulling on her coat.

Violet hesitated. "I'm going to walk there with Clive," she said.

Queenie eyed her jealously. "Clive Betts? Is he your boyfriend?"

"No. He just offered to carry my gramophone, that's all."

"He's sweet on you, though," Myrtle said as she fiddled with the buckle on her shoe.

"Is he?" Queenie asked in a whiny voice. "Oh, bother! I'm sweet on him."

"You can have him," Violet said quickly, then felt a twinge of guilt. "I mean, he's lovely, but he's . . ." Not Sam. He was definitely not Sam. "He's not my type."

"He's my type," Queenie said mournfully.

An awkward silence ensued, then Myrtle said, "Well, you'd best not be late for him, as he's been so kind to offer to carry your gramophone. We'll meet you there."

Clive was waiting between the two pine trees that stood sentry at either side of the entrance, dressed impeccably in a suit jacket and cuffed trousers and wearing a straw boater. He took Violet's gramophone by the handle and held out his elbow for her to hold.

She smiled at him as she took it. He returned her smile, but didn't say anything other than, "Come on, then." For that she was glad.

It was too chilly an afternoon to wear the floaty georgette frock, really, but worth it when Violet saw the appreciative glances men gave her when she arrived at the party and shed her coat. About forty people were there: waitstaff and chambermaids and bellboys, and some strangers. A table had been set up with a punch bowl and cups, and several women had baked biscuits and cakes, and busied themselves offering them around. A red-faced young man with a loud voice saw Clive with Violet's gramophone and called, "The music's here!"

A round of cheers went up and a space was cleared. Violet wound it up and put on her favorite dance record—The Original Memphis

Five—and soon they were dancing. Myrtle had smuggled some apples out of the kitchen and they used them for prizes in a spot dance. Violet let herself sink into the moment, enjoying the movement of limbs and feet and the thudding of her heart as she danced.

Later, she was exhausted, leaning on a wall, munching on a crunchy apple when a recording of Marion Harris singing "Somebody Loves Me" came on. Couples began to pair off; others drifted to the sides of the room. The day was growing dim, and there were no working lights in the house. The partygoers had already listened to all three of her records twice through. She nursed a cup of punch and drifted off into her fantasies of Sam again as she fingered his brooch, and the words wound around her still body.

Somebody loves me, I wonder who, I wonder who he can be . . .

"Violet?"

She looked up. It was Clive, smiling down at her.

"Are you having fun?" he asked.

"Yes. I haven't danced in weeks. It's wonderful."

"You look a bit melancholy."

"No. I'm fine. Just a bit homesick maybe." She could never tell him—or anyone—the truth. *I can't stop thinking about a very rich guest at the hotel who gave me this gift and called himself mine.* Clive would bleed the situation of any pleasure, telling her she was mad or imagining it or in danger of losing her job.

"Missing your mother?"

"Yes, absolutely. I should write to her." Violet realized she was telling the truth. She had been too overwhelmed and busy to write to Mama to tell her she had arrived safely. What would her mother say if she knew Violet was nursing feelings for somebody utterly forbidden to her? Suddenly, Violet felt irritated; everyone around her was such a do-gooder.

And do you always do as you're told?

She smiled as she remembered Sam's words.

"There's that smile. Much better," Clive said.

"Clive," Violet said, "did you know that Queenie has a terrific crush on you?"

The side of his mouth twitched in bemusement. "Queenie?"

"She's mad for you. You should ask her to dance."

Clive shrugged, clearly uncomfortable. His eyes found Queenie across the room. "Queenie's not for me." Then he looked back at Violet, and his brow creased as though he'd had an unhappy thought. "I'm sorry," he said, his eyes sad. "I won't . . . We're still friends, aren't we, Violet?"

"Nothing more, nothing less," she said lightly.

He nodded, then turned and headed off towards the drinks table. Violet felt sorry for him, but was relieved nonetheless that he finally seemed to have accepted that their romance—however brief and faint—was over. She studied the people in the room. Laughter and dancing feet. She hadn't the heart for more dancing but didn't want to ruin the party by taking her gramophone away. Nor would she leave it behind for Clive to bring back—not with her precious note from Sam in it. So instead, she shrugged back into her coat and went outside into the cool, late-afternoon air and sat on the stairs where two other girls she'd never met were smoking.

"Cigarette?" one of them said, holding out a filigree cigarette case.

"Thank you," she said.

The other girl, the one with too much lipstick on, lit it for her, and she drew back the smoke then blew it into a narrow stream.

"That brooch is divine," the first girl said.

"Thank you. Somebody special made it for me."

"Made it?" Lipstick girl snorted. "Hardly. I've seen them for sale on the main street for ninepence. An old lady who lives down at Leura makes them for tourists. It's a local flower, see. A rush lily petal."

Violet's face almost stung with mortification. "Did I say 'made'? I meant 'gave.'" They could surely tell she was lying, but they politely didn't point it out. So, Sam hadn't spent hours gluing and lacquering the brooch. He'd spent exactly ninepence on her.

She sat and smoked and waited for the party to finish, which it eventually did when the sun fell behind the horizon. Then she packed up her gramophone and noticed Clive was gone, so she carried it back to the Evergreen Spa, with Myrtle and Queenie for company. Queenie was in tears because Clive had rebuffed her, and when Myrtle kindly told her Clive was a cad and wasn't worth her trouble, Violet bristled.

"Clive Betts is *not* a cad," she said forcefully. "Just because he isn't interested in her doesn't mean he's a bad person. He's one of the sweetest men I know."

Myrtle was taken aback by the heat in Violet's voice. "Yes, but he's rejected poor Queenie here and—"

"That's life," Violet said. "That happens. To everyone." Then she forged on ahead of them, even though Myrtle's shoes were pinching at her toes. She regretted being so beastly to Queenie, but since meeting Sam her moods had swung so wildly she felt she could no longer find their edges and pin them down.

The Evergreen Spa was a tall silhouette ahead of her now. She knew she'd have to face Queenie and Myrtle again in their shared bedroom, but she hoped by then to have had a long bath to calm herself. Lights were coming on in the hotel windows, and she looked up at the second floor again, her eyes ranging from window to window, just in case . . .

There he was. He sat by the window looking down, an expression of dreamy melancholy on his face.

She willed him to see her, wondering if she dared pick up a pebble to cast at the glass in the hope it would draw his attention.

She needn't have worried. Something about her pale dress in the gloom must have caught his eye. His face lit up. A smile broke out on her lips in return.

He lifted his hand and waved, just once. She waved back, then stood gazing up at him gazing down on her, until she feared Myrtle and Queenie would catch her up and she reluctantly went inside.

Her heart was singing again. *Somebody loves me.*

The door to the coffeehouse swung inward, and Tony ushered Flora ahead of him.

"Ladies first," he said, with the twinkle in his eye she knew so well.

She smiled and went in, and the door closed the wintry wind out behind them. The coffeehouse was outside at the rear of the ballroom, and managed by a Turkish couple and their five sons. The decor was all woven mats and gilded wall hangings and bronze ornaments. Few women ventured down here; it had become something of a men's gathering place at the Evergreen Spa. Flora quickly checked the room and noticed with relief that she wasn't the only woman here today.

Tony's gang sat at a table under the back window, which looked out onto a tangle of vines. They all greeted each other roughly, greeted her less roughly, and then sat down again. The waiters came to take their orders, and Flora cringed at the nonsense the men went on with, especially Tony and Sweetie, who made jokes about their headscarves and their skin color. The waiters took the ribbing with good grace, but Flora knew they were offended by it.

"You really shouldn't, you know," she said to Tony once the waiters had disappeared to make their coffees.

"They love it," Sweetie said, with a shrug of his enormous shoulders. "It makes them feel as though we're all friends."

"I rather think it's cruel," she muttered.

"Beware, you're marrying a shrew," Harry teased. "She'll tell you what to do."

Tony kissed her cheek. "Now, put it out of your head, Florrie. Sweetie's right; they'd worry if we stopped now. Not everyone is a gentle soul who can't take a joke, like your brother."

A ripple of chuckles around the table. Flora didn't respond; she was used to them noticing Sam's difference from them. She supposed he was quite eccentric, but it did tire her to be caught in the middle of Tony and Sam's quarrels. She tried, however, to let it all wash over her as the conversation moved on, their coffees arrived—Flora took one sip and knew she would never try coffee again—and the coffeehouse grew noisy.

After a few minutes Tony leaned out of the conversation and spoke softly to Flora. "You don't mind me making a bit of fun of Sam?"

"I do mind. But I'm used to it." She smiled weakly. "I know you two don't get on."

"I thought I might have hurt your feelings. You're very quiet."

"I just worry about him."

"He's a man, not a little boy."

"He *is* a little boy still. His mind and his heart and his soul haven't quite caught up with his body yet." She spread her hands helplessly. "He thinks he's in love."

"With whom?"

"A waitress named Violet."

"The lass who picked up your pearls?"

"The very same. I've kept him away from the dining room a few days, but I can't forever. He talks about her. Wonders aloud where she's from, what she's like."

"Do you want me to have her fired?"

Flora shuddered. "Oh, no. The poor thing. It's not her fault. I keep trying to tell him it's not real love, that he barely knows her and he's besotted with her appearance and can't possibly have a future with her. He's behaving himself for now, but I know it's not sinking in."

Tony furrowed his brow in thought. "Perhaps you're approaching this all wrong. Let him be in love with her but convince him that it would be very bad for her if they were to get involved. She'd certainly lose her job."

Flora turned this idea over in her mind. "You're right. That could work."

Tony winked. "Don't say I never do anything for you."

"I would never say that."

Flora excused herself shortly afterwards to go upstairs to talk to Sam. The afternoons were growing short, and the sunlight had softened and burnished across the valley, its amber reflection caught in the windows in the stairwell. Flora kept her head down as she walked the corridor to Sam's room, wary as she ever was about making eye contact with other men wandering about. She knocked, waited a moment, and reached for her key.

But she didn't have to worry. Sam was coming down the hallway from the bathroom, dressed only in a towel, his hair wet and sticking out at strange angles.

"Sissy!" he called brightly.

She stood back and let him ahead of her to open the door. "You ought to dress before you go running about," she said.

"There's nobody here to offend."

"What if a young woman was down here? Like I am."

"Then she'll see only what God in his good grace chose to make," he replied, opening his arms, then quickly catching his towel before it fell off. "Come in and sit by the window while I dress."

Flora followed him into the room. A quick glance around told her the opium pipe and lamp were nowhere in sight. Her heart remained cautious, however. If he were really in the throes of with-drawal, he wouldn't be so bright and talkative. Sam dropped his towel and she averted her gaze out the window. "Really, Sam. A bit of decorum."

"You used to bathe me," he said. She heard him open his ward-robe door then close it again. "It's nothing you haven't seen before. There, I'm decent now."

She turned to see him clad in a rich red dressing gown, made of silk and embroidered with dragons. He had brought it back from China along with his opium habit. He crouched on the floor next to the bed and brought out his silver tray from beneath.

Flora leaped to her feet and stayed his hand. "Wait," she said. "Just wait until I've said what I need to say. While you're still think-ing straight."

"I always think straight, my lovely Sissy," he said, but nonetheless he left his tray on the floor and straightened his back to look her in the eye. "Go on."

"I've been thinking about Violet."

He smiled, and the warmth that came to his eyes was achingly familiar to her; she had seen it in him since he was a little boy. It was the expression he wore when a passionate interest filled his mind. "Violet," he said. "I've been thinking of her, too."

"I know. It's obvious. I wanted to say . . . don't hurt her."

"I wouldn't dream of it."

"If you do think well of her, remember her station. Remember that to return your interest might cost her her job."

"Then I would look after her. I have plenty of money."

"Sam, no—"

"If you came here to tell me whom to love, then you have wasted your time." He scooped up the tray and sat on the bed with it, light-ing a match and holding it over the wick of the lamp.

"Please be sensible," she said, biting down frustration and fear.

"For what purpose?" He shook out the match and reached for the bottle of opium.

"So that you don't hurt those you love. Those who love you."

"They're fools if they love me," he replied.

"Will you leave her be?"

He exhaled roughly. "I have left her be thus far, have I not? Because you told me to?"

She had to admit it was true. She nodded.

"Then let it go. Perhaps you should have a taste of my pipe, Sissy?"

"No!" she exclaimed quickly. "Never."

He chuckled, drew a lungful of smoke. "You always do the right thing."

Flora wasn't sure if the last comment was an insult or a compliment, but she didn't want to stay around to talk to him more. She couldn't bear him in his stupor. "If it is true I can trust you, I will meet you at the dining room for dinner tonight. We don't have to eat in our rooms anymore."

He waved her away with an elegant figure eight. "Stop worrying."

Much easier for him to say than for her to do.

Flora returned to her room, unlocked the door, and breathed in the sweet scent of the fresh roses Miss Zander left for her every Wednesday. Her hand went to pull the light switch just as her foot struck something on the floor. She looked down and saw a bundle of letters. This week's mail.

Flora sat at the little bureau beside the bed and pulled open the top. She untied the letters, then sifted through them. Two from her father. One from her friend Liberty, who was traveling in America, and another from her old school mistress, who loved to write long, rambling letters about nothing interesting. Finally, the account from Dr. Dalloway. Will.

She slit that one open first, but there was no account. Just a hand-written letter.

Dear Flora,

Rather than bill you for my time, because you took so little of it, I want to extend an invitation for you to consult me again on any day, without an appointment, if you should find you need reassurance or assistance with your terrible burden. I will help you in any way I can.

Yours faithfully,

Will

Flora folded the letter carefully and slid it away. She veered between feeling angry at his presumption, and touched by his offer of help. Neither Sam, nor Tony, nor her father seemed to care much how she fared with this enormous responsibility upon her shoulders. That a stranger should offer to help her in her troubles showed up the lack of support evident everywhere else. She couldn't help but feel embarrassed by his warmth.

Flora placed the letter in one of the nooks in her desk and tried to put it out of her mind.

CHAPTER SEVEN

Violet found her thoughts turning to Sam again and again. In sensible moments, she told herself that she had exchanged only a few words with him, and that she must keep her head. But the sensible moments were few and further apart as the days went by. She didn't see Sam in the dining room: his sister and her beau were often there, but Sam wasn't. Once she saw him wandering through the foyer and out the front doors with a glazed look on his face, but under Miss Zander's watchful eye she couldn't approach him.

So she started to spend her break every day hanging about on the bushwalking path; she had seen him at the Falls once, and she hoped he might go there again. She saw many other guests, most of whom glanced at her uniform curiously as they walked past, but there was no sign of Sam.

Her first two weeks as an employee of the Evergreen Spa passed. She did as she'd promised Clive and worked hard. Miss Zander often gave her a nod of approval as they passed each other in the corridors. She posted money to her mother and attended Queenie's going-away party in the staff dining room, guilty but satisfied to have ongoing work. There was still the problem of the winter break, but that was several weeks away and she hoped to find something up here in a shop or a restaurant to tide her over so she didn't have to go back to Mama empty-handed.

Then one day, loitering by the kitchen door chatting to Myrtle after the lunch shift, she thought she saw Sam. He was crossing the tennis courts and heading down the stone stairs towards the bush-walking path.

"So I decided I would have to hem it again," Myrtle was saying, "because it was simply too short. I suppose you think me a terrible wowser."

"Hm? Oh. No, Myrtle. Not at all."

"I just don't have the legs for it, you know. That scar on my knee, from where I fell last year—"

"Your legs are fine. But . . . I'm sorry, I think I'm . . ." Violet gestured to her forehead. "Headache. I might go for some fresh air."

"Lovely idea. I'll come with you."

"I . . . No, maybe . . ."

Myrtle frowned. "Well, you only have to say if I'm boring you."

Violet grasped Myrtle's hand, squeezed it once, and said, "Sorry. This isn't about you," and started to run.

All of the entrances to the bushwalking paths led to the same place—the fingerpost—and that's where Violet caught up with him. Blessedly, they were the only two on the path.

"Sam!" she called.

He turned, saw her, and stopped. He didn't seem surprised. It was almost as if he'd been expecting her.

She hurried towards him and he gave her a brilliant smile. "There you are," he said.

"Yes," she said. "Here I am."

"I'm going to the Falls. Have you seen them?"

She shook her head. "Not up close."

He took her hand and pulled it. "Let's go."

He began to walk so fast she had to run to keep up, and then when she started to run so did he, over the gravelly path. She hoped her shoes wouldn't trip her. He was laughing, the sun in his hair, and she was almost too puzzled by his strange behavior to relish the feel of his hand over hers. But then the breeze caught her cheeks and she was laughing, too, laughing at how mad it was to be barreling down the bushwalking path in her waitress uniform, hand in hand with a man she barely knew but who had bruised her heart with his dark, dark eyes.

Down the path and up the winding ways they went, the crash of the Falls growing louder and louder. There wasn't time or breath for conversation, though he occasionally exclaimed, "How beautiful!" She was never sure which particular feature of their environment prompted this exclamation—birds or flowers or smells or sounds—but she loved it about him nonetheless. Passion and fire. He was perfect.

Finally, they came to a halt on the flat rocks around the top of the Falls. Little cascades fell into a dark eye of cold water, which then poured over the edge of the cliff and into the valley more than three hundred feet below.

"Do you like to swim, Violet?" he asked.

"I do."

"Go on, then," he said, gesturing to the water hole.

"It'll be freezing."

"Are you scared?" he teased.

She lifted her chin, beaming at him. "You go in. Or are *you* scared?"

He grinned and began unbuttoning his shirt. She remembered seeing him naked here and a flush of warmth rose up through her body. As he shed his clothes he walked to the sandy edge of the water hole. She followed him, already working at her own buttons, alive with fear and desire.

He stripped to his long johns, then stopped, suddenly modest. His body was lithe and pale, thinner than she had expected. She stepped out of her shoes and her dress, unrolled her stockings, and slid out of her petticoat, and dropped them on the rocks. Then she was down to her singlet and bloomers, which were tied with pink ribbons just above her knees. A wave of cold sobriety caught her, then, and she crossed her arms over her chest.

Sam approached her, took both her hands in his, and spread her arms wide. Her small breasts, something that made dresses fit her wonderfully, suddenly seemed a terrible handicap. Her singlet looked as though it were hung on two nails.

"Look how beautiful you are," he said, dropping her hands.

Violet caught her breath. Heart thudding madly, she turned and began to walk into the water. It was freezing, and she braced herself, then waded farther and plunged into the deepest part. Down and down into the dark, icy depths. The cold knocked the breath out of her. She shot to the surface and beckoned him. "See? Not scared."

"Is it cold?" he asked.

"Not in the least. But you can swim, can't you?"

"Of course." A second later he had plunged in next to her. He rose to the surface, hair streaming, and shouted, "Liar!"

She swam away from him to the shallow sides of the pool, and he caught her, pressed her against his body. Her hands went to his shoulders, and she could feel his tight gooseflesh. His lips were an inch from hers.

"May I kiss you?" he asked.

She nodded dumbly, and his lips pressed against hers with all the passion and force of the Falls. The heat of his mouth was searing, making her forget the cold water. He slid his tongue into her mouth—no boy she had kissed before had done that—and she found herself pushing her breasts and thighs against him.

"I knew you'd taste sweet," he murmured into her mouth, then redoubled his force on her lips. His hands cupped her buttocks, kneading them violently.

Suddenly, he released her. "Violet, it's too cold."

Yes, it was too cold. She nodded, and they climbed out of the water hole. She turned her back to him and stripped off her wet singlet, scooping up her petticoat to put on. Then she wriggled out of her bloomers and kicked them off on the rocks, feeling both embarrassed and thrilled. The water on her body was already evaporating, her skin puckered with goose bumps. When she turned around, he was dressed, his wet long johns in a heap on the ground next to her sodden bloomers.

Something about this sight made her laugh, and he grabbed her around the waist and squeezed the breath out of her. "You are so beautiful," he said.

"Let's leave the clothes here for people to wonder about," she said.

"I know somewhere we can go," he said, releasing her, and she had the distinct feeling he hadn't heard or hadn't listened to her. "Come with me."

He grasped her hand again, as he had before, pulling her along in his wake, back up the bushwalking path, her legs aching from the ascent. But then he took a detour, over rocks and ferns, and a few moments later they stood at the mouth of a cave.

Violet grew wary. "It looks dark."

"Yes. Nobody will see us. I come here all the time."

She allowed herself to be taken into the cave.

"I want to show you something," he said. "Look."

Near the entrance was a large rock with a smooth back. She squinted in the gloom and realized he was showing her a carved shape on its surface. As she looked closer, she realized it was a love heart with hard angles where soft curves should be.

"Did you carve this?"

He shook his head. "No. I found it. This is granite. Imagine, somebody had to carve this with a hammer and chisel, to prove his love to his girl. Ever since I found it, I've thought of this cave as Lovers Cave. Do you not think it's wonderful? The passion?"

She ran her fingers over the chiseled lines, not telling him that she found the love heart a little ugly. When she turned, Sam was unbuttoning his shirt again. A stab of desire, but also a wave of caution.

"Sam? Why are you taking your shirt off?"

"We're going to make love," he said.

Her head swam, but the cave floor was cold, and she was certain the cave was home to ants and spiders.

"No," she said, softly but firmly.

He paused in his unbuttoning and frowned. Was he angry with her? Cool regret. Now she would lose him.

"I'm sorry," she elaborated. "Not here. Not now."

"Well, nobody's ever said no to me before," he remarked, fingers falling away from his buttons, leaving his shirt half open.

"Sam, I've never said yes before," she replied slowly, so he understood.

"Is that so? Are you saving yourself for marriage?"

"For love," she said.

"Is that so?" he said again.

"I hardly know anything about you," she said.

"We'll rectify that right now. Come on, sit down here with me. Don't worry, the soil is quite soft. You can put your head in my lap. There."

Violet relaxed into his lap, and he laid his coat across her shoulders and began to stroke her hair softly.

"What would you like to know?" he asked.

"How old are you?"

"Nearly twenty."

"So am I," she said.

"Keep going. More questions."

"Where do you come from? Tell me about your family."

"I live with my family on one hundred thousand acres of farm-land in New South Wales. We are very wealthy and well known, apparently. I have more money than you could count." He laughed at this comment, though Violet wasn't sure why. "My father is an evil old schemer, and my mother is a pretty doormat. My poor sister, whom you have met, is kinder than she ought to be, given her provenance. My father has arranged to marry her off to the oily son of one of his business associates, a man who is not her equal in brains or good nature, and who will no doubt fill her belly with a dozen Catholic babies and use her up until she's a husk. What about you?"

She was painfully aware of the difference in their fortunes and prospects. "I have a mother with arthritis who works as a laundress and seamstress. She can make a dress in a day, and is often required to do so by the family she works for. But they pay her very little and her hands don't work like they used to. I send her money, but I can see a time where I'll have to work for both of us . . ." Violet trailed off. Speaking the awful truth aloud made her feel miserable and lost.

Sam had grown quiet. She turned her head to look up at him, and his gaze was thoughtful.

"Do you love your mother?" he asked.

"Of course I love her."

"Then don't worry about it. Because anyone you love, I love, too, and I have enough money to fix everything. So, never worry about it again, because I can't bear to see you fret. I will fix everything with my money. It's easy for me, and I love you."

The declaration of love was buried at the end of such a confusing statement that Violet almost didn't register it. He loved her? Her heart sped. He loved her.

"More questions," he said.

She took a moment to gather herself. "Um . . . what are you doing at the Evergreen Spa?"

"I have some health problems that don't bother me but they bother everybody else. I am here to resolve them. We've been here two months now. It's Flora and Tony's first holiday together, but he keeps traveling to Sydney to visit prostitutes, although he tells her they are business trips."

"That's horrible."

"*He* is horrible."

"Have you told her?"

"It would hurt her too much. And she wouldn't believe me. But I heard him bragging to his vile friends. Come on, more questions. About me. Not them."

"Do you believe in God?"

His hands left her hair for a moment and he flung them in the air. "Yes! I worship the poppy god."

"I've never heard of him."

"Perhaps the poppy god is a woman," he said. "She has such a way about her. Next question."

"Do you really love me?"

"Oh, yes. The moment I saw you. The moment I saw you."

He closed his eyes, a rapturous expression on his face, and Violet's body was traversed with happiness and longing and wild peaks of feeling. She loved him, too. Mad as it seemed, she loved him, too, and had since their eyes had met that evening in the dining room. Others would say she was foolish: Myrtle or Clive or her mother. But *they* were the fools. What ignorance to think that love must be somehow sober and orderly, unfolding in a slow, set pattern so one didn't get too much of a shock. Love was a thunderbolt, crashing down on her with its brilliant, savage force. It was ancient and eternal and it peeled back the mundane layers of the world and showed her the wet, beating heart of reality beneath.

"I love you, too," she said.

"Of course you do," he replied. "You understand me."

She reached up towards his chin and touched him gently, her heart giddy. "I will lose my job if we're discovered."

"I don't care. I have enough money for both of us."

"I do care," she said. "Just for now. Just until things are more . . . certain."

"Then I will be very careful." He opened his eyes and smiled down at her. "Sissy is watching me. She would decidedly not approve. Nor would my mother and father. It's delicious, isn't it? A love that is forbidden tastes sweeter and sharper."

"Maybe you're right. But, Sam," she said gently, "I have to go and get properly dry and dressed for work."

"Let's go back to the hotel, but not together," he said. "You go a hundred yards ahead of me, as though we were simply out walking at the same time and don't know each other. I can watch the sweet sway of your hips the whole way."

"All right," she said, climbing to her feet. "I'll go first."

At dinner that night, she and Sam tacitly agreed to play a game. She swapped tables with Myrtle, who agreed grudgingly because she was still hurt about Violet cutting her off earlier that day, and Violet waited on his table as though nothing had passed between them. He sat with his sister—who watched Violet like a hawk—along with the Italian man and his entourage, the opera singer, the beauty queen, and the writers. Flora dressed very soberly, in a long gray skirt and buttoned blouse, with her long hair pinned in a tidy bun. It was hard to credit that she and Sam were siblings. They all laughed and talked happily, including Sam, who didn't meet her eye once.

And yet . . . as she moved past he would casually brush her hip with his forearm; as she stood and leaned in to clear plates he would press the side of his calf against hers. Each touch was hot and electrifying. Lucid in her mind were the memories of the day, of being naked with him, of kissing him, of his open desire to make love to her. She shivered with it. In all her nearly twenty years, she had never considered having sex. Mama had drummed into her that "getting in trouble" led only to misery: indeed, she was proof of that. Violet had had many boyfriends. Some had tried to get fresh, and she'd slapped their hands or sometimes their faces. But Sam awoke a hunger in her that she had never imagined she would experience. How she wanted to be naked with him again, to press the full length of her soft body against his hot, hard one. Consequences didn't exist in her imagination: there was only the desire, liquid and searing.

After her shift, she lay for a long time in bed with that desire swirling in her body, keeping her awake. She wondered if she'd ever sleep well again.

The staff dining room always had a peculiar smell at breakfast time. Bacon and toast, yes, but also a yeasty, damp smell from having been locked up all night. Despite the cold, Violet opened a window a crack. The windows down here were almost at ground level, but a sweet sliver of fresh air made its way in nonetheless. Violet leaned at the window a moment, letting the cold air refresh her tired eyes after a night of tossing and turning. Other staff were making their way to the buffet and to tables, talking and laughing and clinking crockery and cutlery. But suddenly there was silence.

Violet turned. Miss Zander stood at the door, looking out of place with her immaculate hair and elegant pearls. She surveyed the room, and each staff member held their breath, wondering if she was looking for them.

"Ah, Violet," she said, when she spied Violet by the window. "Have you eaten?"

"No," said Violet, pulse pricking at her throat.

"Have some breakfast and come straight through to my office." Then she turned and left without further comment.

The others eyed Violet with pity. Clive was with her a moment later. "What's going on?" he asked.

"I don't know." She considered last night's game with Sam. Had Hansel caught on that she was flirting with a guest? Had Myrtle told tales? Or was it worse than that? Had somebody seen them kissing, or standing at the Falls nearly naked?

"You'd better eat something, then," Clive said. "Sit down, I'll get you a plate."

How was she supposed to eat with this worry hanging over her head? Her tired brain couldn't grasp it. She just wanted to go back to bed and sleep until it was all over.

"Go on. Sit," Clive said again, pushing her gently towards the women's side of the dining room.

Violet sat and Myrtle joined her. Bless Myrtle; she sat close to Violet and gave her a squeeze. "I'm sure it's nothing," she said. "Miss Zander's always putting the fear of God into us for no good reason."

Clive returned with a plate of bacon and steak. Violet picked around the edges, then pushed it away, sliding off the bench. "I have to get this over with," she said.

"Good luck," Myrtle replied softly.

She made her way up the stairs and through the foyer to the pale blue door of Miss Zander's office. She knocked and waited. At last, Miss Zander opened the door.

"Yes, good. Come in, Violet."

Violet followed her in. Miss Zander took her place behind her gleaming desk, upon which papers, books, ink well, and pens were arranged precisely in parallel lines. Miss Zander didn't invite Violet to sit, so she remained standing, hands clasped and clammy.

"Is there something the matter?" she asked. Here it came, the accusation of fraternizing with a guest. If she lost her job, would Sam really come to her rescue?

"I have spoken to several of my guests," she said, looking at her papers.

Violet was almost deafened by the sound of her blood rushing past her ears. She didn't dare speak.

"There are enough who have no firm plans to leave over the winter that I have decided to keep the hotel open with a skeleton staff in place. Ordinarily, you see, we would close after Christmas in June celebrations, and reopen again on the first day of spring."

Because it wasn't the accusation of misbehavior she expected, Violet wasn't sure what to say.

"I'm very happy with your work, and I'm inviting you to continue to work through the winter."

The relief washed through her like warm water. "Oh, yes!" she exclaimed. "Yes, please. That's wonderful news."

"Good girl. Now, keep it to yourself because there's plenty who have worked here a lot longer than you who aren't getting the extra work. Myrtle, for example. As far as I can tell, we will have fewer than a dozen guests to service. You may need to double up some duties. I hope you don't think yourself above some chambermaid work."

"Not at all. I am most grateful for this opportunity and I won't let you down."

"I know you won't," Miss Zander said with a smile, and Violet's heart lifted.

With a startling clang, the wood-and-brass candlestick telephone on Miss Zander's desk came to life. Miss Zander reached for it with one hand, shooing Violet out with the other.

"Thank you. Thank you," Violet mouthed, backing out of the room.

She closed the door behind her and stood against it a moment, her eyes closed. Now she could write to Mama and promise her money over winter. Mama's arthritis was worst during winter, and every year she feared the family she worked for would put her off. Violet opened her eyes and headed off to work, letting her mind turn to other things. Would Sam be one of the guests staying over winter? Her heart couldn't stand not knowing.

A sharp rap on her door startled Flora out of her reverie. She had been sitting at her desk, a half-written letter to her father in front of her. How was she to frame the news that Sam was no better or no worse? Should she confess that she couldn't stop him smoking opium? Was it worth including Dr. Dalloway's testimony? Or was Father still unaware that Sam's woes were largely self-inflicted? If so, to tell him would shock him so badly he might do something unforgivable, such as disown Sam. What then for her younger brother? Would he have to live on the street, like the filthy beggars she had seen in Sydney?

The knock was a welcome distraction. She rose and opened the door to Miss Zander, the elegant manageress.

"Good morning, Miss Honeychurch-Black," she said, briskly.

"Forgive my intrusion, but there is a telephone call for you in my office."

"A telephone call?"

"Mr. Honeychurch-Black. That is, your father."

Flora felt the blood drain from her face. "My father," she whispered. "Is everything all right?"

"Yes, yes. I was engaged in writing him a letter precisely when you knocked. It's a shock, that's all. As though I made him come to life." She laughed nervously, realizing she sounded foolish. "Kindly show me the way."

She followed Miss Zander downstairs and across the foyer to her office, where Miss Zander indicated the phone and politely left her alone. The door closed behind her.

Flora picked up the handset in one hand, the receiver in the other, and perched on the edge of the desk. "Hello, Father?"

"Florrie, my dear. How lovely to hear your voice."

"I was just writing you a letter. What a coincidence."

"You're a good girl. Letters take too long, and I needed to speak to you about two pressing matters."

Flora swallowed hard. "Go ahead."

"I've had two pieces of correspondence that trouble me somewhat. One from your brother and one from your fiancé."

"Tony wrote to you?"

"Why don't we save that one for last, eh? About Samuel. He says you are staying a little longer in the mountains."

"That's right," Flora said, her pulse prickling guiltily at her throat. "I was going to tell you myself. I had no idea Sam wrote to you."

"He does from time to time. Long, rambling things that don't make a good deal of sense, but he always did have an odd imagination. Am I to take it from your extended stay that his condition is improving?"

Flora opened her mouth to speak, to tell him her brother was an opium addict and she could no sooner make him better than she could fly to the moon by flapping her arms, but fear held her tongue. She had to protect Sam. "A little. A very little."

"Then that is enough." His voice sounded so relieved that Flora could have cried for him.

"Father, his condition is . . . I consulted a doctor who has offered his support to me."

"Well done. With that and the fresh air and spa water, he will be back to himself in no time. I have every faith you can resolve this."

She was keen to change the topic but also wary. "What about Tony's letter?"

His voice became stern. "I don't think you've been perfectly honest with me, Florrie."

"What do you mean?" She glanced out the window, at the white winter sunlight in the crisscross of pine branches. It looked cold out there, bitterly so, though the office was warm.

"Tony has asked to bring the wedding forward."

"Oh."

"But you told me he wanted it put back six months. I've just sent a letter off to him now asking him to explain, but thought it might be quicker and clearer if I spoke to you."

Father had written back to Tony? A disaster. Tony would know she'd delayed the wedding. "I said *we* wanted it put back," she explained limply.

"By 'we,' you meant 'Flora,' is that right?"

"Yes," she said softly. "I didn't talk to Tony about it. I didn't realize he minded. He thought it was your decision."

An exasperated noise. "What on earth can you hope to gain from putting the wedding off, Florrie?"

"I don't know," she said, and it was true. It was all coming, whether she liked it or not. She would be a wife and then a mother, she would manage a house and attend charity balls and grow old by Tony's side, neatly fulfilling her duty as a member of the Honeychurch-Black family, even with her new, more exotic, surname.

Her father's voice grew gentle. "Could you speak to Tony, please? Set a date. Sometime this year."

Her breath compressed in her lungs. This year was already half over.

"Florrie?"

"He's in Sydney for a few days, but I'll definitely speak to him. Don't send the letter to him. He'll think me a liar, or he'll think I don't love him. I do love him."

"I'm afraid it's too late. It went in this morning's mail. But perhaps that's a blessing. Best to have it out in the open. A marriage doesn't thrive in the shadows. Talk to him. Write to me with a date. I expect a letter by the end of next week. Will you promise me?"

"Yes, yes," she said, dreading Tony's return. "I promise you."

After the breakfast shift, Violet returned to her bedroom and noticed her pillow had been propped up against the wall. Curious, she picked it up and found underneath it a small white linen bag with a red drawstring.

She untied the string. Inside the bag were sweets. Conversation sweets. Back in Sydney, she and her friends were always trading them with each other at dances or at the cinema. Violet tipped them out on her bed and sorted through them. Pink ones, white ones, yellow ones. On each one was stamped the words *I love you*.

Violet could barely contain her smile.

*   *   *

The early evenings were the worst. Flora had no idea which version of Sam she would find when she went to fetch him for dinner—smiling and acquiescent, irrational and cross, or lost to the world in his eyes-half-closed golden bubble. Flora sat in her room very still, willing the butterflies in her stomach to do the same. Finally, she rose and made her way to his room.

She knocked, and he opened the door almost immediately, wild-eyed and flushed. He was wearing a half-unbuttoned shirt and crumpled trousers that she suspected he had found on the floor or under the bed.

"Sissy?" he said, seemingly puzzled.

"Why aren't you dressed for dinner?"

"Not coming. I have to see a friend. He's been away and . . . I really need to see him."

"A friend? What friend?" Sam didn't have friends; he never had.

"Just a fellow I know from the village. I'm off to see him at six. Is it six yet?" He pulled out his pocket watch. "Twenty minutes. Twenty minutes, then I'm off."

Flora grew suspicious. "What's this friend's name?"

"Never mind. You are terribly nosy sometimes. You go down to dinner. I heard Tony and his entourage pass by just a few minutes ago. I'll see you in the morning at breakfast." He moved to close the door in her face, but she held out her forearm to stop him.

"Sam, I spoke to Father today. You really must stop writing him strange letters."

"Did I write him a strange letter?"

"He says you did."

"I dreamed I wrote him a letter. Or perhaps that was real." He frowned.

She dropped her voice low. "Do you see what the opium does to you? You can't tell the difference between sleeping and waking."

With a hard expression, he pushed her arm out of the way and slammed the door. Flora stood a moment on the other side, and made her decision.

She considered going to the dining room to tell Tony's friends she wasn't coming down for dinner, but they wouldn't even notice she was gone, or perhaps they would ask questions and take the opportunity to sneer at Sam; so instead she took her coat from her room and, without telling anyone, went to wait outside.

The shock of cold air hit her as the heavy double doors closed behind her. The last orange sliver of sun had almost extinguished behind the valley, and stars emerged on the eastern horizon. She positioned herself between two pine trees along the front fence—they stood just over eight feet high—and watched the front door from the shadows.

An icy breeze ran over her, and she jammed her hands into her coat pockets, wishing she had stopped for her gloves or some sturdy boots. A few minutes later, the door opened, allowing out a finger of light, and Sam emerged, hunched into his coat. She watched as he walked briskly up the road, then she began to trail him a hundred feet behind.

It had been a long time since she had seen him move so fast. In the past year he had become languid and idle. His head was down, and if he heard her footfalls behind him, he gave no sign.

They went up the hill then crossed the train tracks. The station was empty and still, the EVERGREEN FALLS sign rattling in the breeze. The grass was long here, and damp with dewfall. Dusk had given way to night, and Flora alternated between watching Sam and watching her feet carefully so she didn't slip.

At last he began to slow, glancing up at the houses on the left as though unsure which one he was supposed to visit. Finally, he stopped. Flora drew as close as she dared, then hung back behind an oak tree. Yellow and brown leaves showered down over her in a gust of wind. Sam ascended the five front steps to the low veranda of a dilapidated house. A lamp burned on either side of the steps, and another sat on the floor next to a long sofa on which an Oriental man was stretched out, stroking a fluffy ginger cat.

Flora strained to hear.

"Malley," Sam said to him, "you're back."

"Back with everything you need."

It was as she suspected: this man—Malley—was the supplier of Sam's opium. How she wanted to run up there and scream at them both to stop, but instead she could only watch. Sam sat next to Malley, and as he did so and the lamplight hit the man in the face, she could see he wasn't Oriental at all. He was as white as she was, but he was dressed in loose black pants and an embroidered Manchu jacket. He wore his long, black hair in a tightly contained ponytail, and his goatee beard and mustache were long and wispy. The beam of the veranda railing obscured what they were doing, but she supposed they were exchanging money and goods.

Flora sagged against the tree, the rage and pain boiling inside her. How dare this horrid Malley peddle poison to her brother, and all with such a relaxed smile on his face? She took deep breaths, waiting for Sam to finish his business and hurry off into the night. Then, instead of following him, she detached herself from the shadows and stormed up the front stairs of Malley's house.

He looked up at her blearily. "Who are you?"

"I'm Samuel's sister, and I absolutely demand you stop selling him opium."

He smiled slyly, and the heat of her anger cooled enough for her to remember that she didn't know this man, she was out here at night alone, and nobody knew where she was.

"Why do you think that's what I was selling him?" Malley asked.

"Because . . ." she stammered. She had no proof. "I know you were. Don't try to be clever."

He rose, and she backed down two steps, her heart hammering. But he wasn't coming after her, he was opening his front door and slipping inside.

"I'll tell the police about you!" she cried.

"Then I'll tell them about your brother," he answered, spreading his hands in a gesture of innocence. "Prison would suit him, don't you think?"

With that, he closed the door with a soft snick, and left her standing on his front stairs shaking with cold and fear and anger.

She turned and looked around at the starry sky, the dark tree branches fretting in the wind. Her throat seemed blocked up with some terrible scream she was never allowed to release. Her vision swam and she feared she was about to faint. She realized she was only a block or two from Will Dalloway's house. He had said she could call on him any time, hadn't he?

She began to run.

A few minutes later, she was thundering on his door. "Will! Will! Let me in!"

The door opened, spilling out light and warmth and the smell of something good cooking. He looked at her in alarm, catching her in his arms and then setting her upright on the hallway floor while he locked the door behind her.

"What's happened? Are you injured?"

"No, I'm not, I'm . . ." She realized she was sobbing, her face was damp and hot. "I'm not sure what's wrong. It feels as though I'm falling apart. I'm . . ."

He steadied her, brought her inside through the door marked PRIVATE, and set her on a wing-backed chair. "Sit," he said, striding to a drinks tray on the mantelpiece. "You aren't falling apart, but you're hysterical. Here." He returned with a glass of whiskey, which she duly gulped.

"Now. What happened?"

She handed him the whiskey glass and told him, finally expressed aloud the cruel corner into which she was painted. Sam was an addict; she had to help him to keep their father's favor but couldn't help him without exposing him to the law, or to disavowal by his family, or to some other horror that she hadn't yet managed to imagine. Either way, no matter what she did it could not be the right thing. As she spoke she wept openly, as though she had lost her propriety on Malley's front steps and would never get it back. But it felt so good to have said it all, and to have cried so openly.

All the while he sat in front of her on an embroidered ottoman, the lamplight flaring in his Harold Lloyds. When she had finished, the mortification crept in.

"I'm so sorry," she said, "I really shouldn't have—"

"My mother drank," he said quickly. "To excess. When I came home from school every day, I didn't know if she would be sober and guilty, or drunk and angry. I tried everything I could to fix her. I tried to be good. I did well at school. I wrote her stories. I begged her to stop. I thought if I could just figure out the one thing that would bring her to her senses, I could help her. In the end, of course, there was nothing I could do. My father packed my sister and me up when I was fourteen and he left her. She tried to contact me a few times, but then I heard nothing until news of her death reached me, just last Christmas."

Flora looked at him, blinking hard. He had delivered the whole story in a voice holding firm against a surging tide of emotion.

He drew breath, and his voice returned to normal. "So you see, Flora, I know how you feel. You need never be sorry for it."

She nodded, afraid to speak lest she cry again.

"Another whiskey?"

"No, I'd . . . I should return to the hotel. Nobody knows where I am."

"Let me drive you. You oughtn't be out after dark alone."

"No, no. It isn't far."

"I insist. Please, Flora, let me help you."

She placed her fingers on her forehead, unable to think straight. "All right, then. All right."

Only ten minutes later she was back at the entrance to the hotel, watching as Will's car pulled away up the hill. He had driven her in warm, sweet silence, despite the cold, oily smell of the car. Something had shifted inside her, and it was with a surprising sense of regret that she watched the last flash of his Nash sedan's headlamps turn the corner and disappear out of sight. What a different life she could have had. Simpler. Better. But Tony was back tomorrow or the next day, and they had to choose a wedding date.

Then, the rest of her life would come rushing towards her, stealing her feet from under her, like a current too strong to fight.

CHAPTER EIGHT

Tony returned on a Saturday afternoon. He seemed perfectly fine and happy through dinner, and kissed Flora warmly on the cheek before he went to bed that night, telling her he loved her. She counted the days and was certain Father's letter would have arrived already if it was going to, so she allowed herself a sigh of thanks. Father must have somehow retrieved it from the mail, to save her embarrassment.

On Sunday, Karl invited them all for a trout-fishing expedition in the cold streams and water holes ten miles north of Evergreen Falls. Because the challenge of organizing enough space in cars and sulkies for all of them became too confusing, they decided it would be a lark to catch the train with all their fishing rods, buckets, and bags. Sam refused to come, of course, leaving Flora in the company of Tony, Sweetie, Harry, Vincent, and Vincent's girlfriend, Eliza, who had come up from Sydney for the weekend. Eliza and Flora sat together on the long train seat, ladylike in their knee-length box-pleated skirts, with picnic baskets on their laps. The boys in their straw boaters mucked about, putting their heads and arms out windows, bragging about the size and number of fish they would catch. Vincent occasionally sent a friendly wink over to Eliza, but Tony seemed to have forgotten Flora was there. It was no matter; she liked to see him happy.

They alighted two stops up the line and began the long walk down to the stream. The day was cool and clear, and the sun shone a little warm light from far away. A kookaburra called in the distance, and the boys all attempted impersonations of it, making themselves laugh until they were doubled over. At length, the group came to a large watering hole. The boys kicked off their shoes and rolled up their trousers to wade in, while Flora and Eliza scouted for an appropriate place to set up the picnic, settling on a large flat rock to lay the tablecloth and spread out the cutlery and plates. The food stayed wrapped for the time being.

"It will be too cold for them to stand in the water for long," Eliza observed.

"I don't know if the goal is actually to catch fish," Flora answered. "I think the fun might have already been had."

"They are certainly in high spirits."

Flora turned to gaze at Tony, who had his back to her. The sun caught highlights in his dark hair. His broad back was flexed and his hips square, as he cast his line into the cold water. His back. When she was married, she could touch his back. Not just through his shirt, as she had once or twice boldly while he kissed her. It gave her an odd, awkward thrill.

"When are you two getting married?" Eliza said, sitting on the edge of the rock and crossing her ankles.

"I'm supposed to make a date as soon as possible," Flora replied, turning back to the picnic. "I have to talk to Tony about it. He's been away on business in Sydney."

Eliza nodded, seemed as though she wanted to say something but didn't. Instead, she smiled. "You love him?"

"I do. How about you and Vincent?"

"I keep hoping he'll ask me to marry him, but he doesn't. It's been ages. Six months. It doesn't help that he's been up here for so long."

"That might be my fault. Or perhaps my brother's fault. Sam won't leave, so I can't leave, so Tony stays on, so they all do. But don't worry, we're all coming back down after Christmas in June. Just two more weeks. Perhaps then Vincent will do the right thing."

Eliza shrugged. "I don't know. Do men really even know 'the right thing' to do?"

"I hope so."

She dropped her voice. "Flora, if you knew that Vincent was . . . doing the *wrong* thing . . . would you tell me?"

Flora was taken aback by the question. "Vincent is the kindest man, Eliza. You have nothing to worry about."

"But would you?"

"Would you want me to?"

Eliza nodded emphatically. "I would want to know if he did something he oughtn't."

"Then, yes, I would."

Eliza's gaze went over Flora's shoulder, and she turned to see Tony emerging from the water.

Flora beamed at him. "Giving up already?"

"Had a few nibbles." He nodded at Eliza. "Mind if I steal your companion a few minutes? I need to talk to her."

Eliza said, "Of course," but Flora had the distinct feeling some animosity passed between them.

Tony took her by the arm, and they headed into the woods. As soon as they were out of earshot, Flora asked, "Don't you and Eliza get on?"

"Eliza? She's a silly thing. Vincent can do better. I don't like it when she gossips and whispers like that."

"You heard her?"

"She has a shrill voice that carries. I heard her whisper, though I didn't hear what she had to say. I don't care to know, Flora. Just be wary of her." He stopped, turned her to face him. "But I didn't bring you here to talk about Eliza."

A cool edge touched his voice, and Flora's stomach flipped over. "No?" A breeze picked up and fretted in the branches above them. A deep smell of eucalyptus and dank soil reached her nose.

"I received a letter from your father when I arrived back yesterday."

The letter. The cursed letter. Flora squirmed. "Why didn't you mention it yesterday?"

"I thought I might see if *you* mentioned it first."

Flora shook her head. "Don't be cross. I know I've been silly."

"I want to get this straight. You told your father that *I* wanted to delay the wedding?"

"Yes."

"And you told me that *he* wanted to delay the wedding?"

"Again, yes."

"But all along, the only person who wanted to put the wedding off was you?"

This time she simply nodded, cheeks heating with shame despite the chill air.

Tony turned half away from her, his lips set in a hard line, shaking his head with anger.

"I'm sorry, Tony," she said, reaching for his shoulder.

He flicked her off. "Can you tell me why?"

"Everything seemed to be going too fast."

"Do you not want to marry me?"

"Of course I want to marry you. I love you."

"Then I simply don't understand."

She took a deep breath. Maybe Tony would understand if she

told him. They were to be married, after all. Partners for life, confidants. "Do you ever feel that your life isn't your own? That you are floating along helplessly on a course already set out for you?"

"Must you go on with such nonsense, Florrie?" Tony said, moving from anger to exasperation. "All these starry-eyed notions—they're the reason your brother is such a mess. I expect you to be more practical. It's what I love about you."

"You've never felt it? You've never felt that you're unfairly compelled to work in your family business rather than pursue some greater passion? That you've been forced to marry me rather than meet the girl of your dreams?"

"I don't believe in girls in dreams. They only come when I'm sleeping," he said hotly. "Is that what this is about? Are you holding out for a dream man?"

"No, that's not at all what I meant."

"Flora, our fathers are great friends, that's true. They introduced us because we suited each other, not because this is a nineteenth-century novel and we have to marry against our will. We get along, don't we? We like each other's company?"

Slowly, it dawned on Flora that Tony was hurt by her doubts.

"Don't you see?" he continued. "Other troubles go away when we marry—mine and yours. With me as your husband, your father can cut you out of his will later on and it doesn't matter. We'll still be fine. He's promised to buy us a house, for heaven's sake. With you as my wife, I get invited into society more readily. I'm not 'new money' anymore; I'm an honorary Honeychurch-Black. Flora," he continued, touching her shoulder, letting his hand wander lightly to her breast, "there are other things that I really don't want to wait for anymore." Then he lifted his hand away, ever the gentleman.

Blood thudded in her head.

"What would you do, Flora?" Tony pressed. "If you didn't marry me, if you didn't live the life your family dreamed for you, what would you do? You'd be a fish out of water."

"I'd be a doctor," she blurted.

Now he laughed. "You? A *doctor*?"

Her face stung with indignation. "I'm very clever and I like helping people."

He shook his head, laughter dying on his lips. "Flora, I do love you. But you are being ridiculous."

A loud cheer in the distance alerted them to the fact that somebody had caught a fish.

"I'm not being ridiculous," she said softly, but he didn't seem to hear.

"Let's get back," he said. "I forgive you for bending the truth. Put it out of your mind."

"September," she said, with sudden, decisive courage. "We'll get married in the spring."

"Perfect. Choose a Saturday near the middle and let your father know." He put his arm around her and led her back out of the woods. "Aren't you glad we had this little chat?"

She nodded mutely. She couldn't find fault with any of his arguments, so she didn't entertain that little shred of protest inside her that said, *But what about my dreams?* Tony was right. Dreams came only when sleeping. Tony had woken her up, and it was time to get on with life.

Flora called in at Sam's room that afternoon to tell him about the wedding date.

"I'd say I'm happy for you, Sissy," he said, "but I'm too miserable at the idea that Tony DeLizio will be my brother-in-law until the day I die."

"Don't be like that, Sam," Flora said, sitting on the bed next to him. She noticed a book on the bedside table, folded open. She was pleased that he'd been reading, and that she could not detect any smell of opium smoke in the room. "I have to grow up sometime."

"So, a spring bride, eh?" He snapped his fingers. "You should get married up here! This place is easily big enough and posh enough for a society wedding."

Flora frowned. "We'll be gone long before September," she said. "We're leaving straight after Christmas in June."

"Are we?"

"You promised me. Also, the hotel is closing down."

He spread his hands eagerly. "It's not. Not entirely. I was talking to Lord and Lady Powell this morning. They're staying on—Lady Powell is trying to finish her book. And of course, she's terribly good friends with Mrs. Wright, the opera singer, who has said she's staying, too. And Miss Sydney has adopted Mrs. Wright as a mother figure, so she and her odious fiancé will dig in as well. Miss Zander told them she's retaining a skeleton staff. Imagine? A handful of us rattling about with the hotel all to ourselves."

Flora was shaking her head through this entire speech. "No, no, a thousand times *no*, Sam. The Christmas party is the twenty-fifth of June, and we are leaving on the twenty-sixth."

"You can go without me," he sniffed.

"I can't. Father won't allow me to leave you here and I—"

"But, Flora," he interrupted, placing his index finger over her lips. "I'm feeling so much better. I'm smoking less. I'm sure it's the mountain air."

She narrowed her eyes.

"I know you want me to stop altogether, but that's so hard. Instead, I'm slowly cutting down the number of pipes I smoke. Look at me now." He dropped his finger and stood in front of her, and she did have to admit he looked well.

"Really?"

"It's Violet," he said. "She makes me want to be a good person."

"Violet? The waitress?"

Once again his index finger returned to her lips. "Don't say a bad word against her. She's done this to me. She's done what you never could."

How his words hurt her, gouged her deep in the belly. But if it was true that his love for the waitress inspired him to smoke less, then she had to accept it. "Please be careful with her," she said.

"I wouldn't do a thing that wasn't right and good," he replied. Then smiled a boyish smile. "Well? Can we stay?"

"I'm not getting married up here."

"We can stay over the winter?"

Tony wouldn't like it, but that mattered little. Sam's health was her first priority. "As long as you continue to cut down."

He pressed his hand fervently to his heart. "I give you my word."

"Then we'll stay," she said, and regretted it immediately.

Dances at the abandoned house had become a regular Saturday-afternoon occurrence, and Violet, owner of the gramophone, was expected to come. She didn't mind so much: she loved to dance, and spending all week in a black-and-white uniform was terribly dull. It was nice to put on some color and do her hair.

Today, the room was buzzing with excitement about the upcoming Christmas-in-June celebrations. The staff were considering their own celebrations before the winter break, and word had it that Miss Zander had given permission for the staff to mingle with the guests at the afternoon Christmas party. Somebody had brought new records—they'd all tired of Violet's three—and the music was fast and fun, and Violet hit the dance floor to dance the black bottom, the Saint Louis hop, and the Charleston. Evening was coming. One of the chambermaids had brought along a bag full of cracked glasses from the hotel that were destined to be thrown out, and she went around the room setting them out with candles in them, adding a little flickering light to the interior. A foxtrot came on, and Clive approached her hopefully. She let him take her in his arms, but tried to keep a cool distance between them. It made their steps awkward, but he didn't seem to notice.

"I'm not supposed to say anything," Clive confessed, "but I simply must know if Miss Zander has asked you to stay over winter."

Violet glanced around. Nobody was listening. The music and chatter were loud anyway. "Yes, I am. She didn't want me to tell anyone, though."

Clive grinned. "Me, too," he said. "We'll both be here."

"I'll be glad to have a friend here," she replied guardedly, knowing he wanted more. Clive was a good man, a kind man. But now she had known feelings of a different order; Clive would never be enough. "I don't know if Myrtle is staying. I daren't ask her."

"Where is Myrtle today?"

"Back at the hotel with a sprained ankle. She slipped in the kitchen this morning. She really is accident prone."

"I'll say she is. Why, just last week she . . . Who's that?"

Violet turned, following the direction of his gaze. Her heart grew hot. It was Sam, standing at the entrance to the house, searching the room with his eyes.

"Isn't he a hotel guest?" Clive asked.

Sam found her and strode over. The crowd parted, still dancing but eyeing him curiously. Murmurs passed from lips to ears. Sam extended his hand for Violet, not even looking at Clive. "Will you dance with me?"

"I . . ."

Clive tightened his grip on her for a moment, then took note of the expression on Violet's face and realized he'd been bested. He let her go. "If you want to, Violet. Don't let me stop you."

Violet moved swiftly into Sam's arms, but the foxtrot ran for only another half minute and then they stood for a few moments, still holding each other, gazing at each other, waiting for the next song.

It was a waltz: "It's Time to Say Goodnight" by Henry Hall. He pressed her to him, his warm hand on the small of her back, and they started to move. The party, the crowd, receded into the distance. There was only her body and Sam's body, perfectly in time with the music. His good breeding meant he danced like a dream, twirling her and catching her, pulling her back against him. Her feet may as well have been on clouds. Such happiness, such lightness inhabited her. Finally, the last line of the song rang out and silence came. The record had finished, but still they danced, the waltz's rhythm faultless in their hearts and bodies as they danced from one end of the room to the other and back again, while the crowd parted and stood on the sides watching them.

As if waking from a sleep, Sam blinked rapidly, realizing the music had stopped. He released Violet, picked up her hand, and kissed it once. He leaned close to her ear, whispered two words, then turned and left through the same door he had come. Another record went on, and slowly people began to return to the dance floor. She stood where Sam had left her, and several of the other girls eyed her curiously, jealously. Judging her with their gazes.

Clive joined her. "That's Samuel Honeychurch-Black, isn't it? You know him?"

"Only from serving his dinner," she lied.

Clive looked to the door, then back to Violet. "How very strange for him to turn up here like that."

Violet cleared her throat, pretending she was anything but deeply affected by dancing with Sam. "Yes. He does seem a little odd. But he's a very good dancer."

"Be careful Miss Zander doesn't hear about this. Fraternizing is—"

"Strictly prohibited. Yes, I know. But everyone saw him come to me. It wouldn't have been polite to refuse him, given he's such an important guest."

"I suppose so." Clive smiled. "Another dance?"

"I'm quite exhausted," she said. This was true, but Violet also now knew that dancing with anyone but Sam from now on would feel like dancing on leaden feet. "I'm going to sit a few out."

She took to the back stairs and smoked a few cigarettes. The girls outside hadn't seen Sam arrive so didn't feel the need to gossip with her about him. She kept her thoughts and feelings to herself, but if any of them had known what she was planning, they would have thought her mad.

Late, late at night. Myrtle slept across the room, snoring softly. Violet particularly didn't want to wake Myrtle, because Myrtle suspected something was going on. When Violet had returned from the dance, Myrtle had told her incredulously that one of the guests, Mr. Honeychurch-Black, had come looking for her. It was Myrtle who had directed him to the dance.

"What did he want?" Myrtle had asked, and Violet's ineffective dismissals and disavowals had only intensified Myrtle's curiosity.

Violet rose and dressed quickly. No time for a singlet and bloomers—her skin prickled at the thought of it. Just a slip, a dress, and her bare feet on the cold floor. She glanced out the window, through the crack between curtains. Moonlight and shifting shadows in the wind. Violet took a breath and quietly left her bedroom, closing the door behind her.

She tiptoed along the corridor. It was close to one in the morning and everyone was asleep. But he would be waiting for her.

Come tonight. That's what he had said before he left her at the dance. There was not a force in the world that could stop her from fulfilling this command. Somewhere at the back of her mind lurked warnings—about her soul, her body, her future—but desire drowned them all in a molten gold river. *Come tonight.* She was coming.

Her feet creaked on the second set of stairs. She paused, waiting to hear if any doors would open, any questions would be asked. But the sleeping silence remained unbroken, and she was more careful and light as she ascended.

Along the corridor in the dark, counting the doors until she realized there was only one with a yellow light shining under it.

She stopped outside it, realized that if she knocked she would draw attention to herself. Instead, she turned the handle. He had left it unlocked.

The scene that greeted her was wholly unexpected. Completely clothed, he lay asleep on top of his bedspread. His hands were folded over a silver pipe of some kind. A tray next to his bed was full of unfamiliar metal implements.

Before she could get any closer to look, he roused, saw her, smiled. "You came."

"Yes."

He put the pipe on the tray. "I fell asleep waiting. I told myself if I woke in the morning and my light was still on, it meant you didn't love me. Come here." He spread his arms, still lying on the bed.

She hurried over, sank into his arms, her lips hungrily seeking his. With his hands hard on her upper arms, he pulled her down against him. His hair smelled like molasses and old plant cuttings, an intoxicating exotic smell she couldn't place. He kissed her as though he wanted to climb into her mouth and dissolve in there, then rolled her over on her back and sat up, his knees spread on either side of her hips.

"Take off your dress," he said.

She struggled to a half-sitting position and plucked her dress up at the hem, turning it inside out to get it over her head.

"Take off your slip," he said next.

Her body shuddered with pleasure. She pulled it off, and was now naked.

"Lie back," he said.

Once again, she did as she was told, folding her arms behind her head, feeling open and exposed. "I've never done this before," she said.

"All the better," he replied, bending over her, his lips on her left breast, his mouth closing over her nipple. Then he moved across to the other side, and suckled at her with such bruising force that she gasped and squirmed violently.

His mouth descended, across her ribs and belly, then farther still until he pushed her thighs apart and buried his mouth in the sweet, hot crevice between her legs. Violet had never felt such sensations. She bucked her hips and moaned, her eyes fluttering closed. The pleasure was so intense and scorching that she thought it might kill her.

After a time he sat up, and she groaned when the sensations drew away. She opened her eyes and saw he was stripping out of his clothes, standing up and kicking off his trousers. "I must have you," he said, taking his erection in his hand. "Roll over."

She rolled over, and he positioned himself behind her, lifting his hips so her bottom was in the air. Once again, she had the wonderful wicked sensation of being exposed to him, then he entered her and she cried out in pain.

"It'll only hurt for a moment," he said as he started to move, and he was right. He had a hand on each of her buttocks and she let the tide of desire and pleasure rock through her. As his pace grew faster, he moved one of his hands under her hip so he could touch her between her legs, in a spot that seemed so dense with sensation she wondered that she'd never found it before. With a minute of deft rubbing, she suddenly exploded into a shattering pleasure that would have made her fall flat on her face on the bed were he not holding her hips up. She cried out, and, seconds later, he did, too.

He laid her gently on the bed, turning her over to look down at her face.

"That was incredible," she gasped.

"You are so beautiful," he said. "To see and hear your pleasure is the most beautiful thing in the world."

She let her head fall back and started to laugh. "I never thought . . ."

He stroked her hair away from her face. "Never leave me."

"I never will," she replied.

"I will find a way to be with you."

"I believe you."

They fell asleep with the lamp still on, curled together on top of the bedspread.

CHAPTER NINE

2014

After eight straight days on the breakfast shift, I was looking forward to a sleep-in. The mornings were growing cooler and darker, and I was snuggled a long way under covers and layers of sleep when my phone rang. I jolted awake, looked at the clock: 4:57. Was it Tomas? No, it was my mother.

"Mum," I croaked into the phone. "Everything okay?"

"Yes, just thought I'd catch you before you went to work."

"No work today," I said, trying to keep the irritation out of my voice. "Having a sleep-in, then lunch shifts all week."

"Oh, dear, I'm sorry. Still, you can go back to sleep shortly, can't you? I've just made myself a cup of coffee and thought, *I'll sit down and call Lauren*. It's so nice to hear your voice now you're not around anymore. It's a bit lonely here this morning."

I sat up, rubbing sleep out of my eyes and yawning. "Where's Dad?"

"He's on his way up to Sydney for a conference. He's going to drop in on you this week sometime."

"Tell him to call me first. In case I'm working."

"Will do. I'm hoping he'll meet that boyfriend of yours."

The ground suddenly became tricky. I said, "Hm," in a noncommittal way, my sleepy brain grasping around for a change of topic.

"Lauren? Would that be all right? You've never had a boyfriend before and we want to know that—"

"Tomas is in Denmark."

"He's gone home?"

"Temporarily."

"Why?"

Just lie. Just lie to her. "An old friend of his has been in a car accident. She's seriously hurt. He's gone to be with her."

"Oh. A female friend? They must be close."

"He calls me every day."

"Still . . ." She let the word hang, and it did the work she wanted it to do. *Still.*

He wasn't here; he was over there, with his ex-wife. Sabrina had survived surgery, was stable but still in a medically induced coma. Tomas had managed to track down one of her cousins, who was making arrangements to fly in from America to join them. Sabrina's best friend from high school had shown up, and several of her workmates were in and out visiting her. So it wasn't just Tomas and Sabrina alone in the hospital room together. But he still wasn't talking about coming back. "It was only a few dates, Mum," I said. "Mightn't go anywhere."

"Sounds like he's leading you on."

"I don't think so."

"Ah, none of them can be trusted. They break your heart. You're better off without them."

"You married Dad."

"He's a rare one. I got lucky."

I didn't reply. There was little point in contesting the issue with her. Mum could see only a world in which bad things awaited her children. I lay back on my pillow and turned on my side, and as I did so I noticed the photograph of Adam and Frogsy, which I had propped beside my alarm clock. Here was the change of topic I'd been hoping for. "Hey, Mum," I said. "Did Adam ever mention a friend named Frogsy? Or a friend named Drew?"

"I don't know either of those names," she said.

"From before. When he lived up here in the mountains."

A brief silence. Then, "He had a lot of odd friends at that time, Lauren. I don't remember their names."

"What kind of odd?"

"Just . . . odd. People who wanted to lead him astray. I noticed not a single one came to see him when he was sick."

I didn't point out that she'd made it nearly impossible for people to see Adam when he was sick, and that the Blue Mountains were a long way from Tasmania. I picked up the photo and gazed at it. That day, with its sunshine and wind, had passed. The dark future had come. Every moment was a moment like this one: a held breath before whatever came next, good or bad, entirely unpredictable. I thought about Tomas's ex-wife and her car accident, how she had left the house assuming she would return safely. I closed my eyes. No wonder Mum worried: a million possibilities hung on every moment. Today, home alone, she must be out of her mind with formless anxiety. "You must be lonely without Dad there," I said. "I'm going to make a cup of tea and then we can have a long chat. It'll be almost like being together."

I could hear the smile in her voice. "What a lovely idea."

I needed to find Frogsy and Drew. I needed to know these "odd" people who had been Adam's friends before he got sick. I surmised that Frogsy might be a pet form of a surname, and went through the local phone book looking for names beginning with Fro. Frockleys and Frohloffs and Frombergs. I called a few, explained who I was looking for, and was met with numerous rebuffs, some curious, some gentle, some puzzled and irritated all at once. I tried rhyming surnames: Boggs and Toggs and Vogs. Loggins and Coggins. Still nothing, and I'd spent half a day feeling increasingly embarrassed and annoying. I opened all Adam's books one by one, checking for more dedications and shaking them for loose photos, but found nothing. I pinned the photograph on the fridge with a magnet, to remind me to take it to work tomorrow to ask Penny.

I got on with my day, catching up on laundry and washing up. I was taking the recycling rubbish out to the bin when I saw Lizzie struggling with her woodpile, which was down the same graveled side path as the bins.

"Hang on," I called, jogging up towards her.

"Thank you, dear. The deliveryman came today and he stacked it too high."

Logs kept rolling off the top and onto the ground. I tidied them up, stacking the thicker round ones upright, and containing the others behind the wire fence. "There you go," I said, dusting my hands off on my jeans.

"I think he thought he was doing me a favor, leaving me extra. We old ducks get cold in the autumn. Not working today?"

"Day off. Want to come in for a cuppa?"

"I think it would be most cruel of me to have you make me tea on your day off."

"Don't be silly. I'd love to have you."

"Well, all right, then."

She followed me back to my flat and looked around while I made a pot of tea. "You've made the place look pretty," she said.

"I've not really done anything to it," I replied.

"Light and air and books. That's all it takes. It seemed quite sterile before. I hadn't let it out for a year or so, not after the last mob."

"Why? What did they do?"

"I think they were drug dealers. Cars pulling up at all hours. Nice to have a straight arrow in here."

"Well, you couldn't get a straighter arrow than me. Do sit down."

She didn't sit down. "What an odd collection of books. These are your brother's?"

"Yes. He read widely. When he was sick." I watched her pull out books and slide them back, then she came to stand in the kitchenette while I poured the tea.

"Who are these handsome lads?" she asked, pointing at the photograph on the fridge.

"That's Adam on the left and a mystery friend. You don't know him, do you? It was taken about fifteen years ago. Did you live here then?"

"Yes, I moved here just after my mother died. But I don't recognize the friend. Your Adam has a sweet face."

"I'm keen to know about his friends. This one is named Frogsy, probably a nickname. He had another named Drew. I know even less about him."

"If they're still in Evergreen Falls, somebody will know them," Lizzie said. "It's a small town."

"I suppose. Though fifteen years is a long time."

"No, it isn't. It's gone in a blink."

My past fifteen years hadn't been a blink so much as a long, drawn-out sob.

"Why do you want to find them?" Lizzie asked.

"Just to see if they have any interesting memories of Adam. I was only fifteen when he got sick, and so my impression of him is limited. Mum said he had 'odd' friends up here, and that interests me. Mum's threshold for odd is pretty low, I might add."

I arranged the teapot and cups on a tray and ushered Lizzie

into the sitting room. We sat and poured tea and talked about the weather, but then she asked, "What's happened to Tomas? I haven't seen him for a little while."

I told her the whole story, including how I missed out on my first-ever third date, and she listened and nodded, her blue eyes bright and sharp. I left out the business about the key to the west wing and the room with the love letters, simply because I didn't want to get Tomas in any trouble with the developers. He had asked me to be discreet in my investigations. The gardeners had been clearing the grounds for the past week, so I hadn't had a chance to go back in.

"So," I finished, "now I don't know when he's back or if he'll even be interested in seeing me again."

"Why would you think that?" Lizzie said, pouring herself a second cup of tea.

"Well, he's been with his ex-wife. I mean, my mum said he can't be trusted."

Lizzie frowned. "Dear, he didn't go back to her to fool around. She's been seriously injured. What a man he is to put aside any ill will between them, any concerns of how his return might be interpreted by the small-minded, and do the right thing. Lauren, that's not a man to mistrust; that's a man to trust with your life."

Her view, so at odds with my mother's, lit up the room. She was right. She was right and Mum was wrong, because Mum could see only through the prism of her worry.

"Let me tell you about my father," she said. "He was the most steady, loyal, good man you can imagine." Her voice stretched across tears, and she had to catch her breath. "But . . ." She trailed off, waved a hand. "Every family has secrets, I suppose. No point in airing them. You wouldn't be interested."

I was *so* interested. But my curiosity was for salacious details, and it wasn't fair to extract them from Lizzie if she wasn't comfortable.

"But I did adore my daddy," she continued. "He never let me down. Not once, not until the day he died. He was meant to pick me up from the train station, and he didn't come. I'd been away with a friend, and my friend's family came for her and they offered me a lift, but I said no, Dad will be along . . ." Again the tears. "Gosh, you must think me a silly old duck, crying all over the place."

"Not at all. Let me get some tissues."

"No, I always have a bumfle," she said, reaching up her sleeve for a handkerchief.

"Bumfle?"

"It's an old word for the lump a hanky makes in your sleeve," she said, laughing now. "You've never heard it?"

"No, never. But I'll use it all the time now."

She smiled and now seemed more composed, so I ventured a question. "So, how old were you when he died?"

"Twenty-five. Mum outlived him by more than forty years, but she never remarried. Couldn't have met another man as good as him. I met my husband shortly after that, and he did struggle to live up to Dad. It was all a bit of a disaster. We finally divorced once the children had left home. One more thing for Mum to disapprove of. The shame."

"There's no need for shame."

She smiled at me. "You are a sweet girl. But I must be getting on with my day and so must you."

I saw her off at the door and returned inside, standing for a long while to stare at the photograph. Fifteen years, gone in a blink. Where were Frogsy and Drew now?

My next shift was a lunch shift, and as I cleared plates away I noticed that the big industrial bin outside the west wing was gone. "Have the gardeners finished out there?" I asked Penny.

She peered out the window. "Seem to have. I thought it had been quiet."

On my break I went out and walked the length of the west wing through the newly cleared garden. They'd lopped branches off the pines and cleared decades of needle and leaf fall. The beds had been weeded and the flagstones had been pressure-hosed. On the strip closest to the road, they had laid new turf, and yellow-and-black caution tape kept pedestrians off it so it could settle.

I came back the same way, glancing at the door to the west wing. They had also renewed the caution tape around the entrance. The flagstones between the two pine trees had been dug up, right down to the clay, presumably to get to the tree roots.

But the gardeners had gone, and that meant that this evening, after my shift, I could go back in.

The café was busy for a Tuesday afternoon. Schoolkids and their mums moving tables together to make large groups who wanted impossible-to-remember orders: double-shot latte with soy; strawberry milk shake divided into two plastic cups with straws; hot chocolates that needed to be anything but hot. I was run off my feet, and yet I heard it.

As I walked past a young woman—overbleached hair, nose ring, sweet face under all that eyeliner—I overheard a snippet of the conversation she was having on her mobile phone. "Yep, sure. Will Aunty Drew be back by then?"

Aunty Drew. I dragged my feet as my mind began to race. I'd assumed Drew, Adam's friend, was a man. But of course it was a woman's name, too. I tried to hang back to hear more of the conversation, but right then a little boy knocked a milk shake all over his school uniform, and I had to rush off to clean it up.

I was putting the mop away when I saw the young woman get up from her seat and head for the door. Before I knew what I was doing I ran after her and caught her just as she stepped out onto the street.

"Excuse me," I said.

She turned, cocked her head curiously.

"Look, I'm sorry if this sounds . . . creepy. But I overheard you talking about somebody named Drew."

She narrowed her eyes. Yeah, I sounded like a crazy person. All that time calling Frombergs and Boggses had done it to me.

"Do you often listen to customers' *private* conversations?" she asked.

I put my hands in the air. "I know how it sounds, but my brother knew somebody named Drew, here in the mountains fifteen years ago. I'm trying to find anybody who knew him then. Could you just ask her for me? Ask her if she knew Adam Beck? And if she did, and she's in town—"

"She's in London," the girl said. "Won't be back until the end of the year. But yeah, she did used to live here fifteen years ago," she conceded.

"Would you ask her for me? If she knew him, could you give me a number I can call her on?"

"Adam Brett," the girl said.

"No, Beck. Adam Beck. Here—" I pulled my order pad out of my apron, wrote the name down, and handed it to her.

"Got it."

I watched her go, wondering if I'd ever see her again.

I stayed back late that afternoon, helping Penny restock for the next day. She was anxious to get away on a date with a new man. I offered to finish filling up the cup dispensers and the plastic-spoon holders and emptying the dishwasher so everything was good to go for breakfast.

It was close to seven o'clock when I locked up, munching on a left-over piece of banana bread that I'd decided would make a nutritious dinner. My legs were tired from the long, hard shift, but it was a pleasant ache that told me I'd been useful and productive in the world. It was raining lightly, and the drops lit up to silver and gold in the beam of the security light over the front door of the café. I kept my head down and walked directly across to the west-wing entrance, and ducked under the caution tape. The bare soil at the entranceway had turned to mud. I reached into my handbag for my torch and shone it about my feet so I didn't trip on anything as I made my way to the door.

As I closed the door behind me, the rain intensified, gushing down hard on the windows and roof. With my torch beam to guide me, I made my way down to the storeroom, which Tomas had said I could sort. It smelled musty and damp, and I thought I could hear a drip somewhere up the stairs.

I stood in the doorway, shining my torch beam slowly from the left side to the right, wondering where to start. Wondering whether to start.

I began by clearing everything off the table, placing the items neatly in the hallway. Then I opened the boxes and crates one by one, my nose itching madly from the dust. Old teapots and frying pans and rusted kitchen utensils and broken candlesticks. No more letters. At the bottom of every box I would stop and repack everything neatly, then stack the box against the wall to make room for the next one.

When I'd finished with what was on the table, I started with what was under the table. I nearly pulled my shoulders out of their joints trying to lift what turned out to be an old Singer sewing machine in a wooden case. More boxes and crates. This time I found a stack of postcards—all black-and-white pictures of the hotel and its gardens—and my heart leaped, but none were written on. I kept sorting, finding nothing.

The rain hammered on outside as I began to grow tired of sorting boxes in the cramped hallways. As I stood and stretched—my back was sore from being hunched over—the sound of the drip grew more pronounced. With my torch shining its beam in front of me, I rounded the storeroom and stopped at the bottom of the stairs. I shone the beam up. Nothing.

I tested my weight on the first step, then told myself I was being silly: the building had stood here for over a hundred years; it was structurally sound. Still, I held tightly to the tarnished brass rail as I made my way up to the first floor.

I found myself standing at one end of a long corridor. Bare floorboards. Doors on either side. It must have once been a guest wing. I ran the beam across the ceiling but couldn't see the drip. I closed my eyes and listened. It seemed to be coming from the closest room to my left.

I tried the door, and it opened readily. I found myself in a moldy bathroom. The rain was making its way in through the corner, running along the ceiling a little way then dripping on the tiles. A large puddle had formed. I pulled out my phone and took a photo to send Tomas. Then I poked around the bathroom. It was large, with three steps up to a platform where a bath must have once stood. All the fittings had been removed, but marks on the wall indicated where they had been, and I tried to imagine the sink, the vanity, the shelves, the mirror.

I retreated back to the hallway, curious now to see if the rooms were also unlocked. I tried every door but not one of them gave. I tried my key but it didn't work. It would have been quite easy to pick the lock or force a door, but I didn't want to do that. Tomas had said everything had been cleaned out of them anyway.

But now I was at the opposite end of the hallway, and I found myself standing outside a room with French doors, their paint peeling. I shone my torch through and saw books, shelves and shelves of books. I tried the door and found it locked. I rattled the door, and it moved freely and alarmingly. I looked closer and saw that the hinges on one side were completely detached from the door-frame, and the only thing holding the door up was the tongue of the lock. Carefully, I pulled the edge of the door out of the frame, slid through, then leaned it back into place.

I was standing in a library in a corner of the building. The boarded windows covered two walls, and I imagined how amazing the room must look flooded with natural light and surrounded by views of trees and gardens. What a fabulous place to read.

Behind the glass doors, the shelves were stocked, and here and there a plastic tag had been placed between books. Three desks—oak by the look of them, with green leather inlays—were placed around the room, and on one of them was a thick modern-looking binder. I sat on the desk and picked it up. A business card stuck to the front of the folder read *Gerald Makepeace, Book Historian. Library, Collection and Document Valuation.*

I flipped open the folder. In large capital letters on the first page it read: *LIBRARY REPORT AND VALUATION, EVERGREEN SPA HOTEL.* The date on the report was only four months ago. From skimming it I figured that the developer hadn't known what to do with the extensive library when he'd bought the hotel. Neither selling the books off nor throwing them away had seemed an option, so he'd brought in the book historian. The report had recommended the developer keep the books as a significant heritage collection, difficult to sell and more valuable as a "distinctive and integral feature of this historical building." What followed were pages and pages of tabulation, listing the books and any notes about them. It seemed that the plastic markers were a way of finding particular books now that the historian had organized them.

I flicked through a few pages, until a subtitle caught my interest. *Guest registers.*

I ran my finger down the column, my heart ticking a little faster. Only 1912 and 1924 were missing. That meant 1926 would be here—according to the table, in *5A lower drawer.* I shone my torch across the books then down. Each bookcase had deep drawers in the bottom. The plastic markers showed me which one was 5A lower drawer. I opened the drawer and took in a second.

I sat back on my haunches and flipped it open. Guest names had been written in by hand, and the ink was faded and the handwriting was tight and thin. My eyes were going to give out if I kept trying to read by torchlight, so I did something that Tomas might not have wanted me to do: I tucked the 1926 guest register and the bound library report under my arm and took them both home.

God bless electric light. I sat on my couch as the rain cleared overhead, late into the night, and read through the lists of names and dates—hundreds and hundreds of them. Given that the handwriting was almost impossible to understand, my head started aching and my eyes started swimming. I closed my eyes and put my head back, just for a moment.

When I woke, the rain had set in again, my sitting room light was still on, and my neck was cricked from sleeping at a strange angle. The guest register had slid off my lap and onto the floor, where it lay closed. I hadn't made a mark of where I'd been up to, and I swore softly at myself.

I leaned over to pick it up, opened it right in the middle, and scanned the names to see if any seemed familiar so I didn't have to read them again.

At the top of the page, I saw his name.

Mr. Samuel Honeychurch-Black.

SHB. It had to be. To confirm it, the name directly beneath his read, *Miss Flora Honeychurch-Black.* His sister, the one he'd mentioned in the letters. I couldn't contain my smile—not only had I found him, I also knew which room he had slept in, because it was written right here in front of me.

But it was late now, and far too wet to go back out. I marked the page with a Post-it Note and headed to bed. I sent a text message to Tomas, who wrote back a minute later.

Well done! Now we have to find her.

Her. Samuel Honeychurch-Black's lover. Was she a guest, too? I didn't have any initials to go on, but I could certainly make a list of women who were at the hotel during his stay. All these thoughts tumbled over in my head as I lay down to sleep. I didn't get there until nearly dawn.

CHAPTER TEN

Because I'd never had a job before, I'd never called in sick before. I was familiar with the concept, having seen it on television sufficient times. But I was unprepared for how guilty I felt, even though I was genuinely sick. Lack of sleep had given me a thumping headache, and I couldn't face another afternoon shift like yesterday's.

Penny, for her part, was sweet and concerned, and offered to drop me in some food on her way home that evening, but I told her not to bother—I was worried I wouldn't look sick enough when she arrived.

After I called I went back to sleep for a few hours, and so it happened that I was slouching around in my pajamas at ten o'clock, thinking about making a bowl of cereal to eat on the couch, when there was a knock on my door.

I put the milk carton down and went to answer it, reminding myself to look weak and pale just in case it was Penny.

"Dad!"

"Hello, darling," he said, folding me in a hug. There wasn't much of Dad: he was slender and narrow-shouldered, with a full head of gray hair and a gray beard that had grown wispier every time I saw him. He wore his familiar brown corduroy coat and pants that hung loose.

I stepped aside to let him in. "Mum was supposed to tell you to call me first. I mightn't have been home."

"She told me she'd let you know. Check your phone. Maybe she left a message."

Dad was notoriously phone-averse, and I knew what had happened. Mum had *wanted* him to surprise me. It was her way of checking up on me, making sure I wasn't doing what I oughtn't. She knew I wasn't working mornings this week, so she'd told him to turn up before eleven. But none of this would have been conscious on her part. She had no concept of privacy, especially where I was concerned. She had only a primal urge to keep me safe, and if that meant sending my father in unannounced to make sure I wasn't climbing a ladder while smoking marijuana and juggling knives, then that's what she would do.

"Come and sit down. Can I make you a cup of tea or coffee?"

"No, just your company, love. Don't hover. Sit with me. I have a few things to tell you."

I sat on the arm of the couch with my feet on the seat, looking at him. "That sounds a bit ominous."

He smiled, deep lines traversing his face as he did. I loved it when Dad smiled, partly because it had happened so rarely during those awful years of Adam's illness. Nor did I ever see him cry. Only once, at the funeral, as though all the years of sadness were finally allowed to emerge. The thought of it caught my heart unexpectedly, and I slid into the seat next to him to give him another hug.

"You look well," he said. "Life up here is agreeing with you, I take it."

"I have a job," I said. "That's new."

He patted my knee. "Good for you."

"Though I called in sick today. Had a rotten night and woke with a headache."

"I have some aspirin in my wallet if you want some," he said.

I waved his offer away. "I've already taken something. You said you had some things to tell me. Come on, out with it."

"Ah. You're not to worry, because it's all fine now."

I frowned. "Okay."

"But I had a bit of a scare. A . . ." He cleared his throat. "Cancer scare."

"Oh, Dad!"

Both hands went up. "Don't worry, don't worry. The biopsy proved negative and . . . it's all a bit embarrassing. You know. In the waterworks."

"I won't ask any more questions," I said. "Except, you are definitely fine?"

"Definitely."

"Mum must have freaked out."

"She didn't know."

"Are you serious?"

"How could I tell her, Lauren? She would have died of fright. You know what she's like."

"It's not her fault. Adam's illness made her that way."

He twisted his lips in a rueful smile. "Actually, she was already a little that way, though you probably don't remember. She and Adam were always fighting. She thought he should live his life a certain way, and he didn't always agree."

"I can't believe you managed to keep it from her, though. That must have taken some planning."

"Yes, I took care of the whole thing without her knowledge. Specialists, medical procedures, all under the smoke screen of work, conferences, so on. I tell you, I could have an affair and she'd never know." He laughed at his own joke, but it was a bitter laugh.

I touched his arm. "I'm sorry you had to go through that alone. You should have told me."

"I was even *less* likely to tell *you*, sweetie. You have your life to live. I'm acutely aware that your freedom has been a long time coming. Which is why . . . you know I don't like talking much on the phone. I can't stand the silences. Your mother's always there listening. I wanted to come and talk to you alone. When have we ever been alone together?"

I shrugged. "Almost never." When Adam got sick, Dad had always functioned more like an accessory to Mum rather than a whole person. After fifteen, I didn't have the dad memories other people did. I had some from when I was younger—he liked taking me grocery shopping with him, or getting me to time him as he ran up the hill near our house, or showing me how to make batter for corn fritters, always slopping lots of beer in the batter and theatrically cautioning me not to tell Mum.

"Exactly. Lauren, during this health scare, when I feared the worst, I realized something. If I got sick and died, your mother would make you come back. She wouldn't rest until you were home, and then you'd never be able to leave again. It plagued me, almost more than fear of my own early death plagued me. My Lauren, just starting to bloom so late. She'd take it all away from you and she would never realize she was doing anything wrong; and you would do as she said because you're a good girl. Such a good girl." He dropped his head and pinched the bridge of his nose, a gesture I was very familiar with. Then he breathed in, lifted his head, and continued. "Promise me that whatever happens, you'll never *ever* come home."

"But, Dad—"

"You can visit, of course. You're always welcome, but if you do, stay at a hotel. Don't come back to Tasmania to live, and never *ever* come back to live in that house with your mother. No matter what happens."

What a curious feeling I had then: I was being set free. My move to the Blue Mountains had always felt forbidden, something I was expected to get out of my system so I could return to life with Mum. But now, with Dad's blessing, the world suddenly seemed lighter, wider.

"Thanks, Dad," I said, kissing his cheek. "I promise."

"Right. Well, I'm going to have to head off late this afternoon to catch my flight home, but I thought we could spend the day sightseeing. You can show me around Evergreen Falls."

"Ah . . . that's kind of awkward. I'm supposed to be home sick. If Penny sees me . . ."

"How about I smuggle you into my rental car, then, and we'll head back down the range to Leura?"

"Sure thing," I said. "Just let me get dressed."

Dad dropped me home around four and continued on his way to Sydney. My headache had lifted, and I sat down once again with the old guest register and traced the Honeychurch-Blacks' stay at the Evergreen Spa for 1926. To my surprise, they stayed for months. Page after page of the register listed their names, next to the same room numbers, and all written in the same thin, sharp handwriting. Samuel and Flora. The register gave me no further information, so I grabbed my phone.

Google did not return any entries for Samuel and Flora, but I did find the Honeychurch-Black family. Old, old, old money. At one stage they owned so much land in New South Wales that they might have made a claim as the state's sovereigns. There were still Honeychurch-Blacks in Australia, and they were still very rich. As I was writing down a few names my phone tinged with a text message from Penny.

Coming by with leftovers. Not taking no for an answer.

I smiled. My stomach was gurgling with hunger. I hoped she had banana bread.

"Hey, sickie," Penny said when I opened the door to her ten minutes later. "I've got tabouleh, a turkey-and-cranberry sandwich, and banana bread in here."

I took the plastic bag from her. "Thanks so much. Do you want to come in?"

"No, I'm on my way to the gym. But . . ." She reached into her pocket and pulled out a piece of paper, an order slip from work. "A girl came in today looking for you. The one you chased out the other day. She gave me this to pass on."

I unfolded it. It was the order slip on which I'd written Adam's name, and beneath it were the words *Drew Amherst* and a phone number in England. "Oh, fantastic. Thanks." It was her. It was *the* Drew who had given the photograph to Adam.

"You feeling better?"

"Yeah. The headache went away. Sorry about leaving you in the lurch."

"No problem. Susie covered your shift. Was pretty quiet anyway." Penny gave me a quick peck on the cheek. "See you tomorrow, then?"

"Definitely."

I closed the door after her and took the food to the kitchen. The salad and the sandwich went into the fridge for later, but I picked at the banana bread while I made a cup of tea. My phone told me it was a decent hour of the morning in London, so it was safe to call Drew Amherst. I dialed and waited, trying to stop my leg from jiggling.

"Hello?" She had a small, sweet voice.

"Hello, may I speak to Drew?"

"This is Drew."

"Drew, this is Lauren Beck, calling from Australia. I think your niece told you about me."

"Ah, yes. She said you're Adam's sister? Is that right? I haven't seen Adam in forever. How is he?"

"He's . . . um . . . Adam died last year." I got up and started to pace.

A shocked silence. Then she said, "I'm really sorry. Was it an accident?"

"No, an illness. He was sick a long time. And now I've inherited his books, and in one of them I found a photograph of him, up in the Blue Mountains. You had written on the back. I know nothing about his time up here and was wondering if you did."

"Again, I'm sorry. I didn't know Adam all that well. We had one mad summer, a bunch of about seven of us, all staying at my grandfather's house. Granddad was away in Perth, and everyone just started showing up, sleeping on the floor, you know. We were completely feral, ate nothing but cheese sandwiches, went swimming at the Falls for hours every afternoon. It was a crazy time, but then Granddad came back and I got a job in Sydney and I didn't really see any of them again."

I stopped in front of the fridge, in front of the photograph. Maybe that's what my mother meant by "odd" people. "There's another boy in the photograph with him. It says on the back his name's Frogsy."

"Yes, I remember him. That wasn't his real name. What was it? Sorry, my memory's not great. It was something French, that's why we called him Frogsy. He and your brother were inseparable. I bet if you could find him, he'd have some better memories to share."

French. Would I be reading through the phone book for every French surname I could find?

"Anton!" she said suddenly. "Anton something-beginning-with-F. Fourtier, perhaps? If you give me your phone number, I'll let it turn over in my mind a few days. It might come back to me."

I already had the phone book open to F, my finger scanning down ahead of my eyes. "Fournier?" I asked. *AG Fournier. 78 Fallview Road.*

"Yes, that's it," she said. "Nice work. Anton Fournier. Frogsy. He and Adam did everything together."

"I've got the phone book in front of me. He still lives in Evergreen Falls."

"Is that where you're calling from? Evergreen Falls?"

"Yes, I came up here because . . . it was the last place Adam was happy before he got sick."

Her voice was kind. "Well, I'm certain if you can find Frogsy, he can tell you what made your brother so happy."

I thanked her and ended the call, then immediately dialed Anton Fournier. The phone rang and rang, long past when an answering machine might have cut into the line. Finally, I gave up, vowing to try again tomorrow.

After work the next day, my dirty apron stuffed in my bag, I let myself in to the west wing and made my way, bravely, up two flights of stairs and along to the room Samuel Honeychurch-Black had once stayed in. The door was locked, so I gave it a good hard rattle. It was old and half hanging off, but I hadn't the strength to break it. Which is why I'd brought the screwdriver from home.

I held my torch between my teeth, feeling a little like a spy as I crouched down to insert the screwdriver in the keyhole. I wasn't sure what to do next, but I jiggled it with all my might, and to my horror the door handle dropped off with a thud and rolled a little way across the wooden floor.

Now all I had to do was insert the screwdriver where the handle had been, give the tongue of the lock a poke and . . . *click*. The door was open. I was aware I'd gone from sneaking where I shouldn't, to stealing things, to breaking things, and I was surprised by how little guilt I felt. As I climbed to my feet and crossed the threshold I supposed it was good that Tomas was a long way off in Denmark so he wouldn't be implicated if anyone caught me.

Of course, the moment I stood inside the room I realized it had been pointless coming here. Many decades had passed; the room had been stripped of furniture, and this was now just another empty room like all the other empty rooms. I walked the floorboards carefully from one end of the room to the other, feeling with the toes of my sneakers for loose ones beneath which love letters might be stashed. I ran my torch and my fingers over the windowsills looking for carved initials and love hearts. I spotted a peeling strip of wallpaper and pulled it loose to check behind for scribbled declarations of love. I even stood in the center of the room and closed my eyes and tried to *think* the secrets out of the walls, but of course that was fruitless, too.

I felt deflated and mildly foolish, not to mention guilty for breaking the lock with no good reason. I closed the door behind me, made my way down the stairs and out into the soft evening. The wind was up and roaring through the pines. It smelled like rain was on the way again, and the air was cold. I shoved my hands in my pockets for warmth and headed home to go through the guest register again. I tried not to think about why I was so determined to know the identity of Samuel Honeychurch-Black's lover. Was I living vicariously through them? Nobody had ever felt for me anything like the mad passion represented in the letters, and I wanted to know what kind of woman aroused such feelings. Would Tomas ever feel that way about me? I couldn't imagine it. He hadn't sent love letters, though we had had some lengthy text exchanges. He rarely called me to speak, and I wondered and worried if that was because my conversation didn't interest him. But then I reminded myself that he spent a good portion of time beside his ex-wife's hospital bed and probably didn't want his conversations being overheard.

Making a liar of me, Tomas phoned me just as I was going to bed, and I told him (without mentioning breaking the lock) about my futile trip to Samuel's room.

"Any likely candidates for the love interest?" he asked.

I pulled my notebook close so I could read my notes. "There

were plenty of other guests staying around the same time, but only a handful of women who stayed the whole winter like he did. I've checked them out. Lady Powell was here with her husband. She's quite a well-known writer and she was in her sixties at the time, so I can't really imagine her being involved in a torrid affair with Samuel Honeychurch-Black."

"You never know. Don't underestimate the silver foxes."

"I'm not. It's just that in one of the letters, Samuel says his sister thinks he's "far too young" to know what love is. So, I'm thinking he would have been a teenager or in his early twenties. Hardly compatible. That also goes for the opera singer, Cordelia Wright, who was born in 1868 according to Wikipedia. There was Miss Sydney, but he mentions her in the third person in his letters, so they can't be addressed to her. Then there's his sister. Obviously not her. The other guests who stayed through winter were all men, and . . . well, you've read some of the anatomically correct descriptions of what they did. His lover wasn't a man."

"Not even a man with rosy nipples," Tomas joked.

"I guess it could have been somebody who wasn't there over winter, but it seems unlikely. They needed time to fall in love. My understanding is that people in the twenties didn't fall into bed with each other quite so readily as . . ." I trailed off, feeling a little embarrassed.

Tomas didn't seem to notice. "Maybe it wasn't a guest, then. Maybe that's why it was forbidden. Maybe he was in love with one of the staff. Are there staff records in the library?"

I eyed the folder on the kitchen bench. "There might be. I'd have to go through the library report." I yawned. "I remember the days when I used to complain I hadn't enough to do in the evenings."

"I'll let you get off to bed."

"Wait. How's Sabrina?"

"No change."

I wasn't sure what to say, so I said, "I'm sorry." Then remembering what Lizzie had said, I added, "You're a good man. Not many men would do what you're doing."

"That's a generous thing to say, Lauren. I have my reasons for being here, and they make sense to me. I can't stop to consider what others might think."

I wanted to ask him about the reasons, but I didn't want to sound pushy or jealous. Instead, we said good night, and I took the library report to bed with me.

Pages and pages went by, and I found no mention of staff records. I was growing more and more frustrated, when a bold heading caught my eye at the top of a page. *Honeychurch-Black Map Collection.*

I ran my fingers down the page. Apparently in 1926, Flora Honeychurch-Black had deposited a collection of twenty folio books of maps in the library as a gift to the Evergreen Spa. Maps?

I couldn't wait to get back to the library to look at them.

I rang Anton Fournier's number so many times I knew it by heart. He never answered, and I began to wonder if he was away. Fallview Road was only two blocks from me, so before work the next afternoon I took a stroll past it.

His house was positioned a long way back on the block, a high-set marvel of glass and wood. Its position told me that Anton Fournier would have an uninterrupted view of the Falls and the cliffs and the valleys, and that he probably had a lot of money.

I don't know quite when I decided I would go and knock, but it was possibly when two spotted whippets appeared from around the side of the house to play happily in the front garden, which told me that somebody was home.

The dogs bounded up to me, barking happily, and he opened the door before I could ring the bell.

"Can I help you?" he said. I recognized him from the photo, the handsome set of his nose. His dark hair had a few streaks of gray, and he was wiping his hands on a tea towel. The dogs were barking so loudly they drowned out my first attempt to speak, and he shouted, "Romeo, Juliet, down!"

The dogs came to heel, looking a little ashamed.

"I'm sorry for dropping in unannounced," I said, coming up the three front steps to the veranda. "I tried to ring, but—"

"The landline? I haven't used it in centuries. Sorry, who are you?"

"My name's Lauren. Drew Amherst gave me your name. You knew Adam. Adam Beck."

His face softened, and his eyebrows twitched almost imperceptibly. "Adam? There's a name I haven't heard in . . . He died, didn't he?"

"Yes, last year."

He exhaled softly.

"I'm Adam's sister and I—"

"Wait. You're his sister?"

"Yes, and—"

His whole mood changed. His hazel eyes grew flinty and his body grew stiff. "I have nothing to say to you or anyone in your family."

"Pardon?"

"Go. Get off my property." He withdrew into the house. "Go on. Go." Then he slammed the door, leaving me standing on his porch, wondering what on earth had just happened.

CHAPTER ELEVEN

1926

A frost fell overnight, silvering the fallen leaves and making the grass glisten. Violet made her way to the post office carefully, breathing fog into the cold morning and trying to stay in the patches of sun that lined the way. Her eyes felt gritty from lack of sleep. Sam had woken her at four in the morning and urged her back to her own room, but she'd been too stirred up to return to sleep. Over and over in her imagination she replayed their encounter. How she longed to do it again. The time between now and when she might see him again, hold him again, stretched out forever.

The post office was a small stone building on the main street, and Violet took her place in the queue then dutifully sent her mother a short letter and some money. She was surprised she hadn't heard from Mama yet, and she hoped her own letters were getting through. She also hoped Mama wasn't expecting her home for winter.

"Cold this morning, isn't it?" said the silver-haired woman behind the counter, eyeing Violet's scarf. "You'll be needing something a bit warmer than that soon. First winter up here, I take it?"

"Yes. This is the thickest scarf I have."

"You ought to start knitting, precious. They're saying it'll be one of the coldest on record."

Violet grew excited. "Will it snow?"

"Almost certainly. Last year we just had sleet. We're due a big snowfall." The woman counted back Violet's change for the stamp, and Violet snapped her purse shut and headed out into the street.

She needed a new coat. A new scarf. Gloves. A hat. She checked her savings, and revised her wish list. Her old coat wasn't pretty, but it would do; and surely there was nothing in the world warmer than her fur-lined cloche. But scarf and gloves were a must. Maybe even boots. She wandered down the main street, dropping in and out of stores to browse and daydream and spend a little money. Everywhere, people were talking about the frost, the sudden turn towards cold after an unseasonably warm start to winter, about how the last time conditions had been like this the snow had come thick and often throughout July. Violet had never seen snow, and her heart glowed at the idea of having a good job in a snowy place through winter and having Sam to keep her warm. She couldn't remember ever being this happy. She bought boots, even though she could barely afford them. Perhaps by next winter, she and Sam would be married. Then she could have new boots whenever she wanted. Guiltily, she squashed the thought.

When she returned to her room, she found a letter Sam had left under her pillow. She unfolded it eagerly and read it with flaming cheeks. He recorded in detail all that he had done to her last night, all that he intended to do to her tonight when she came to him—1 a.m. was the appointed time again—and declared a love for her that weighed more than the moon. Violet carefully folded the letter away in its envelope and tucked it into the back of her gramophone. She could imagine the scandal if Myrtle read it accidentally.

Somehow she made it through her shifts, tired though she was. Sam's sister was at dinner, but Sam wasn't. Violet didn't mind. Soon she would have him all to herself. She fell into bed at ten, promising herself she would wake up at one.

She woke at two, dressed in a silent panic, and rushed upstairs to see him.

He was sitting up in bed when she opened the door. That sweet smell she had come to associate with him filled the room. He sucked on a long, silver pipe.

Violet quietly closed the door behind her.

Sam exhaled, slowly. His eyes were half closed. "I waited," he said, in a thick voice. "As long as I could."

"I'm so sorry," she said. "I was tired from last night, from a day's work. I slept too long." She sank down next to him, and his spare hand moved to untie her dress.

"Is that smell tobacco?" she asked.

"Take everything off but your bloomers," he said.

"It's a very sweet-smelling tobacco." She slid her dress over her head and took off her singlet.

"Lie down," he said, finishing his pipe and putting it away.

Her skin shivered. He remained completely clothed, his eyes dreamy and far away. He took her wrists and moved her arms above her head on the pillow, then lay down by her armpit, his face nestled against her left breast. His warm breath on her bare skin was intoxicating. He dragged idle fingers gently back and forth across her nipples, lost in some rhythm of his own. He kissed the side of her breast, his breathing slowing so much that she would have believed him asleep were his hand not still moving, cherishing her breasts at every curve and peak. She tried to roll towards him to gather him in an embrace, but he pushed her back, pinning her arms above her head now and moving his mouth over her breasts. She thought she might die from the pleasure.

"Take your clothes off," she gasped.

"I'm too tired for that," he said, his hand creeping up the hem of her bloomers. "Tired from chasing the dragon." He slid his fingers inside her underwear and she closed her eyes as he touched her and rubbed her until he brought her to climax, pressing his mouth over hers to drown out her cries of pleasure.

Afterwards she lay quietly, watching through half-closed lids as he rolled away from her and prepared another pipe. As he smoked, he fell deeper and deeper into hazy languor. Violet knew that it wasn't tobacco, and she also knew now what he'd meant by chasing the dragon and worshipping the poppy god. But what was she to do? Should she ask for some? She didn't want him to think her a coward.

"Can I try it?" she asked, hesitantly, but he was shaking his head before her sentence was finished.

"No. Never."

"Why not?"

He rolled on his side to face her, his eyes glazed, and said in a very small voice, "It destroys me."

"Then why smoke it?"

"Because I love it. I never give up what I love."

They lay, knee to knee, forehead to forehead for a long time. She had thought opium smokers must be dirty people or members of razor gangs, not fiery-eyed angels such as Sam. A small niggle of anxiety, like the edge of a loose thread, had started in her belly, but she chose to ignore it lest it ruin this most perfect of moments. The sweet smell and the sound of his breathing lulled her, and she was almost asleep when he said, "You mustn't sleep here, Violet."

She sat up. "Why not?"

"Because one day we will forget to wake up, and then we will be discovered. My sister . . . she would destroy our happiness."

"She would?" Flora Honeychurch-Black had always looked a kind woman to Violet.

"She will tell my father lies about you. Anything to stop us from being together. I'm a grown man and I can decide who I want to be with, but she can't stand the idea that I'll be happy." His brows drew down and his words tumbled out with violent passion. "She will take that happiness from me. She will say you're a thief or a prostitute, and Father won't let me be with you."

Violet bristled at the idea of being called either of these things.

"So, we must keep our love secret from her, do you understand? Just until I can convince Father that you and I are destined for each other. Then . . ." Here his brow smoothed, and the dreamy look came back to his eye. "Then we will lie in bed every day until three, and servants will bring us fruit baskets to feed each other, and there will always be an orchestra playing somewhere." He moved his fingers as though they were playing a tune. "But until that day, I must look as though I'm behaving."

Violet kissed him. "I love you."

"And I love you. That's all that matters."

After four nights in a row of visiting Sam, Violet was more tired than she had imagined possible. Interrupted sleep took its toll: she became clumsy and irritable, forgetful and slow. Hansel shouted at her twice on Wednesday evening, then when she confused another order, he took the unprecedented step of punishing her by making her wash dishes.

Long after the other waitstaff had gone to their rooms, she continued to wash and pile dishes in the echoing kitchen, while the scullery boy sat on the stairs behind her, watching and eating an apple. Finally, Hansel came over and told her she could go to bed. She wiped her raw hands on her apron and made her way across the kitchen.

Miss Zander blocked her way.

"Oh," Violet said.

"Hansel told me he's been having problems with you." She took Violet's chin in her soft, elegant hand and turned from one side to the other. "You look pale and tired. Are you ill?"

"I . . . ah . . . I haven't been feeling the best." Except between the hours of one and three in the morning, when the world slept and she and Sam stripped each other and made bruisingly sweet love.

Miss Zander dropped her hand and took Violet by the elbow, pulling her against her side. "Hansel! This is unacceptable. The girl is not lazy, she is sick. She's to take the rest of the week off."

Hansel said something in German that Miss Zander brushed off. "I want to see some color back in your cheeks," she said to Violet. "Go to bed and *stay there*. Do you understand?"

Stay there. But Sam expected her at one.

Sam, who could sleep all day if he wanted to. She was simply too exhausted. If she didn't come, he would smoke his pipe and drift off into that dreamy world he loved so much. "Yes, Miss Zander," she said. "I will."

Later that night, deep in the dark, Violet woke to warm breath on her face. Sam's hand was over her mouth in a split second so she couldn't call out and wake Myrtle, who slept on in the bed across the room.

His lips went to her ear. "You didn't come."

"I'm exhausted," she whispered through his fingers.

He slid under the covers and pulled up her nightgown, then rolled her on her side. Without preparation or warning, he eased himself out of his trousers and pushed his way inside her, his hand still over her mouth. Her heart raced. It was at once both thrilling and embarrassing. If Myrtle woke, Violet would die of shame. Sam was soon finished, though, and then without a word he kissed her cheek and left. Violet stared up at the dark ceiling a long time, before finally drifting back to sleep.

*   *   *

The letter came the next morning. Myrtle delivered it to Violet in bed, along with a cup of tea and a handful of strawberries.

"Mail for you," Myrtle said with a gentle smile. She gave no outward impression of knowing that Sam had visited the room in the early hours of the morning, but still Violet felt uncomfortable meeting her eye. She focused instead on the envelope, the handwriting on which she recognized straightaway. It was from her mother.

"Now," Myrtle said, sitting on the edge of the bed, "I need to ask you something and I want you to tell me straight, and I promise I won't tell anybody."

Violet held her breath.

"Has Miss Zander asked you to work through the winter?"

She nodded, letting the breath go.

Myrtle set her mouth in a line. "I know it's not your fault, Violet, but it's very unfair. She's not asked me or many of the other staff who have been here years and years. She favors you."

"She does?" Violet bit into the first strawberry. It was sweet and juicy.

"She's terribly hard to please, makes life unpleasant for so many others. But . . ." Myrtle waved her hand to indicate that Violet was lying in bed instead of working the breakfast shift. "She gave you half a week off."

"I'm sick." The guilt was acute, but it was true she did need to rest.

Myrtle sniffed. "Hardly. I haven't heard you so much as sneeze, let alone have a good vomit."

"I don't know why she likes me."

"Because you're pretty. Miss Zander has always liked the pretty girls." Myrtle tossed her head. "Well. There's nothing much I can do about how God made me. But I work hard and could have used the money over winter."

"I'm sorry," Violet offered. And she did feel truly sorry: Myrtle had been a kind friend.

Myrtle patted her knees through the covers. "As I said, not your fault. Enjoy your strawberries. They just came up this morning on the flying fox. I pinched them before the Austrian sliced and sugared them. I've always preferred them as nature intended."

Myrtle left, closing the door quietly behind her, and Violet turned to the letter.

Dear Violet,

I need you to come home. My fingers have become too slow, as I knew they would, and the Ramseys have said there is no more work for me here. I told them you have just been offered well-paid winter work in the mountains, so they have promised to keep me on until the end of August, but then, my dear, you must return to Sydney. Life is very unfair, I know, but I can only write this plainly. It is time for you to give me what I gave you—all on my own without the benefit of a husband—for the first fourteen years of your life: a place to live and food on my plate.

Darling, I would work if I could, but my hands have become unforgiving knots. They are the same hands that soothed you to sleep at night as a child. I know that will count for something with you, because you are a good-hearted girl.

With love,
Your mother

Violet put the letter aside with shaking hands. She didn't want to go back to Sydney, to rent a dingy flat with her mother. She didn't want to leave her job here in the mountains, at a fine hotel with even finer guests. She didn't want to leave Sam.

She took deep breaths, holding back tears. Sam would save her. She called to mind the fantasy Sam had indulged—servants with baskets of fruit and an orchestra—and tried to imagine where her mother would fit in that picture. She must ask Sam, quite plainly, to make clear his intentions towards her. If he really loved her, if he really was going to tell his father he had chosen her, would marry her, then all would be well. But she needed that to happen before the end of August, and she wondered just how hard his father would be to convince.

Flora's bedroom window—where she spent a good deal of time curled up in her chair, a book open but unread on her lap—looked out over the blue mists and shifting shadows across the green valleys and sediment-lined cliffs. From the side window she could see down to the tennis court, and this morning she watched Tony, Karl, Sweetie, and Vincent engaged in a doubles match. Harry had returned to Sydney for the week, and Karl, the spa's Swiss medic, had happily taken his place in Tony's retinue. Tony had that kind of power over other men, a power Flora had never quite understood but supposed was something to be prized. A leader. A man to be admired.

She was alternating between watching the view and watching the tennis when she saw one of the bellboys run at full pelt across the tennis court, disrupting the game. Tony berated him—she couldn't hear, but his hand gestures were clear—but the bellboy ignored him, instead grabbing Karl by the arm, his whole body tense. Karl, too, adopted the urgent posture, and then they both hurried off the tennis court. Flora frowned, and heat flashed across her heart. Sam?

She raced to her door and pulled it open, in time to hear the clatter of feet on the stairs up to the men's floor. She hurried after them, then paused at the end of the corridor. Doors were opening left and right as men came out to see the commotion, and there was Sam, alive and well, standing in his doorway with his back to her and looking towards the bathroom at the end of the hallway, into which Karl had just disappeared. Flora didn't call to him, didn't want to draw attention to herself amid so many men, some wearing only singlets or long johns. She backed down the stairs, her heart returning to its normal rhythm. Her face felt flushed now, so instead of going back to her room, she went downstairs and crossed the foyer to the front door. Outside, walking between the pine trees, the chill air cooled her blood.

Because one day it would be Sam, wouldn't it?

No, that was by no means certain. He still smoked opium, but not as much. She was fairly sure of that. She crossed the lawn and sat on a stone seat among a bed of roses. Weak afternoon light fluttered between the empty oak branches. It was cold, too cold to be out. But she sat there a while nonetheless, not wanting to go back in the hotel where some awful drama was unfolding. She breathed, and the minutes ticked by.

The sound of a car engine caught her ear, and she glanced up to see Will Dalloway's sedan bumping over the semicircular driveway to pull up near the entrance. He seized a black bag from his front seat and, squashing his hat over his auburn hair, ran to the front door.

Here, Flora rose. She followed him inside, but he had already hared up the stairs, and she stood, uncertain, in the center of the foyer.

Miss Zander glided over, all gleaming pearls and lavender. "Miss Honeychurch-Black? Can I help you?"

"What's happening?" Flora noticed that other guests had gathered near the bottom of the stairs and were whispering to each other.

"One of our guests has taken unwell."

"Drowned himself in the bath, I heard," a man at the bottom of the stairs said archly. "If that's 'unwell' to you."

Miss Zander didn't blink. "I always respect our guests' privacy, no matter what the circumstances. Nonetheless, Miss Honeychurch-Black, it's nothing for you—nor any of *you*," she said, looking directly at the assembled guests, "to be concerned with. Please, come through to the dining room, where the hotel is offering complimentary afternoon tea."

Flora allowed herself to be carried along on the tide of guests—about a dozen in all—to the dining room. Miss Zander had somehow seamlessly and quickly organized cucumber sandwiches and tea, and waitstaff to pass it all around with plastered-on smiles. Flora suspected there was a lot of shouting and scurrying in the kitchen, but here in the dining room it was almost pleasant, were it not for the speculation about the drowned guest that passed around the tables.

"He fell in love but she gave him the icy mitt."

"His wife was a nag and he did it to spite her."

"I heard he lost all his money in a bad business deal."

"He was always a miserable bastard."

Flora tried not to listen. She sipped her tea and watched the waitstaff. Young Violet, Sam's latest infatuation, was not here. Flora hadn't seen her for a few days and began to hope that she had gone, and that particular disaster had been forestalled.

Cordelia Wright, the opera singer, found her. "Ghastly business. Everybody speculating like schoolchildren. Nice to see you, Miss Honeychurch-Black."

Flora smiled. She liked Cordelia. "Yes, it is ghastly. The poor fellow."

"Indeed. Nobody suicides unless they're terribly unhappy to start with, and that's the real tragedy. To be so unhappy and have nobody to talk to."

Flora maintained her outward smile as she thought about what Will had said, about opium addicts and suicide, but she didn't have long to contemplate and worry, because Cordelia opened up with a barrage of chatty questions about weather and gowns and Flora's plans for winter, and Flora was grateful for the company.

After half an hour or so, the door to the dining room opened to reveal Will, his eyes scanning the room and stopping when they found Miss Zander.

As Miss Zander hurried out, Flora was seized by a strong desire to see Will, to talk to him. She excused herself and made her way down the hall and through the foyer, but Will and Miss Zander were nowhere to be seen. Without stopping to think, she hurried outside once again into the cold winter afternoon and crossed to Will's car, where she perched on the running board on the driver's side to wait for him.

Time passed slowly in the chill air, and the afternoon shadows lengthened around her. But still she waited, not caring if Sam was looking for her, or Tony, or that her fingertips were turning icy. She wanted to see Will, and though she was unsure why it seemed so important, she didn't change her mind. She wasn't the kind of woman to change her mind.

At length, he came. He saw her the moment the entrance doors shut behind him, and offered her half a wave and half a smile. She stood, smoothing her skirt, as he walked towards her.

He stopped in front of her, a little closer than he might have if they'd never met. She was aware of his body in that slightly familiar space.

"Is it true? Did he drown himself?"

"It would seem so."

"Is that not terribly sad?"

Will opened his car door and slid his bag onto the front seat. He took off his glasses and folded them on the dashboard. "Yes, it is sad."

"Was he young?"

"No. A man in his forties."

"Do you know why he did it?"

"There was no note left, no explanation. I expect his loved ones, when we find them, will know why he did it."

"What happens now?"

"We've moved him back to his bedroom, and the undertaker is on his way. Miss Zander is handling it beautifully, I must say. She said there's never been a death here before, but she's taking it in her stride."

Flora looked towards the hotel, then back at Will. A beam of orange sun shot low through the trees and hit him in the eyes, and he raised his hand to shield them. In the sunlight, his eyes looked very green. Then the wind shifted the branches, and the beam of sun was gone. But the image stayed with her, the amber light on his face, his shining eyes.

"I'm sorry you've had to deal with such an awful business," she said.

He smiled, that warm smile that sneaked under her defenses. "You are too kind, Flora. How is your brother?"

"A little better, I believe."

"That's good news."

Silence stretched out. "Well," he said, "I must be on my way."

Flora stepped aside as he crank-started his car, then climbed in and drove off. Only then did she turn and head inside where it was warm.

By dinner that evening, word of the tragedy had surely spread to every hotel guest. Rather than causing them to be sober and reflective, it seemed the unhappy event had awoken a party spirit. They ate and drank and danced as though warding off their own mortality. Even the orchestra played with unusual vigor.

Flora sat close to Tony, but he spent most of the evening turned away from her, talking, offering her little comfort. Sam, however, paid close attention to her and seemed almost eager in his rehashing of every detail.

"Imagine, Sissy, that's the same bath I sometimes bathe in."

"Don't, Sam, you're making my skin crawl."

"He went in, filled the tub, just as I would . . . but then—"

"Please don't. He must have been so unhappy."

"I saw him when they brought him out, all wrapped in towels like an Egyptian mummy. One of his hands was free, though, and dragging on the floor. It was all blue and wrinkled."

Flora pushed his shoulder roughly. "I said *don't.*"

"Steady on. No need to get violent with me." Then his eyes were drawn across the room, and Flora noted with an inward groan that the pretty waitress was back.

"She's not for you, Samuel," she said quietly.

Sam turned and gave her a bright smile. "You know, I think you're right."

Violet served the guests at the next table, not once looking Sam's way. Flora watched discreetly. Had they had a tiff? Perhaps nothing had ever passed between them. Perhaps, just once, Sam had been able to control himself.

As the evening wore on Tony paid her a little more attention. Vincent pined aloud for Eliza and passed around a photograph of her in a swimsuit that left very little to the imagination. Sweetie was up to his usual nonsense, making off-color jokes about the photograph. Cordelia Wright and Lady Powell were head-to-head on the other side of the table, oblivious to everyone but each other. Flora felt a pang, missing her close friend Liberty, who was so far away.

A bump against the back of her chair startled her, and she looked around in time to see Violet leaning over at an awkward angle at the next table—and Sam rubbing the back of his elbow across her buttocks. A spark of rage ignited inside her. She slapped Sam's shoulder.

"Ow. Why so rough this evening, Sissy?"

"I saw what you just did," she hissed near his ear.

"I did nothing!" he protested.

"You rubbed that girl's bottom."

"Nonsense. I can't help if the young woman is a little clumsy."

"You're doing it on purpose. Both of you. I've a mind to report her to Miss Zander."

"Why would you do that? On an imagined caress? Have you such little faith in me, Flora?"

Flora had less than a little faith in Sam; she had none at all. But he continued to protest his innocence, eyes wide and hands spread, until Flora was forced to back down. She excused herself to go to the powder room.

On her return, she nearly ran straight into Violet, who was ferrying a pile of dishes back to the kitchen.

"Oh, I'm sorry, ma'am," Violet said, with a little deferential nod, and kept moving.

"Wait," Flora said, grasping her arm and holding her in place. "You're Violet, aren't you?"

"Yes." She had the most unusually colored eyes under her black lashes: somewhere between blue and violet, and Flora found herself wondering if she had been named for the color.

"I'm Flora. Sam's sister. You know Sam, don't you?"

Violet nodded. "I know both of you. You have been here the whole time I've been here. I know many of the guests."

"I know what you're doing."

Violet glanced down at Flora's hand, firm on her upper arm. "What am I doing?"

Flora dropped her hand. "Flirting with him."

"I assure you, ma'am, I'm not—"

"You both think I'm a fool. But I can see, with my own eyes, that something is passing between you. Some lovey nonsense."

Violet took a step back, drew her spine very straight. "With all respect, ma'am, you know nothing about me, and you ought not think to judge me."

"I don't judge you. I'm trying to warn you."

Violet turned and stalked back to the kitchen, leaving Flora standing awkwardly between the tables and the powder room.

Then Tony was there. "Well, that went badly," he said.

"Did you hear?"

"No, I saw. Let them be, Florrie. It's not worth it."

She leaned her head on his shoulder. "What a strange day it's been."

"Come and dance, my dear. That will take your mind off the shadows."

That night, in Sam's room, Violet sat naked on the end of his bed, laughing about Flora.

"And she got all puffed up and said, *I know what you're doing . . .*"

"I told you. I told you she'd try to destroy our happiness."

"*I'm trying to warn you*, she said. Warn me! Oh, what a lark. All because you, terrible boy, couldn't keep your hands off my bottom."

"It's a lovely bottom, Violet. All pale and plump. I want to kiss it all over."

She leaned over him, snuggled against his chest. "Warn me," she said again. "Of what, I wonder? You're not dangerous, are you, dear?"

"Not a whit."

"Then all will be well."

"Yes," he said. "You'll see."

She hesitated, then said, "Sam, will we really be together?"

"I know we will. It's written in our stars."

"No, not stars. Not dreams. Real life. Will you stay with me? Will we make a life together? Will you take care of me when I grow old?"

"Of course," he said. "You'll never want for anything."

She smiled, then hesitated again before speaking. "My mother can't work anymore."

"She won't need to. I'll buy her a house next door to ours." He slid down and kissed her collarbone, stirring her desire from the embers. "I'll give you whatever you want, because you've made me so happy."

"Do you promise me?"

"Cross my heart and hope to die," he said against her lips. "Now kiss me, or I'll think you don't love me."

She offered her mouth to him, with all the passion she felt in her heart.

CHAPTER TWELVE

Sam wandered into the dining room for breakfast just as Violet was clearing away the last of the crockery from the empty tables. Aware that Hansel was lurking nearby, she forced a polite smile and said, "I'm sorry, Mr. Honeychurch-Black, but breakfast service is finished. Can I have something sent to your room?"

Sam glanced around, then leaned in and said, "Meet me at Lovers Cave as soon as you're free." Then he straightened his back, nodded at Hansel, and headed back out, closing the dining room door behind him.

"What did he say to you?" Hansel said, in his clipped German accent. "Does he want something brought up?"

"No. No, he said . . . he's not hungry."

Hansel looked puzzled, but Violet ignored him, taking a last tray of plates to the kitchen. The morning's flying fox had just arrived, and the back door was open so Cook and the kitchen hands could bring in the crates. This was the first time Violet had seen such an operation in a hotel kitchen. Certainly, she had seen dumb waiters, large enough for a tray or two of food, that went between floors. But this was another operation altogether. The cables were anchored on points all the way down the rocky outcrops into the valley of farm-land below. Every morning, one of the farm managers would fill several crates with fresh produce: cuts of meat, freshly picked fruit, bottles of milk, and sacks of vegetables. Then one by one, with a system of pulleys, the crates would be hauled up inside a metal box to the top of the escarpment. Miss Zander called it the next best thing to living beside the farms. The process cut out hours of winding trips by car or sulky every day. Violet loitered while the boxes were opened, and then swiped a couple of apples and hid them up the leg of her bloomers before grabbing her coat and making her way out of the hotel and down to the bush track.

It was a bright, clear morning, mild in the sunlight but cold in the shadows under the rocky overhangs and trailing ferns. Birds and lizards crackled in the dry, fallen leaves, and insects buzzed and cricked. At length, she found her way through the gap to Lovers Cave, where he was waiting inside. He'd brought a blanket—she recognized it as a hotel bedspread—and had his tray of opium-smoking equipment beside him. But he wasn't smoking, and he wasn't in his glazed torpor. He sat with his knees tucked under his chin, his arms wrapped around himself, in thoughtful contemplation.

"Hello," she said.

He unwound himself. "Sit down. Do you like it?"

"It's very nice," she said. "If a little cold. How did you get the bedspread here without somebody stopping you?"

He shrugged. "People usually let me do what I want."

She pulled out the apples and gave him one, and he bit into it eagerly. She sat down on the bedspread and leaned into him.

"I've missed you," he said.

"It's only been a few hours."

"I miss you every moment I'm away from you. It's as though my skin craves your skin." He ran his hand over her arm, but the gesture was dulled by the heavy weight of her coat. They sat quietly a few minutes, finishing their apples. Then he went to the entrance of the cave and flung the core as hard as he could. It arced out over the ledge, then rolled and thudded away. She joined him and threw her apple core, too, but she wasn't as strong as he was, so hers didn't make it to the valley three hundred feet below; instead, it landed on the bush track in front of them. She giggled. He encircled her waist with his arms and drew her back against his chest, his hot breath in her ear. "Come and lie down," he said.

She hoped he didn't want to make love; a cold cave in broad daylight was not to her taste. But it seemed he really did simply want to lie down, and they lay with limbs entwined listening to the quiet forest and the soft wind.

"I've been coming down here a lot," he said suddenly. "I'm afraid to go back to my room."

"What do you mean?"

"Ever since that man died up there . . ."

"Are you superstitious?"

"Not at all. It's just . . . there's a bad feeling up there now."

"What kind of bad feeling?" Her fingers reached for his cheek and stroked it gently.

He closed his eyes but didn't answer.

"It will pass, my love," she said.

"Have you ever seen a dead body?" he asked.

"No."

He opened his eyes and spoke urgently. "I saw the dead man's hand. It didn't seem real. It seemed like a puppet's and somebody had forgotten to pull the strings. I keep thinking about it." He tapped his temple. "I don't want to go into the bathroom where he died. I've been using the one at the other end of the hall."

"You could ask Miss Zander to move you."

"Yes, but . . . I don't want to be away from it either. It's as though . . . if I turn my back, something bad will happen."

Violet struggled to understand. He was making little sense—perhaps it was the opium—so she didn't argue with him. "You've nothing to worry about, Sam."

He closed his eyes again and snuggled against her breasts. "If I could just lie here, with your hands in my hair . . . ah, that's it. That makes the bad feelings go away." He grew quiet, his breathing rhythmic. Despite the cold and the lumpy ground, Violet felt herself drifting off. The constant nights of interrupted sleep were taking an unforgiving toll. Some days, while in the middle of some mundane task, a flash of memory would come to her, and she would be unable to say for certain whether it was a real memory or a shred of a dream. Her whole mind was filled with Sam, with his skin and his mouth and his pale arms.

She woke with a start sometime later. Sam lay on his side, smoking his pipe, watching her. The cave smelled of sweet smoke.

"You looked so peaceful," he said.

"I'm tired all the time, Sam."

He frowned. "Why is that?"

She sighed. It was too much to expect him to know what a day of physical labor was like, let alone five or six days a week of it. "Because I only sleep a little every night. I come to you at one, then go back to my own room before dawn and try to catch a few hours before work."

"Are you saying you don't want to come to me at night?" His face hardened, an expression she hadn't seen before.

"Of course I want to come. I live for it. But perhaps not every night. Perhaps every second night."

"So, my spell is wearing off already?"

"No, Sam. Don't be upset. I work. I work hard, all day. I can't sleep when I want to like you can."

He continued to draw on his pipe, his eyes fluttering closed. "I knew it couldn't last," he said. "It never does."

Violet's heart lurched. "Don't say that! I still love you as much as I ever did. Forget I mentioned it. I will be there for you tonight."

"Reluctantly, no doubt."

"No. Eagerly. Wanting you. As I always do."

He waved her away. "Don't bother."

Violet searched her mind for something to say that would reassure him, but he was slipping away into his private oblivion, so instead she simply stayed close, laying his head in her lap and stroking his hair while he floated away on a river of bliss.

Violet became desperate to show Sam that she loved him. She thought of writing him a letter, but she wasn't as good with words as he was, and besides, she couldn't get in and out of his room to put it under his pillow. He could do it because he was rich. As he said, people let him do what he wanted. If Violet was found in possession of a love letter for one of the guests . . .

No, she needed to find another way, to do something that showed her love was passionate and undying. The idea came to her in a flash: the love heart in the rock at Lovers Cave. *Imagine, somebody had to carve this with a hammer and chisel, to prove his love to his girl.* Well, she could do the same, to prove her love to her man.

Violet hadn't seen Clive much of late. It had become too cold for dances in the drafty, unheated house; and he had finished repairs on the windows and was ensconced in his workshop over on the eastern side of the back fence most days. She had seen him once or twice in the staff dining room, but her enforced bed rest and then several days straight of breakfast shifts had meant they didn't often cross paths there anymore. She presumed, though, that he would still be glad to see her. Perhaps glad enough to loan her a hammer and chisel for a few hours.

Between shifts the following day, she left through the back kitchen door and followed the path beside the low stone columns that lined the escarpment. On the tennis court, two men and two women were engaged in a game of doubles, laughing and teasing each other, their voices carrying away on the wind and the sunshine. Christmas in June was only ten days away, and then most of the guests would head back down the mountain. The tennis net would come down and the court would be closed, the remaining guests would be relocated into the west wing—Sam's wing—and the orchestra sent home. The dining room dividers would be slid into place, and staff would pack their bags. Violet had gleaned all this from overheard conversations in the staff dining room, or in directives from Miss Zander. When Myrtle left, so would most of the other waitstaff. Only Hansel and Violet would be left. Alexandria, Miss Zander's elegant deputy, was heading home for the holidays. Most of the staff who were wintering over were men, and they occupied the bottom of the east wing. It would be quiet. She would have to work hard, but there would be a special freedom that came with the quiet: she would have no wait for the bathroom and privacy in her bedroom, and she could more easily sneak out to Sam's room.

The workshop door was open, but Violet still knocked. Clive, who had his back to her and was hunched over something on his workbench, turned and smiled.

"Violet! What a lovely surprise."

"I haven't seen you much lately. I've been on breakfasts." She glanced around the dim space: a wall of tools; another wall with a rack that hung with overalls, waterproof gear, fishing equipment, buckets, mops, and brooms; racks full of bits and pieces of metal and wood.

He grimaced. "I've been up and down the valley, perched in precarious spots, refitting all the flying-fox anchors. Good thing I'm not afraid of heights, eh?"

She sidled up next to him, peering over his shoulder. In front of him was a collection of brackets and screws. "What's that?"

"Brackets for curtain rods. They need repainting. I was supposed to have this done by the end of May. I'm a little behind."

"Miss Zander works you too hard."

"I'm glad to have a job somewhere nice. She's very kind to me. There will be time to catch up over winter, when there are fewer guests breaking things." He smiled.

"Can I borrow a hammer and a chisel?"

He blinked, his smile fading. "Ah . . . why?"

"I can't say."

"You're being mysterious."

"Not on purpose."

He put his tools down and turned to face her fully. "If I loan you a hammer and a chisel, will you promise not to break anything that I have to come to fix later?"

"Oh, I absolutely promise. I'll bring them back same time tomorrow. Before, if I can."

"You won't tell me what for?"

"I'm sorry, I can't. But it's nothing sinister. Trust me."

He sighed. "I do trust you, Violet."

"You're a good friend."

"Yes, it seems I am. Here." He climbed to his feet and went to the tool rack, fetched a hammer and chisel, and handed them to her. "Take your time. I have spares."

She beamed. She wanted to kiss his cheek but thought better of it; it would give him the wrong impression, and, besides, she was fairly sure that Sam wouldn't like it.

The next morning, just at dawn, when she was sure Sam was sleeping off their passion-fueled excesses, she picked her way down the bush path, scarf wrapped high around her ears and cheeks, hat pulled low, and fingers shivering even in her new leather gloves.

Violet was unprepared for how much work it would take to make an impression on the rock. She wanted the letters to be as deep as the love heart in which she was impressing them, and it took ages simply to make the first groove, the top of the S. The rest of the S, a lightning strike, came a little easier now she had learned the best angle on which to lean the chisel. Then she stopped and considered her work. She had intended to write SAM, but remembered that he always signed his love letters SHB. The H was easy enough, but the B looked a mess, like some kind of uneven Viking rune. Nonetheless, one hour and two aching wrists later, it was done.

Violet sat back and admired her work. Yes. She had chiseled her love for him into stone. He would understand how much it meant, and he would never doubt her love again.

She rose, stretching her legs, only to look up and see Clive standing at the entrance to the cave.

"Oh!" she cried, startled, her hand going over her heart. "How long have you been there?"

He inclined his head slightly. "I followed you down. But I didn't approach until I heard you stop chiseling. I'm sorry, but I was worried about you."

"Worried?"

"It's an odd thing to ask for, Violet. I didn't know what you were up to, what trouble you might get yourself into. Forgive me."

He advanced into the cave, and Violet moved her body to stand in front of the rock. "Here are your tools," she said, offering them to him.

"You may as well move. I'll just come back here later to look."

Violet stood aside. "I didn't carve the heart. Just the letters."

Clive looked at the letters a long time, and said nothing.

"Please don't tell," she said.

"I have nothing to tell," he replied, forcing a smile. "It's obviously in a language I don't understand."

Violet was grateful for his feigned ignorance, and for keeping his judgments about her behavior to himself.

"I'd best get these back to the workshop," he said, turning on his heel.

"We're still friends aren't we, Clive?" she called after him.

"Perhaps not," he called back, over his shoulder. "Perhaps that's not best for either of us."

She hurried after him, then changed her mind and hung back. Yes, perhaps it was not best for either of them. He was still sweet on her; of course he was. She knew it. She had taken advantage of it when she'd gone to borrow the tools from him. Once she'd been sweet on him, too, but the remembrance of their one chaste kiss was almost laughable next to the passionate kisses she and Sam shared.

It was time to let Clive go.

"Flora!"

Flora, who was sitting in a sunbeam near the fountain in the garden, turned to see Tony waving to her. At his side was Eliza, Vincent's girlfriend, whom Tony had brought up from Sydney with him, grudgingly. The happy news that Tony had finished with meetings until after the wedding and could spend more time with Flora was tempered by the sad news that Eliza had come to take Vincent off the mountain for good. He had finally asked her to marry him.

Flora rose and walked towards them, admiring Tony's well-cut suit and dashing hat and hoping he had done as she had asked and purchased a special Christmas-in-June present for her to give to Sam. "Did you bring it?" she asked.

"I brought more things than you can imagine," he said, smiling. "I've had them sent up to your room already."

"Dear Flora," Eliza said, leaning in to kiss the air next to Flora's cheek. "Happy to see you."

"Indeed. And happy to hear that you'll be heading down the mountain to get married."

"You two won't be far behind, I take it?" Eliza said, glancing at Tony.

Tony grinned. "Father Callahan said yes. September the eighteenth it is. Write to your father and let him know. We'll take the Wentworth for the reception. My assistant is organizing it all." He brushed his thumb lightly across Flora's chin. "All you need to do is buy a wedding gown."

Flora's body tingled. Was it excitement or fear? They were similar enough. It must be excitement.

"Go on, you two," he said. "Run off and do your women's business. But Flora, do look in on your brother's Christmas present. I must catch up with Karl for coffee at three."

Eliza linked her arm through Flora's. "Come on, up to your room," Eliza said. "I'm dying to see what was in that trunk on the backseat of the car all the way here. Tony wouldn't tell me a thing, the grump."

"A trunk? Golly, I just asked him to get an atlas for Sam. A nice one."

They went inside and up the stairs, and sure enough, in the middle of Flora's room sat a trunk. She felt for the latch, then opened the lid. Inside were two dozen gold-embossed, leather-bound books. She pulled the first one out—it was enormous—and opened at a random page. Maps. The books were full of maps. She and Eliza pulled a few out and browsed the detailed, richly illustrated maps of continents and countries, islands and archipelagos.

"Oh my, Sam will love these!" Flora exclaimed as she stacked them on top of each other on the floor beside her. "Though I'll never be able to wrap them." She looked at Eliza. "I can't imagine what possessed Tony to acquire such a gift. He and Sam don't get along."

"That explains it, then," Eliza said. "When I asked him what was in the trunk, he said it was a peace offering."

"He wants to make peace with Sam?"

"I expect so. Now that the wedding isn't so far away. They'll be brothers."

"They have so little in common. It's like they're from two different species."

"Men are men," she said, diffidently, not meeting Flora's eye. "I say, let's go down to the games room and have a few hands of gin rummy."

"I don't much like playing cards," Flora said, sliding the books neatly back into the trunk.

"The tearoom, then? I'm gasping for a pot of tea."

The tearoom was open only on weekends, and was the favorite haunt of the older ladies, including Cordelia and Lady Powell. "Of course, if that's what you want."

She flipped the catch on the trunk and quickly checked her hair, and then she and Eliza descended the stairs and walked all the way to the end of the east wing to the tearoom. The thick, red drapes had been caught back with gold braided ties, letting sun fall through the hip-to-ceiling windows, and opening up the view out over the cliffs. The room smelled of cinnamon and butter, and buzzed with well-dressed ladies in silk and beads heaping delicacies onto china plates. Flora felt quite plain in her knitted cream jumper and paneled skirt. Long tables had been laid out with platters of sandwiches and scones and fresh fruit. A waiter showed them to a free table and brought them a pot of tea, and Flora had no idea at all from Eliza's demeanor and conversation of the horror that was coming.

Finally, when they were alone, Eliza said, "I brought you here so that when I tell you what I have to tell you, you will be forced to keep your head and not make a scene."

"What do you mean?" Flora's blood iced over. Eliza's face had become so serious. "What's happened?"

"I have known about this for some time, but only now that Vincent is quitting Tony's 'admiration society'"—she said these words with barely disguised loathing—"am I free to tell you."

"Please," Flora said, because she didn't know what else to say, "be easy on my heart." She reached for Eliza's hand. "Please."

"Your fiancé has not been faithful to you."

Flora let this sink in. She found that it didn't immediately cause pain, the way finding out her mother had died or Sam had been exposed to the police might. She nodded. "He has a lover?"

"Would that it were one, my dear. He keeps the regular company of ladies of the night when he is in Sydney."

Flora shuddered.

"A good friend of mine is the wife of his assistant, the man who is charged with procuring and paying for these ladies. By his word, Tony doesn't do a lot of work in Sydney. It is rather more pleasure. Worse, Tony's father is the same. A man who lives off the fat of his business, pays cleverer men to do the hard work, and spends a lot of time in brothels." Eliza exhaled loudly. "There, I've said it. I've been wanting to say it for a very long time."

Flora recalled their conversation in the woods near the trout lake, Eliza's doubts about men being able to do "the right thing." Her cheeks flushed with embarrassment. "Does Vincent know?" she asked.

"They all know," Eliza said.

"Then why haven't they stopped him?"

"Because they don't judge him. They think it natural for a man such as Tony to have what he wants. I have told Vincent, very clearly, that it is *not* natural for him to want such things and that I will wring his neck if he goes near another woman. *Any* type of woman."

Flora's cheeks stung. Eliza was right, though: being in a public place made her repress any urge to cry and rage. She folded her hands on the table in front of her.

"Tea, dear?" Eliza said.

"Thank you."

"I'm sorry to be the bearer of this news."

"It's better that I know."

"Will you still marry him?"

The question surprised Flora. It hadn't even occurred to her that she wouldn't. Her father wanted it, Tony's father wanted it, they loved each other, the date had been set and the church booked. "I imagine I will," she said. "Many men . . . do that. Even after they are married."

"You make sure he stops before the wedding," Eliza warned. "He'll bring home the clap and give it to you."

Flora found herself repulsed. The idea of being intimate with Tony, which so far had been a vague, dreamy fantasy on the edge of her mind, now seemed ugly and wet and too real.

Eliza poured her tea. "Now, we are going to sit here until I'm sure you are able to keep yourself composed."

"I'm composed."

"Are you angry?"

"I don't get angry. It's impractical."

"Are you hurt?"

Flora considered her feelings as though from a distance. "I'm . . . sad. I think. And embarrassed."

"It's him who ought to be embarrassed." Eliza leaned forwards and grasped Flora's hands. "Will you talk to him about it?"

"I don't know. Perhaps it doesn't matter. Perhaps my feelings don't matter." She wondered if Tony ever sang opera songs to his lady companions.

Eliza sat back. "*You* matter, Flora. If you want him to stop, you have to tell him."

Flora sat, mute and empty. She suddenly wished that Eliza had never told her. She wished she'd minded her own business.

"Will you tell him?"

"I don't know," Flora snapped.

Eliza arched a perfectly penciled eyebrow. "I thought you said you didn't get angry. Now, drink your tea like a lady. Whatever you do, make sure Vincent and I are gone before you confront him. With Tony's bad temper, who knows what he'll do."

Flora drank her tea. It tasted bitter, or perhaps bitterness was all she could taste.

CHAPTER THIRTEEN

Flora paced her room. Around and around. The trunk full of books sat in the middle of the floor. How could he? *How could he?* Pacing, pacing. How she hated the trunk of books, how she hated the idea that he had bought them out of guilt, rather than out of a desire to mend a fractured bond with her brother.

A knock at the door. It would be Tony; she knew it. How could she even look at him? Head down, she answered the door.

"Miss Honeychurch-Black?"

"Oh. Miss Zander. Is everything all right?"

"Well, no. May I come in? Or you could come down to my office if that's more agreeable."

"No, no. Come in. I'm . . . not busy."

Miss Zander closed the door behind her. "It's about your brother."

Flora steeled herself. There couldn't possibly be more bad news today. "Go on."

"Some of the ladies on this floor have complained about him using their bathroom."

Flora was confused. "Using the ladies' bathroom?"

"Yes."

"On this floor?"

"So they say."

Had Sam smoked so much opium he couldn't find his own bathroom?

"I'd approach him myself, but . . ." Miss Zander trailed off. "I'm unsure how to broach the topic sensitively, and I know you are very protective of him. He's much younger than you, isn't he?"

"Five years," she muttered. "But yes, he lacks maturity. I will certainly speak to him. It's probably a simple mistake. My brother's sins are more often of omission than commission, Miss Zander. Try not to think too ill of him."

"I think nothing but good things of your family, Miss Honeychurch-Black," she said. "Good day."

Flora took a moment to gather her thoughts. Tony. Sam. Both gave her nothing but sorrow; why did she love them both, then?

Down the stairs she went to Sam's room. He wasn't there. She hardly saw him about anymore, and she found it curious that he had discovered the pleasures of nature and the outdoors at precisely the time the weather had turned too bitter to leave the hotel.

She returned to her room for hat, coat, and gloves, and after an hour wandering around the grounds and shallower mountain paths, trying to clear her head, she made her way back, past the coffeehouse. As she glanced in the window she was surprised to see Sam sitting alone at a table, gazing out. Gazing right through her. She waved, and the movement caught his eye and he half smiled, but she could tell already he had been smoking. His mind was roaming a long way away.

Rather than invite him out where he might stumble and fall, she went in. The heating was up very high, and her skin prickled under her warm blouse. She hung up her coat and glanced about anxiously for Tony's mob, but they weren't there. She slid into the seat opposite Sam, wondering how he'd managed to find his way here without her help.

"Sam, are you all right?"

"Yes."

"You've been smoking."

"An hour ago. Coming down now."

"Why aren't you in your room? It isn't like you to come out . . . in this state."

He shrugged.

"Sam, Miss Zander came to see me. She said there have been complaints about you using the bathroom on the ladies' floor."

His head snapped up. "It was only once!"

"Why on earth were you up there?"

"I don't want to use the bathroom closest to my room. The other bathrooms on the men's floor were occupied. So, I went upstairs." He dropped his voice. "I really needed to go, Sissy."

"Why don't you want to use your bathroom?"

"Because that man died in it, and now it's haunted." He said this matter-of-factly, as though he'd described it as dirty or too small.

"Haunted?"

He nodded.

"But you don't believe in ghosts, Sam. Why would you think it's haunted?"

"Because he died in there."

"Great-grandpapa died on the sofa in our sitting room back home, and you were always happy to be in there. And to sit on the sofa, for that matter. I remember finding you there in an embrace with Mrs. Hanover."

"Great-grandpapa didn't *haunt* the place, Flora. It's different altogether."

Flora spread her hands on the table. The noise of men talking and the smell of coffee brewing whirled around them in the heated room. "You'll need to explain. What have you seen or heard?"

"Nothing. I haven't seen or heard anything. But I can *feel* it. I can feel my skin prickling. It's cold in there. The sensations echo about."

Even though it wasn't rational, Flora's own skin came out in goose bumps. What dark imaginings he was capable of. "It's a bathroom," she said forcefully, as much to reassure herself as him. "Bathrooms are always cold."

"I'm not going back in there."

"Just promise me you'll stay out of the ladies' bathroom."

He shrugged.

"Miss Zander can decide we are too much trouble and send us home, you know."

"She wouldn't do that."

"What if she did?"

"All right, all right. I'll stay away from the ladies' floor." He ran his hands through his hair. "I haven't been sleeping right. I've been having dreams. Ever since he died."

"It's the shock. We were all upset by it. You've always been more sensitive."

"Yes, yes. That's it. That's it and nothing more. Thanks, Sissy." He covered her hand with his. "How are *you*?"

Should she tell him? No, he already hated Tony. She made herself smile. "I have your Christmas present in my room."

"Christmas isn't for months."

"Christmas in June, remember?"

"Oh. I'd best find something for you, then." It had always been the way with Sam. She lavished him with gifts, and he would give her an old book he'd found under his bed or buy the first ugly thing he saw.

"Don't worry about it, Sam. The best gift you can give me is to keep smoking less, and stay away from the lass."

"You can count on me," he said, unconvincingly. But today, too many other worries took precedence, and she could not bring herself to probe him further.

Flora wasn't entirely sure what she was doing outside Will Dalloway's house, but now she was here she may as well go in. It was freezing on the street, and she knew he wouldn't turn her away.

Inside, three patients waited on the long wooden bench. One of them coughed violently as Flora took a seat at a distance, trying not to show she was leaning away. She left her gloves and hat on, in case she decided this was a bad idea and fled.

Will emerged after a few minutes with an elderly woman who was thanking him profusely. His eye caught on Flora, and he lit up. "Miss Honeychurch-Black," he said, reverting to her formal name in front of his patients. "What a delight to see you. I can take you in straightaway if you need me to."

Flora looked at the wretched patients ahead of her and shook her head. "I shall wait my turn, Dr. Dalloway. It isn't urgent."

He smiled, and she saw that he was pleased that she hadn't jumped the queue. She felt the particular warm glow that came from gaining the good favor of somebody important, and settled in to wait her turn.

A loud clock ticked away the time, and she wished she'd brought a book to read. One by one, the patients went through and more arrived, though Flora shuffled up to the end of the bench closest the surgery door to make it clear she was next. Finally, Will showed her through.

She sat on the other side of his desk while he settled into his chair and opened his notepad.

"How can I help you today?"

Flora picked up the rope of beads around her neck, worried them between her fingers. "It's Sam."

"Go on."

"He's seeing things. Well, he says he's not seeing things but *feeling* things. He talks about a ghost in the bathroom where that man died, about awful dreams. He seems afraid to be in his room, and once he's there it's almost impossible to get him out without him shaking and turning pale."

Will put his pen down and joined his fingers in a steeple, leaning his forehead on them.

"Is it the opium doing this to him?" she asked.

He looked up. "It's hard to say. The drug affects people differently. They say that under the influence it's possible to feel strange things, but they are usually nice things. Opium is associated with euphoria."

"He said he's cut down."

"That might have something to do with it. As I said, it's hard to say. We haven't nearly enough studies on opium. We really only know it's very addictive and eventually turns ordinary people into desperate wretches." He checked himself. "I'm sorry."

"Could it be sending him mad?"

This time he chose his words carefully, forming his lips several times before actually speaking. "He may have already been on the way, if you take my meaning."

"I don't."

"The very thing that drew him to opium—to that euphoria, that escape from everything—might have been an underlying lack of mental stability."

"Are you saying . . ." The awful weight of her worry threatened to crush her.

"He may have started talking about ghosts anyway. But certainly, yes, the opium makes such things seem acute to him. It can take whatever dread is natural to a man and amplify it."

Flora thought back over her life with Sam. He had always been odd, out of step, off with the pixies. "Is there anything we can do? Could you give him some medicine for it?"

"There are specialist doctors who treat disorders of the mind, but none up here in the mountains. I can give you the names of some in Sydney, but your problem, once again, is getting Sam to attend his appointments."

Flora slumped forwards in her seat, letting her forehead rest on Will's desk.

"Flora?"

"I am so overburdened, Will."

"Take heart. He's young. He may recover."

"It's not just that." *Don't tell him. Don't tell him just because he has warm eyes and says he cares.*

"Then, what else is wrong?"

She sat up again. The sun through the leaves outside the high window dappled onto his shoulder. Through the glass she could hear a bird calling, and she was taken by a longing to be a bird. Carefree, flying away up high above the buildings and streets and the people and their endless neediness.

He dropped his voice low. It was no longer a doctor's voice; it was the voice of a confidant, and Flora registered the moment as one of potential danger. The crossing of a ship into uncharted waters. "You can tell me anything."

"But I oughtn't."

"But you can."

"It's about Tony. My fiancé."

He nodded.

"He's been . . . seeing prostitutes." The words, in escaping, churned up nausea in her throat.

Will blinked, clearly struggling for the right words. "This makes you unhappy."

"Desperately. Desperately unhappy." She glanced away, not wanting to see the pity in his eyes. "Is it normal? Do most men—?"

"*I* certainly don't," he said hotly. "If I were engaged to be married to a good-hearted, intelligent woman such as yourself, I would count my blessings and treat her like a queen and not subject her to the risk of certain diseases that—" Then he dropped his eyes. "I've said too much," he continued, shuffling the papers on his desk. She could see his pulse flicking at his throat. Her fingers itched.

"No, you said just the right thing," she replied softly. "Thank you."

She rose, and he stood quickly and blurted, "Will you still marry him?"

"I suppose I must," she replied. "But I will make my terms very clear to him."

"Good," he said.

"I've held you up long enough."

"You are always welcome. At any time."

Her eyes met his, and warmth passed between them wordlessly.

"I know," she said.

Miss Zander called a staff meeting on Friday afternoon at three o'clock, and Violet dutifully filed in with her workmates to the guest dining room, where they took seats around the gleaming tables under the chandelier.

When all were settled, Miss Zander called them to attention with a short series of sharp claps. She waited for perfect quiet. Violet glanced over at Clive, but he was looking the other way. Myrtle sat with her, giving her a broad smile, all animosity over missing out on winter work forgiven.

"Now," Miss Zander started. "I've called this staff meeting to discuss our Christmas-in-June celebration, which is coming up in five days."

She held five fingers aloft theatrically. "Most of the preparation is under way, but I need two male volunteers to help erect the tree with Mr. Betts, and six female volunteers to help me decorate the long room."

Hands shot up all around her. Violet wondered if she should volunteer, but it was all over quickly. Miss Zander took down names on her clipboard, then quieted the group once more. "Next, I need ideas for activities throughout the day. I already have a full schedule of games and so on, but I wondered if any of you know how to read fortunes or draw portraits or some other bit of fun the guests might like to indulge in."

There was much head scratching and murmuring.

"It's worth a Christmas-in-June bonus," Miss Zander said.

Violet raised her hand. "Clive Betts can draw portraits."

"Thank you, Violet. Clive, you weren't going to tell me?"

"They're not very good, ma'am." He deliberately avoided Violet's gaze.

"They don't have to be, but please don't insult the guests by making them look too deformed."

Thora volunteered to read gypsy cards, and Miss Zander offered her a real gypsy costume, with ribbons and bells. Others got into the spirit, offering everything from fortune cookies to French braiding, and Miss Zander happily took down all their suggestions and promised to call them in if she needed to discuss it further.

"Finally," she said amid the excitement, this time bringing quiet to the room with more difficulty, "you are all invited to the Christmas-in-June celebration. The roster will be up tomorrow, and you will work short shifts so you can attend at least an hour of the activities. Of course, the Christmas lunch in the afternoon will be for guests only, but the events are open to all of you. Consider it my way of saying thank you before the winter break."

A cheer of many voices and a shimmer of applause went through the room.

"Sh, sh," Miss Zander said, palms up. "Great responsibility comes with this invitation. You are all ambassadors for the hotel. You will wear your uniforms. You will not drink a drop of liquor. You will be polite and mingle with the guests, but you will not flirt with them, ask them for money, offer nor ask for any confidences. Behave at all times as though I am standing directly behind you, with this expression on my face." Here she drew her eyebrows down in such a glower that everybody laughed uproariously, Miss Zander included.

"Any questions?"

Happy silence.

"Very well. I look forward to celebrating the day with you."

Myrtle squeezed Violet's hand. "What fun!"

Violet turned Miss Zander's warning over in her mind. *Mingle, don't flirt.* How she longed for her relationship with Sam to be out in the open, not hidden away and guilty. She would love to wear a beautiful frock and attend the Christmas dinner with him. But the past two nights he hadn't unlocked his door for her. Had he not seen her carving? Or had he seen it and cared nothing for it? She read and reread his love letters, searching for answers to questions she couldn't articulate. All were full of promises, but she was starting to wonder if he was even capable of keeping such promises—so readily bestowed by him, and so desperately grasped by her.

That evening, as Violet lay on her side in bed, nursing her misery alone while Myrtle worked, she heard a light knock on her door. The moment she opened it Sam gathered her in his arms.

"I found it," he said. "I found your beautiful present. You wonderful, wonderful girl. I asked for a sign. I said, *God, if she still loves me, give me a sign,* and there it was, hewn in rock."

Her ear was squashed against his chest, and she could hear his heart pounding. "I've never stopped loving you." She extricated herself, glanced up and down the hall nervously. Myrtle wouldn't be back for hours, but the chambermaids were still around. "What are you doing down here?" she asked.

"You weren't working the dinner shift, so I thought you might be here. I made an excuse and left dinner and . . . oh, Violet, Violet." He took her hands in his, and she noticed they were clammy. "Everything has gone badly." His mouth and jaw began to tremble, and she realized he was on the verge of sobbing.

"What do you mean? What's wrong?" His vast plummet in mood, the change in his demeanor, was so violent that it frightened her. "Do you want to come in?"

"No, I want you to come out. A long walk in the night."

"Down the cliff? I don't think that would be safe."

"No, into town. I'll explain on the way."

She hesitated, and he squeezed her hands more forcefully. "Don't doubt me, my love, don't doubt me. Everybody else does. I couldn't bear it if you did, too." He was pale and shaking.

"You don't look well. Perhaps you should come in and sit down."

"I'm not well, Violet. I'm not well. I need to go see a friend, and I need you to come with me. I've tried, I've tried so hard. But then the ghost came and I'm falling into ruin. Help me. Will you help me?"

Violet's ribs contracted. "Of course, of course. What do I need to do?"

"Put on your coat. Come with me."

Violet reached behind the door for her coat and scarf, hat and gloves. "Won't you be cold?" she asked him.

"I can't feel the cold. All I can feel is the need."

"We have to leave separately anyway," she said. "Why don't you go and get your coat and meet me out front?"

"Yes, yes. Good Violet. You understand. You know what to do.

I knew I could come to you. I'll meet you outside. I'll go and get my . . . I can't. I'm afraid to go up there."

Violet glanced around her room, then grabbed her bedspread and wrapped it around his shoulders. "Go. I'll meet you at the corner in two minutes. Don't despair, Sam. Whatever the problem is, I'll help you. I love you."

"I love you."

She watched him make his way up the corridor and disappear into the stairwell, the blanket tight around his shoulders. Her heart hammered. What was wrong with him? What did he mean about ghosts and falling into ruin? The seconds ticked by agonizingly slowly, then she hurried off, calling out to Alexandria that she was off for a brisk walk, and headed out into the cold.

He pounced on her from behind a pine tree, and she clutched at her heart.

"You gave me a fright."

"We're going to see a friend," he said. "His name is Malley." He began to walk briskly, but the blanket kept slipping off his shoulders and he had to stop to hitch it.

"Where does he live?"

"Other side of the rail line, a block or two from that house where you go dancing. Violet, he sells me my opium. You don't mind, do you?"

"I mind that you are so agitated. Why do you talk of being ruined?"

"I've been trying . . . trying so hard, for you. And for Flora. Poor Flora."

"Trying?"

"To give up the pipe. I cut back from twenty a day to ten a day. I got down to eight. Violet, nobody has ever inspired me to get down to eight a day! You are an angel, a goddess!"

She was in no mood to feel pleased with herself over his compliment. Rather, she was cold and worried.

"But it's not enough. My guts are hurting. I itch all over, but the itch isn't on my skin, it's under it, in the layers of my flesh that I can't see. I've started . . . feeling things. Things I don't like. I hear footsteps and I imagine they're him, coming down the hall, all waterlogged and blue."

"What a horror story! Who are you talking about?"

"The suicide. Self-murderers don't rest in their graves, you know. Why, it was only last century they were still regularly tied into their coffins to stop them rising from the dead."

Despite the fact that she believed none of this, Violet still felt a chill at his words. She forced her voice to be even and rational. "Sam, none of that is real. You must be sensible."

"I dream about it, over and over. I dream about the bath, him in the water with his eyes closed and his hair floating about him. I can't stop the dreams, and I think they are coming because I'm trying to stop smoking. I had a little opium left. I hoped it would be the last I would smoke, but I can't stop, do you see, Violet, my love? I can't stop." He raised his hands, made a cage around his head with his fingers. "Without it, the world is a nightmare. Everything has sharp edges. All that is good in the world seems foreign and forbidden to me. The ghosts come. The dreams come. Oh, oh, Violet, don't make me stop."

She reached for him and hitched the blanket around his shoulders. "I never asked you to stop, Sam."

He was quiet a few steps, then said warily, "It's true, you didn't."

"I don't like to see you in such misery. Let's find your friend and see what he has to say. Is he a doctor?"

"No, he's a criminal. You do understand, don't you, that opium is not legal? Or do you not even know that much about the world?"

Violet smarted from his casual chastisement. "I don't know much about much, I'm afraid. Is it very dangerous?"

"What you see before you," he said. "But only if I stop."

Violet didn't know what to think or what to say, but her instinct to relieve Sam's misery was greater than any other. Through the dark they hurried, as the cold wind rose and tore the last leaves from the oaks along the way and hissed harsh and flat through the pines. Soon they came to a house with a long settee on the veranda, and tall Chinese lamps either side of it.

"This is Malley's house," he said, and palpable calmness began returning to his limbs. "Malley will make the ghosts go away."

They climbed the stairs and knocked, waiting in the cold dark. Violet began to fear that Malley wasn't home, but then the door opened and he was there, smiling down on them.

"Samuel," he said. "Who's your pretty friend?"

"This is my Violet. She is a delight, but you aren't to give her any of your potions, you understand. She is pure and will remain that way."

"Wouldn't dream of it. Come in."

Malley was tall and thin, with a long ponytail and beard, dressed in what appeared to be red silk pajamas. Violet wasn't sure where to look. His house was cramped and smelled odd—a sweet smell laid over something old and decaying—and was full of Asian objects: woodprints and pots and jars and silk hangings and the opium pipes and lamps and awls and scissors she recognized from Sam's room. He indicated they should sit on the floor, where a thick rug was laid out and big soft cushions were scattered around.

"I'm in a bad way," Sam said to him. "I've been trying to cut back . . ."

"But the dragon is roaring. I know, I can see by looking at you."

"Can I have a pipe here? I need . . . oblivion."

"Oblivion? Then I've got something for you. Something you'll love."

Malley disappeared into an adjoining room and seemed gone for an age, as Sam sat next to Violet shivering and shuddering. Then the tall man returned with a green leather pouch that unfolded to reveal what looked to be medical implements.

"What is that?" Violet asked, wary.

"That is the easiest path to heaven," Malley said. "It's called heroin. Much like the opium you smoke, but this . . . this goes straight into your blood with a hypodermic syringe."

It sounded dangerous, and Violet opened her mouth to caution them, but Sam was eager.

"Will it make the ghosts go away?"

Malley smiled, showing two gold-capped teeth. "It will chase them away with such power that they'll be afraid to ever come back."

Violet watched as Malley prepared the solution and the syringe, and she held Sam as Malley injected the substance into his arm. Sam leaned into her, and she could feel the tension drain out of his body as he became limp and heavy.

"Are you all right?" she whispered in his ear.

"Lie down," he said, and so she lay on her side next to him, and he stroked her face with his hand. "Beautiful Violet."

"You look so peaceful," she said.

"Can we sleep here a little while?" But he was already drifting off, and she watched him flutter out of the world, leaving his horrors and his ghosts behind. His face in repose gave no indication that just half an hour before he had been shaking in her doorway. She tried to take comfort in his peace, although her heart harbored many other fears.

CHAPTER FOURTEEN

Violet resumed her visits to Sam's room in the dead of night, but only every second night. "That is the price we pay for forbidden love," he said, finally accepting her need for more rest. "Stolen moments."

On the nights she didn't come, he would write her furiously passionate love letters and leave them under her pillow with flowers pressed between tissue paper, or sweets, or pretty stones he'd found.

Sam returned to smoking whenever he wanted, and he evened out. She asked if he was going to see Malley for another injection, and was relieved when he told her he preferred his pipe to a needle and now he had enough opium to get him by for a while. He said his fear of the suicide's ghost had also gone away, but he declared it in an airy tone she suspected was false bravery, and he still refused to use the bathroom in which the man had drowned. His illness and itches had left him, and he had an air of calm about him. But something else went away, too: the edge of his spirit was dulled, he seemed less interested in everything. Her desire for him was undimmed, but sometimes he needed to be persuaded to touch her. Violet began to grow embarrassed by their interactions, stripping her own clothes off, pulling at his until he seemed to wake a little and realize she needed his caresses.

The day before Christmas in June, she arrived at one in the morning to find him sitting on the floor surrounded by open books.

"Look at this, Violet," he said. "This is what my sister gave me for Christmas. Is it not wonderful? Come and sit by me."

She sat with him and listened as he pointed out the places in China he had visited, the places in Africa he dreamed of going, and all the farms and meadows his family owned back in England and Wales.

"Is there somewhere you've always wanted to go?" he asked her.

"I should like to see Paris, I think."

He found the book containing maps of France, and showed her Paris, pointing out where the Eiffel Tower had been built, and describing the different character of each of the arrondissements. "I will take you there one day," he promised. "You will see it with your own eyes."

She kissed him and he pushed her over on the open map and made love to her in Paris. She closed her eyes and imagined they were really there, conjuring the smell of the Seine and the sound of accordions from Sam's descriptions. Afterwards they sat up and pored over more maps, fingers tracing dreams they hoped to fulfill together one day. He was very taken with his gift, the way a small child might be taken with a treasured toy on Christmas morning.

At four, she returned wearily to her room. She slipped off her dress and pulled on her nightie, then lay down in bed. The last thing she expected was Myrtle's voice in the dark. "Where have you been?"

Violet's brain was too tired to think of a good excuse. "Nowhere," she said.

"Were you nowhere the night before last, too? And two nights before that?"

"Nowhere interesting. I haven't been sleeping well. I get up and walk around."

"You come back smelling like opium smoke. Are you smoking opium?"

"Of course not! How do you know what opium smoke smells like?"

"Because we've all smelled it on Mr. Honeychurch-Black."

Violet didn't respond. Her pulse seemed very loud in her ears in the quiet room.

"I don't want you to get in any trouble," Myrtle said.

"I won't. So long as you don't tell anybody."

"Not that kind of trouble," Myrtle answered. "A different kind of trouble. The trouble girls get into when they aren't careful enough around men."

"How dare you?" Violet said hotly. "What kind of assumption is that to make about me?" She felt embarrassed and a little foolish.

"I don't mean to offend, only to warn. I'm your friend, Violet. I won't be around this time next week, so . . . so, I have to speak now. I know you're seeing him. I know he leaves you little notes. I saw him in here putting one under your pillow. He scuttled off quick smart, but I'm not an idiot. Does he say he loves you?"

Violet didn't answer, caught in the hot moment of being exposed, angry and fearful all at once.

Myrtle continued anyway. "He may well love you, but he *can't* love you. A man like him wouldn't be allowed to love a girl like you. You aren't anybody. Men like Samuel Honeychurch-Black marry fancy ladies whose fathers are barons, women who have been to finishing schools and know a bit about the world. They don't marry girls like you and me, Violet. It's a fact of life."

"You know nothing about him. Nor me. Nor us," Violet exploded.

"Be as angry as you like," Myrtle responded. "I don't really care. I'm not saying all this to make myself feel superior to you. I'm saying it because for some foolish reason you haven't thought it through yourself."

Violet flipped on her side, roughly pulling the covers over herself. "I'm not listening to you anymore," she said.

"Never mind. I've said my piece." Myrtle grew silent and soon settled into the sleep of the righteous.

Violet, however, chased sleep fruitlessly until dawn. Not because she was angry with Myrtle, but because she feared that every word Myrtle said was true.

Violet had spent her whole life in and around Sydney, where Christmas was hot and bright. Of course she knew about cold Christmases because all the cards and decorations depicted Christmas this way, but until now it had seemed a remote or impossible way for Christmas to look. But when she stepped into the long room for Christmas-in-June celebrations, she was charmed by a sense of cold and wonder. The long room was used for occasional art exhibitions and community celebrations, and was really a conservatory that ran along the valley side of the east wing. The glass had caught and held much of the morning sun's warmth, but two fireplaces had been lit and were crackling merrily. Wreaths of holly and ivy hung from the mantelpieces, and pretty red-and-green paper chains draped from the ceiling. A huge Christmas tree—one of the spruce pine saplings from the nursery—sat between the fireplaces, adorned with glass and glitter balls and handmade angels. Through the windows, Violet could see the cold day. Frost laced the hedges in the shade and the wind shook the bare branches of the crepe myrtle tree in the garden. A trio of singers rang bells and sang carols, and even though she knew it was not really Christmas, Violet let herself pretend.

Violet was on the first shift, and so began her work of carrying around large silver platters of star-shaped biscuits and slices of fruitcake iced thickly in marzipan. The guests converged around the fireplace and the tea table, and exchanged small gifts with laughter and cheeks made rosy from the cold and the fire. Or they gravitated to the three activities taking place at various parts of the room. In the far corner, under the spreading branches of a tree that dropped leaves relentlessly on the glass, was Clive with his easel, drawing portraits; in another corner, close to the fireplace, sat Thora in her gypsy costume, reading cards; and over by the bookshelves one of the bellhops made little wood carvings of elves. Violet focused as hard as she could on the task at hand but was alert for Sam's arrival. He had said he would definitely come, so where was he? His sister was here, standing by the tree with her fiancé and his entourage. Flora wore a beautiful dress of silk and beaded netting. She didn't look happy, which made Violet suddenly worry that Sam might be ill or in some kind of trouble.

Then the door burst open and he was there, looking slightly disheveled but alert, which was a good sign; perhaps he hadn't been smoking. Violet kept her head down, and within moments he had come over to take some cake and smile at her lovingly.

"Did you make this?" he said.

"No. I'm not much of a cook," she replied.

"We'll have servants."

She blushed happily, then remembered her place; for now, *she* was the servant. But he had veered off, in order not to draw attention, and Violet kept working, ferrying sweet treats and then Christmas lunches to and from the kitchen via the long walkway outside, in and out of the heating until her poor body didn't know whether to shiver or sweat. But then, once the main courses of roast beef, Yorkshire pudding, potatoes, and cauliflower were out, she was off shift and able to sit back and enjoy the carols and something to eat.

The party continued after the meal. Even though Miss Zander had allowed them to mingle with the guests, it was clear that the guests weren't particularly interested in the staff. Violet saw Myrtle talking to Miss Sydney, and Alexandria in close dialogue with Cordelia Wright, the opera singer, but the rest of the staff hung together, chatting and laughing among themselves. Violet didn't want to get caught up with them—she wanted to be free to duck away if Sam needed her—so she ambled about the room, stopping to look at the fire or admire the decorations on the tree.

Then she saw Sam and Flora up near Clive, watching him draw his portraits. She felt awkward in her own body, wanting so much to walk up there and join them, but feeling strangely shy about it. Usually she and Sam were alone together at odd hours or in strange places.

But then, wasn't Clive an old friend? She could go and speak to him, watch him. Yes, he had said they weren't friends anymore, but surely he would have cooled off by now. She knew she was telling herself lies, but she didn't care. Taking a deep breath, she made her way down to the corner of the glass conservatory.

The light gleamed in Clive's fair hair. He was concentrating on his easel. In front of him, with her back to Violet, was Lady Powell, sitting in an embroidered armchair. Violet joined Sam and Flora at a polite distance behind Clive as they watched the drawing appear on the paper.

My, but he was good! Violet had had no idea. She'd only ever seen him draw trees and buildings and bowls of fruit. But this portrait of Lady Powell captured everything about her haughty demeanor and the intelligent brightness of her eyes. She had to catch her breath, and the sound alerted Sam and Flora to her presence.

Sam looked up and smiled. Flora looked up and scowled.

"He's very good, isn't he?" Sam said.

This made Clive glance up. He saw Violet and quickly turned back to his work.

"Oh, yes," Violet said. "I'm so impressed."

Clive ignored her compliment, adding some finishing shadows to his drawing and then lifting the paper off the easel. "Here you are, Lady Powell," he said, deferentially.

Lady Powell took the drawing and assessed it with her nostrils drawn down. Then the corners of her little mouth twitched up in a smile. "Well done, Mr. Betts," she said.

He nodded, and she called Lord Powell over, who pressed a handful of shillings into Clive's hands despite his protestations. Flora had wandered off, but Sam still stood next to Violet. Even though they were several inches apart, she was sure she could feel the magnetized heat of his body.

Clive sat down again and looked up at Sam. "Mr. Honeychurch-Black? Would you like a portrait?"

"I should like one very much, Mr. Betts," Sam said. "But not of me. Of Violet."

"Oh, not me," Violet said, glancing around nervously.

"I'm only supposed to do drawings for the guests," Clive said.

"You will be. For me. I will keep the portrait once it's done, to remind me of my favorite waitress."

"No, Mr. Honeychurch-Black, I really insist—" Violet started.

"No, *I* insist," he countered, raising his voice a little, and then Miss Zander was there and Violet was sure she was going to lose her job.

"What seems to be the matter?" Miss Zander said.

"I'd like your artist to draw Violet," he said. "I like to watch him draw."

"Then perhaps we can get him to draw your sister?" Miss Zander suggested lightly.

"But I want to watch him draw *her*. I've seen him draw fine ladies, and now I want to see him draw a waitress. I want to see if he can capture any dignity or bearing in someone of his own class."

Violet stung. Not a fine lady. A waitress. *His own class.* She knew Sam might be saying these things to manage Miss Zander's suspicions, but they were true and they both knew it.

"Very well, then, Mr. Honeychurch-Black," Miss Zander said,

conscious of the interest that their conversation seemed to be provoking. "Violet, do sit down. Clive, your best work, please."

Violet reluctantly sat in the embroidered chair, a little flushed and embarrassed by the handful of guests who had drifted over to watch her and Clive, and a little proud and vain that she had been singled out from all the staff. She kept her eyes down until Clive said, "Violet, you'll have to look at me."

She lifted her gaze. He met it, and there was such sadness in his eyes that her heart twinged. She remembered the reason he'd given for never having drawn her before. *Because a page is too flat and too small to capture you.* Was he thinking that now as his eyes appraised her face?

"Keep your head up, please," he said, as his eyes went down and he began to draw. Violet looked past him to Sam, who stood with his back against the glass, smiling at her knowingly. She smiled back. Surely anyone who saw them like this would know they were in love. Was it an open secret? Maybe everybody knew and nobody cared. She relaxed her chest and shoulders, and her blood raced through her more freely. Being in love, reciprocated love, was pure bliss.

A small crowd had gathered, mostly guests. But Belle, the chambermaid, also approached and squeezed in next to Sam. She turned and smiled at him, then said something—Violet thought it might have been a simple, "Happy Christmas in June, Mr. Honeychurch-Black"—but he didn't reply to her. He acted as though he hadn't heard at all, but then Belle tapped his arm to get his attention, and Sam physically recoiled, giving Belle a look of contempt that Violet wouldn't have believed possible if she hadn't seen it with her own eyes. Belle lowered her gaze and scuttled away, and then Sam gathered some bluster and said to the crowd of guests, "Let's leave Mr. Betts to do his work in private," and wandered off. Violet felt deflated. The others dispersed, leaving her and Clive alone in the corner of the conservatory.

"Eyes front, Violet," he said.

She did as he instructed, feeling her heart thudding softly in her throat. The silence was strained over words that couldn't be said.

Finally, Clive spoke. "Mr. Honeychurch-Black seems quite taken with you."

Violet couldn't think what to say in reply. She glanced around the room, but she couldn't see Sam.

"I think he will be happy with the portrait," Clive continued. "I think I've managed to capture some *dignity*, despite your low class." All this was said without a hint of a smile. It was meant to warn her. Or hurt her.

"Eyes front," he said again, in a whisper.

"Sam is a lovely man," she said, defensive.

"You know that, do you?"

"Yes, I do."

"Then I shan't interfere."

The minutes crawled by. The carollers began again, and the music provided some relief from the long, awkward silence. Violet wanted very much to look around—to see if Sam was back, to see what was going on—but Clive had her pinned to the spot. She wondered if he was taking an age on purpose, then reminded herself that each portrait had seemed to take him half an hour, and probably only half that time had passed since she sat. The room seemed too warm.

Finally, Clive sat back. "It's finished," he said.

She gave him a bright smile. "Can I see?"

"Yes, but I can't give you the drawing. It's for Mr. Honeychurch-Black."

"Of course." She rose and stood behind Clive's shoulder, looking down on the portrait. She had seen photographs of herself from time to time and was always surprised—they never seemed to capture how she thought she looked—but this portrait . . . it was strange.

There was the softness about her cheeks and the directness of her gaze that she knew from looking in the mirror.

"It's very good, Clive," she said. "Thank you."

"Don't thank me, thank your patron. Ah, here he comes." Clive stood and plucked the drawing paper from the easel, just as Violet turned to see Sam approaching. As he passed her, she caught a distinct whiff of opium steam. So, that's where he had been.

"Ah, marvelous. Marvelous," he muttered, admiring the drawing then rolling it up and tucking it under his arm. "Well done, Mr. Betts. I haven't any cash on me to tip you . . ."

"I don't need a tip, sir. I'm paid well for what I do." A hint of wounded pride in Clive's voice went unnoticed by Sam.

"Good-o, then." He turned to Violet, nodded once. "Thank you, Miss Armstrong. I'll . . . ah . . . see you soon." Then he scuttled off and out of the conservatory.

"He seemed to be in a hurry to get away," Clive said, his head down, rearranging the papers on his easel.

Violet narrowed her eyes, prepared to retort, then changed her mind. Clive was jealous; that was all. So instead she moved away, back towards the fireplace, and joined Thora in her silly gypsy costume and Myrtle who was eating a Christmas-tree biscuit. They pointedly didn't ask her why she sat for a portrait for Sam, and she was glad not to have to make any more excuses.

Flora watched Sam leave, with the portrait rolled under his arm, and wished she could leave, too. She stood alone by the back conservatory corner, opposite the kind-faced handyman who was drawing portraits. What a torture today had become. Trapped with Tony and his friends, with preening Karl joining them after lunch. Mixing with the staff had aroused their most smug and mean-spirited jokes, and they egged each other on to more and more outrageously snide comments. If one of the staff came to talk to them, they would politely smile and offer compliments as though they were the loveliest fellows in the world; but the moment the person walked away, they would snigger and gossip in the most unsavory terms. Flora was quite sick of it. Sam's company, too, had been good only for a brief moment. But as soon as he'd seen Violet, he'd become belligerent and sullen. She'd spent a good deal of time sitting by herself trying to look as though she was enjoying the carollers, or trying to get a word in edgeways in conversation with Cordelia Wright.

"Isn't the cold bracing?" Cordelia was saying, picking a cherry off a biscuit and popping it into her mouth. "You know, they're saying it might snow. I do love snow."

Snow? Now she'd never get Sam out of here. This cold weather wasn't Christmas as Flora loved it. Christmas was warm sunshine and aching blue skies and waving grass and the throaty buzz of cicadas, relatives visiting and roast lamb and damper on the long back veranda of her parents' rambling manor in the country, with brandy pudding after. What would Christmas—the real Christmas—be like this year? Married to Tony, living in the city, surrounded by his awful friends.

Would he stop seeing the other women? (She couldn't even bring herself to *think* the word *prostitutes*.)

Flora itched to get away, and at last she resorted to feigning a headache.

"I'm sorry, Miss Wright," she said, "but I think this Christmas brandy has gone to my head . . ." She pushed herself away from the glass wall.

"Oh, you poor dear. You just need more practice." Cordelia winked and moved off, and Flora was just about to escape when she saw Tony approaching, the awful entourage in tow.

"You're not leaving?" he asked, smiling that heart-melting smile, his hands spread casually.

"I'm not feeling well."

"We've hardly spoken two words today. I have a little Christmas gift for you."

She allowed herself to smile, then looked pointedly at Sweetie and Karl. Tony made a buzz-off gesture with his hands, and then turned back to her. The afternoon shadows grew long outside, and the wind freshened and rattled against the big glass panes. The light in the room changed, and as Miss Zander bustled about lighting lamps, Flora couldn't shake the feeling that the approaching darkness was somehow significant to her. Perhaps it was being alone with Tony. She felt she couldn't be herself around him anymore. Her mind was always creating pictures of him with other women: hard-faced women who had no modesty. Was that what he liked? Were her dignity, her decorum, her decency liabilities?

He stood close, kissing her cheek. He stank of alcohol. "Have you been avoiding me today?"

"Your friends are buffoons."

"It's just a bit of fun."

"You know I don't like cruel fun."

He smiled, reaching into the pocket of his jacket. "Maybe this will make you happy."

The small box was wrapped with a ribbon, and she plucked it open. She knew she should be excited, but instead she found herself anxious. What level of obligation would attach itself to this expensive gift?

Inside the box was a gold necklace with a large, rectangular emerald in its center. "It's beautiful," she said, trying to sound enthusiastic.

"Would you like me to put it on you?"

"Maybe later. I don't want to draw attention to us."

A look of irritation crossed his face, but he didn't push her to put it on. She snapped the box shut and smiled at him. "Thank you so much, my dear."

His voice dropped low. "What's wrong?"

"Nothing's wrong."

"There's been something wrong all week. You don't smile at me with your eyes anymore. Now, what is it?"

The words bubbled up her throat. Her vision went white around the edges as she wondered if she would tell him. Then it occurred to her very brightly: What if Eliza was wrong? Or what if she had made it up to spite Flora? Certainly Flora didn't know her very well, and people often did strange things for strange reasons. What if she asked him, and he reassured her that it wasn't true?

Flora realized that long seconds had passed since he asked his question. She took a deep breath. "Eliza Fielding told me you see . . . ladies of the night . . . in Sydney."

Tony blinked. She took a last loving gaze at his beautiful face in case everything changed for the worse after this moment.

"Men do that kind of thing," he said.

All the breath left her lungs. "So, it's true?"

"I'm a natural man. I have needs. You've put off our wedding for a long time. I can't wait forever to have my needs met. It's perfectly natural."

Flora felt sobs building up in her chest, but she wouldn't cry. Not here in public. She tried to push past him, but he caught her.

"You aren't to judge me for this, Flora. I could have denied it. I told you the truth. All of the other men do it, too. Sweetie does."

Flora thought of Will Dalloway's words: *I certainly don't.*

"Let me go," she said.

"Don't go getting hysterical. Women and men are different."

She peeled his hands off her, but stood her ground in front of him. "Will you stop?"

"When?"

"Now. Will you stop now? Our wedding is only a few short months away and I . . . I won't have it, Tony. Either you stop, or the wedding is off."

His eyes darted away. "All right. I'll stop."

A victory. Why didn't it feel like one?

"Also, you must be tested and treated against any . . . illnesses you might have acquired."

"I haven't any such illnesses," he protested, but she merely shrugged, staring at him icily.

He sighed, his shoulders softening. "Yes, yes. All right. I have to say, I didn't know you had this much mettle in you."

She felt the corner of her lip twitch.

He sensed her softening. "I'm glad I'm marrying you," he said.

"I predict we'll make a good life together, Tony. But I expect impeccable behavior."

"You shall have it. I make that promise to you."

"Thank you for the necklace. Really. Thank you. It's beautiful."

He caught her again, this time gently and lovingly, around the waist, and pulled her close against him, stroking her hair. "I'm sorry, my love. I never intended to hurt you."

Flora felt pierced by guilt for having told Will about their troubles. It wasn't right for him to know so much about her personal life and feelings. She simply had to stay away from the doctor.

"Merry Christmas," she murmured against his shoulder.

"Merry Christmas, Flora."

CHAPTER FIFTEEN

The Evergreen Spa was due to close on the first of July, and the staff quarters were busy with activity as people packed and moved out. The mood was sometimes light and sometimes miserable, depending on whether staff had somewhere to go for the holiday or work to tide them over before their return in spring.

Myrtle was in high spirits as she packed her things. She told Violet about visiting her sister in northern Queensland, where the weather was warm and mild and where the beach was only a ten-minute walk away.

"Imagine, you'll be up here in the snow, and I'll be swimming in the sea," Myrtle gloated, and Violet had to admit that swimming in the warm sea sounded very appealing indeed.

"It might not snow."

"Well, I've never seen the snow here, to be honest," Myrtle said, snapping her suitcase clasp on her finger. "Ow!"

"You really are clumsy, Myrtle."

She sucked her finger. "I was going to say," she continued, "that everybody's talking about snow and lots of it. One of the coldest winters predicted. I'm glad to be getting away."

Violet closed her case for her. "There. What time does your train leave?"

"In an hour. I have to wipe down the drawers and my dresser now. Miss Zander insists on it. You can't leave a thing behind, not so much as a hair."

Violet pitched in to help and they busied themselves meticulously cleaning out the drawers Myrtle had used for the past year. "I'm quite looking forward to being on skeleton staff," Violet said, "though I have to make the beds on the ladies' floor every day."

"Only a handful," Myrtle said. "There aren't many staying."

"I suppose."

Myrtle wrung out her cloth in her bucket again, and kept working. "The Honeychurch-Blacks are staying, are they?" she asked in a too-casual tone.

"As far as I know," Violet replied, equally casually, as though she and Sam hadn't passionately celebrated the fact that they would be together another two months in a near-empty hotel.

"She's nice, isn't she? Miss Honeychurch-Black? She has a lovely way about her, and she's a bit . . . queenly."

"I don't know." Violet stopped dusting and drew her brows down, thinking of Sam's warnings that Flora would try to stop them being together. "I think she's quite bossy."

Myrtle stopped and turned. "She's not bossy. I've served her dinner most nights for weeks. I've never met a less fussy, more kindly guest." She put down her cloth and fixed Violet in her gaze, and Violet knew there were warnings and judgments coming.

Violet sighed. "Go on, then," she said. "Say your piece."

"Miss Zander called me in to see her, directly after Christmas in June. She asked if there was any chance I could change my plans and stay for the winter."

"So?"

"I told her no, and I asked her why. Was she expecting more guests? But she just shook her head and said it was 'a passing concern.'"

"What does that mean?"

"Don't you see, Violet? I'm a waitress. You're a waitress. She was thinking of replacing you with me. Now, I don't know if she changed her mind when I said no, or if she asked all the other waitstaff and none could change their plans . . . but she's not stupid, our Miss Zander. The business with Mr. Honeychurch-Black demanding a portrait of you . . . she's not stupid."

Violet's heart grew hot. "You think she suspects?"

"Absolutely."

"Am I going to lose my job?"

"Not yet, you're not. Put yourself in Miss Zander's shoes: she wants to keep her very rich guests happy, and she knows that Mr. Honeychurch-Black likes you and that if she fires you while he's here, he'll be anything but happy. But after he's gone, there's nothing to protect you."

Violet drew her back up tall. "*Sam* will protect me."

Myrtle cocked her head to one side. "You're sure of that?"

Violet nodded, and Myrtle turned back to her drawers. "Then there's nothing to worry about, is there?" Myrtle said.

Violet lay back on her bed. No, there was nothing to worry about. The job at the Evergreen Spa couldn't last either way. At the end of the winter, when Sam had sorted it out with his family, she would be engaged to him. Or else she would be heading back to Sydney to look after Mama. She wished she could be certain of the first, because the second was a sad, measly horror.

Sam's words returned to her: *Don't doubt me, my love, don't doubt me. Everybody else does. I couldn't bear it if you did, too.* No, she wouldn't doubt him. Provided they played it carefully for just a little longer, Violet had nothing to fear from Miss Zander.

"There," said Myrtle. "All done. I'll go empty this bucket and then . . . would you walk me to the train station?"

"I'd love to."

The air was cold and crisp outside, and Violet's cheeks stung with it. Other staff milled about on the platform trading gossip and jokes, but Violet noticed that many of them seemed wary of her. Perhaps she herself had been the subject of recent gossip. She kept her head high and didn't let it bother her; in fact, she was almost a little proud.

Finally, the train was ready to leave, and Myrtle enfolded Violet in a soft, rose-scented hug. "Good-bye, Violet. I shall write to you."

"Go swimming for me," Violet said, through a mouthful of Myrtle's hair. "I should love to go swimming."

Myrtle put her mouth close to Violet's ear. "Mind yourself, dearie. You are precious. Mind yourself. I don't want anything bad to happen to you."

Violet fought to keep the irritation out of her voice. "It won't," she said. "Now, off with you. Enjoy your warm winter."

She stood on the platform until the train had gone. She had an overwhelming longing to be on the train with Myrtle, to be heading north to Queensland, where the sun was warm on the sea and all of this uncertainty was behind her. But then thoughts of Sam took over again, and her mind and senses were filled with the memory of their late-night encounters, and the yearning to be with him again burned through her like fire.

Footsteps constantly moving up and down hallways and stairwells, voices calling good-bye to each other, car doors closing and engines starting. It was a busy few days and everybody who could be pressed into service was. Violet even found herself carrying suitcases for guests like a lowly bellhop. One tall, fleshy man with an arrogant mouth had watched wordlessly as she tried to maneuver his two trunks into his car for him. They seemed to weigh a ton, but he said not a word in thanks. Clive, who was also helping out on leaving day, saw her at the last minute and raced over to help.

"Thanks," she whispered. "I was afraid I'd drop one."

"Stick to helping the lady guests," Clive said. "Silk doesn't weigh as much." He winked at her then went back to his own duties.

She was already exhausted when Miss Zander came to fetch her to clear the emptied guest rooms.

"This is Agnes's last day," Miss Zander said, roughly jerking free a sheet while Violet tipped a pillow out of a slip. "She'll launder all this today and hang it out, and I want you to bring it in tomorrow, then come up here and change all the beds for our remaining guests."

"Certainly. How many are there?"

"Just three on the ladies' floor, and five on the men's. Lady Powell and Lord Powell share the regency suite on the upper floor. I know you think it's beneath you, but I do expect you to do your best. Sheets, floors, rugs, dusting, and so on. Mr. Betts will be cleaning the bathrooms. Your work shouldn't take too long, and of course your waitressing load will be lighter with so few here. So, don't be asking me for extra money."

"I wouldn't dream of it." Violet hid her disappointment. Yes, there were fewer guests, but fewer staff, too. She'd have to work breakfast, lunch, and dinner as well as tidy rooms and boil sheets for six rooms. But then she reminded herself that this was better than not working at all, and she would still be close to Sam.

In fact, she would have access to his room. This thrilling thought fell flat almost immediately as she realized the access to his room was for the purpose of changing his sheets and cleaning up after him, so she tried to buoy herself by imagining that they were married, and she was simply looking after him as a good wife would.

"Right, take these," Miss Zander said, shoving a rough ball of sheets into her arms. "Put them in the trolley outside."

Violet did as she was told, emerging from the room at precisely the same moment that Flora exited her own room, wearing a wool hat and a sumptuous fur coat. She looked at Violet with pale, startled eyes.

"Good morning," Violet mumbled.

Miss Zander was right behind her. "Now we'll take these down to—" She stopped, and her tone changed immediately. "Oh, good morning, Miss Honeychurch-Black. Off to town?"

"Yes, I . . ." Flora touched her hat nervously, put her head down, and moved away, not finishing her sentence.

"A lovely woman," Miss Zander said. "So beautifully bred, so accomplished."

Violet wordlessly shoved sheets into the bag on the trolley, feeling low and servile.

That night, she dragged herself out of bed exhausted at midnight, and crept up the stairs to Sam's room. She was determined to extract some kind of promise from him about when he would ask his father if they could marry. The uncertainty overwhelmed her. She opened his door and found him lying on his side on his bed, smoking his pipe. Underneath the lamp was the portrait of Violet that Clive had drawn.

Violet was disappointed. When he smoked, he went off to his own world and was impossible to talk to sensibly. "Hello," she said softly, closing the door behind her.

Sam fixed her in narrowed eyes, then exhaled slowly. The warm, organic smell of the opium steam filled the room. "He's in love with you, isn't he?"

Violet was taken aback. "Who?"

Sam tapped the back of his knuckles on the drawing. "Clyde."

"You mean Clive?"

His voice rose sharply, suddenly deafening in the quiet. "Don't correct me! I don't care what his name is and nor should you!"

Alarm lit Violet's heart. "Sh, Sam!" she whispered harshly. "Somebody would have heard that."

"I don't care."

"Why are you so angry with me? I don't understand."

"Look at it. Look at it!" He tore the paper out from under his lamp, nearly upsetting his pipe, and flung it on the floor at her feet.

Violet picked it up and looked at it. She had no idea what she was looking for, but her pulse was pounding and she fixed her eyes on the paper nonetheless, hoping he would settle down before he woke the other men on the floor.

"Well?" he said.

"I'm so sorry, my darling, but you're not making sense," she said, as gently as she could.

"He's in love with you. Can you not see it? In every line, in every curve. The care, the detail."

Violet chose her words carefully. Of course Clive was in love with her, but she had never known it to be so dangerous a problem before now. "But he showed as much care and detail in his drawing of Lady Powell. You saw that."

"This is different. Look, he had the cheek to sign his name on the bottom."

Violet peered at the bottom, where she saw Clive's name crossed out.

"He crossed it out."

"No, I did."

"Well, then," she said, "it's gone. Anyway, what would it matter if he did love me?" she continued boldly. "Because I don't love him. I love *you*, and my heart is constant."

Sam put his pipe on the bed and climbed to his feet, sending the tray containing the scissors clattering to the floor. His face was desperate, the expression of an uncertain boy. "Do you promise, Violet? Because my heart cannot stand the thought of losing you."

She handed him the drawing. "I promise. Of course, I promise."

He beamed, then took the drawing to his writing desk. "Well, then." He scrabbled around for a pen and ink, and wrote something on top of the drawing. "My Violet. Not his."

"You never need to doubt me, Sam, I—"

Her sentence was cut short by a soft knock at the door.

Sam's eyes widened, and Violet's blood flashed with heat. Sam dropped his pen and, without a word, grasped her shoulder and pushed her towards the wardrobe. She opened the door and climbed in, between suit jackets and trousers folded over coat hangers, and crouched in the bottom. Sam shut out the light, and she put her arms tightly around herself and tried to be very still and quiet.

The door opened. "What is it?" Sam said.

"Everything all right in here?" a man asked. Violet didn't recognize his voice.

"Yes, why?"

"I heard shouting. It woke me up."

"You must have dreamed it," Sam said, and Violet detected for the first time a note of fear in his voice.

"Have you got a lady in here?"

"As you see, I don't."

"Are you sure? I wouldn't mind sharing her." Then a sound she couldn't place, like somebody patting down their trousers.

"Stop it," Sam said.

"Or you'll do what?" The sound continued.

"Just leave me be."

Then an unmistakable slapping noise. "You're a mental case," the unknown man said.

"Leave me be."

Violet's heart beat fast. What was the man doing to Sam? Should she break out and call for help?

"Next time, I'm coming in," the unknown man said. "I'm taking my share of whatever it is you shouldn't be doing here."

Sam didn't answer. The door closed, and when Violet heard only silence, she emerged from the wardrobe.

"Who was that?"

"One of my future brother-in-law's goons," Sam said, straightening his hair and climbing back on the bed. "The one they call Sweetie."

"What was he doing to you?"

"He slaps me around. The shoulders, the head. It's not the first time, and it won't be the last."

"Then you should report him to the police!"

"They'd never believe me. Flora didn't believe me. Tony protected him. He just likes to have his sport with me, then he goes soon enough. I would never let him lay a finger on you, so don't worry about that."

Violet remembered the one called Sweetie; he was much bigger than Sam, and she doubted Sam would be able to stop him if he got it in his head to search the room for her. Sam was lighting his lamp again, preparing another pipe with shaking hands.

She lay down next to him. "Sam, in a day or so I'll be the only woman left on the staff floor. Why don't you come to me from now on? You can spend the whole night. We don't have to worry about Sweetie or anyone else."

He looked dubious, so she said, "You'll be away from the bathroom where that man died."

"That's true," he said, drawing in the sweet opium steam. "I just want to be with you, Violet," he said.

"It's the same for me, my love. All I want is to be with you." She thought of all the other things she wanted to say: that she was unsure, that she couldn't imagine Flora ever welcoming her as a sister-in-law, that he needed to explain how they would overcome their differences in class and breeding, that she wanted reassurance she would always be enough for him. But as he smoked himself into oblivion, all of it went unsaid.

"To be together. It's a simple wish, isn't it?" he said, eyes flickering.

"So simple," she said. Then why did it seem so impossible?

Sam coming to her room made all the difference. She was no longer braced against discovery. Nobody else was down here, and Miss Zander never ventured into the staff quarters at night. They were still cautious but were much more relaxed. More importantly, it meant Sam could now spend the whole night. No stumbling back to her room at three in the morning. Her back curled into his front, she slept in a haze of happiness, his breath behind her, his hands softly caressing her breasts and belly.

Nor did he bring his opium pipe with him. Sometimes when he turned up, she could tell he'd been smoking, but those times weren't so bad. Usually then he would just want to sleep, and Violet needed the sleep. She was run off her feet with chores, busy from seven until seven every day, but in that first week or two of the winter period, she began to feel rested again.

They were so content with one another, so peaceful and cozy, that she didn't want to upset it all by asking pointed questions about their future, though sometimes it was difficult. They talked about light things, made love, slept in each other's arms, and were happy for a short time. Violet tried not to cling to the happiness too desperately.

Quiet settled on the Evergreen Spa Hotel. Flora didn't mind it; she'd grown up in the country and was used to having few people around. Tony said he felt unsettled by it, as though they'd all been left behind, cut off from the world. Mealtimes were intimate, now. The dining room had been divided by a line of Oriental-themed silk screens on wooden frames, and only one large table was set for all of them. Not everyone came down, but at breakfast on the fifth day, they were all there: Flora and Tony, with Tony's entourage pared down to Sweetie and Harry now that Vincent was gone (Karl, technically staff, still wasn't allowed to sit with guests in the dining room); Lord Powell, being steadfastly ignored by Lady Powell, who was engaged in intense discussion with Cordelia Wright and young, wide-eyed Miss Sydney; Miss Sydney's beau, a sweating businessman whom Flora still hadn't properly learned the name of—Mr. Duke? Or was it Mr. Earl?—who tried to get a word in but was simply not allowed by the older ladies; and then there was Sam, dear Sam with his messy hair and slightly bewildered expression, sitting at the table but looking a million miles away. Her heart panged. How she loved him and worried for him. The fire was roaring in the grate, and the world seemed gray and flat outside the windows.

Lord Powell, seeming to give up on retrieving his wife's attention, leaned across his bacon and said to Tony and his entourage: "They're predicting the coldest winter they've seen."

Tony visibly shivered. "Up here?"

"Yes. Won't be pleasant. I trust our Miss Zander will know how to keep us warm. That woman is a marvel."

"I'm betting our Miss Zander knows all kinds of things we can't even imagine," Sweetie said, and he and Harry shared a chuckle.

Flora was puzzled. They seemed to be hinting at some sort of rude nonsense, but she didn't know what and she didn't want to ask.

Lord Powell was oblivious, continuing in his praise of Miss Zander. "Yes, it's true. She certainly knows how to please her guests."

"Especially the ladies," Harry snickered.

"Though I'd be happy to teach her a thing or two about gentlemen," Sweetie responded, and the two of them burst into laugher.

Lord Powell sniffed indignantly and was saved by his wife, who turned to ask him a question.

Flora, however, was left with their uncouth nonsense.

"Ah, but she's not interested in the gentlemen," Harry said.

Tony laughed. "Is that so?"

"What do they mean?" Flora asked, leaning close to Tony, but her question was heard nonetheless.

"He means, dear Miss Honeychurch-Black, that Miss Zander is unmarried not because she didn't find a husband, but because she didn't want one," Sweetie said with a salacious wink.

"Surely that's not a thing to be rude about," Flora shot back. "A woman can choose how—"

"Flora," Tony interrupted, closing his hand over her wrist. "They mean she's homosexual."

Flora had never heard that word said aloud before, and it shocked her. "Really?"

"Of course she is," Sweetie said, and he seemed to take cruel pleasure in her shock. "Haven't you seen her eyes following all the young ladies? Miss Sydney here? Even you sometimes!"

Flora thought about Miss Zander and found she didn't mind at all if the woman wanted to find love with somebody other than a man. What happened in people's private lives was their own business, and Miss Zander was a good woman who deserved happiness. But why did Sweetie have to go on with such lascivious expressions and gestures about it, making it all seem so sordid? Why did Tony have to play along, laughing and egging him on?

"Oh, leave her be," Sam snapped. Flora hadn't been aware he was listening. "You know nothing for sure, and if it's true, that's a hard road for her to walk. Love is love wherever you find it, and nobody should be censured for it."

This declaration sent Sweetie into peals of laughter, and Harry followed suit. Tony, aware he should protect his fiancée's brother, intervened. "Enough," he said in a low but authoritative voice. "That's enough now. We're not at a bar. There are ladies present."

"Luckily for Miss Zander," Sweetie blurted, which set Harry off again and this time even Tony.

Flora watched them as though they were strangers. Watched Tony and saw an unpleasant side of him she often chose to ignore. Even though she knew Tony could be a perfect gentleman and moderate his behavior, he would always be surrounded by buffoons like Sweetie. For the rest of her life, she would have to put up with Sweetie or somebody like him. The thought exhausted and diminished her.

Sam looked at Sweetie with unsheathed hatred, and Flora felt at once proud of him for defending Miss Zander, and sad that his declaration—that nobody should be censured for finding love—wasn't true for him. He would eventually have to marry, and it would likely be somebody of their father's choosing. Because Lord knew he wasn't capable of choosing the right girl himself.

In the middle of all this, Miss Sydney's beau leaned across the table and addressed them. "Are you all staying?"

"Staying?" Tony asked. "As you see."

"Even with the news?"

"The news about the cold? We can handle a little cold," Harry said, with swagger. He had an obvious infatuation with pretty Miss Sydney, and was puzzled and angry that she had chosen to take up with a plump man more than twice her age.

"Snow. There's snow coming, and lots of it. I'm heading back down to Sydney today. I can't afford to get stuck up here. I have a business to run."

Miss Sydney pouted. "I don't want to go home yet."

Cordelia Wright put her arm around Miss Sydney. "Stay here with me, dear. We can finish that quilt we've been working on. It'll be cozy."

"You wouldn't mind if I stayed?" she asked her beau, and he shook his head.

"Who else is staying?" Harry asked.

Flora turned to Sam. She knew what he'd say. With Violet here, she would never prise him free.

"I'm staying," he said.

Tony rolled his eyes, and Flora flared with anger at the expression but said nothing. "I am staying with Sam," she said.

"Then I'm staying with Flora," Tony said.

Sweetie and Harry began to hem and haw, talking about the possibility of being stuck here, about business in Sydney, until Tony finally said, "I don't care what you do. Stay, go. It doesn't bother me. Be men. Choose your own path."

"I'm going," Harry said quickly.

"I'll stick around," Sweetie said.

Flora sighed a little in relief; at least one of those horrid men would be gone at last. Maybe if she could encourage Sweetie to spend the majority of his time with Karl, she might get to see more of the real Tony.

"You can come down in my Studebaker," Miss Sydney's beau said to Harry. "Anyone else?"

Lord Powell looked pointedly at Lady Powell. "There's only one road out," he said.

"There's a train line. We'll be fine."

Lord Powell turned to them. "We'll be staying."

Now there would be just eight of them. That afternoon, the two men packed the car and headed off, leaving a strange, cold quiet to come over the hotel, as it shivered under grim skies on the mountain's edge. Flora wished for winter to be over.

CHAPTER SIXTEEN

2014

For the first time in as long as I could remember, I phoned my mother before she phoned me.

Still reeling from being booted off Anton Fournier's front steps, I punched in her number as I walked home.

"Hello?"

"Mum? It's me."

The edge of panic hit her voice. "Is everything okay?"

"Yes, yes," I said, forcing the irritation out of my voice. "I'm fine."

"You don't normally phone me, that's all."

You don't give me a chance. "Mum, I'm going to say a name to you, and I want you to tell me what you know about him. Okay?"

"What? Why?"

"Just go along with it, please."

"You're behaving mysteriously."

"Anton Fournier. Mum, who is Anton Fournier?"

There was a half second's pause before she spoke. "I've never heard that name," she said, but I knew she was lying. I'd heard the fear and anxiety in the pause. It came down the line as clear as a bell, because my mother was highly practiced in conveying her anxiety to me. I *had* heard it.

"Come on, Mum, who is he? Why does he hate us?"

"Hate us? What are you talking about? I told you, I don't know who he is. Has he contacted you? You should call the police if he's threatened you."

I stopped, turned in a circle, my long shadow at my feet. The trees in the breeze. Mum would never, *never* tell me, especially not if I bullied her. And if she got to Dad before I did, he'd never tell me either: he was a servant to her anxiety as much as I was. But she knew who Anton was—I was certain of it. I'd bet all I owned (which admittedly wasn't much) that she was the reason Anton Fournier had snarled at me as though I were some kind of fiend.

"Lauren?"

"Forget it, Mum," I said.

"But is he—"

"I said forget it. Tell Dad I love him. Talk soon." I ended the call and slid my phone back in my pocket. I longed to go back to Anton's house, calm him down, get him to talk to me. What on earth had my mother done to him?

But I couldn't go back there. I couldn't call him. So, my only option was to write him a letter. I hurried home.

Dear Anton,

I know this letter will be unwelcome, but please read it. I don't know why you are angry with my family, but I do know that my mother can be overprotective and interfering, and perhaps she is the one who has upset you. For my part, I am four years younger than Adam, and was little more than a child at the time you and Adam were friends, so I promise I've never done anything to hurt you, or to hurt Adam, of course. He was my brother and I really loved him.

I stopped writing, put down the pen on the kitchen bench. *I really loved him.* It was too wishy-washy. Anybody could say they "really loved" somebody. It didn't capture anything: the way my love for my brother existed in every pore of my skin, every strand of my DNA. I picked up my pen again, scribbled out the last line and started a new paragraph.

I was born in love with Adam: he was there before me, like my parents. But unlike my parents, he never nagged me to brush my teeth or told me I was getting too rowdy or that I should sit still because I was giving my mother a headache. Adam was on my side. Even though he was a boy and even though he was older, he never brushed me off or called me a brat or a dumb little girl. Granted, he never hit the school bully for me either. You know how skinny he was—he probably needed somebody to protect him from bullies. But he was protective of me in other ways. He was protective of my heart, of my ego. He was unfailingly kind to me when we were children, in a way I realize now was well out of the ordinary for a young boy.

I have all these memories that bubble to the surface when I think about Adam. We grew up on a big rambling property twenty kilometers outside of Hobart, and much of our playtime was spent imagining we were other people. One summer, we became obsessed with playing a game we set at a strict boys' boarding school: St. Smithereens Boys School. He played the part of the clever senior, always outwitting the wretched teachers; I played the part of the wide-eyed junior, an accomplice to his brilliant plans who spent most of the game saying, "You are the smartest boy I know." I worshipped him, in the game and out of it.

I put the pen down again, slumped forwards on the bench, and let myself cry. I would come back to the letter later, when I didn't feel so raw. In the meantime, I would ask around about Anton Fournier. It was a small town: somebody must know something.

I knocked on Mrs. Tait's door at ten the next morning, my day off, and she answered it with a smile. "Hello, dear."

"Would you like to come over for a cuppa?" I asked.

"Why don't you come in here? I have a lovely new teapot."

"I'd love that." Secretly, I was relieved. There wasn't much room at my place, and I could smell something wonderful baking in Lizzie's house.

"Come on in, then. I've just made a batch of scones for the library fund-raising committee. We can steal a couple for ourselves."

Sitting in Lizzie's sunny kitchen drinking hot tea and eating fresh scones with jam and butter was a lovely way to spend my morning off. I had chores to do—grocery shopping, cleaning my bathroom—but they could wait. We chatted for ages about family, life, work, movies (it turned out Lizzie was a crime-thriller film buff), and then I finally asked what I'd been intending to ask all along.

"Lizzie, do you know of somebody named Anton Fournier who lives up on Fallview Road?"

"Is that the rather handsome fellow who runs a record company?"

"He's handsome, yes. I don't know what he does for a living."

"It's the big timber-and-glass mansion."

"That's him."

"I don't know much, I'm sorry. Just that he travels a lot for work, overseas and so on. He keeps to himself."

"He's the man in the photo. With Adam. The one I showed you."

"Is he? Is he indeed? Yes, now I think of it, it *is* him. I didn't recognize him in the picture with all that long hair. He's filled out a bit."

"I suppose he was only a teenager back then."

"So, he knew your brother?"

"The most curious thing: I went to see him, to ask him what he remembered about Adam. He got really angry at me and told me he wanted nothing to do with me or my family."

Lizzie tipped the teapot up to her cup again, but only a trickle came out. "Did he now? There's a mystery for you."

"Something happened back then. I don't know what. Can you think of anyone in town who might know some more about him?"

"I think he has a young fellow who stays there with him, some of the time or all of the time, I'm not sure. He looks after the house and the dogs when Anton goes away. Can't recall his name, but Penny might know. But apart from that, I can't help."

"No wife I could speak to? Children at the local school?"

"Not that I know of, dear. Sorry to be so useless."

I beamed. "You're not useless. You're wonderful. Shall I refill the pot?"

"That would be lovely."

Penny had nothing either.

"I've seen the guy Mrs. Tait mentioned," she said to me, after hearing the whole story. "I remember chatting to him outside the bakery one day when he was walking the dogs. Two whippets, isn't it? He mentioned Anton being away in Hong Kong. I think he said his name was Peter, or perhaps Patrick. Started with P. Anton has been in here once or twice, but my impression was that coffee isn't his thing. He was after vegan food and herbal tea."

"But he's a record executive or something?"

"I couldn't say. Travels a lot. Not often around in town and very private when he is, I imagine. You could try Amelia at the health-food shop; there's a good chance he's more frequent there."

"Thanks. Thanks, I might do that." I tied on my apron and got to work. I was starting to understand that asking about Anton Fournier wasn't going to achieve much. Whether or not he was a record executive who went to health-food shops, whether or not he owned whippets, or had a dogsitter named Peter or Patrick—none of these things told me why he'd had such a violent reaction to my presence. All I could do was keep working on my letter and try to put it out of my mind.

"Hey, I'm driving down to Sydney on Monday morning," Penny said.

"You want me to cover your shift?"

"No, Eleanor's going to do it. I wanted to know if you want to come for the drive. I've got to see a solicitor in the city. You could go shopping. It's a long way by myself, and I'd be grateful for the company."

An idea glimmered, driving thoughts of Anton Fournier out of my head temporarily. "Will we be anywhere near a library?"

"A library? Evergreen Falls has a library."

"I want a big library."

"There are libraries at the university."

"Then I'll definitely come."

When Adam left to take the job in the Blue Mountains—I presume that's when he met you—I was bereft. I was a spotty teenager, very awkward, and he was always so smooth and so sure of himself. He was a beautiful boy, wasn't he? I look back at pictures of him and he has a glow about him, a softness about his face. I have a photograph of the two of you, all long hair and faraway looks, up on the viewing platform above the Falls. He looks happy, content. That's why I wanted to talk to you. I wanted to know what he was doing at that time in his life, when he was far away from us. He never let go of the idea that he might go back one day, though that wasn't to be.

I wish I could say Adam was always lovely, patient, kind, and gorgeous, as he had been as a boy and then in his young adulthood when you knew him. But unfortunately, it wouldn't be true. The illness took such a toll on him, it's impossible for you to imagine. He was at times bloated and red-faced, at other times bony and pale. The light left his eyes around his twenty-second birthday, with his first bout of cancer caused by the anti-rejection drugs. Maybe up until that point he'd thought one day he'd get better, but after that, he grew negative and—

I stopped for a moment. I knew what I had to write. Frightened. He grew frightened. I tapped my pen on the desk, deciding that only brutal honesty would win Anton Fournier over, and continued.

—frightened. His fear was one of the worst aspects of his condition. We were all afraid, too, of course we were. We were afraid for our hearts, afraid of the empty future without him, afraid of how much it was going to hurt when he died. But his fear was far more primal. He looked death in the face every day. Every single day. The rest of us think about death every now and again, and it gives us a chill for a few moments and then we're off about our lives, making ourselves busy. But Adam lay there every day and breathed every breath alongside that shadow, and I'd be lying if I said he eventually got used to it or made his peace. He didn't. There wasn't any peace. That made him a little cruel, and very demanding. That made the corners of his mouth turn down perpetually, creating permanent creases in his beautiful face—that face that had never even seen a pimple—and it made him sometimes say or do hurtful things.

I took a deep breath and pinched the bridge of my nose as some of the memories came back to me. Adam's voice, shrill with pain, telling Mum she'd ruined his life, telling Dad he was a bumbling oaf, telling me I was a stupid little girl who knew nothing about the world. I suppose, at least, the last accusation was true. I didn't write any of this down. It was too private.

Through it all, I loved him still. I loved him and wished and hoped for improvements. Not for recovery, because we all knew that this was a train that had only one destination. But I wished for happiness for him, and sometimes he had it. Sometimes in a gentle mood we would laugh and talk as we had as children. We'd reminisce about St. Smithereens or about television shows we'd watched together like Monkey *and* Doctor Who. *He was still in there, my lovely brother. When I got a chance to see that side of him and spend time with him, I felt like the happiest girl alive.*

Anton, one thing I know about Adam is that Evergreen Falls is the last place he was happy. When I asked him about why, he would just say because it was beautiful and he had good friends there. Is that true? Or was there more? Drew told me about the mad summer you all had. I would love to know more. I would love to hear everything you can remember about Adam, because memories are all I have now that he is gone. I'll write my phone number and address below if you change your mind.

Kind regards,
Lauren Beck

I wrote my phone number, my address and the address of the café, and then I folded the letter, went to Lizzie's for an envelope and stamp, and walked to the corner to post it. Once it had slid into the postbox, there was nothing more I could do, so I vowed to put my own family mystery out of my mind.

I had a mystery from the 1920s still to solve.

*   *   *

The vast university library I walked into on Monday morning was nothing like the small community library where I used to find books for Adam. Nor would I have to return home to wash my hands with antibacterial gel and spray the books with disinfectant, causing Adam to curl his lip when I handed them to him. "Did you get these from the library or the hospital?" he would say. And I'd say, "You're welcome," and he'd crack a little smile and start reading.

I let the memories flow through me and turned back to the task at hand, which was trying to figure out the state-of-the-art software with which I had to try to find books. Keyword search? That might be the one.

I typed in *Honeychurch-Black*.

I got hundreds of hits and my heart leaped. Was there that much written on them? But no, there was a Honeychurch-Black Agricultural Institute that published mostly science books, and every one of them had turned up on my list.

I tried excluding them and ended up with zero hits, so I tried again, adding new search terms instead. *Family. History. Australia. 1920s.* Eventually, with a bit of ingenuity and a lot of luck, I found a book called *Great Farming Families of Australian History*, published by the Honeychurch-Black Agricultural Institute.

The air-conditioning in the library was cranked so high my fingers were turning blue. I buttoned up my cardigan as I walked up the stairs to the book stacks. Swarms of students passed me, going up and down. The young women didn't seem to be wearing much. Was I becoming an old lady? Perhaps I was just jealous that super-short cutoffs wouldn't look good on me. The staircase echoed with their voices, but up among the stacks it was very quiet, the carpet absorbing any hushed sounds. I ran my fingers along spines until I found the book I was after.

I didn't bother sitting back down. I stood right there between the shelves flicking through pages. Births, deaths, marriages . . . I moved from the 1800s to the 1920s with one flick. There they were. With photos. My heart pressed up against my ribs to see him. Samuel Honeychurch-Black. His soul in his eyes, black hair flopping over his forehead. Born 1906 at Curlew Station, outside Goulburn in regional New South Wales. Died at home in 1927 of pneumonia. His father also died of pneumonia at the same time. It made me sad to think that he lived only to twenty-one—but at least he got to have that passionate affair at the hotel. Flora Honeychurch-Black was born in 1901 at Curlew Station, married in 1927, and had four children. She died in 1989. I studied her picture. She was pale, like me. Not pretty. Again, like me. But there was something about her face: I saw goodness. Her brow was calm, but a tiny smile touched the corners of her lips. Her eyes were clear and intelligent. I compared her to her brother, who was dark and sad-looking.

But maybe I was projecting all this onto them. He died young; she didn't. His letters made it clear that his sister had a strong sense of duty and dignity.

I held the book to my chest as I stood in the queue for the photocopier. I gazed out the narrow window and saw students milling about. I would have liked to finish my university course. I'd studied business communication, with an idea that I might work in a big firm somewhere, writing documents and correcting everybody's grammar. The thought was laughable now. Me in a big business firm? Wearing power suits and meeting "key performance indicators"? It was well beyond me. The same illness that robbed Adam of his youth had robbed me of mine. All this time I had told myself it wasn't too late to go back to university, that I might get there one day, but as I stood here surrounded by students and books and learning, my heart sped a little. I was nearly too late for everything.

For study, for husbands and children, for backpacking in exotic places. I was on track to die alone.

I steadied my breathing, told myself not to be an idiot. What Adam would have given still to be alive. I lifted my eyes, watched the elms bending in the wind, the sun shining on their leaves. I was like Flora, the sister who survived. I should be grateful and live my life gratefully.

That's when it occurred to me: Flora's children might still be alive. Or if not her children, then her grandchildren. They might be keen to see Samuel's letters. A generation or two had passed. Nobody would be shocked anymore, surely. Also, they *might* know who Samuel's lover was, and then I could solve the mystery, and share it with Tomas.

I flipped to the back page of the book, looking for names. I discovered that the book had been written by Graeme Dewhurst, who was the husband of one of Flora's grandchildren. He'd thanked her in the acknowledgments: Terri-Anne Dewhurst. By the time I'd made my copies, I'd decided on a course of action.

I sat down at one of the computers and searched for the Web site of the Honeychurch-Black Agricultural Institute. I composed a message to Terri-Anne, in which I told her about the letters and offered to send them to her, and then sent the message to the institute's inquiries address, asking them to forward it to Terri-Anne. I was hoping that if she called, she might be willing to talk or share memories.

Or maybe I would get the same kind of reception I'd received from Anton Fournier.

It didn't matter. I hit Send. The letters were written by her great-uncle. They belonged with his family.

The wind changed in the night, turning and swirling in, cold and dry, from the south. I'd left my window open when I went to bed, and the wind blew the curtain in wildly, rattling the rail and waking me up. I checked my phone: 3 a.m. I closed the window and lay for a while, expecting to drift back to sleep, but it seemed that my brain had decided it was the perfect time to obsess about all my problems. Around and around in my head they went. Mum. Dad. Tomas. My future. Anton Fournier. An hour passed.

I sat up, reached for my phone. In Denmark, it was probably a reasonable time of the day. I always waited for Tomas to contact me; I'd never been so bold as to contact him. Before I could think better of it, I tapped out a text message.

Can't sleep. Thinking of you.

It whizzed off into the night. I waited, but nothing came in response. I obsessed a little longer, then got up and dressed. There was a whole collection of map books at the Evergreen Spa west wing library waiting for me.

I wasn't prepared for the cold—that particular cold characteristic of the hours before dawn, when the world seems emptied out. The wind howled through the pines, whipping my hair into my face. The streetlight through the branches of the oaks along the main road created constantly shifting shadows. A few leaves loosened and streaked off down the road. My fingers were numb. I hurried towards the hotel, my head down, wishing I'd stayed in bed.

I let myself in and shut out the cold, caught my breath gratefully, then switched my torch on and headed up to the library.

The library report had given the location of the maps, so I carefully shone my torch on the tags inside the glass-fronted bookshelves until I found them. Three shelves of folio-sized books, bound in red leather. I opened the door, carefully pulled out the first one, and took it to one of the big oak desks.

As I turned the heavy pages, a squall rose outside, shaking the windows on the other side of the boards. If there weren't so many of these map books, I'd have taken them home where it was warm and I could switch on an electric light and make a pot of tea. Book after book, page upon crackling page of detailed maps, but no notes in margins, no love letters stashed between pages. It was just a set of books.

By the time dawn came I was beginning to feel despondent. I left the maps for the time being and went to the big drawers at the bottom of the shelves. Here was where the librarian had stacked old records, and it didn't take me long to find a set of well-worn staff registers, dating back to the opening of the hotel in 1888. I plowed through the drawer until I found the one that covered Samuel's stay. The binding had rotted away and pages were loose and falling out. I opened it and carefully ran my torch over a few of the pages. Names, dates, duties, pay rates. I put it aside to take home and pore over, and continued looking through the drawers. I soon found a leather-bound letter book, brimming with typewritten letters and swollen with age. Each letter had been pinned in, and all the pins were rusty. Every piece of correspondence was signed off *Yours faithfully, Miss Eugenia Zander, Manageress*. I looked closer, and realized they were all carbon copies. Miss Eugenia Zander had kept a copy of every letter she had sent.

I flicked forwards; the book ended in 1925. The next one in the drawer started in 1927. The only one I was really interested in—1926—was missing.

I had two choices: go through all the drawers one by one, or go home and look through the library report to see if correspondence for 1926 had been catalogued.

I chose to go home, reasoning that if I started pulling things out of drawers, I increased the chances that I'd mix it all up putting it back. Besides, my stomach was grumbling, and I fancied some toast and tea.

I shone the torch around and realized I'd left one of the map books out. As I picked it up off the desk to return it, my sleep-deprived, clumsy fingers let it slide out of my grip and it landed with a thud on the floor, pages splayed.

"Oh, no," I sighed in the dark. I knew I'd bent pages; I just hoped I hadn't damaged the spine. I crouched and picked it up carefully, and something slid out.

I sat back, looking at it. It was a portrait of a woman. Written across the top in faded ink, in handwriting I recognized from the love letters, was *My Violet*.

Samuel's lover had a name.

CHAPTER SEVENTEEN

I know I shouldn't have, but I took the picture home, tucked inside the staff registry. My stash of stolen treasures from the Evergreen Spa was growing. I intended to take it all back, of course, eventually.

I made myself some breakfast while dawn struggled into the sky. It was a gray day. By the fluorescent glow of the kitchen light, I studied the portrait of Violet.

Violet.

I now knew for sure she was a staff member. In the portrait she wore a maid's uniform. She was pretty, achingly so. A sweet, round face with a slightly pointed chin, wavy dark hair cut to her jaw, large eyes with long sweeping lashes. There was something familiar about her; perhaps she looked like a movie star of the time—they all seemed to have a similar look. The artist had been very good. He captured the light in her eyes and something—was it uncertainty?—around her brow. I wondered if Samuel had drawn this, but I could make out another signature at the bottom, though it had two thick lines struck through it. The first initial was a C or an E, and the surname Betts. Why was it struck through?

I turned to the staff register, careful not to soil it with the peanut butter from my toast. I knew the dates I was looking for, and was delighted to find that an *Armstrong, V* had commenced work as a waitress in the autumn of 1926. My excitement built as I searched but failed to find anyone else with the initial V—it must have been her. And there was something unusual about her entries in the register: her name stopped appearing in July of that year, with no explanation. With other terminated employees, the register would include a date of termination and a reason (and some of the reasons were intriguing in themselves: "caught smoking for fifth time," "too dull-witted," "left to pursue the man who got her in trouble"). But in Violet Armstrong's case, her name simply stopped appearing. She was paid her usual salary at the end of July, and after that . . . she disappeared from the record.

I finished my breakfast and turned to the library record, to see if a collection of letters from 1926 had been catalogued. It hadn't. Curious.

I stuck Violet to my fridge with magnets, next to my photo of Adam and Anton. All my mysteries collected conveniently in one place. I was considering them when my phone rang. Tomas.

"Hello?"

"It was lovely to have a message from you. Why can't you sleep?"

"Now I'm too excited. Guess what I found?" I told him everything with growing pride that I had solved the mystery (well, mostly) while he was away.

"So, they had a brief affair but never married? No happily ever after?" Tomas said.

"Not according to the book I read at the library yesterday. He was dead the following year, and she . . . I don't know. There's no record of what happened to her, but she stopped working at the Evergreen Spa that winter. Oh, and Tomas, she was so pretty. I'm going to take a photo and message it to you. I have one of Samuel and Flora, too."

"You've done amazing things. Well done."

"I have a few last parts of the mystery to solve." I told him about the missing correspondence from that year. "I suppose I don't really need it now to identify Violet, but it would be interesting to read it all the same."

"You know, I seem to remember from when I first went into the west wing on my walk-through that an office off the foyer had some books and papers that the librarian missed. Perhaps you could check in there."

"I will."

"You can wait for me to get back if you like."

My heart stopped. "Really? You're coming back?"

"Sabrina's cousins are here now, and some friends she works with. She's showing signs of improvement every day. I don't think I need to be here anymore."

"Don't you want to be there when she wakes up?"

"I'd love to be," he chuckled, "but my employer expects me back at work as soon as I can be. Delays cost them a lot of money."

I was secretly grateful that such practical matters could bring him back to me soon. "So, when . . . ?"

"I'll be back next week."

Next week. It was already Tuesday. Nearly Wednesday. "I will be really glad to see you," I said, boldly.

"Really?"

"Yes."

"You never call me or send me messages. I had started to think you'd gone off me."

I blushed, despite the thousands of kilometers between us. "I didn't realize I could," I said, honestly. "I'm really not very good at this stuff."

"Third date," he said. "Next week."

"I can't wait," I replied.

*   *   *

I dropped in on Lizzie on my way to work, to tell her that Tomas was on his way home. But she didn't answer her door, and it wasn't until I arrived at work half an hour later that I discovered why.

"Hey," Penny said. "How is she?"

"Who?"

"Mrs. Tait," she replied, her face echoing my confusion.

"What do you mean?"

"She went into hospital. I thought you must have known. It happened on the weekend."

I felt like my blood dropped two degrees; people going into hospital was one of my least favorite things. "Hospital? Is she okay? I mean, obviously she's not okay if she's in hospital but—"

"I'm not sure, that's why I was asking you. She's at the private clinic at the bottom of Arthur Street, apparently. One of the nurses mentioned it."

I looked anxiously at the clock. I was rostered on all day.

"It's okay, go if you need to. I can manage. Eleanor's coming in soon."

"Would you mind?" I asked, already untying my apron. "I wonder if she's lonely. Frightened."

"Go," she said. "See you tomorrow. Hopefully with good news."

I raced off, just in time to catch the local bus that rumbled down the main road. It dropped me off at the Anzac Park, and I walked through it to reach the back of the private clinic. The gray clouds still hovered, but it hadn't yet rained.

After checking in at the reception desk, I was directed down the pale-pink-and-green corridor. My dread lifted a little. This was a lovely clinic: it smelled like roses instead of disinfectant. Adam had never been in a hospital that smelled like roses.

I found her lying on her side, turned towards the window. The television was on, but the sound was down. I thought she might be asleep, so I hesitated in the doorway, but then she moved and I could hear her humming softly to herself. She had an IV line in her hand, a big bruise on her crepe-like skin.

"Lizzie?"

She turned, then when she recognized me the corners of her mouth turned up slightly. "Hello, dear. How nice of you to come."

I slid into the padded chair next to her bed. "Why didn't you call me?"

"Oh, it's nothing. Besides, I don't have your number."

I was pretty sure this was a lie. She had all my contact details because she was my landlady. "Have you called anyone else? Your kids?"

She shook her head. "It's nothing, really. Just a little operation and it'll all be over, they say."

"Operation?" The calming effect of the roses wore off and was suddenly replaced by concern. "What's wrong?"

"It's a problem with my lower intestine. I've had it before. I always knew a day would come when I'd wind up in here about to be carved up. Really, I'd rather not talk about my guts. It's very undignified, don't you think?"

"So, you were raced off to hospital and you didn't tell me? I could have come with you in the ambulance."

"I caught a taxi, dear. I wasn't worried. Nor should you be, and certainly not my children."

"You're not getting rid of me," I said. "I'm going to call your children. You may as well just tell me where I can find their phone numbers."

She sighed. "My house key is in the bag in that drawer there. If you'd water the plants, too, I'd be most grateful. Their numbers are all pinned to the wall next to the phone. In case of . . . emer-

gency. Call Robbie—he's the eldest and the bossiest. He can tell
the others."

I reached for her hand. It was very cool, and her fingertips very
smooth.

"Gosh, I hate this," she said. "What's the point of me? What's the
use of being as old as I am? I'll disrupt everybody's lives, and for no
good reason. I'll either be fine or I won't. Life goes on."

"When's the operation?"

"Your guess is as good as mine. They keep changing their minds.
I thought it was tomorrow, but now they're saying Friday. They say
my condition has to stabilize first. It might even be next week."

Next week. "Tomas will be back next week," I said.

She smiled, the first genuine smile she'd given me today. "Lovely.
You'll need to get your brows seen to again. They're getting pale."

I laughed. "He's going to find out sooner or later my true eyebrow color."

"Put it off as long as you can."

I don't know what I expected of Lizzie's son. The way she'd spoken
about her children, I'd feared he might be dismissive, maybe even
hostile. But, in fact, Robbie was a soft-voiced man who spoke to me
with gentle gratitude. Two hours after I'd made the call, he phoned
back to say they were all on their way from their various locations
in the world, and to ask me if I'd keep Lizzie company as much as
I could until they got there, which of course I promised I would.

Four days of lunch shifts were followed by four long visits at the
hospital with Lizzie, who remained in good spirits though she occasionally fell into her negative spells about how inconvenient it

all was for everyone and how the doctors had put off the operation again. But I could tell she was grateful for the company, and the fact that her children were coming.

On the fifth day, her daughters Christie and Genevieve arrived from New York and Vancouver respectively. I embarrassed myself by asking if they'd caught the same plane, to which they smiled in a puzzled way before one of them (Christie, I think) explained that Vancouver was all the way over the other side of the continent from New York, and actually in a different country.

As I have said repeatedly, my knowledge of the outside world was fairly limited.

So, I had a whole day to wait for Tomas to arrive, and no shifts at the café. I boldly let myself in to the west wing during daylight hours.

I checked and double-checked that there was nobody looking when I unlocked the front door, and propped it open with a loose brick. Cracks of light shone above and below the boards over the windows, illuminating a polished floorboard here, a grimy window-sill there. The dusty smell of the place had become pleasant to me, wrapped up in memories of my exciting discoveries. I stood in the foyer looking at three doors lined up, and presumed these must be the offices of which Tomas had spoken.

The first two rooms were small and empty, but the third was a spacious office with an old, beautifully carved desk pushed up under the boarded window. Opposite the door was another door, which opened onto a cupboard with six shelves. Tomas was right: there were still books and papers in the cupboard.

I sat my torch on the desk to give me a little light, but then I grew bold. The board over the lower part of the window was loose at its top corner, where the nail had come free. I put both my hands on the loose corner and pulled. With a heave, all the other corners detached with a crack, and light flooded in. Through the grimy glass

I could see the line of pines outside, and gray swirling clouds. The desk was thick with dust. I drew a swirly pattern in it with my index finger, then immediately regretted it as I was overcome by sneezes.

Back to the cupboard. I was daunted by the sheer volume of papers in here. It was so much easier up in the library, where everything was catalogued. I immediately dismissed the thought of going through all the boxes and piles: right now all I was looking for was a leather-bound letter book, like the ones for 1925 and 1927. While rain moved overhead I worked in the dim, dusty light, carefully moving piles of papers and stacking them around me in a semi-organized fashion, trying not to hurry. Some I glanced at, and found they were mostly supplier records listing food and linen and washing powder and so on, bought in bulk. I found Eugenia Zander's address book, and of course I skimmed through the H entries for Honeychurch-Black, but it wasn't there.

Perhaps it was curious or perhaps it was random, but the letter book I wanted was the last thing I found. It was beneath everything, inside a box, sandwiched between invoice books. The rational part of me said that it was probably flung there long after Eugenia Zander's time, by somebody who neither knew nor cared what it was. The excitable part of me said that it was hidden: well, semi-hidden. That Eugenia Zander deliberately made it hard to find, though her passion for record keeping meant she couldn't dispose of it altogether. In my vivid re-creation of the events of 1926, Violet Armstrong went missing and Samuel Honeychurch-Black actually died of a broken heart.

I knew, of course, that I'd be disappointed at some stage. Real life was a lot less exciting than that.

At the precise moment that I pulled the 1926 letter book from the file box, I heard the front door of the west wing open.

I wish I could describe precisely the reaction my body went through at that sound. At first, a faint hope that it was Tomas. Then, remembering I had his key, the awful realization it was *someone else*, someone I didn't know. Then, glancing around and seeing the enormous mess I'd made of this room, a room I wasn't meant to be in, inside a hotel I also wasn't meant to be in, a feeling of dread. Piles of papers and books, a board ripped off a window, and in my hand an old leather-bound journal that belonged in a library. At this last thought, I stuffed the journal in my shoulder bag and pushed it down under my spare scarf. Now my heart beat even more guiltily as I tried to think of an appropriate pose to adopt for my inevitable discovery. I settled for at least looking like I was putting everything back. So my back was turned when the voice said, "What are you doing here?"

I turned around and—because I'd seen it on police shows—put my hands in the air.

The security guard, an incredibly buff man in his fifties with a thick handlebar mustache, burst into laughter. He gestured that I should lower my hands. I think I smiled or maybe I grimaced.

"What's your name?" he asked.

"Lauren Beck." I reached into my pocket and pulled out Tomas's key. "I have a key."

He switched off his torch and looked around at the papers and boxes. "Are you working with the librarian?"

I almost nodded. Perhaps I should have. But I didn't trust my ability to lie. "No. Tomas Lindegaard gave me his key for safekeeping while he was away. I came in to look through some old records. I'll put everything back."

He frowned, held out his hand. "You'd better give me that key. Not that I don't trust you, Miss Beck, but . . . well, no, I don't trust you. I don't know who you are, and I do know that Tomas Lindegaard is in Denmark—"

"Tomas will be back tomorrow," I said, dropping the key into his palm. "You can ask him then."

"All right, I'll do just that. In the meantime, I'll take down your name, address, and phone number, and escort you out."

Oh, the shame. Thankfully, the rain had eased. An elderly couple with a Maltese terrier looked at us curiously as we walked out of the building. I tried to tell myself that it wasn't obvious I was being evicted—it wasn't as though I had my hands in cuffs and a gun at my back—but my guilt and embarrassment must have been glowing like a beacon. The security guard led me to his car, where I faithfully gave him my contact details, which involved me proving my identity by fishing out my driver's license from the bottom of my bag: a tricky operation because—God help me—there was a stolen book in the way. Of course my driver's licence still listed my old address in Tasmania, and the best person to prove where I lived was Lizzie, who was in hospital. I was about to mention Penny at the café, when the security guard said, "Show me your phone."

I handed it to him, and he did something tricky on it and got my number off it somehow, and wrote that down.

"All right, I have all I need. I'll talk to Mr. Lindegaard. I'm sorry if I've inconvenienced you, Miss Beck, but I'm just doing my job. The insurance wouldn't cover you if you fell or hurt yourself in there, you understand."

"I understand," I said.

"Can I give you a lift home?"

I shook my head. "I'm really sorry."

He shrugged, said good-bye, and got in his car, leaving me standing outside the hotel—locked up now, no way of getting back in—wondering if Tomas was going to be pleased or angry with me. As if on cue, the rain started again. I walked home.

I was so ashamed that I couldn't bring myself to look at the letter book straightaway. I left it in my bag and lay in the bath for a long time. When I finally emerged, I checked my phone and saw a message from a number I didn't recognize. I immediately thought of Anton Fournier and played it back.

"Hello, Lauren. It's Terri-Anne Dewhurst here responding to your message. Could you call me at your earliest convenience? I'm very keen to talk to you." Her voice was quiet, almost girlish.

I quickly toweled off and threw on my pajamas, even though it was only four p.m., then grabbed the letters from Samuel to Violet and called her back.

She answered on the first ring.

"Thanks for calling me back so quickly," she said. "I've just had your e-mail forwarded on to me, and I have to say I'm very excited."

"I have the letters right here," I said. "I should warn you, I guess, that they are very . . . um . . . sexy."

"Really? Brilliant! I'd be more than grateful if you could send them to me. I can't believe you found them. Are you sure they're written by Sam?"

"Sam? Is that what they called him? Not Samuel?"

She laughed lightly. "You know how there's an amateur genealogist in every family? That's me. And yes, Great-Uncle Sam has intrigued me for years. That's how I've always thought of him because that's how my grandmother, his sister, referred to him. When she spoke of him, that is."

"Well, I'm sure it's him. I've been investigating old guest registers, and the facts check out." I thought of being caught out today and shuddered with embarrassment again, but then I told her everything I knew. About Violet, about the portrait, everything. "I've become quite caught up in the mystery of it, I confess," I told her. "I was hoping you might know more. What happened to Violet? I know Sam died of pneumonia the following year, but—"

"No, he didn't," Terri-Anne said, and maybe I imagined it but I'm

pretty sure she dropped her voice conspiratorially. "That's a conve-
nient family myth, started by my great-grandmother, Sam's mother.
I uncovered the lie when I was quite young, poking around in old
family records."

"But why? Why would they—?" Then I guessed it. "He disappeared, didn't he?"

"Yes, in 1926. Never came back from the Evergreen Spa. And do
you see? If these letters prove he was in love, well, we might finally
know *why* he disappeared."

"The records run out on Violet as well," I said. "No note of her
resigning or being fired. One page she's there, the next . . . gone."

"Maybe they ran away together," she breathed. "Maybe I have
relatives I've never even met. Honestly, Lauren, I've never been so
excited. I can't thank you enough."

"What was your grandmother like?" I asked. "Flora? In the letters
he calls her Sissy, and he seems to think she's a bit stern and moral-
istic."

"She was the sweetest, happiest old lady you could imagine,"
Terri-Anne said with tenderness. "Though she refused to speak
of Sam, and became very distressed when I turned up the medical
records that showed her father had died of pneumonia but made no
mention of Sam. That was my first hint that something was amiss.
It didn't take much to find out it had all been a lie. But I couldn't in-
vestigate it until Grandma died; it would have upset her too much.
I've been wondering my whole adult life about it."

We chatted for a few more minutes, and it occurred to me that
these people about whom I'd been speculating for weeks were real,
and not characters in a book. I liked Terri-Anne: she wore her heart
on her sleeve. I organized to send all the letters down to her by cou-
rier—at her expense—and she gave me permission to make copies
for myself, and begged me to keep poking around for her.

The whole conversation made me feel better about having been caught in the act that day, and as soon as I hung up I took out the 1926 letter book from my bag.

Rain settled in overhead as I curled up on the couch. I didn't bother starting at the beginning. The love affair had taken place in winter, so I started on the first of June, flicking through page after page looking at the addressee of each letter. It took me less than a minute to reach August, to a letter addressed to Mrs. Thelma Honeychurch-Black, who I knew from my investigations was Sam and Flora's mother.

Dear Madam,

I acknowledge your correspondence and will keep this letter brief, the sooner to assuage your anxiety. In short, madam, you have nothing to fear from me. I have always taken pride in my discretion, and the personal knowledge I have of all my guests, past and future, will accompany me to my grave. I respect your wishes, and assure you that all involved are committed for their own pressing reasons never to speak of it again. The events were tragic; their repercussions ought not be felt more widely, lest that tragedy magnify. We are of one mind on this.

Yours faithfully,
Eugenia Zander

I read the letter over and over, and each time my skin shivered. *Never speak of it again. The events were tragic.* What exactly had I uncovered? And what did it have to do with Sam and Violet?

CHAPTER EIGHTEEN

1926

The snow came, as predicted, but not in great thick drifts that made travel impossible. Rather it floated down two nights in a row, soft and light as though spun from crystalline spiderwebs. In both cases, it had melted away by morning. Violet was enchanted with this kind of weather; she had never seen it before, and even though she found being out in it stark and unbearable, she loved to watch it through the windows, prompting Hansel to become very cross with her when she was supposed to be collecting meals to deliver. But not as cross as he used to be. The quiet seemed to make everybody calm, almost cavalier. Winter was here, and they were a handful of humans sharing a big, empty space. The mood was light, collegial. Even the guests, including the ordinarily caustic Cordelia Wright, were friendlier.

Mind you, Violet had now seen inside Cordelia Wright's room, when she'd gone in to polish the furniture and change the linen, and had decided the opera singer had no reason to be cranky. Beautiful dresses and furs were flung over the bed or hung haphazardly in the wardrobe, and dazzling jewels were crammed in the jewel case. Of course, Violet shouldn't have seen any of this, but alone in their rooms, she succumbed to curiosity. Flora's room was immaculately tidy, her desk neatly arranged with pens and inkwell and note paper. Lord and Lady Powell's bed always looked as though they'd been wrestling in it all night (she couldn't bring herself to believe that they'd been making wild love for hours). Miss Sydney's dresser was crammed with more beauty products than Violet had known existed in the world: creams and potions and pills, and even a soap labeled DOCTOR POTTER'S SLIMMING SOAP whose packet promised to melt away fat *and* age at the same time. Tony's and Sweetie's rooms were exactly as she'd expected: messy and with a pervasive musty male scent. Not like Sam's room, with its scent of sweet maple, damp earth, and plant clippings. Even though she knew it was the smell of opium steam, she didn't mind, because it was the smell of his happiness and hers. Her first week of chambermaid work was fascinating, but thereafter it became merely tedious and, she believed, beneath her.

The extra work made her tired; tired so deep in her muscles that, by the third week, she could only get through the day if she napped for a half hour in the afternoon. Keeping her eyes open during Sam's nocturnal visits also became a problem, and more than once she nodded off while he was telling her some grand story about his great-great-uncle who fought in a war with Spain or his mad great-grandmother who kept a hundred cats in a manor home and fed them all cream. He could still bring her alive with his touch, but the imperative to sleep weighed on her more and more heavily.

"You're bored with me, I can tell," he said one night, as they lay side by side in her narrow bed in the dark.

"No, never," she said.

"Sometimes I feel as though you aren't even listening to me."

"I'm tired, Sam, that's all. It must be after midnight. The rest of the hotel is asleep."

"Asleep. Asleep and empty. We could do whatever we wanted."

She propped herself up on her elbow and looked at him. There was too little light for clarity; he was dark gray and indistinct, his black eyes the only thing she could fix upon. "What do you mean?"

"Have you ever danced in the grand ballroom?"

"Of course not. I carry plates around in there."

He flicked back the edge of the cover. "Come along, then."

"You're not serious." A golden thrill beckoned, the same thrill she'd had at the start when everything seemed to be made liquid and sparkling by his presence.

"I'm serious."

"I'll get dressed."

"Nobody is going to see us. You said yourself: it's after midnight. They're all sleeping. You can dance in your nightgown. In fact, I insist on it."

She rose, giggling. "We must be careful and quiet."

"I have no intention of being discovered," he said in an urgent voice, picking up his dressing gown from the floor. "Discovery would ruin us." He moved to the door, opened it, and listened into the hallway. "All clear," he said.

She pulled on her wool nightgown and snuggled up behind him, breathing in his scent. "Are you sure this is a good idea?"

"It's a stupendous idea," he asserted, grasping her hand. "Let's go."

They hurried on silent feet along the hallway and up the stairs, then down to the end of the next corridor. Sam opened the door that led into the next wing, and soon the dining room door stood before them. Sam tried it.

"It's locked," he whispered.

Disappointment. She sagged against him for a moment, until she remembered. "Hansel has a key. It's in the kitchen."

"Show me the way."

They retraced their footsteps until they came to the kitchen, where Violet took down a hurricane lamp from the top of the pantry and lit it. She opened the top drawer and found the key nestled among ingredients lists and old recipes written on scraps of paper. Sam seized the lamp in one hand, Violet's hand in the other, and they raced back to the ballroom.

Violet unlocked the door, her pulse thudding hard at her throat. She would be in so much trouble . . . but then, would it really matter now? At the end of winter she'd either be engaged to Sam or heading home to find a new job. In that moment she felt completely free as she threw open the door.

The tables, all empty of linen and cutlery, sat mute in the dark. Sam walked to the middle of the dance floor and put down the hurricane lamp, while Violet closed the door behind them.

"We have no music," Violet said.

He pulled her close and placed her hand upon his chest. She smiled as she felt his heartbeat through the soft silk of his dressing gown.

"My blood is the music," he said. "I can hear it. Can't you?"

She couldn't hear a thing, but she said yes anyway, because the moment was hot and dense, and she wanted it to be perfect. He began to dance, and she fell into step with him. At a sedate pace at first, but then faster, he spun her around and around the dance floor, while the hurricane lamp flickered at the center. She watched their whirling, flickering shadows as they danced, madly, long after she was too tired to continue. Finally, she begged him to stop, and he stopped abruptly and pressed his mouth over hers, inflamed to a level of excitement she hadn't seen since that first night they'd made love.

"I want you," he breathed into her mouth.

"Not here."

"No?"

"Back to my bed."

Hurricane lamp in hand, they returned the key and made their way back to the staff quarters, where Sam made love to her with bruising force.

Afterwards, before he dropped off to sleep, she said to him, "Sam, you do love me, don't you? Real love that lasts forever?"

"Real love that can move the stars," he said.

"Real love that endures illness and old age?"

"Real love that is brighter than the sun."

"Real love that overcomes obstacles and finds a way?" She willed him to answer her sensibly. His passion was compelling and beautiful, but she was certain that Sam had not yet communicated with his father about her—and she wasn't sure if he ever would.

"Blazing love," he said instead, covering her face with kisses. "Incandescent love. Mad, mad love."

Mad, mad love. That's what it was. That's what it always had been.

Violet's least favorite job was boiling the sheets, which she had to do once a week in the laundry at the end of the east wing. She took all the sheets up the long corridor in a trolley, then had to wrestle them down a set of stone steps outside in the cold, then back into the laundry where she lit and boiled the copper. Perspiration sheeted off her as she used a long wooden paddle to stir the linen among the soap flakes, her arms aching and her hands turning red. Afterwards, she had to drag them out into the laundry tub to rinse, then feed them through a mangler to squeeze as much of the water from them as she could. Only then could she hang them out, which involved moving from the hot, sweaty laundry into the frigid air outside. Her breath fogged the air and she could see steam rising off her arms as she shook and pegged the sheets. The cold wind caught them, making them flap madly. In the open space between laundry and workshop, even where the sun was brightest, there was no warmth. Her fingers grew raw. In and out of the cold and heat.

As she pegged out the second load, Clive called out to her from his workshop, and she gave him a brief wave and then kept working, wanting the task to be over as soon as possible. Back inside, her head felt light from the heat again. Sheets through the mangle. She wiped her forehead with the back of her arm. Her head swam a little and she steadied herself on the rough edge of the stone sink. Outside, she shook the sheet and reached up to peg it, and suddenly everything around her went gray and a whistling noise rose in her ears.

The next thing she knew, she was lying on the dewy morning grass with Clive bent over, saying her name over and over again.

She tried to speak, but only a whimper came out.

"Wait here and don't move," he commanded, and she wanted to say that it wasn't possible for her to move, that all her limbs were lined with lead and her head screeched with pain. Clive raced off, and she could see a sheet lying on the ground and all she could think was, *I'll have to wash that again.* But then she closed her eyes and listened to her own breathing a few moments because thinking was too hard.

Within two minutes, Clive was back and Miss Zander was with him. She knelt over Violet with an expression of concern.

"Violet, can you hear me?"

"Yes, I'm feeling a little better. It was just the heat."

"Don't try to get up; I don't want you to faint again. Clive, can you carry her?"

"I think so."

"Bring her to her room. I'm going to go ahead and telephone Dr. Dalloway. I don't think Karl will be much help here."

"Violet," Clive said in a gentle voice, not meeting her eye, "could you put your arms around my neck?"

"I can walk," she protested.

"You're not walking," Miss Zander said in an authoritative tone. "Do as you're told."

Violet put her arms around Clive's neck and he lifted her easily. She could feel his heart thudding where she was pressed against him as he carried her across the lawn and back inside. Miss Zander hurried ahead, her heels clicking on the wooden floor, Clive carried Violet around the ballroom where only last night Sam had danced with her until her head spun, and then down the corridor and the stairs to the ladies' staff wing.

"Which room is yours?" Clive asked.

"Fourth on the left. Really, I can walk."

He checked that Miss Zander was gone, then set her carefully on her feet, keeping a steadying hand under her elbow. "All right, but I'm going to stay with you until Miss Zander arrives."

"Fine."

She opened her bedroom door and gratefully sank onto her bed. Her knees were weak. Clive sat opposite, on the bare mattress that was once Myrtle's bed, his hands folded together between his knees.

"How are you feeling?" he asked.

"My head hurts."

"You fell on your side."

Violet became aware of a throb in her right arm. "My elbow hurts, too. I get so tired, Clive. Don't you? The extra shifts are killing me. The laundry, the bed making, the polishing. I know that meals are quicker and easier to serve, but—" She stopped herself before tears started. "I'm just so tired."

"Are you eating properly? Getting enough sleep?"

"I don't have much of an appetite. I'm always rushing off to do something. But, yes, I sleep well enough." With Sam beside her. Though his nighttime arrivals and departures meant she woke up frequently, and he took up so much of her bed that she slept lightly.

"The doctor will know what's wrong."

"But what if he says I need to rest? Miss Zander won't cope without me. She's sent everyone else home."

"There are still a few men over in the east wing," Clive said. "Don't worry so much. There's always somebody who can do what you do. They say Miss Zander knows how to do every job in the hotel."

"I can't imagine her waitressing," Violet sniffed.

"I can. She's got a way about her."

Violet chuckled. "Hansel wouldn't dare shout at her."

They sat for a few long moments in silence, then Miss Zander was at the door. "Clive, Dr. Dalloway is on his way in his motorcar. Would you go out front and keep an eye out for him? He'll need to know where to go."

Clive hurried off, and Miss Zander shooed Violet into bed. "Come along, now, take your uniform off and hop under the covers. A day in bed is what you need."

Violet undid her buttons. "But what about—"

"Violet, I'm not a fool. I know how to staff a hotel. Winter colds are common. I have enough staff here to cover for you. We have only eight guests left, after all. The only eventuality I'm never prepared for is if I get sick, so I refuse to get sick." She smiled. "You work hard, dear, and I appreciate it. Your rewards will come. But don't kill yourself. Somebody else can do the laundry next week. One of the boys. I'll work it out."

Violet slid between her covers and put her head down. Her pillow seemed very soft. Miss Zander sat on the end of the bed. "I'll wait here with you for the doctor," she said.

"Thank you."

"You've been working like a Trojan. I might give you a pay rise after winter." Miss Zander smiled, revealing the gold lining on her back teeth.

But her offer only made Violet's heart sting. After winter. There was no "after winter" for her. Her uncertainty about Sam, which she usually refused to acknowledge directly, was like a painful wound inside her, and its edges now festered. Tears sprang to her eyes.

"Oh dear," Miss Zander said, and it was the first time Violet had seen her look bewildered. "Whatever is wrong?"

"I don't know what's going to happen to me!" Violet cried, and now it was as though floodgates had been opened. "My mother is very ill with arthritis. She can't work anymore, and she says I have to come home after winter to look after her." Her nose began to stream, so she searched under her pillow for a hanky then rubbed her face with it vigorously. "But I don't want to go back to Sydney. I want to stay here."

"Then stay here," Miss Zander said, as though it was the most obvious thing in the world. "Why would you go somewhere you don't want to be? A girl like you has so few choices in her life anyway. Why would you even consider throwing some of those choices away with both hands?"

Violet sniffed, puzzled by her logic. "But it's my mother. She looked after me until I turned fourteen. Now I must repay her."

Miss Zander shrugged. "No, you don't. Not if you don't want to. Did she make you sign a contract when you were a baby? Did she say, every time she put a spoonful of mush into your mouth, *One day, dear, you'll have to repay me*? No. Parents ought not expect recompense from their children. How very unfair, to haul somebody into the world without an invitation, then to try to determine what she does." She huffed. "If she wants you to look after her, then she can jolly well catch a train up here and find a little flat. You'll be on good money, and there may be other opportunities in a year or so if you behave yourself."

"Mama will never leave Sydney. The cold makes her arthritis worse."

"Then tell her to stay in Sydney and look after herself." Miss Zander sniffed. "Really, I get quite tired of the way girls get carried along on the wills of others so easily. I expect better of you, Violet."

Violet felt the burn of Miss Zander's disapproval, and quickly filled the silence. "You've given me much to think about," she said.

"Good. I must say your color has come back, and you don't look so frighteningly pale. A day or two in bed, then up and about. What do you say?"

Violet was going to say something to assure Miss Zander that she'd do whatever it took to stay in her good favor, but then remembered the warning: *girls get carried along on the wills of others so easily.* She had to appear to be more independent. "I will be fine after a rest, I'm certain."

"Good girl."

Miss Zander's offer of a pay rise, along with her commonsense solution to Violet's problem with Mama, served to intensify Violet's guilt over sneaking about with Sam. When he suggested more dancing by the hurricane lamp that night, she refused.

"You've not become a scaredy-cat, have you?" he teased, lying knee to knee with her in bed. He tapped her nose playfully.

"No, I just really need to keep my job."

He shrugged off her concern. "I have so much money you'd never spend it all."

"Are you going to marry me?" she asked boldly.

"Steady on. The man is supposed to propose, not the woman."

"It's not a proposal, it's a question," she said.

"Have I not reassured you sufficiently of my love? Here, let me show you again." He began kissing her, and, as ever, desire washed her good sense away.

He dozed after, curled around her. But whirling thoughts kept her awake, even though she knew she needed to sleep.

"Sam?" she said, in the dark.

"Hm?"

"Where will we be in a year?"

"Sailing to Antigua. Swimming in the Seine. Anything you'd like to do."

She tried again, bringing the imagined time frame closer. "Where will we be at the end of winter?"

"Here," he said.

"After here?"

"There."

"Where is there?"

"I'm growing tired of these questions. Go to sleep. All will be well. If you keep asking me questions, I'll think you don't trust me."

She fell silent. Tired, bone-tired. She told herself to focus on the moment, his warm body in the dark, the lovely forbidden thrill of their affair. Her love, which was hot and bright and piercing. She told herself not to think of weddings and babies and—

Babies.

When had she last had a monthly visitor?

Her panicked brain couldn't focus for a moment. No, surely she was overreacting. Being tired and off her food was not unusual given how busy she'd been. But still her brain struggled to count backwards. Myrtle had still been here. Was it before or after Christmas in June? Before. Long, long before. Hot fear flooded her mind. This wasn't happening to her. She'd assiduously avoided thinking about it, so it couldn't *possibly* happen to her. Apart from the first time, Sam had never spilled his seed inside her. He said that had always worked, and she'd been so upset at the idea that he'd made love to other women that she'd taken him at his word and never asked for further details.

Counting, counting . . . six weeks. She hadn't bled in six weeks.

Sam slept on behind her, softly snoring. She wouldn't wake him. What purpose would that serve? He would either run a mile or feed her some more nonsense about golden cribs lined with ermine and angels singing above the child's head.

A sneakier thought crept in. Now Sam would have to marry her.

But she dismissed it. Sam would do nothing he didn't want to. A family like his could do whatever they liked, and if they chose to deny the child was his, that would be that.

So she was trapped in the searing moment of horror all alone, watching her possibilities dwindle to nothing. Only minutes ago, life had been carefree. Now, reality was crushing down on her. Twenty years old, pregnant to a man who would never marry her.

Violet lay awake a long time.

In the early hours of the morning, after Sam had left and Violet finally descended into a dreamless sleep, the snow came. Falling softly, white and clean, and settling this time. Settling in fine, powdery layers around the fountains and gardens, on the lawns and tennis courts. Forming soft piles on the branches of the pines, and clumping around rocks and scrub on the walking tracks. The guests and staff of the hotel woke to a world that had turned white, and they chatted with delight and excitement to each other over breakfast.

All except Violet, for whom the world stayed black.

CHAPTER NINETEEN

The tearoom and the coffeehouse were closed for the winter, so Lady Powell had taken it upon herself to purchase a tea set and serve tea in her rooms every afternoon at three. She and Lord Powell shared an apartment on the top floor, with their own sitting room and bathroom. Flora resisted going most afternoons but would have appeared rude if she didn't show up once in a while. The gentlemen, of course, had nothing to do with such a gathering, which Sweetie characterized as nothing more than a chance for women to talk about diets and face creams. Flora took offense at this: she had never once discussed either, with anyone. But as the conversation in the room took its predictable turn towards Miss Sydney's beauty routine, Flora found herself agreeing silently with Sweetie.

"Your skin is so smooth," Cordelia said to Miss Sydney.

Miss Sydney giggled and started talking about fruit soaps, and Flora tuned out, sipping her tea, glancing around the room. Flocked wallpaper, Oriental-patterned carpet, four comfortable sitting chairs. Father had suggested she and Sam share one of the apartments on their stay, but Sam had insisted on having his own room, away from Flora. So he could smoke without her knowing, she supposed, though she always knew.

Miss Sydney continued to hold forth, the older ladies hanging on her every word, as though she had the power to grant them the return of their youth. Flora was surprised that Lady Powell should be so interested in such things, given the terribly turgid books she was famed for writing. But then, word had it that she had been a beauty in her day, and women valued for their beauty naturally tried to hold on to it for as long as they could. A curse that Flora would never have to endure. She supposed it very boring of her, but she placed much greater value on the possession of good morals, a quality that would not dwindle over time.

A silence alerted her to the fact that everyone was looking at her expectantly. She had been asked a question. What was it?

"I'm sorry, I was gathering wool," she said, trying to laugh off her inattention. "Did you ask me something?"

"Tony," Miss Sydney said. "He has such lovely hands. We've all noticed. Clean, well-trimmed nails, soft skin. We wondered if you looked after them for him."

Flora pushed down the urge to laugh. Had to push it down very hard, because this seemed the most absurd, inconsequential thing anyone could think about.

"No," she said, "I've never touched his hands."

Cordelia smirked. "But have his hands ever touched you?"

A ripple of wayward laughter went around the room. Flora tried not to think about how Miss Sydney knew Tony's hands were soft. She had seen Tony and Sweetie hanging about her a few times since her fiancé left. She was beautiful, so Flora couldn't really blame them, but she did despise the way Sweetie spoke to her, all his words laced with innuendo and ribald laughter. For her part, Miss Sydney seemed to thrive on his silliness. Perhaps she was enjoying being away from her beau, who was old enough to be her father.

Yes, the mood had changed since the winter closure. There was something a little lawless about all their behavior, as though they all enjoyed pushing at the boundaries of the codes of decency that usually kept them in check. Well, Flora wouldn't be part of it. She let the laughter die away then rose to her feet. "I must go," she said. "I promised my brother I would sit with him this afternoon." It was a lie, but it would do.

"You're not angry with us, are you?" Miss Sydney asked, fluttering her lashes the way she did to Sweetie. And Tony, for that matter.

"No, really. It was a good joke. Of course I've touched Tony's hands, and of course he's touched mine. I simply meant that I've never manicured him, and I'm fairly certain he gives his fingers scant attention, as there is really nothing less important in the world than how a man's hands look."

"I disagree," said Cordelia Wright. "One of my husbands had the tiniest, pale hands. Let me say, little hands predict little things elsewhere."

More laughter. Flora couldn't stand it anymore. She nodded once and left without another word. So what if they thought her rude? She thought *them* rude.

She flew down the stairs, deciding a few breaths of the frigid air outside were in order. It had been snowing steadily since the very early morning, and now inches of it were piled up. Just as she reached for the door, a voice behind her called, "Flora! Miss Honeychurch-Black!"

She turned to see Will Dalloway approaching, his leather bag and hat on one arm, his overcoat folded over the other.

"Dr. Dalloway," she said, aware Miss Zander watched from behind the reception desk. "It's a pleasure to see you."

"Are you off out into the snow? You'll freeze."

Good point. "Just for a bracing breath, then straight back where it's warm," she said.

"How's our Violet today?" Miss Zander called.

"Much improved," Will answered. He turned to Flora, handed her his overcoat. "Here, take this for your bracing breath while I talk to Miss Zander."

She smiled and took the coat gratefully, then slipped it on and went outside.

Violet had been ill. She wondered if Sam knew. He'd become very reclusive since the hotel had closed. Some days, she didn't see him at all until dinnertime, when he yawned through food and conversations as though he hadn't slept in years. She had no idea how much he was smoking, and kept hoping it was only a little.

The snow came down soft and slow, but steady. Flora stood under the eaves and watched it. The white of the snow made other colors stand out more vividly: green pine needles, dark-brown trunks, cold gray bricks. The air tingled on her cheeks, and she huddled into Will's overcoat, becoming very aware of the smell of it. A warm smell, a male smell. Spicy but clean. She turned her head to the side and took a deep sniff, letting her eyelids drop.

Then she shook herself. Here she was, judging the silly ladies up in Lady Powell's sitting room, or Tony's friends with their lewd nonsense, and she was no better than them. Sniffing Will's overcoat and thinking of him too fondly. Far too fondly.

She shrugged out of the coat, just as the door swung inwards and Will stepped out.

"Here," she said tersely, offering it to him.

"Aren't you cold?"

"I don't mind it."

He took the coat, smiling at her. "Your brother? He's well?"

Of course she had encouraged his interest, and none-too-subtly. She had sat in his office and cried about her cheating fiancé. She had let him too far into her life, her heart. If she didn't want to fall into the same casual unruliness in which everyone else was indulging, she had to push him back out. "All is well in my life, thank you, Dr. Dalloway. I will let you know if there is anything I need from you, so you need not inquire further."

His eyes flickered behind his glasses, and she had to swallow down hard. She'd hurt his feelings. It was for the best.

"Good day, then," he said, pressing his hat on his head and hurrying off to his car.

She stood shivering in the snow for a few moments longer, knowing she'd done the right thing but feeling bereft all the same.

Even with the ballroom divided in half and the fire roaring in the grate, the cold seemed close, gathering in the corners of the room and up in the high ceiling. The candlelight and firelight gave the room a shifting, amber glow. A gramophone had replaced the orchestra, and it gave the room an emptied-out feeling, as though they were the last people left on earth. Flora sat close to Tony, listening as he told the table a story about the day he met the prime minister. Nobody seemed to mind that they'd heard it before: they had all had dinner together so many times it had become acceptable to recycle stories.

Flora glanced at Tony's hands. They were very clean and tidy; she hadn't noticed before. Sam's, by contrast, were pale, with ragged nails and cuticles. Even though he sat at the table, he seemed off in his own world, rocking slightly, thumbnail in his mouth, distracted gaze, messy hair. She watched him a few moments, then saw him straighten and remove his hand from his mouth, his whole countenance becoming light and engaged. She didn't need to follow the direction of his gaze to know it was Violet who effected this change in him.

Flora turned and watched Violet approach. She was pale but didn't look particularly ill. The girl worked hard, and Flora admired that about her. She obviously made Sam happy, and it was the longest any of his love affairs had lasted. For the first time Flora found herself wondering if it would be the worst thing in the world if Sam married a woman like this. If she made him happy—given it was so hard to make him happy—surely that would be a good thing.

Of course, their father would see things differently.

Violet brought out their meals, careful to avoid eye contact with any of them. Flora could see Sweetie eyeing the young woman lasciviously, and she had to turn away. What a horrid ape he was. By contrast, Sam, eyes aglow, watched Violet with gentle affection, and Flora couldn't help but smile.

After Violet had returned to the kitchen, Flora leaned across to Sam. "You are quite taken with her, aren't you?"

"Life is a cold, vast ocean without her."

Flora was well used to Sam's dramatic turns of phrase; at times ordinary expressions of human feeling seemed beneath him. For once, she didn't tell him that Father would never approve. For once, she just let him love her.

The conversation turned again. Lady Powell, a few too many champagnes past good sense, was holding forth on the idiocy of book reviewers while Cordelia Wright agreed emphatically about opera reviewers, and Sam's agitation increased to the point where Flora knew he would soon spring out of his chair and stalk off, wordlessly, to his room and his opium pipe. Sure enough, his meal half finished, he did just that. The others watched him go, Miss Sydney with one eyebrow lifted disapprovingly. Perhaps she couldn't understand why Sam didn't ogle her like the others did. However, all were so used to his disappearances that it went unremarked.

The evening wore on, and there was much talk about the weather. Violet came to clear their plates, and Flora noted the disappointment on her face when she saw that Sam had gone.

"Miss," Lady Powell said, tugging the hem of Violet's apron, "what is our dessert tonight?"

"Toffee pudding," Violet answered.

"Oh, none for me," Miss Sydney said. "I'll just have tea."

"I'm having pudding," Lady Powell harrumphed. "Toffee pudding is my favorite."

"I feel like something sweet," Sweetie said. "Are you on the menu, dollface?"

Tony and Miss Sydney sniggered. Violet smiled politely and ignored it. "Only toffee pudding, sir, but I can bring you tea or coffee if you'd prefer."

Sweetie, either unable or unwilling to read the situation, pressed on with an aggressive glint in his eye. "I'd prefer a taste of you."

Flora saw a look of weariness come over Violet's face, and wondered how many times in the past men like Sweetie had made comments like that. Flora had never had to endure such treatment, but for Violet it was probably regular. She remembered that the girl had been ill—ill enough to warrant a visit by Dr. Dalloway—and she spoke up.

"Really, Sweetie, that's enough. You're embarrassing yourself."

Sweetie shot back, "Why should I be embarrassed?"

"The girl is obviously not interested in you. You're an oaf."

A grim silence descended on the table. Violet kept her head low and scuttled back towards the kitchen with their empty plates.

"Steady on, Flora," Tony said quietly. Threateningly.

This inflamed her. Flora was not a woman to lose her temper, but week upon week with these people, especially odious Sweetie, had worn upon her nerves. "I won't *steady on*. The world does not belong to him, nor to you, nor to any of you. We share it. We share it with people like Violet, who has a right to do her job without Sweetie insulting her."

"Too right!" Lady Powell said, raising her glass.

"I wasn't *insulting* her," Sweetie spat. "I was flattering her. She loved it."

"She did *not* love it. She was embarrassed and probably frightened. She won't say anything because she's afraid of losing her job."

"If she didn't love it, why was she smiling?"

"She's paid to smile at you. She probably hates you. Lord knows, I do sometimes. But I suppose you're used to paying women to be pleasant to you."

Sweetie turned to Tony and snarled, "Get your woman under control."

Tony put his hand under Flora's elbow. "Come on. We're leaving before you insult anyone else."

Flora allowed herself to be thrust out of her chair, but shook Tony off as they crossed the dance floor. She noticed Violet lingering at the staff entrance opposite, having witnessed the whole exchange. Defiantly, she gave Violet a broad smile, then held her head high as Tony marched her out.

They were outside her bedroom door before he said a word, and by then Flora had had time to regret speaking so sharply to Sweetie in front of all their friends.

"Really, Flora," Tony admonished, but gently. "Sweetie is one of my oldest friends."

"I'm sorry if I embarrassed you," she said, "but even you must admit he goes on with such rude nonsense. It's not fit for a table full of well-bred ladies, and it's cruel in the extreme to lower people like waiters and waitresses, who dare not speak up for themselves. I won't tolerate it anymore. Speak to him and get him to stop it." Her heart thudded a little in her chest, but she was glad she'd said her piece.

"I can't stop him doing anything," Tony said.

"Yes, you can. He hangs off you. They all do. He's still here, for goodness' sake. He could have gone back to Sydney, but he worships the ground you walk on. The level of behavior you overlook is the level of behavior you condone. I should hate to think I am marrying a man who would turn a blind eye to such incivility."

Tony drew his eyebrows down, and Flora felt a tiny note of alarm touch her heart. But then his anger seemed to melt away, and his eyes crinkled at the corners, and his mouth turned up as though fighting a smile. Then he started to laugh.

She was too bewildered to join him.

"Oh, Florrie, you are *fierce*. How I love you." He pulled her into his arms and kissed her forehead, her cheeks, and then moved his lips to her mouth.

She breathed out. "Well, I wasn't expecting that."

"Sweetie's face," he said, "was priceless. I don't think he expected in a million years you would speak to him like that. Yes, he had it coming. But please, please don't do it again."

"You'll talk to him?"

"I will talk to him. I will make sure he behaves in your company, and in the company of the other ladies."

"Thank you, my dear." She kissed his cheek and turned to unlock her door, but he grasped her wrist.

"May I come in?" he said, and the question seemed heavy with intent.

Flora considered his request. He had asked before, of course, and she had always said no. But at this moment she felt very close to him, her blood was warm and her spirits high. "You can come in for a *little* while," she said, equally layering her words with hidden meaning. "Understand?"

He smiled and nodded. She unlocked the door and they went inside.

She switched on the lamp next to her bed and stood in the center of the room, not sure what to do. Tony put his hands around her hips and pulled her close against him.

"Let me kiss you. Really kiss you," he said.

She offered up her face, and his lips descended hungrily, his tongue darting into her mouth. Liquid heat moved in her groin. She told herself to relax as his hands moved and cupped her buttocks through her skirt, pressing her against him. These were all things he had done before, when she let him.

"Can we lie down?" he asked, close to her ear.

Wordlessly she nodded, and he led her to the bed. He laid her on her back and settled beside her, kissing her fiercely, stroking her hair, running his lips along her neck. She closed her eyes and surrendered to the sensation. There was something wonderful about being appreciated in this way by a man—a handsome, powerful man like Tony. Of course, Tony had appreciated other women this way, too, and the thought made her sad. Wouldn't it be nicer to be the only one a man had ever been with? She wondered if Will Dalloway would find her as attractive as Tony did.

Her eyes flew open. Where did that thought come from?

"What's wrong?" Tony asked, propping himself up on his elbow.

"Nothing. Why?"

"You went stiff."

"Oh. No, I'm fine. Just . . . you know I have trouble relaxing when we . . ."

"You like it, though, don't you?"

"Oh, yes."

He teasingly moved his hand onto the curve of her waist, running it up over her hip. "You like that?"

She smiled, nodded.

"You have a beautiful shape, Florrie. Miss Sydney, our beauty queen, is shaped like a pencil. I know it's the fashion to be thin, but women should have hips and bottoms. And breasts." His hand crept up towards her breast.

She pushed it away. "Fresh," she said gently, smiling.

"You'll like it. I promise you."

She closed her eyes. "What I didn't see didn't happen." Her skin prickled in anticipation. She had never let him caress her breasts before.

His warm hand moved smoothly up over her ribs and closed over her left breast. Her heart sped. She tried to be in the moment, and not think of how many other women Tony had done this to. *He loves me. He loves my shape.* Once again, she found herself thinking of Will, if *he* liked women with hips and bottoms and breasts.

Tony's hand disappeared, then reappeared at the hem of her blouse, pulling it loose and creeping up over her stays. "You are a long way beneath the surface," he remarked. "I want to touch your skin."

Boldly, she sat up and pulled her blouse over her head, then lay back down. Closed her eyes. "This and no more," she said.

He undid the first few hooks on the front of her stays and slid his hand inside. The thought of him touching her there was almost as thrilling as the touch itself. He molded her nipple between his thumb and forefinger, and she gasped involuntarily.

"I told you you'd like it," he murmured.

She sat up, brushed his hand away. "Enough," she said.

He laughed. "Too much?"

"Too . . ." She couldn't think of the word. All she knew was that she felt a strong tickling urge between her legs that she'd never felt before, and she was afraid that one more moment of Tony's touch would make her say yes to anything.

"We'll be married in a few months anyway," he said. "It's snowing outside and so warm in here. You and me, curled up together, in love. Why not let me stay?"

"Because that's not how I was raised."

He shrugged, then he kissed her cheek. "You are beautiful, you know, in your own way."

"And you are handsome, in a way everyone can see," she said. "But that's not why I love you."

He rose as she pulled her blouse back on. "I'll have you eventually," he said.

"Yes, you will. But not now." She deliberately made herself think of Tony with those other awful women, to pour cold water on her warm desire.

He left and she went to her window to watch the snow fall. So much snow. Hours upon hours of it. Surely it would clear overnight. This was Australia, not Switzerland. She would have thought snow rare, though she supposed she didn't know all that much about mountain weather. The lights of the hotel lit up the flurries. Beyond them were dark streets. Now she let herself think of Will. She wondered if he was standing by the window of his room, too, watching the snow fall out of the night sky. She let herself imagine that he was, and the thought made her smile.

But then she told herself that was enough nonsense, and turned to get ready for bed.

Violet woke to a cold that the small radiator simply couldn't keep away. Her window, small and dim at the best of times, was completely covered by snow. She curled herself into a ball under the blankets, hanging on to the last sweet scrap of sleep, where she was warm and her future unfolded with calm ease. The last thing she wanted to do was get up for the breakfast shift. But then she remembered that the kitchen would be roaring with warmth and good smells, and she threw back the covers. She went to the bathroom to wash and dress, then headed upstairs.

Miss Zander was in the kitchen, which was uncommon. Usually she let the cooks and waitstaff be, but then Violet realized she was in urgent discussions with Hansel.

"What's happening?" Violet said, sidling up to Cook.

"The flying fox is stuck down in the valley. They think the snow is blocking the cable hoops."

Miss Zander turned and saw Violet, gave her a smile. "I wonder if your friend Mr. Betts is up to working in the snow," she said. "We'll need that fixed or we'll have nothing to eat!"

"Does it always snow this much?" Violet asked.

Miss Zander shook her head. "Violet, it *never* snows this much. Or it hasn't in forty-eight years. We had sixteen inches of it overnight. If it doesn't stop today, the roads will be impassable. If the winds turn southerly, we're going to have a storm on our hands."

"How do you know?"

"Because I lived at Evergreen Falls the last time it snowed like this. I was only six, but I still remember the storm that came that afternoon." Miss Zander's face looked pinched. It was the first time Violet had seen her look anything less than perfectly in control.

Violet shivered, and moved to the kitchen table that had been pulled up close to the fire. Cook put a plate of bacon next to her. "Eat up," he said. "The radiator's busted in the staff dining room, so we're going to have to eat in the kitchen till it's fixed."

Eating was the last thing she felt like doing, but she picked at some bacon anyway. There was a baby inside her now, trying to grow, and she was responsible for it.

Clive came in, fetched by the last of the bellhops, and discussed with Miss Zander the best way to go about getting the flying fox moving. After Miss Zander bustled away, Clive sat down.

"Morning," he said, reaching for the bacon.

"Are you sure it's safe, fixing the flying fox in this weather?"

"Of course it is. Just a bit cold." He forced a smile. "Not worrying about me, are you, Violet?"

She looked at her plate. "I don't want anything bad to happen to you," she said. She wondered what Clive would think if he knew how much trouble she was in.

"Your concern is very sweet. I'll be fine. If I can get the cable moving at this end, it will shift all the snow off along the entire length. I think it's just that the pulley wheels are frozen and need oiling."

"Well," she said, not meeting his eye, "do be safe."

The kitchen grew busier as the day started, but there was a subdued feeling about. At first Violet didn't notice it, so involved with her own ruminations was she. But after breakfast she realized the staff were dragging their feet, continually going to the windows to look out at the slate-gray sky and the constantly falling snow. Clive came in, having been unable to move the flying fox more than a few feet. He shook snow out of his hair and off his gloves, his cheeks red and his eyes wild. "I've never felt anything like it," he said.

By three o'clock they heard that the roads were closed. Miss Zander gathered them in the kitchen and announced that anyone who wanted to head out of the mountains and down to Sydney should pack immediately and leave on the five o'clock train.

"Are you going?" Clive asked Violet.

She shook her head. How could she go back to Mama in this state? Besides, how could she bear to be apart from Sam? It would happen, but not yet. Not yet.

A flurry of activity followed. Bags were hurriedly packed and rooms left in disarray. By that evening, the only staff left were Miss Zander, Cook, Clive, and Violet.

"How will we manage?" Violet asked.

"Oh, we'll manage, my dear," Miss Zander said. "We've lost Miss

Sydney and Mrs. Wright, too. Four staff is ample for six guests. In any case, it's only in the short term. The snow will ease and the roads will open again, and they'll all be back. But I can't keep them up here in the freezing cold when there's a chance we'll be cut off, especially with the flying fox out of action."

Violet went to the kitchen sink and leaned on the cold porcelain, gazing out the window. Dark fell and the snow continued, pouring out of the sky white and soft and relentless.

CHAPTER TWENTY

Around midnight, the wind changed direction and howled over the hotel. Violet woke at the noise, then slept fitfully thereafter, as internal doors banged and windows rattled and the cold penetrated through any crack it could find.

She didn't know how long it had been—perhaps three or four hours—when a thundering crash woke her with a start. Instinctively, she curled into a ball under her covers as the noise went on. The wind seemed to have redoubled its force. Her heart sped, and she was now far too frightened to go back to sleep. If only Sam had come to her tonight. Pressed against his body, nothing would seem so bad.

Violet threw back the covers and pulled on her dressing gown. Maybe if she crept up to his room, like she used to do, the fear would ease.

She was emerging from the staircase to the staff quarters when she saw a light bobbing in the dark across the foyer. She paused, waiting, and a moment later Miss Zander's silhouette emerged.

"Violet!" she said coolly. "Good, you're here. I need you to wake all the guests and get them to assemble immediately in the ballroom."

"What? Why?"

Another huge gust shrieked over them, and Miss Zander clutched at Violet's arm protectively. As it passed, she thrust Violet gently away. "Go. Take this lamp," she said. "Part of the roof on the east wing has fallen in. Our electricity has been cut, and so has our phone. The ballroom has the domed roof. It's the safest place for us all to be until this storm passes."

Violet nodded, and headed up the stairs with the hurricane lamp. She would be waking Sam after all, but there was no need for secrecy. No time for embraces.

The ladies' floor was first, and she knocked hard on Flora's door. "Excuse me. Wake up, ma'am. It's an emergency."

The door opened a second later. "Violet?"

"Sorry to wake you, ma'am," Violet said, embarrassed to be standing in front of Sam's sister in her champagne-colored silk dressing gown.

"As if I could sleep. What's going on?"

"We're all to assemble in the ballroom. There's been a roof collapse on the other wing. The safest place is under the dome."

"Of course, of course. Do I have time to dress?" Another immense gust. Flora shook her head. "I think I'll just go as I am. Here, you go up to tell the Powells, and I'll fetch Sam, Tony, and Sweetie. That will save some time."

"Thank you, Miss Honeychurch-Black."

"Flora," Flora said. "Please, call me Flora. Our surname's rather a mouthful."

Violet smiled at her, and Flora returned her smile in the shifting light of the lamp flame. Then Violet hurried off upstairs to wake Lord and Lady Powell.

By the time she came back down to the ballroom, Miss Zander had illuminated the room with half-a-dozen hurricane lamps, had the fire burning in the grate, and had piled up pillows and blankets by the fire.

"Come in, come in," she said to Violet, who was hesitating a few steps behind the Powells. "No standing on ceremony tonight. Staff and guests all together. Safety first. See, our handyman and cook are already here."

Violet looked around for Sam, who sat on a pillow by the fire gazing intently at her. When their eyes met, he gave her a weak smile. Her ribs contracted, and it occurred to her very brightly that love was actually a kind of pain that one didn't feel at first through the euphoria. She acknowledged him with a nod, then went to sit by Miss Zander, who sat at one of the dining tables with a sheet of paper and pen and looked elegant even in a thick wool dressing gown.

"We'll need to do some rearranging, Violet," she said. "The boys from the east wing will have to be moved."

Violet glanced up and saw Clive and Cook huddled together, chatting by the room dividers.

"With roads and rail out, our flying fox almost certainly disabled, no phone and no electricity, we can expect it to be a long time before somebody can come and look at the roof over there. Wonderful as Clive is, I think it's a bigger job than he can manage himself. So, I'm going to move the male staff into the female staff quarters, and I'm going to move you up to the ladies' floor. I've already spoken to Miss Honeychurch-Black, who's the only woman up there now, and she has no problem sharing the floor with you. You will take the east bathroom and she the west, so you'll likely rarely see each other. I'll move my own things up on the top floor next to the Powells." She made lists as she spoke. "The gas appears to be working still, so we can cook and heat the rooms." Miss Zander stopped for a moment, put down her pen, and sneezed loudly. "Oh, for heaven's sake," she said. "The last thing I need is to get sick. Violet, feel my forehead. Do I feel warm to you? I've been feeling congested and woolly all day."

Violet pressed her palm over Miss Zander's brow. She was on fire. "You're very hot," Violet said. "You should go and lie down. I can take care of things here."

"No, I'll simply will it away," Miss Zander harrumphed.

Violet grew insistent. "You'll make yourself sicker if you don't rest."

"How inconvenient," she said. "And Will Dalloway may as well be a million miles away. Even if it stops snowing tomorrow, the route between here and there will be impassable. Perhaps in the morning, when the storm's over, I can get Clive to go over to Karl's offices and see if there's any medicine there for a fever." She sneezed again. "Good grief, the timing."

Violet smiled at her. "I'll set you up a little bed on the floor."

"No, and I mean *no*. I can't have them all seeing me lying down looking ill. I am the only person here who won't lie down. When Eugenia Zander collapses, so does the whole hotel. I'll just put my head down on the table for a little while. Would you be a dear and make sure everyone is settled? We'll be safe in here." Then Miss Zander did just that, laying her head gently on the table and closing her eyes.

As the wind screamed overhead, shaking the windows, Violet went to the guests one by one—including the odious man everyone called Sweetie—to offer them pillows and blankets and cups of tea. Sam took the opportunity to caress her hand softly as she handed him a pillow, but apart from that they neither touched nor spoke. Cook went off to the kitchen to prepare toasted crumpets and tea, and Clive kept the fire stoked. He was wearing a long, maroon wool robe and slippers, and Violet felt a stab of fondness at gaining a small glimpse into the private man he was.

Nobody slept, and gray light glimmered outside the windows a few hours later. Dawn was accompanied by a sudden drop in the wind, and by the time Cook had brought in plates of steak and eggs for breakfast, the snow had stopped altogether.

Violet saw Clive heading for the exit and followed him. "Where are you going?"

"Outside for five seconds, to see," he said.

"I'm coming."

Lord and Lady Powell overheard and joined them. What a strange group they made: the noble writers, the waitress, and the handyman, all in their robes, gingerly opening the front door to the hotel—letting in a spill of snow that had piled up—and peering into the daylight.

The sky was pale blue and mostly clear, with gray clouds disappearing on the horizon. The frozen air was still. The sun was weak, and it gleamed wanly off the snow. The east wing looked no different from outside, but Clive told Violet a section of the roof about twenty yards across had collapsed under the wind and the weight of snow. As for the rest of the world: it was a different landscape from the one they were used to. Where paths and roads and rail lines had been, there were instead softly undulating snow hills. It was so pretty, Violet almost didn't mind that they were cut off from the outside world.

"We should have gone back to Sydney yesterday," said Lord Powell.

"The move would have disrupted me too much," Lady Powell answered. "My novel is just getting to a crucial point."

Lord Powell huffed. "Don't marry an artist," he said to Clive, then shuffled back inside, followed by Lady Powell.

Clive turned to Violet. "Sorry I got you into this."

Violet looked back at him puzzled, then realized what he meant. "Don't apologize. I made my own messes," she said.

"You didn't make it snow."

"Yes, that's true enough." But for everything else, she blamed only herself.

It was a strange day, strange and silent. The guests retreated to their rooms, and the staff packed and relocated as instructed. Miss Zander grew paler by the moment, until finally she took herself to her new room at the top of the stairs, leaving Cook in charge until morning.

Violet didn't have a moment to enjoy the luxury of her new room. After she finished moving she was busy making beds and serving meals, then as evening fell, she ran about organizing lamps for all the guest rooms, and finally waitressing at the small dinner in the dining room, which Sam did not attend. She took Miss Zander's evening meal up to her, then ate her own dinner afterwards in the kitchen with Cook and Clive. Clive, too, had started to look distinctly unwell.

"Not you, too, Clive?" she asked.

"I'll be fine. Don't tell Miss Zander."

Without thinking, Violet reached across to feel his forehead. It was only as her skin connected with his that she remembered their history, and how intimate the touch might seem. She jerked her hand away. "You're very hot," she said.

"So hot that I burned you?" he said with a smirk.

She wasn't in the mood for jokes. "You should go to bed. Cook and I can manage."

After an hour of cleaning up, Violet finally climbed the stairs to the ladies' floor. Wearily she fetched her things from her room and took them with her hurricane lamp to the guest bathroom. It was so different to her own grim, lightless bathroom downstairs that she put the lamp on the ground and gazed around. Gleaming white-and-green tiles, here and there with a stylized pine tree engraved on them. Long green curtains caught back around a tall window. An elegant white sink with brass taps. A deep bath with shining clawed feet. And the bathroom rug—her feet seemed to sink inches into it. Two huge radiators warmed the space. She started to fill the bath and waited, sitting on the carved wooden toilet lid, letting the day drift away from her.

When it was full, she stripped off and slid into the bath. The lamp gave a soft, amber light, and she closed her eyes and tipped her head back to let her hair trail in the water. She was used to taking baths in a cramped tub with peeling enamel, in a room with no windows and no heating. This was bliss.

If only . . . If only . . .

Everything was going to change. When? She looked down at her breasts. They were already heavier, the nipples darker. Would Sam notice? Would she soon burst out of her uniform? Her stomach was still taut, her hip bones still prominent. Could it be possible that she would swell up like a melon? Could it be possible that she would give birth to a squalling baby? Then what?

But she knew what came next. What had happened to her mother came next: a long, thankless haul raising and educating a child, while youth and beauty bled away. *Look at me*, her mother used to say. *No wonder I'm lonely. You've stolen my looks and figure, and no decent man would have aught to do with me.*

That's what waited.

Violet let herself cry, for the first time in a long time. Really cry with big heaving sobs, which echoed around the bathroom. But after a few minutes she sniffed them back. She splashed water on her face and climbed out of the bath. She dried off by the light of the lamp. She wasn't sure if Sam would visit her tonight, or if she should visit him. Everything was topsy-turvy while they were cut off from the world, but she ached for the comfort of his arms.

As she emerged from the bathroom in her robe, she nearly ran into Flora coming the other way.

"Oh, I'm sorry," Violet said, bowing her head.

"No, I'm sorry. I thought this was . . . Miss Zander said the east bathroom?"

"She told me the east bathroom, too."

"She probably had a lot on her mind. I'll head up to the other bathroom. Not that I . . ." Flora trailed off. "I don't want you to think that I wouldn't share a bathroom with you because you're . . ."

"Oh. No, I wouldn't have thought that."

Flora looked at her more closely. "Are you all right? You look as though you've been crying."

Violet shook her head, but at the same time she said, "Yes, I'm in such a mess . . ." The tears came again. What was she doing? She couldn't cry to Sam's sister about her troubles. Sam had always said Flora would destroy their happiness, but she had been so kind, and she had such a sweet, gentle face.

"Oh, dear. Oh, dear," Flora said, putting an arm around Violet's shoulder. "Come with me. You oughtn't be alone. Come with me." She led Violet to her impeccably tidy room and sat her at the desk. Flora crouched in front of her. "Would tea help?"

"I . . ."

"Tea would help. Let me get it. Is there anyone down in the kitchen?"

"Cook should be there."

"Now, it will take me a few minutes. Promise me you'll wait here for me? Don't race off anywhere."

Violet nodded. Her hair dripped onto the collar of her dressing gown.

Flora patted her shoulder and hurried off.

Violet tried to get her feelings under control. She'd been up since the early hours of the morning, and extreme weariness meant everything had taken on a nightmarish hue. Her heart clenched with despair and hopelessness, and now here she sat in Flora's warm room, waiting for tea. If she hadn't promised Flora she would stay, she would have run right then.

But she had to tell someone, and like as not Flora would know as soon as Sam did. She couldn't put off telling Sam much longer.

Flora was back in a flash. "Your cook had just made some for himself," she explained. "He gave it to me. How kind of him."

Violet didn't tell Flora that it wasn't kindness but obedience on Cook's part. Guests always came first; Miss Zander would have it no other way. She watched as Flora poured tea, then she pulled up a chair opposite Violet and said, "Go on: drink."

Violet sipped the tea in silence for a few minutes. It made her feel marginally better.

"Would you like to tell me what made you cry?" Flora said. "I don't want to be nosy . . ."

"I'll tell you," Violet said, putting aside her cup. "But only because it involves Sam."

"He's broken your heart, hasn't he? He's done it before, to others. I'm sorry. I would have warned you if I could."

Violet shook her head. "He hasn't broken my heart. Though I suspect he might." Her voice cracked and she breathed back a sob. "But it appears I'm to have his baby."

Flora's mouth dropped open a little, and she sat there for a long time by the lamplight, her lips forming a perfect, surprised O.

"I'm sorry," Violet said.

"No, no," Flora said, galvanized back into life. "No, *I'm* sorry. Sam should be sorry. But . . . oh, my dear girl. This can't end in any good way."

"What do you mean?"

"My father, if he finds out, will cut Sam off." Her voice dropped to a whisper. "Me, too, I'm afraid."

"He will?"

"Without a doubt. My mother has a big heart, but my father has a small mind. I would be fine, I'm to marry a rich man. But Sam . . . What kind of father will he make? Oh, what a mess. What a mess. He can't stop smoking that pipe. How can he be a father?"

"So, he won't marry me?"

"He could never have married you," Flora said, but she said it gently and for that Violet was grateful. "Or at least, he could have, but then he would have nothing."

"He would have had me."

"Yes, yes, that would be something. But . . . Violet, you know Sam. I have no illusions anymore that you two stay apart from each other. Imagine him. Imagine him without a penny to his name. He can't work. He can barely leave his room most days. That is what you'd be married to."

The full weight of despair fell upon Violet, crushing her. The last hope that she and Sam would raise their child in luxury had now fled. She put her head in her hands and sobbed.

At length, Flora said, "I have an idea."

Violet lifted her head, wiping her nose with the back of her hand. "What is it?"

"If we keep it a secret, then I can help you. I can't say what Sam would do, but you can trust me."

"I don't know what you mean."

"If we keep the baby a secret from my father, Sam and I will have the money to help you. We could buy you a little place, send you money. But you must promise never to do anything that would let my father find out—" Flora stopped, bit her lip.

"You can trust me," Violet said. "I promise you. I won't ask for anything much. I just want to be able to keep working. I just want a future." Again she cried, and Flora clasped her hand and stroked it softly.

"You and your baby will both have a future, Violet," she said. "I will make sure of it."

CHAPTER TWENTY-ONE

Violet woke the next morning, in the gray just before dawn, feeling light. The despair had lifted. She burrowed under the blankets for a while, enjoying the softness of the mattress, replaying the conversation with Flora in her mind. A small, cautionary voice told her not to trust Flora completely: she may feel sympathetic now, but as the years passed she might be less and less inclined to help. But it didn't matter as much as Violet thought it would, because what Flora had helped Violet to see was that she would get by somehow. She would *not* be her mother. She was still young, could still work, and was not afraid of working hard. Certainly she couldn't waitress with a big belly, but maybe Miss Zander would let her come back after she'd had the baby. She didn't need to live at the hotel, she could find a little flat. Mama would simply have to leave Sydney and come to live with her so she could watch the baby during Violet's shifts. If Mama refused to come, so much the better: instead of buying dresses, Violet could pay a girl as mother's help. Or perhaps she wouldn't have to work in a hotel at all. Perhaps she could work in a shop, something that sold expensive, fine things like scarves or shoes or Miss Sydney's silly beauty products. If Flora really did buy Violet a home, or even pay the rent on one for a few years, so much the better. Violet was not educated, but she was clever. She was not high born, but she had a strong spirit. Mama's problem wasn't that she'd had no choices, it was that she had refused to see them.

A light knock at the door startled her. She flicked back the covers and listened, wondering if she'd imagined it. Miss Zander, if she were up, would simply let herself in. Was it Flora?

"Violet?"

It was Sam. She rose, gathering her courage. She had to tell him. Whatever came next she would take in her stride.

She opened the door, and he practically fell in, his head down and burrowed into her shoulder. "Oh, Violet, Violet," he said. His skin was damp with perspiration, his body shaking. Had he come down with the same cold that Miss Zander and Clive were fighting off? How much longer could she stay well with so many sick people around her?

Violet quietly closed the door behind him and led him to the bed. "What's wrong? Are you ill?"

He nodded. He was pallid, dressed in a sweat-stained red dressing gown. "I've run out."

"Run out?"

"Of opium. Malley was supposed to be back from Sydney with more the day before yesterday, on the last train. The weather must have prevented him. Now the trains aren't running, and there's no way of getting out of here and—"

"Sh, sh, slow down," she said, trying to still her own heart. "How long has it been?"

"I smoked my last pipe twenty-four hours ago." He threw himself against her again, his cheek pressed against her breast. "Oh, God, Violet, oh, God. It feels as though I'm falling apart."

Through the haze of alarm, she realized that she couldn't tell him now about the baby. "What do you want to do?"

"There's nothing I can do. I have to go through this. Maybe it's best. Maybe it's best. I could really get off it this time. What do you think, Violet? Am I stronger than the dragon?"

She imbued her voice with force. "Of course you are. You are the brightest star I know."

"Oh, God, oh, God." He shuddered against her. "Electricity. Horrible cold electricity all through my body. Under my skin. I'll never be calm again."

"Yes, you will. You will." She stroked his hair, trying to soothe him.

He sprang to his feet, paced the room in ever-decreasing circles. "You don't know," he said. "You know nothing. All of you who have never tasted it, you know nothing. How can I *be* after opium? How is the world to smell and taste? There is nothing on earth to interest me after it's gone. I can't stop. I can't." He stopped, suddenly. "You must help me."

"I'll do what I can."

"Help me stay strong. It will pass. Days, maybe weeks. It *will* pass."

"I know you'll be well again."

He sat on the floor in front of her, his legs splayed, and began to sob. "It's awful. I hate it. It's awful."

She came to crouch beside him, rubbing his arms.

"Don't," he said, flinching away. "My skin is crawling."

"You *can* overcome this," she said.

"The roads are cut. The trains are staying away. Malley's gone," he said with a horrible sigh, as though he had heard of the death of all he loved. "I have no other choice."

Flora came down to breakfast with a headache. She had barely slept the night before, turning over and over in her mind the idea that Sam was to be a father. In some ways, she was surprised it hadn't happened before now: he'd had plenty of opportunities to get girls in trouble. But Violet wasn't like the other girls, and Flora saw that now. Why, Flora was half in love with her herself: Violet's steady gaze and girlish vulnerability, coupled with a bright spirit that imbued even her weary movements with an energetic grace. She didn't doubt Sam was in love, for real this time. Though whether it was real love was, unfortunately, irrelevant. Father would never welcome a waitress into the Honeychurch-Black family.

Violet was at breakfast, in her black-and-white waitress uniform, pouring tea for Lady Powell. Flora nodded good morning, and noted Violet looking at her urgently, but then Tony appeared and no opportunity arose for Flora to seek Violet out alone. Instead, she sat through the meal and put up with Sweetie's rough complaints about having to endure being cut off like this. Sam hadn't come down, heightening Flora's anxiety that Violet had told him about the baby and he was off smoking himself into a stupor.

Before she cleared their plates, Violet stopped in front of their table and said in a brave voice, "Excuse me, ladies and gentlemen."

Tony whispered something to Sweetie, who laughed loudly. Flora elbowed Tony and sat to attention.

"I have an announcement from Miss Zander. I'm terribly sorry to say that of our four staff, two are bedridden with flu, including Miss Zander. Only Cook and I are well. Meals will continue as usual, and I will do my best to have all beds made as soon as possible after breakfast. But we still have no electricity, no phone, and no way of knowing when roads might be cleared or the rail station might reopen. It might be today, or tomorrow, and Miss Zander thinks no later than the next day. So, we all beg you for your patience in responding to your needs."

Lord Powell huffed. "Don't worry, girl. We're hardly going to revert to savagery."

"I've been feeling a little unwell myself," Lady Powell said.

"Well, this is completely unacceptable," Sweetie boomed. "Do you *know* how much we pay to stay here? More than your yearly salary, I'd wager."

Flora watched in admiration as Violet refused to be intimidated. "I understand your frustration, sir, and I'm sure Miss Zander intends to compensate all of you for your inconvenience. If you need one of us, we are most likely to be in the kitchen."

"Steady there, Sweetie," Tony said smoothly. "The young lass here can hardly control the elements. Thank you, my dear," he said to Violet. "Pass on our best to Miss Zander. She's a fine woman."

Flora beamed at him, her heart light.

They finished breakfast, and Flora made an excuse to hang back and walk down the corridor to the kitchen, where Violet was scraping plates.

"Violet?" she said.

Violet turned, saw her, and moved towards the threshold, wiping her hands on her apron. "It's Sam," she said.

"What's happened? Did you tell him?"

But Violet was already shaking her head. "I didn't have a chance. He came to me . . . he's very, very ill. He says he's run out of opium. He looks dreadful."

Flora suppressed a groan. She knew what happened next. She'd seen it before. "God save us all, then," she said. "It will be awful."

"It already is."

Flora patted her arm. "You're not to worry. I'll go see him."

Violet nodded, and Flora hurried away to Sam's room.

When she didn't find him there, Flora's first thought was Will Dalloway's warning about suicide. But as she stood, frozen, in the corridor, he emerged from the bathroom, pale and shaking.

"Sam!" she cried, racing to his side and guided him towards his room.

"My insides have turned to lava," he said.

"Come to your room. Let me help you."

"Help me?" he cried, his voice loud and harsh. "You'd make me just like you, wouldn't you? Don't you see? I can't be like you. I can't be one of the ordinary mob who don't know." He spread his shaking hands. "I have seen . . . paradise. Now I must give it up."

"You will be glad that it's over," she said, stilling his hands and drawing him into his room.

He roughly shook her off, and went careening down the corridor to the bathroom once again. She stood where she was, trying not to hear the awful sounds of him vomiting, of him crying out in pain and despair. In time, he emerged and slunk past her to his bed.

She closed the door behind him, then opened the curtain.

"No," he said. "No daylight. My eyes sting." He flipped from one side to the other, then back again, then rose and paced. "Everything hurts me, even these wretched blankets. Pain. Pain is everywhere."

She didn't know what to say that she hadn't already, so she simply watched him and waited. The back of his shirt was soaked in sweat.

"The nightmares I had. Oh, God save me from them. That man who killed himself, shuffling into my room all blue and cold. Over and over, he came. Shuffled up to my bed and stretched his hand out to me with a hissing noise. I woke up every time only to fall back into the same horror." He began to weep. "All is lost, Sissy. All is lost."

"All is not lost, I assure you," she said. "Trust me. Haven't I always looked after you?"

He stopped, leaned over her, and kissed her head. "Yes, you have. My dear sister. My dear sister. You will stop the pain for me, won't you? Malley isn't there, but he might have left something behind, something that can—"

"Surely you're not suggesting I go out in three feet of snow, Sam?"

"If you loved me, you would."

"I love you, and so I will not. Dr. Dalloway told me the with-drawing pains can't kill you. So, if it doesn't kill you, and at the end of it you are free of that wretched substance, then the last thing I will do is end your misery now."

He drew his hand back and slapped her hard across the face. "Get out!" he shouted.

Her cheek stung, but she told herself not to be angry with him. This wasn't Sam; this was the opium leaving his body, piercing every fiber of him as it left. She stood and spoke calmly. "You know where I am when you need me. I can bring you food, love, whatever you want. But don't ask me to bring you opium."

Of course it was hard to leave him like that, but she told herself over and over it was for the best. If left to give up the opium on his own, there would never be a right place or time. But here, cut off from the world by hills of snow with hardly anyone around . . . it was almost perfect.

Flora walked away, hearing his sobs through the door.

Violet took the tea tray down the stairs to the staff quarters where just a few days ago she had slept. She wasn't sure which room Clive was in, so she knocked on all the doors softly until he called out, "In here."

She balanced the tray on her hip and pushed the door in. She had just delivered tea to Miss Zander, who was laid flat on her back with a fever that had soaked her nightgown but still she managed to give orders as Violet stirred sugar into her tea.

"Cook is experienced, but he's not good with people. Make sure you're there at every meal, smiling at everyone. Reassure them. Use my name often. I'll be up tomorrow, I'm almost sure of it. Have you heard anyone yet? Any tractors or trains? Somebody must come to clear the roads soon. Surely they haven't forgotten about us."

Clive had far less energy.

"How are you feeling?" she said, laying the tray on the dresser beside his bed.

"Wretched," he said, then as if to emphasize the point, he coughed loudly. It was a deep, wet cough that might have alarmed Violet had she not been with Sam just an hour before and seen how sick he was. Her chores today seemed a waste of time that should be spent with Sam, holding him and stroking him and reassuring him.

Still, she said, "Good grief, that's a terrible cough."

"I'll be fine in a day or so. Are you well? And Cook? We aren't going to have to let the guests fend for themselves, are we?"

"I'm sure it won't come to that," Violet said, smiling. "Can you sit up? I'll pour your tea."

He struggled into a sitting position. He was wearing navy pajamas, and one of his buttons was missing. She could see through to the sparse hair on his chest, and it made her feel awkward and blush. She turned to the tea tray, poured him a cup, and added a spoon of honey.

"So, you remembered how I take my tea?" he said, as she handed him the cup. She noticed he had adjusted his pajama shirt so it no longer gaped.

She smiled. "Of course I did. Black with honey. You must have told me a hundred times when we worked at the Senator."

"Only because you kept giving me milk."

"Who drinks tea without milk? Only oddballs," she teased.

He smiled weakly and sipped his tea. "The Senator would never have been snowed in and cut off."

"A lot of things wouldn't have happened at the Senator," she said wistfully, sitting on the opposite bed.

"Is everything all right with you, Violet?"

She sighed deeply. "No, but thanks for asking."

"You could tell me, you know. I'll listen."

She looked at him, and remembered when she'd first met him. How she'd thought him sweet and merry, and how she'd happily gone on dates with him. But she'd always had a fickle heart, until she met Sam.

"Are we friends again?" she asked in a quiet voice.

He nodded. "I'm sorry if I was angry with you. It was out of concern, not jealousy. Or at least I hope it was. I like to think of myself as a decent man."

"You *are* a decent man," she said. Then, before she could change her mind, she said, "Clive, I'm pregnant."

Bless him. He tried hard not to look shocked. "Ah," he said. "That's rather a spanner in the works, I imagine."

She braced her chin so she wouldn't cry, and nodded unhappily.

"Will he marry you?" Clive asked.

"I don't know. He's sick at the moment and I haven't told him yet." So sick. Sicker than she'd ever seen. "But I suspect . . . I suspect he won't. That he never could have anyway."

"I'll marry you," he said, without missing a beat.

His offer speared her heart. "Why on earth would you say that?"

"Because it's true. Because your baby needs a father and because I've always loved you . . . Come now, Violet, none of this is a surprise, is it?"

Violet dropped her head. How much easier things were back at the Senator, when she and Clive were sweet on each other. If she'd stayed with him, life would have unfolded with so few complications. "I can't marry you, Clive, because I don't love you. Flora has promised to send help with the baby."

"But will she keep her promise?"

"I don't know. I don't know anything." She didn't even know if Sam would survive his illness. "It's all a bit . . . bleak."

Clive fell silent.

"You *are* a good man," Violet said.

"And you are a good woman," he countered. "Good will come to you."

"You won't tell Miss Zander, will you? I mean, I can't keep it a secret forever, but you'll keep it to yourself?"

"Of course I will, Violet. Of course I will."

She rose. "I'll come back for your tray later. I have a thousand things to do."

"Do take care of yourself."

"I'll do my best," she said, and left the room. She stood in the dim corridor for a few moments, catching her breath.

There were other things to do, but Violet couldn't help gravitating back to Sam's room. She paused outside his door, listening to the voices within. One female voice. Flora. Violet hesitated, then knocked lightly.

Flora opened the door a crack. "Yes?"

"I wanted to see how he is." She craned to see behind Flora. Sam was sprawled on the bed.

Flora moved to block her view and dropped her voice to a whisper. "This is not your concern right now. Come back and see him when he's well again."

Violet bristled. Even though Flora's tone was gentle, it was underpinned with steel. How unfair of Flora to speak to her so; she'd thought they were friends now. "I want to help him get well," she said.

"He will get well on his own. Please, you must trust me." Flora's voice was determined, but Violet sensed a note of desperation. "He *will* get well. It's better if you don't see him like this. Better for both of you."

Violet was so unsure. Was this just another attempt to keep them apart? Was Flora's concern of the previous evening just a ruse to get information out of Violet about their relationship? Were promises of help and money insincere?

"Go, please," Flora said, her eyebrows scooping upwards. "This is a family matter."

"I could never be family. I understand," Violet said, turned away, and marched down the stairs. She half hoped Flora would call her back, but she didn't.

Night came and still they were cut off. Violet kept imagining she could hear the whistle of the train approaching the station, or the rumble of a tractor. Every time, she raced to the window and opened it, listening out into the silent, frigid air. But every time, she was disappointed. It had started to snow lightly again. She kept telling herself that when Miss Zander was better, things might seem more normal, more in control. But with each meal, the remaining guests grew more and more exasperated. Especially the horrible man called Sweetie.

"Potatoes? Again?" Sweetie said as she laid his plate in front of him.

"I apologize, sir, but our flying fox isn't working, and we can't get fresh food until it is."

"This has gone on for two days now!" he roared. "Why hasn't somebody simply walked to the village for help? Get Miss Zander. I want to give her a piece of my mind."

Violet gritted her teeth. "Miss Zander is ill, and so is one other staff member. Cook and I are doing everything we can. Besides, there are two or three feet of snow out there, and the village is several miles away."

"Yes, don't be unreasonable," Lady Powell said to Sweetie. "It's

inhospitable out there." Then Lady Powell turned to Violet. "Now, I distinctly tasted powdered milk in my afternoon tea. Can you ensure I have fresh milk tomorrow?"

Violet was bewildered that a woman as clever as Lady Powell hadn't figured out where the fresh milk was. She glanced at Flora, wondering if she would come to Violet's defense. But Flora had her head down and was absently pushing her food around her plate.

"As I said," Violet repeated slowly, "the flying fox that brings our fresh produce up from the valley is not working."

"So, you're out of fresh milk?"

Violet nodded. "We are out of many things. I must ask you to be patient just a day or two longer. We aren't that far from civilization, so this isolation won't last."

Lord Powell came to life, his gruff voice booming in the empty, lamp-lit room. "It seems to me a hotel of this caliber should have prepared better for such an emergency."

Violet was tired of explaining, weary to her marrow. So, she simply repeated that she and Cook were doing the best they could and then slipped away to the kitchen.

"They're complaining again," she said to Cook.

Cook, who was sitting at the kitchen table with his head in his hands, looked up. "I think I'm getting sick, too."

Horror flooded Violet's body. "No. I can't be the only one standing. I can't cook! What will I do?"

"Perhaps I'm just tired," he said. "A good night's sleep might sort me out."

"Go, then. Go now. I'll finish up here."

Violet collapsed into bed very late, very tired. She left her door unlocked in case Sam visited in the night. Despite her anxiety and uncertainty, she immediately fell into a deep, dreamless slumber.

The knock didn't wake her. The door opening didn't wake her. In

fact, she didn't wake until Sam was sitting on her bed, shaking her shoulder. "Violet, wake up," he said.

She hauled herself out of sleep, reached for him. "What's wrong?" she said. "Are you better?" She couldn't make out any detail in the dark, but an unpleasant smell clung to him. A sour smell, so at odds with his usual sweet odor that she almost wondered for a moment if it really was Sam.

"No, I'll never be better." He began to sob, and she reached for him. Her hand made contact with a cold, sweat-soaked back. "Let's put a light on," she said, climbing out of bed. With the hurricane lamp on the desk by the window, she could see how very ill he looked. His pallid skin, his eyes encircled by dark shadows, his frame weak and shaking. He wore only a singlet and long johns.

He lay down on her bed and groaned. "Can I stay here tonight?"

"Of course."

"He's come for me. He knows that's my room. I can't go back there, not during the night."

"Who are you talking about, Sam?"

"The ghost. He's stepped out of my dreams and now he's in my room. Standing, grinning in the corner. Blue with the cold, bloated from the water."

Freezing alarm touched Violet's heart. "Sam, tell me you know that's not true."

"I've seen him with my own eyes. I'm not going back there." He cried out in pain, then leaped up and began to pace.

She came to his side and tried to still him, but he shrugged her off violently. "No, don't hold me down. My legs and arms, they are racked with cramps. The only thing I can do is move them. The pain is . . . oh, God. I can't do this. You must help me. You must."

"I'll do anything."

He lay down again. His arms twitched and flailed as though he

wasn't in control of them. "But for an hour of sleep. A moment of respite," he gasped.

"How can I help? Tell me. I'll do anything."

"Kill me."

Violet recoiled. "No."

"I beg you. I beg you. I don't want to live anymore, not without my opium. I saw . . ." He raised his hand and it shook. "I saw all the way to the other side of reality. It was beautiful, so beautiful. What is my life now? Pain, unending pain. I can feel my body dying all around me." As if on cue, his legs started to shake uncontrollably, and he had to shoot to his feet and pace again. "This is all there is," he said, "until the pain kills me. It would be a mercy for you to press a pillow over my face and let me die."

"I'm not going to kill you."

"I'm going to die anyway. He's come for me. That's why he's in my room. He's come to take me with him. I don't want to die with him grinning at me. I want to die looking upon your sweet face."

Violet gulped, the heat of her fear blinding her. He did look like a man very close to death. But never in a million years would she help him die. No. She would help him live.

Violet knew exactly what she had to do.

CHAPTER TWENTY-TWO

Watching Sam go through the pains of withdrawing from opium was a living horror, but Flora comforted herself with Will Dalloway's words: withdrawal wouldn't kill him. *The far greater danger is that he keeps taking it.*

First thing in the morning, she rose and sat outside his door. He no longer wanted her in his room, but she heard him. She heard his groans and thundering steps as he paced around and around trying to shake out the cramps that racked his limbs. She heard as his groans turned into shrieks, pleas to God for mercy, pleas to Flora for death. Every one pierced her heart, but she sat there all morning and let nobody come near. Shortly after breakfast, Violet stood at the top of the stairs looking at Flora, eyes pleading and tearful. But Flora waved her off. She would explain to the girl later. This was for the best.

And so, with snow two or three feet high outside, and food running out, and no electricity in the dim hallway, Sam yelped like a madman in his room, and Flora sat with her head against his door, and willed her heartbeat to stay even and calm. One more day of this, perhaps two, and surely—*surely*—he would start to recover.

The door to Tony's room opened. He had declared he couldn't

bear the sounds emerging from Sam's room so had retreated to his room to read. But here he was now, strolling down the corridor towards her with a smile on his face.

"How is the patient?" he asked, settling on the floor next to her. He was smoking a cigarette. Both he and Sweetie had taken up the habit again the moment Miss Zander had disappeared.

"Tearing himself to pieces," she replied, her voice cracking.

"But it's for the best. You said it was for the best."

"Yes. Once he's through it, he can recover. I'm glad for the snowstorm. I'm glad we're cut off from the world. He can't get out. He can hardly walk as it is, but the snow and the cold would stop him and he knows it."

"You'd be the only one of us who's glad we're cut off. Sweetie's climbing the walls."

"Sweetie needs to learn when to surrender to circumstances," she said with a sniff. "Picking on the waitress because of bad weather is very poor form."

Tony narrowed his eyes and blew out a stream of smoke. "You've become very defensive of that waitress. What's her name? Vera?"

"Violet."

"Do you fancy her for a sister-in-law after all?"

Tony was likely joking to try to lighten the mood, but Flora was too deep in a well to respond. "In a perfect world, Tony, Sam could marry Violet if he wanted. But we all know that isn't going to happen."

The quiet of the corridor was punctuated by more shouts from Sam. "Flora! Flora! Where are you? Make it stop! Make it stop!"

Flora's heart iced over. "Oh, this is such a horror," she cried.

Tony put his arm around her shoulder. "Come here," he said. "There, there. It will work out. You've said so yourself enough times."

She shrugged him off—he reeked of cigarette smoke—and called back through the door, "I'm right outside. You'll be fine soon."

Sam started thumping on the door from the other side. "Let me out. He's in here with me. He's in here with me now. Let me out."

Flora scrambled to her feet. Tony looked at her, puzzled.

"He's hallucinating," she told him, before opening the door a crack and looking in on Sam's pale face, his haunted eyes. "It's not locked, Sam," she said. "I haven't locked you in. I'd never lock you in." In fact, she had thought about it, but his door could easily be unlocked from the inside.

"He's here," he hissed. "Get Violet. Violet makes him go away."

"Violet's busy. Do you want me to come in?"

He wrenched open the door. He was wearing nothing but a singlet. Below the waist he was completely naked, and as unashamed as a child. "In the corner," he said to Flora in a low voice. "Can you see him?"

"I can't see anyone, Sam. It's probably just a shadow. Do you want me to get you a lamp to put in the corner?" As soon as she said it she became afraid he'd upend it and set fire to his room.

"A lamp's not going to help."

"Where are your clothes?" she asked.

"My clothes? There's a *ghost* in my room, waiting to take me with him to meet death, and you care about where my clothes are! Here!" He marched across the room and threw a pile of clothes at her. They were filthy and the stench of them was unbearable. It seemed he'd soiled every pair of trousers he owned. "Enjoy them!" he shouted, before pushing her out and closing the door again.

Tony eyed her and the clothes. "What are you going to do with those?"

"Come to the bathroom with me. I'll soak them in the bath."

"Just get one of the staff to do it."

"This is too private." She headed down the corridor to the bathroom—the bathroom in which the unfortunate man had died, the man who was haunting Sam. She had Tony check that nobody was in it—it was the men's bathroom, after all—and went in to fill the tub and leave the clothes in it. Then she washed her hands as thoroughly as she could and leaned back on the sink. Tony stood in the doorway.

"At least this way, your father will be happy," he said. "The visit to the hotel will have cured Sam of his addiction."

"His 'health problems,'" Flora said. "Father never called it an addiction."

"But he knew?"

"It's hard to say. But yes, when all of this is over and we return home, Father will be pleased."

"Pleased with you?"

She laughed bitterly. "In that he's not overtly *dis*pleased, I imagine. He won't cut me out of his will, if that's what you mean."

"It's not what I meant."

Something about the current awful circumstances, the way the isolation had robbed them of civility, prompted her to say, "Would you still have married me? If he'd cut me off?"

"I would," Tony said without hesitation.

"Why?"

"Do you want me to tell you I'm crazy for you? That you're irresistible and you make the heavens bright?"

"I want you to tell me the truth."

He shrugged. Smiled. "A man needs a wife. He needs a woman with a good name and a good heart, somebody who will stand by him and not fuss and carry on. You have a strong moral compass, Florrie. You know what to do. You will be a good wife, and for that I love you."

Another cry rose from Sam's room, and Flora pushed past Tony to hurry back. Sweetie emerged from his room at the far end of the corridor and called out gruffly, "Can you not make him quiet?"

"He's very ill," she protested. "Have a little pity."

"Pity is for women and weaklings," he retorted, and slammed his door shut.

She looked at Tony meaningfully.

"I'll talk to him," Tony said. "He's frustrated, that's all. We all are, cooped up in here."

"Have a little pity, that's all I ask," she said again, quietly, indicating Sam's room and the groans emanating from within. "He's my baby brother."

Violet was crazed from lack of sleep. She'd been up all night in her room with Sam. He'd only left when he heard Flora in the bathroom that morning. Violet had then slept for an hour before being roused by Cook, who told her he was now unwell and that meant Violet had to make and serve breakfast single-handedly.

Clive was weak, but he rose to help her and then went straight back to bed. Miss Zander was alarmingly pale but determined that this would be her last day in bed. At her request, Violet told the guests at breakfast that the hotel was officially non-operational. She would do her best to make biscuits and sandwiches that she would leave in the kitchen for them, but that for the next twenty-four hours they could expect no more than that of her.

Lord Powell and Sweetie shouted her down, but she simply told them, as Miss Zander had instructed, that there would be no charge for staying here this week. "Might I remind you," she said, indicating the falling rain outside the window, "you are free to walk to the village in the hopes of finding a different place to stay." Miss Zander had definitely *not* told her to say that, but she enjoyed the look on the men's faces as they understood that all the shouting in the world would not improve their situation.

After breakfast Violet tried to check in on Sam, but once again Flora was sitting outside his door like a particularly zealous guard dog. Violet tried to keep a lid on her anxiety as she made biscuits and bread in the kitchen, the wood-burning stove keeping the cold at bay. But her mind returned repeatedly to Sam, to the grotesque dance the spasms made him perform, and to her own certainty that she would find something to help him.

She would need different clothes. Her fashionable winter boots would not be warm enough or dry enough out in the snow. Her destination was about two miles away, and she estimated the snow would be thigh deep. She'd need a walking stick of some kind. A waterproof coat. Her plans whirled around her head as she mixed and kneaded and baked and left the food in the kitchen for the guests to help themselves.

Then she put on her warmest clothes, wrapped all her scarfs around her, pulled on gloves and a hat, and headed out the kitchen door to Clive's workshop.

The snow was ankle deep in some places, thigh deep in others. It seemed to take her an age to trudge across, and she began to doubt very much that she could get to Malley's house. What if she did? He likely wasn't there, and even if he was he might not have any opium for Sam.

She considered turning back but then she remembered Sam begging for death, convinced he would die of the pain. She believed him. He already smelled like death. His eyes had already dimmed. She wouldn't be like Flora, doing nothing more than sitting and watching as he slowly died. The thought galvanized her, and she pushed herself through the snow until she arrived at the workshop.

Miss Zander had given her the keys to everything now that Cook was ill in bed, and she unlocked the door and pushed it open. A mound of snow fell in as she did so, and she stepped over it and into the workshop, her eyes scanning the room. She knew she'd seen it somewhere . . . ah, yes. With the fishing equipment. A pair of water-proof overalls, and scuffed Wellington boots. She shrugged out of her coat and pulled them down from the hanger.

Sitting on the wooden floor, Violet unlaced her own boots—now wet and cold—and pulled on the overalls. Her skirt rode up, and she tucked it awkwardly into the legs, then pulled the bib of the overall up and fastened it. It gaped. She pulled her coat back on and fastened it as tightly as she could. Then she slid her feet into the Wellington boots. They swam on her, so she removed the boots and put on the two spare pairs of men's socks she'd found in the laundry. Once her feet were padded the boots were still far too big, but they would have to do. She pulled the overall legs down over the boots and tied them tightly at the ankles. Then she grasped a broom from the stand and prised off its head.

Using the handle as a walking stick, she took her first few steps out into the snow.

She waded away from the workshop, away from the hotel. She couldn't see where the roads were, so she looked out for other land-marks. Trees, street signs, the train station. Her thighs began to ache while the hotel was still in sight behind her. The cold penetrated even the waterproof overalls, and her feet chafed in the boots. Still she pushed on, lifting her feet through heavy snow, pushing herself forward while her hips groaned and her knees burned, hoping against hope that she was going the right way. Sometimes she would come to a short stretch where the snow was only up to her knees, giving her some respite. In places, though, it was almost up to her waist, and she leaned heavily on the broomstick to drag herself through. A light rain started then stopped again, but she barely noticed. Teeth gritted, she pushed on, towards the only thing that could make Sam feel better.

There was nobody at the train station. Nobody moving around outside the small houses that lined the street.

The last time she'd come to Malley's house with Sam, it had taken a little over ten minutes. This time, it was an hour and a half before his house was in sight. Her heart was thundering and her lungs bursting from the effort. But she recognized the house easily enough. The long couch was still on the veranda, and she hoped this meant that Malley was home.

She gratefully shook herself free of the snow as she stepped up on the veranda, taking a moment to catch her breath before knocking hard.

She waited. Her breath made fog. The cold silence spun out.

She knocked again. Nothing.

A loud meow gave her a start. She looked around and saw a ginger cat padding around the veranda. She crouched. "Hello, Puss. You must be hungry." Then she spotted several mouse skeletons under the couch and decided perhaps Puss was not hungry at all. Violet eased herself onto the couch and put her head in her hands. She hadn't come all this way to leave empty handed. She'd hoped for it to be easy, but nothing about this expedition was easy. She lifted her head. All that mattered was Sam. She knew what she had to do next.

She stood and walked to the corner of the veranda, where a lamp stood. Its base was heavy brass. She loosened the glass bowl and took the base to the door. With all her might, she slammed the lamp base down onto the door handle. It made an enormous crack that seemed to echo off every snowflake piled around her. She waited, her heart thudding, for somebody to notice. To come out and call to her.

Nobody did.

She lifted the base and cracked the handle again. This time it came loose. One more blow and it was off, clanging to the floor and narrowly missing her foot.

She kicked the door gently, and it swung in. The house smelled musty and damp, as though it had been locked up for a year, not a week. Deep inside was the faint smell of something rotting. It was silent inside but for the tick of a clock on the mantelpiece.

The night she'd been here with Sam, Malley had retreated to a back room for opium, so Violet went through into a lightless corridor with a threadbare runner, which led off to two small rooms and a bathroom.

She had no idea where to start looking. The bedroom was filthy, with clothes strewn about and a strong smell of cat urine. The curtains were closed, faded to a color between beige and gray. She opened them, and dust floated in the weak daylight. A wardrobe sat unevenly on its legs, the door hanging ajar. Violet opened it and looked inside. More clothes, balled in the bottom. Empty hangers. She searched through the clothes—they all looked like Chinese pajamas—but found nothing.

She searched the scarred dresser next, but again without success, so she moved to the next room.

This room looked promising. Collections of the kind of things Sam used for smoking opium were stored in drawers and cupboards. Trays and lamps and pipes and tweezers and matches. But no jars. She was aware time was ticking on, and she still had to manage the long walk back. Miss Zander would be furious. Violet was the last able-bodied employee, and she'd already been gone nearly two hours. Her hands became desperate, too hasty, rifling through drawers and throwing things out of the way in frustration.

Nothing. Nothing. Nothing.

What a mistake it had been to come here. She stalked into the hallway in her too-big Wellingtons, nearly in tears contemplating the long walk back, the possibility that Sam would die because she couldn't find the drugs he needed. Yes, he had to come off them one day, but slowly and gently with a doctor on hand, when his body wouldn't shake to pieces and send him to an early grave.

The bathroom. It was the only back room she hadn't checked.

A smell of mold. Hair in the sink. A cabinet by the bath. She opened it. Bottles, dozens of bottles. She reached for them, saw again and again that they were empty. Then she saw something she recognized: a green leather pouch. That night they had come to Malley's, he had given Sam something from that pouch, and Sam had immediately been cured.

She pulled it out, unfolded it. Medical things inside. A small, half-full bottle.

"Oh, thank God," she breathed as she refolded the pouch and tucked it inside her overalls. Her body protested the idea of heading out into the frigid world again, but now she had Sam's cure, she had to hurry.

Flora was guarding his door still. Violet could have screamed with frustration. Her blood was icy from the long trudge back through snow. Her hair was damp from the drizzle, and her heart was still thudding from exertion. Flora glanced up as Violet came to the top of the stairs, but Violet backed away quickly before she was spotted. She returned to the kitchen to wait, trying to keep busy peeling and washing vegetables and baking more bread. All the meat had run out and they were down to their last dozen eggs. She had no idea what to offer the guests for dinner, so she made cucumber-and-watercress sandwiches, all the while waiting for night, when Flora would sleep and Violet could get to Sam.

She didn't have to wait for night. At six o'clock, Tony came to the kitchen door and asked about dinner.

"This is all we have," she said, indicating the plate of sandwiches.

"There are five of us for dinner," he said. "That will do. Make us tea to go with it."

They were down for dinner—that meant Flora had left Sam's door. Violet boiled the kettle and served the tea and sandwiches in the dining room, then ran for the stairs.

She knocked quickly at Sam's door.

"Go away," he said weakly.

"It's Violet," she called.

He opened the door. "Violet? You've come! Why didn't you come before?"

"Your sister wouldn't let me see you."

He collapsed back onto his bed. "I'm as weak as a baby. I'm in so much pain."

"We don't have much time," she said quickly. "Flora will be back as soon as she's eaten. But Sam, I've been to Malley's."

He sat up, his whole body tense. "Was he there?"

"No, but I found this. Do you remember?" She held up the green pouch.

He snatched it from her hands. "Violet. Violet. My love. My redeemer." He kissed her, and his mouth tasted sour. "You went out in the snow for this?"

She nodded proudly, then started when she heard footsteps on the stairs. "I have to go. Do you know what to do?"

"I think I remember. Ah, I feel better already, just knowing there's an end to it. Thank God. There's an end to it. Quick. Go. I'll come to see you in your room tonight."

"I can't wait to see you well again." Then she could finally tell him about the baby.

"You saved me," he said.

"I love you."

"And I love you. I always will."

Violet exited the room and hastened to the stairs so she wouldn't be found near Sam's room. But it wasn't Flora coming up: it was Clive.

"Ah, there you are," he said.

"You're up and about."

"I feel a lot better."

"You still don't look well. One more night in bed, eh? There are sandwiches in the kitchen. I'll bring a tray of them and some tea down to your room." She had a spring in her step as they returned down the stairs together. Sam would be better soon. Just for now, nothing could trouble her.

Flora's stomach was still growling after the light dinner. She had skipped lunch and had rather hoped for something cooked and filling. But she wouldn't complain, not to Tony and certainly not to Sweetie, who accompanied her back upstairs to the men's floor. Through Violet, Miss Zander had sent assurances that this hardship wouldn't last much longer. Besides, Sam hadn't eaten for days and was in far greater distress than she was.

"So, you're going to sit out here all night, are you?" Tony asked.

Flora listened at the door. It was quiet. "Perhaps I won't need to. It sounds like he's finally sleeping."

"He'll start groaning again soon enough, no doubt," Sweetie said. "Probably right when I'm trying to get to sleep." He stalked off towards his room and closed the door hard behind him.

Flora asked Tony to listen by the door while she went to bathe and then dress in her nightgown and robe. She returned twenty minutes later to find Tony sitting on the floor, his head against the door, his eyes closed.

"Has he stirred?" she asked.

"No. That's a good sign, isn't it, that he's quiet?"

"I think so. Maybe it means the worst is over. It's been three days. The other times he's tried, he's lasted only one or two. I love the thought that he's sleeping. Now perhaps I'll get some sleep, too. What a horrible few days we've had."

Tony touched her hand. "I'm glad it's over, too. Do you think he'll stay off it now?"

"It's to be hoped. He can be very pigheaded, but surely he won't want to go through such awful withdrawing pains again." She smiled at Tony. "You don't mind, do you? That your future brother-in-law is an opium addict?"

He shrugged. "Every family has a black sheep."

She yawned. "I think I'll have an early night. Should I look in on him?"

"Better to let him rest, maybe."

"I can be very quiet."

Tony climbed to his feet. "Go on, then."

She cracked open the door as quietly as she could. The room was dark, so she waited a few moments for her eyes to adjust. She could see Sam on the bed, the dark splash of his hair against the pillow, his body sprawled on top of the covers.

Something was wrong. Her heart knew it before her head did. Her pulse quickened, but she wasn't sure why. Then she listened. Really listened.

He was far too quiet. Too still.

"Sam," she said loudly, imagining that it would wake him, and she wouldn't care because that would simply mean that he was breathing but she couldn't hear it over her own thundering pulse. "Sam!" she shouted, kneeling at his side and shaking him. Tony came blustering in with the hurricane lamp, and she could see Sam properly then, spread on the bed in a pose of languor, free from the torment of his withdrawal at last.

With skin as cold as a stone.

CHAPTER TWENTY-THREE

2014

I was stepping out of the shower, getting ready for a morning shift, when the phone rang.

For once, I didn't assume it was my mother and groan. For once, I ran, towel loosely held over my wet body, trailing damp footprints behind me. Because Tomas was back today.

"Hello?" I said breathlessly, feeling water drip down my neck.

"I've just landed in Sydney," he said.

"We're in the same country," I replied. "That feels nice. I'm working until three."

"I'll come by the café at three, then." A moment of silence, then, "I can't wait to see you. I missed you."

"Same," I said, relieved. Given that most of our relationship had been played out in late-night, long-distance phone calls and text messages, I wasn't sure how much of a claim I had on him, whether it was acceptable to confess to missing somebody after two dates.

The day crawled. I watched the clock, and it didn't seem to move. Work was beset by grumpy customers, and a blocked steam nozzle on the coffee machine meant Penny and I had to spend a large portion of the day tripping over workmen and apologizing for slow coffees.

But then the lunch trade started to thin out, and right on three the front door opened, letting in the cool air from outside. Tomas stood there.

My heart lifted into my throat. "Hi," I said, from across the café.

Penny gave me a little push in the back. "Off you go."

I untied my apron and stuffed it in my bag, let my hair out of the tight ponytail I wore it in for work, and crossed the floor to meet him.

We stood, six awkward inches apart, and he said, "It's nice to see you."

"Yes," I said. What was the protocol? I had no idea.

He grasped my hand and said, "Come with me."

I waved to Penny, who gave me two thumbs up, and followed Tomas outside.

"I've missed the view," he said. "Can we go over to the deck?"

"Sure."

We crossed the road, still hand in hand. The afternoon sun was behind us, making our shadows long. We waited for a busload of tourists to exit the car park and then we stepped onto the large wooden viewing platform that had been built out of the escarpment, affording a full, magnificent view of the mountains and valleys under shifting cloud shadows.

"Ah, that's beautiful," he said, finally releasing my hand.

"More beautiful than Copenhagen?" I still held out hope that he'd want to stay in Australia.

"There are places in Denmark even more beautiful," he replied with a twinkle in his eye, and then he seized me in a hug, and I surrendered to it gratefully. The smell of him, his heat and his hard body, were intoxicating. I turned my face up for a kiss, and he pressed his mouth against mine. A breeze whipped up, sent dry leaves scuttling over the wooden boards. Goose bumps stood out on my arms.

Tomas let me go. "Let's sit down and talk," he said. "There's a lot to talk about."

I folded myself up on the bench next to him, knees under my chin. "About our mystery? That letter from Eugenia Zander has me utterly baffled. If only I could get back into the hotel—"

But he was already shaking his head. "Sorry. I've been in to work today, and my visiting privileges for the west wing have officially been revoked."

"Ah. That's my fault, isn't it?"

"Technically, it's mine. I gave you the key and told you to go in. I'm sorry I got you in trouble."

"I'm sorry I got *you* in trouble."

He shrugged. "That kind of thing doesn't bother me. They pay me a lot of money and will continue to do so. The developer has simply said it's an occupational safety hazard, and so that's that. Until I start on the design, I'm not going back in." He touched my cheek softly. "Besides, what else could you find that would help?"

"Letters. Records. Anything that tells me what happened to Violet Armstrong. I need to know if she and Sam lived happily ever after."

"If she did, I doubt the hotel would have the records. In any case, that's not what I wanted to talk about."

I heard the serious note in his voice and shifted so I was looking directly at him. "Go on," I said, and his eyes became solemn and unhappy. That was the moment I was certain he was going to break it off with me, that he would tell me it was all too hard or that he was going back to his ex-wife. I told myself to sit there and listen and not interrupt, and maybe just treat it like an anthropological experiment: *this is what it feels like to be dumped*. It was new to me. All of it.

"I need to explain something to you about Sabrina and me. I expect it might have seemed unusual to you that I . . . went so far for a woman I divorced five years ago."

I shrugged. I didn't know what else to say or do.

He rubbed his chin with his palm. "I would have told you all this eventually. When we were a little more established. When we'd got to know each other better. But, Lauren, I really like you. I really see some kind of future with you, as mad as that sounds after a relationship built on text messages."

This was unexpected. Now I was utterly perplexed, and it must have shown on my face because he said, "I'm sorry. I'm not making sense and I need to get to the point. There is something significant about me that you don't know, and I am going to tell you now."

"Okay," I said, trying to look encouraging. The wind was in the eucalypts, making them shake and shiver above us. It would soon be too cold to be out. I wished I'd packed a cardigan when I'd left home this morning.

"Sabrina and I were married when we were twenty-two. We married because we . . . sort of had to."

For a second I didn't know what he meant, but then suddenly I understood. "Oh. She was pregnant?"

"Yes. In fact, we had a baby. We had a daughter." His face knotted, and I realized he was trying to stop himself from crying.

My whole body shivered with heat: he'd had a daughter, but he'd told me when we first met that he had no children. So that meant . . . "Oh, no," I said. "She died, didn't she?"

"She was just a little thing," he whispered. "Only a week short of her third birthday. Her name was Emilia. Emmy, we called her. She fell from a window at her creche. The cleaner hadn't locked it properly; the carer had a moment of inattention. It was a cascade of bad luck. Nobody's fault, really. We didn't blame anyone."

"I'm so, so sorry," I said, and I felt as though I had stepped into a vast ocean that I couldn't feel the bottom of. It was adulthood, a place where people had pain and histories and consequences. I reached for his hand and squeezed it tightly.

"When Emmy fell," he continued, "she was still breathing, her little heart still beating. Sabrina and I saw her at the hospital." He waved a dismissive hand. "You don't need me to tell you how distressing it is to see somebody you love like that. Little Emmy fought on, day after day, and not once, not for one second did Sabrina leave her side. She said, *I will be here until she wakes up or until she dies*, and she kept that vow. I was wild with grief. I could barely be persuaded to go to the hospital. I couldn't look at Emmy. She didn't look like my little girl. I stayed out late, I went to work as though nothing had happened. I quite literally lost my mind. For six days. Just six days. Then Emmy died." He shook his head, wiped away tears. "Fifteen years have passed, and it's still as fresh and as awful," he said.

"That's why you went to Sabrina," I said.

"Yes. I felt that somebody had to be there with her, until she woke up or until she died. Just as she had been for our daughter, when I couldn't be."

"I can't even imagine what such a loss feels like," I said.

"Much like your loss," he said. "Only with a little dash of helplessness and self-blame." He gave a wry smile.

"So, after that, your marriage couldn't survive?"

"Sabrina and I grieved very differently. I cried and raged. She tried to make sense of it, as though if she could make sense of it, she wouldn't have to feel it. She went down a path I couldn't follow. Spiritualists and crazy religions and gurus who took her money and gave her false hopes that she could contact Emmy on the other side. We were still young, really. We didn't make it." He spread his hands apart. "We didn't make it."

"I'm sorry."

"Life is like this, Lauren. Maybe you haven't realized yet because you have been so folded away within your family, with one inevitable outcome that took all your focus. But it's a big mess out here. A big, unpredictable mess, and there's no telling what will happen next." He shook his head. "Sabrina woke up, about fifteen minutes before I left to come home. I got to speak to her. She couldn't talk, but I could tell by looking in her eyes that she knew why I was there. She'll be fine."

"I'm glad."

He smiled. "It feels good to have that off my chest."

"Tomas, you can tell me anything."

He squeezed my hand, and his eyes went to the view. I watched him for a while. I had no idea what I was supposed to do or say after such a big revelation, but I remember after Adam died wanting people just to sit with me, not ask questions or offer comfort. Just sit with me and be another beating heart close by. So I did that.

I sat beside him and let my heart beat.

As the afternoon moved towards evening, jet lag began to get the better of Tomas, and he needed to go home, so I went home, too. It was very quiet, and I had a lot to think about. Tomas's message about the unpredictability of the world ran so opposite to my mother's lifelong teachings that it almost made me breathless. I had lived a life on a one-train track: keep Adam alive for as long as you can. While I understood why Mum wanted us all to think that way, it meant I had fallen into line and stopped looking sideways. I had missed a lot. Adam had missed more. Adam had missed something in particular, something associated with the Blue Mountains. And Anton Fournier knew what it was. If only I could convince him to tell me.

*   *   *

Terri-Anne Dewhurst called me later that evening to tell me she'd received the letters and to express her thanks again.

"You were right, they really are a bit saucy," she said.

"There's certainly a lot of passion there. Look, after we last spoke I found a copy of a letter the hotel manageress wrote to your great-grandmother. Can I read it to you?"

"Of course."

I read her the letter, making sure I paused for dramatic emphasis on the part about everyone involved never speaking of it again. But Terri-Anne didn't need dramatic emphasis to get excited.

"A cover-up!" she cried. "How thrilling!"

"Any ideas?" I said, falling onto the couch and lying back to look at the ceiling. The waistband of my pajamas had lost its elastic and hung down unflatteringly. I was glad Tomas was home in bed sleeping off jet lag.

"No, but I'll bet Grandma knew and never said a word. She was like that."

"I keep wondering if it was as simple as Sam and Violet running off together."

"But that's not tragic," Terri-Anne said. "She specified 'tragic events.'"

"And for your family at that time, it wouldn't be tragic if Sam had run away with a waitress?"

She paused for a while, thinking. Then she said, confidently, "No. Tragedy had a specific meaning back then, not like now when news reporters use it for everything. It meant something awful—death, ruin. I think somebody died."

"Violet?"

"Maybe."

"There's nothing more I can do at this end," I said. "I kind of got in trouble, sneaking around in the hotel."

"Leave it with me. I have lots of contacts and lots of resources. I'll see if I can find out anything about Violet Armstrong: where she was born, what became of her. Perhaps if I can find Violet, I can find Sam."

"Let me know the minute you find anything interesting," I said. "I'm invested."

"I will," she said. "I promise."

Mrs. Tait's operation was the following morning, and I phoned the hospital after the café's lunch rush and was told she was awake and "resting."

After work I walked to the flower stand outside the grocery store to pick up a gift to take to Lizzie. As I approached, I noticed two whippets tied up to a yellow bicycle rack out the front. Anton Fournier's dogs.

I stopped and crouched to pat them. They went mad with happiness, wagging their tails and licking my hands. They were obviously spoiled and happy, which was the sign of a good-hearted owner. If Anton was good-hearted, surely he would talk to me. Eventually.

I peered through the shop door, but I couldn't see Anton. I stood, made still by indecision until a man exited the shop and bent to untie the dogs—and it wasn't Anton.

"They're lovely dogs," I said, trying to hide my curiosity as I looked him over. Lizzie had mentioned a "young fellow" who house-sat for Anton, but I had presumed he was younger, perhaps a teenager, whereas this man was about my age, with short, neat hair and a soft face.

"They are," he said with a smile. "They like you."

"I've met them before," I said.

He raised an eyebrow. "Oh, really?"

I took a deep breath and offered him my hand. "My name's Lauren. Anton kicked me off his front porch last week."

The man smiled, took my hand, and shook it warmly. "I'm Peyton. I heard all about it."

His smile made me relax enough to ask, "Do you know why he hates me so much?"

He released my hand and went back to untying the dogs. "I know everything. I know all about Adam, about the past. The whole story. But it's not for me to tell you."

"Anton won't."

"Of course he will. In his own time. That's what Anton's like."

"Is there anything I can do?"

Peyton wrapped a dog leash around each wrist. Romeo and Juliet strained against him, ready to get going. "The letter you sent had a strong impact," he said. "He's considering it."

"Really? Can you tell him you saw me? That I begged you? Because I swear, I don't know a thing. I have no idea what happened between Adam and Anton and my family, but I really, *really* want to know. Will begging help?"

He smiled again. He had a lovely smile, so warm and relaxed. "I will tell him you begged, but I don't know if it will help him make up his mind quicker. He doesn't like being told what to do. Now, I'd better get these dogs home before they pull my arms out of my sockets."

"Thanks," I said.

"Bye." He turned and began to walk away from me, then stopped and looked back. "He *will* talk to you eventually. Don't worry."

"How do you know?"

"Because you're Adam's sister. That means more to him than you can imagine."

I watched him go. Other people emerged from the shop, looked me over, and went on their way. I must have been standing there a long time. Then I selected a bunch of flowers for Lizzie and went inside to pay for them.

I arrived at the hospital just as the afternoon was turning towards evening. Lizzie's daughter Genevieve was sitting in a pink chair by Lizzie's bed, worrying the edge of her thumbnail with her teeth. Lizzie was half reclined, looking dozy and blissed out.

"Hi," I said.

Genevieve looked up. "Pain meds," she said, indicating Lizzie. "She's a bit sleepy and away with the fairies."

"Ah. Hello, Lizzie," I said, leaning over to kiss Lizzie's powdery cheek. "I brought you flowers."

"Put them in some water," she said in a thick voice. "Genevieve, get the nurse to put them in water. They'll die otherwise. I don't want them to die. Young Lauren has brought them for me."

"Don't worry, Mum," Genevieve said, taking the flowers and laying them on the bedside table. "I'll ask the very next nurse who comes in."

"The operation all went well?" I asked Genevieve. She was one of those striking women in her late forties who looked good in silk scarves. I had never been able to wear a silk scarf without looking as though I was drowning.

"She came through it brilliantly. She's in such good health for her age. We're all so pleased."

"Are you talking about me?" Lizzie said, but her eyes were closed.

Genevieve shrugged. "She's not really with it."

"I might go, then."

"Would you mind waiting ten minutes? I'm dying for a coffee, or what passes for coffee at the cafeteria here. I'll get a takeaway and come right back."

"Sure," I said.

"Thanks." Genevieve hurried off, and I took her place in the pink chair, leaning across to touch Lizzie's hand.

"I'm so glad you're okay, Lizzie," I said.

"Life in the old bird yet. Not like my mother. She lay down like this, and she didn't get up," she slurred, then fell quiet. I sat with her, listening to her breathe, assuming she had fallen asleep, but then she suddenly started talking again. "Genevieve, I have to tell you something."

"I'm not Genevieve, I'm Lauren," I said.

But she paid no attention. "Your granddad: he wasn't my real father. It kills me. I wish she'd never said anything."

"Who said—" I started, then stopped when I realized the message wasn't for me. "Lizzie, it's not Genevieve. It's Lauren. Genevieve has gone to get a coffee, and she'll be back in a minute, so you can tell her then."

Lizzie cracked open one eye and looked at me. "Lauren. You're a good girl."

"Thanks."

"Get those flowers in water."

"I will."

She fell silent again, and this time tuneful snores told me she'd fallen asleep. *He wasn't my real father. It kills me.* Poor Lizzie. She'd always spoken so fondly of her father. I promised myself, though, that this time I wouldn't interfere. Lizzie was old and deserved privacy.

Genevieve returned soon after. The smell of cigarette smoke told me she'd gone for more than a coffee.

"Doesn't she know you smoke?" I asked.

She shook her head. "She'd be so disappointed."

"But *she* used to smoke."

"Did she?"

I put up my palms. "I've said too much. Not my place to share family secrets. While you were gone, she thought I was you and tried to tell me something about your granddad."

"Oh, yes. We already know. On her deathbed, Grandma confessed to Mum that Granddad was not her biological father. I'm afraid she took it very badly and has never really got over it. She doted on Granddad. She told us as though it was a big secret, something to be ashamed of. None of us know who the 'real' father was. Of course we don't mind. Funny that she should bring it up now."

"Well, if it's something she'd rather keep secret, I can pretend I never heard anything."

"Thanks. That would mean a lot."

I left the hospital and headed out into the cool glow of the late afternoon, hoping Tomas wouldn't be too tired for company tonight.

CHAPTER TWENTY-FOUR

Work was crazy-busy the next morning. A busload of Romanian tourists turned up unannounced at ten o'clock, and Penny and I ran ourselves ragged making coffee and toasting banana bread for them. In the middle of it all I heard my phone ring and I knew it was my mother, and I suddenly felt unspeakably angry with her.

Always. Ringing. Me.

I ignored it and made a promise to myself that I would tell her that it was no longer okay for her to call me all the time. I had a life, and she was interfering with it.

When I checked my phone in a quiet moment I saw that it hadn't been her at all. It was a number I didn't recognize, and the caller had left a message. I pressed it to my ear to listen.

"Lauren," a smooth voice said. "It's Anton Fournier. I'm heading off to Hong Kong the day after tomorrow, but if you can be at my house at eleven o'clock tomorrow, I will talk to you. I hope to see you then."

Eleven o'clock. I was rostered to work. I didn't want to call him back and try to bargain on the time in case he got spooked and told me the deal was off. So, instead I went to Penny and begged.

"Please, please, please can I leave at ten thirty tomorrow? I'll be back at twelve or twelve thirty at the latest."

"But we've been so busy. What if we get more tourists?"

"I don't know what to say. A man who holds the key to a family secret has offered to meet with me, and I don't think the appointment's negotiable."

"Is this Anton Fournier?"

I nodded.

"Do it," she said. "I'll cover for you. It can't possibly be worse than today."

I knew one last thing I had to do before I went to see Anton. I had to give my mother a final chance to tell me her version of what had happened. On my break, I slipped outside and sat on a bench looking up at the hotel, and called her.

"Mum, it's me," I said.

"Is everything—"

"Everything's okay," I said quickly. "But I need to tell you something."

"Yes?" she said slowly, warily.

"I'm meeting Anton Fournier tomorrow."

"The man who harassed you? Are you out of your mind?"

"He didn't harass me. If anything, I harassed him. He had to kick me off his property. Last chance, Mum. Tell me what happened."

"I don't know what you're talking about." Then her voice changed, became plaintive. "If you loved me, you wouldn't go. You wouldn't meet with him."

I exhaled loudly and turned my eyes up to the rooms in the hotel, the old west wing. In there, something happened many, many years ago, and Flora Honeychurch-Black had refused to talk about it. Her granddaughter Terri-Anne was still trying to figure it all out. Lizzie's mother had revealed her daughter's paternity on her deathbed, and Lizzie still carried the pain and shame of it. Family secrets had such power, and I wasn't going to let Mum bury ours. A flock of birds arrowed overhead, and I watched them, waiting to see if Mum would relent.

"I always did what was best for you and Adam," she said at last.

"What *you thought* was best," I said.

"You're fine, aren't you?" Her voice was defensive now.

"I don't know. Am I? I'm nearly thirty-one and I've never had sex and I can't drive a car. Is that fine?"

A hot silence. She was angry.

"Mum?" I said, trying to sound conciliatory.

"Meet with him, then. See if I care," she snapped, then the line went dead.

I pocketed my phone, taking big gulps of the fresh mountain air. The guilt wouldn't work this time. I was determined to know the truth.

Tomas, recovered from jet lag, was at my door at seven. I'd cleaned the flat, baked a pie (steak and mushroom), lit a scented candle, dressed in a pretty new cotton blouse and my best jeans, and brushed my teeth two or maybe three times (in my anxiety, I'd lost track). Because this was it, this was the big one: our third date.

"Come in," I said, trying to sound worldly rather than freaked out. We'd had such an odd start to our relationship, and I wanted very badly for everything to go well from now on.

He kissed my cheek and handed me a bottle of wine. "Don't drink it all at once," he said with a little smile.

"Very funny," I replied, following him in and putting the wine on the kitchen bench. "You look rested." He looked very fine indeed, in dark gray trousers and a chambray shirt.

"I feel fine. I functioned normally at work today, which is always a good thing."

"Any more news on the west wing?"

He shook his head. "There won't be until next January. It's only two months before I'm done with the east wing and they send me home for the year."

My mood deflated. He had warned me, but I'd conveniently forgotten. I smiled brightly to cover it up. "Glass of wine?"

"Good idea."

We both reached for the bottle at the same time, and managed to bump it off the bench and onto the kitchen floor. With a smash, red wine began to spread across the tiles.

"I'm so sorry!" he exclaimed, dashing to the sink for a cloth.

I crouched and began to pick up the pieces of broken glass. "Gosh, what a mess," I said.

"Here, let me help."

As he crouched next to me, our knees bumped.

And something happened. I can't explain it, but with that small physical touch, a flame lit inside me. I was such a stranger to desire, that now it hit me I almost didn't recognize it. I experienced it first as apprehension: my go-to emotion. But he had felt it, too, and he was looking at me intently. The cloth was in his hand, the broken bottle was in mine.

Then, with quiet agreement, we both dropped those things and reached for each other. His fingers moved to my cheek, pulling me towards him, kissing me as we stood and then fumbled our way over the spilled wine and out of the kitchen.

We fell onto the couch together, me on top of him, lips locked. I could hardly breathe, but I didn't care. His mouth, his teeth, his tongue—I explored them all with passionate abandon.

My hands moved to his chest, and I began to unbutton his shirt. That's when he gently pushed me back and met my gaze. "Are you sure?" he said quietly.

"I am *so* sure."

"I know it's your first time. I don't mind if you want to wait a bit longer."

"I'm thirty. How much longer should I wait?" I laughed.

He pulled me down into his warm arms. The steak-and-mushroom pie ended up burned, but neither of us really minded.

The next morning, I woke up before Tomas and propped myself up on my elbow, watching him sleep. I had never woken up next to somebody before. My eyes pricked, like I might cry. It seemed such a simple thing to have missed out on for so long.

As though he sensed I was watching him, he began to stir. His eyelids flickered and then opened, and he saw me looking at him. As recognition and remembrance dawned, tenderness—vulnerability—came over his expression, and it induced in me a feeling of falling. Falling somewhere warm and soft.

"I love you," he said, in a croaky morning voice.

"I love you, too," I replied.

I stood outside Anton Fournier's gate ten minutes early. I didn't want to go in and knock in case it annoyed him that I had arrived before our agreed time, so I hung about on the footpath under the shade of an oak tree. I measured my heart rate. A hundred beats per minute. Anxiety had me in its prickly grasp.

I took a few deep breaths, checked my watch again. Only two minutes had passed.

"Are you going to come in?"

I whirled around. Anton stood at the gate, his dogs by his side.

"I saw you from the house," he said, and he gave me half a smile.

"I didn't want to bother you if you weren't ready for me."

"Come in," he said. "I'll make us something to drink."

I followed him up the long front driveway. Romeo and Juliet sniffed me and then ran about before coming back and sniffing me again. We walked up the front stairs and through the open door.

"Oh, wow," was all I could think to say when I saw the inside of his house. The entire back wall was glass, and it gave an uninterrupted view of the valley.

"Yes, I love it," he said. He wore a loose cotton shirt, cotton pants with the cuffs turned up, and no shoes. "When a storm comes in, it's the best place in the world to be. Pity I travel so much."

"Somebody said you were a record producer."

"Nothing so exotic," he said, padding across to his open-plan kitchen. "Head of Asian marketing. I'm practically tone deaf." He switched on his kettle. "I don't drink anything caffeinated, I'm afraid. How about fruit tea?"

"I'm willing to try it."

He found a canister in the pantry and placed it on the marble island bench between us. The sound echoed through the living space, right up to the high ceiling. While he prepared the teapot, I gazed around. Art on the walls, mostly abstracts. Stylish, modern furniture. Bookshelves crammed with paperback thrillers.

"You look nothing like Adam," he said to me, studiously avoiding my eyes.

"No. He looks more like Mum."

His mouth pulled into a line, and I knew that it was my mother who had upset him. But then, I'd already guessed that.

"I mean *looked* like Mum," I corrected myself. "I still talk about him as though he's here."

"I can't believe he's gone. Your letter was beautiful."

"Thanks. It was from the heart."

The kettle began to whistle. "Please, make yourself comfortable.

Sit down. This needs a few minutes to brew." He filled the teapot and placed it on a tray with cups, a jar of honey, and slices of carrot cake. I chose to sit where I was sure spillage wouldn't stain—so, *not* the white couch—putting my back to the beautiful view. One of the dogs curled up on the floor at my feet.

"She likes you," he said, placing the tray on the coffee table between us. "That's a good sign."

"It is?"

"You could do worse than trust a dog's opinion of a person," he said. "I'm sorry I was rude the first time we met. I didn't know how involved you'd been in what happened."

"What *did* happen?"

He sat opposite, fearlessly on the white couch. "You're sure you want to know from me? You could just ask your parents."

"I tried that. Mum clammed up. At first she pretended she didn't know who you were."

He rolled his eyes. "Of course she did," he said.

"So, tell me. Everything. Please."

"Okay. Well, where to start . . ." He poured tea and handed me a cup. It tasted sublime; like hot strawberries with a twist of lime. "How well did you know Adam?" he asked.

"Really well."

"I mean . . . did you know anything about his love life?"

I shook my head. "Well, no. He didn't really have one after he got sick. I suppose he would have liked a girlfriend but—"

"No," he interrupted. "He wouldn't have."

I looked at him, puzzled. Then he put down his teacup and spread his hands apart. "Lauren, Adam was gay."

"He was?" Then it all fell into place. "Oh. You and he were . . ."

"In love, yes. Mad love. Teenage love, I suppose. We were so wrapped up in each other. It was one of the most beautiful times of my life. He was my soul mate." His face worked against tears. "He was a special, special lad. Good God, I still miss him."

I sat motionless, gobsmacked. I'd had no idea, not even the slightest inkling, that my brother was gay. How was that possible? I would never have judged him for it; why didn't he tell me?

But of course I knew why. My mother. My interfering, overly anxious mother.

"What did she do to you?" I asked.

"Your mother? Adam told her," he said. "She went ballistic. She told Adam it was a phase he was going through. She thought I had him under a spell of some kind. She said he'd never have a normal life if he stayed with me and that she just wanted things to be easy for him. She did everything in her power to convince Adam not to be gay." He shrugged. "Like trying to convince the tide not to come in. Your family cut off contact with him, and Adam was bereft. I told him to go and see them in person and sort it out with them. So he did. That was the last time I saw him." The pain in his voice was raw.

"He got sick."

"Yes, he got sick while he was down in Tasmania with you all. I phoned every day, but your mother wouldn't let me speak to him. She said she wouldn't even tell him I called and just to leave him alone. I wrote letters. I don't know what happened to those."

"She intercepted them," I said. "Back then, the mail service was shocking. We had it all diverted to the post office in the village, and Mum went in every day to pick it up. She never let anyone else do it."

"There. One mystery solved. Finally, I caught a plane to Hobart and I hired a car and I just showed up." He stopped for a moment, sipped his tea. The other dog hopped up on the couch near him, and Anton took a few seconds to pat his side, gather his breath. "Your father answered the door. He was in on it. Your mother came out. I tried shouting out for Adam, but I don't know if he heard. They told me he didn't want to see me, that he had to focus on getting well and I was making that hard on him, that I was not and never would be welcome in your family."

These were hard truths for me to hear. I was so disappointed in my parents, especially my father.

"I came home. I sent more letters, phoned less frequently. After a year, when I still hadn't heard a word from him, I started to think maybe they told the truth. Maybe he didn't want to see me. Maybe I was being a crazy stalker. So . . . I let him go."

"You let him go."

"Yeah." He sagged forward.

I could see it now: those first few years of Adam's illness, his sadness, his perpetual air of being lost, wasn't just about being sick. It was about being brokenhearted. "That is . . . really awful," I said.

"Yes. It is. But, please, don't see me as a tragic figure. I got on with life. I met Peyton; we have two spoiled dogs. It's Adam who's the tragic one. He probably thought I'd abandoned him when he got sick. It was the last thing I would have done. The very last thing. I wanted to be there. I wanted to nurse him. I wanted to hold him when he was frightened. I got to do none of those things, give him none of that comfort."

I let his words hang in the big echoing room. Outside, a cloud moved across the sun, temporarily dimming the room, then passed over. A beam of sunshine fell on the back of the dog at my feet. She stirred, then settled back to sleep.

"I'm sorry," I said. "I didn't know anything about it, and I might have been too young to change what happened. But I'm still sorry. For you. For Adam."

He twisted his lips into half a smile. "Believe it or not, that actually means a lot to me."

"If it's any consolation, my mother might have behaved just as badly if you'd been a girl."

"It's no consolation. And I think you're wrong."

I considered this. "Yeah. Maybe I am." Even though I hadn't been the one to stand between Adam and Anton, I still felt sickeningly guilty. "But you know what? I'm really glad Adam had you, even if it was for a short time. I'm glad he got to have a mad love affair. I'm glad he got to taste some of that kind of life. He never stopped thinking of you. He had a huge print of the Falls hanging on the wall of his bedroom. It was the first thing he saw when he woke up in the morning, the last thing he saw before he went to sleep at night."

This time a full smile came over Anton's face. He was incredibly handsome, just the kind of gorgeous creature my brother deserved. "That's lovely."

"You've got to remember," I continued, "towards the end, he was never sure if he would wake up. So, maybe you offered him comfort in other ways."

"I'd like to think that."

"Here," I said, reaching into my handbag to retrieve the photograph of the two of them. "You should have this."

He took it from me and gazed at it a long time, his eyes misting over. Then he looked up at me and said, "Will you talk to your mother and father about this?"

"My word, yes."

Mum didn't answer her phone, so poor Dad felt the full weight of my fury.

"You've got to understand," he protested, when I drew breath for a moment, "your mother thought it was for the best."

"And you? I never had you picked for a bigot."

"I'm not. I'm just . . . your mum is very persuasive. In a way she was right. It's hard to be different, and Adam had chosen maybe one of the most difficult ways to be different."

"He didn't choose, Dad. He was what he was. You and Mum, you broke two hearts. You denied two people happiness."

"We were just focused on keeping Adam alive."

"A life without love. It wasn't your call to make. How did you stop Adam from contacting Anton?"

There was a brief silence. Dad was probably battling with his conscience, with his fear of what Mum would say. Then he said, simply, "He asked us to call Anton every day. We said we had, and that Anton had decided his illness was too much trouble. We knew the relationship had only been short—less than a year. We thought it was kinder that way, for both of them. You'll forgive us, won't you?"

I sighed in exasperation. "I am so angry with you both, right now. Tell Mum not to call me for a while."

"Now, don't be cruel. You know how she worries."

"Tell her I lost my virginity on the third date. To a divorced man. Tell her I'm in love with him and there's nothing she can do to stop me." Then I hung up, my heart beating hard. I didn't feel as good as I thought I would after unleashing my anger. I just felt sad.

Tomas kept me busy. Work kept me busy. Anton and Peyton invited us over for dinner one night, and Tomas revealed himself to be a soft touch when it came to dogs. It was just one more reason to love him. Without the yoke of my mother's endless calls, I started to feel different. More me, somehow. I felt an incredible freedom, possibilities beckoning to me. Tomas talked of me coming to Denmark with him when he returned for six months, "just to see." It no longer seemed like an outlandish idea, something that only an irresponsible person would do. Why shouldn't I go to Denmark? Why shouldn't I go "just to see" if Tomas and I were meant to be together?

Eight days after her operation, Lizzie Tait came home. The last time I'd visited her in hospital, she'd been sure she'd have at least a further week to stay, so it was a surprise when she knocked on my door.

"Lizzie!" I cried, folding her in a hug. "You're back. How do you feel? Come in. Can I make you a cup of tea?"

"I've been back since last night," she said. "They finally let me go, and my children have headed off to their various destinations. No, I won't have a cup of tea. I'm going to enjoy my solitude. I just wanted to drop by and say thanks for visiting. It meant a lot to me."

"It was my pleasure," I said.

"Genevieve told me I got all mixed up one time, and talked to you as though you were her. Is that right?"

I chose my words carefully. "You were a bit high. It looked as though you were off with the fairies. I didn't pay much mind to what you said."

"Well, I'm sorry if I embarrassed you. I just—" She stopped, her eyes fixing on something over my shoulder in the kitchen. I turned to see what she was looking at. It was the sketch of Violet Armstrong, which I'd stuck to the fridge.

"Where did you . . ." She trailed off, pushing past me. She moved into the kitchen and stood, frozen to the spot, in front of the picture. Her face was pale, but I couldn't tell if that was from seeing the picture or from her stay in hospital.

"Are you all right?" I asked.

"Where did you get that?"

"It's a long story. Is everything okay? You look as though you've seen a ghost."

"That woman," she said, pointing at the portrait. "That's my mother."

Cold electricity ran through me. "Your mother?" And then realization dawned. "Oh, God, Lizzie. I know who your father is."

CHAPTER TWENTY-FIVE

1926

"Flora?" Tony moved closer with the lantern.

Reality warped. She stood in a house of mirrors. "He's so cold," she said.

"Oh my God," Tony said, then raced to the door, calling, "Sweetie! Sweetie! Get down here!"

"We need to get him somewhere warm," Flora said.

"No. Flora. He's—"

"The kitchen. That stove will still be burning. If we can just get him somewhere warm."

"Florrie. Florrie. He's dead."

"No, he's just cold." She put her ear to his chest and listened for a heartbeat, but her own pulse was deafening her.

Sweetie appeared at the door. "What's going on?" Then he saw the scene within and drew in his breath sharply.

Flora turned. Why were they not acting? Why were they standing around gasping? "I said, *Get him to the kitchen!*" she shrieked.

"It won't make any—"

"Please, Tony, please."

Tony looked at Sweetie, and Sweetie back at Tony, and at once they seemed to decide they would do this, if just to calm her down. Tony scooped Sam up in his arms and Sweetie grabbed his legs.

"Be gentle with him," Flora said, following them out of the room and downstairs. "He bruises easily."

Neither of the men said a word. Down the stairs, then along the corridor to the empty kitchen.

"Put him by the stove," Flora said, going to the woodpile and seizing an armful of extra logs. She opened the stove door and threw them in, watching her own hands move as though everything were normal, when she knew, deep down, that nothing was normal.

Sam lay on the stone floor in front of the stove. Tony and Sweetie stood back, arms folded. Flora kneeled next to Sam, framing his face in her hands. "Sam," she said. "Sam, you have to wake up now."

Nothing. But his warmth was coming back. Wasn't it? He was just cold, that was all. Cold and sleeping.

"Sam?" she said again, and her own voice frightened her because an edge of hysteria touched it. Beyond that edge was a spinning void that she couldn't allow herself to fall into. She gently slapped his face. "Please, Sam. Please."

Tony knelt next to her, took her hand, and placed it on Sam's ribs. She tried to pull her hand away, but he held it there hard. Moments passed in horrified silence.

Sam's chest wasn't moving. No breaths in or out.

"He's not breathing," Flora said.

"He's dead," Tony replied.

"No, he's just not—"

"Yes. Yes, Flora. He's dead."

Flora pulled her hand from Tony's grasp and fell on Sam, an animal howl escaping her lungs. He seemed so small beneath her, like a child. She could barely cry, could only say, "No, no, no," over and over. Behind her, Tony and Sweetie lit cigarettes and discussed what to do next, as dispassionately as if it were a business deal. They kept saying "the body" and Flora thought this might make her scream and never stop. Speaking in whispers that were not quiet enough, as men did, they said it over and over. "We can't have *the body* simply lying in a room here." "If we put *the body* in the bathing pool, then it might appear to be a drowning." "But when they examine *the body* they'll find no water in the lungs." And so on. All the while Flora, locked in the grim prison of her mind, unable to comprehend anything since she discovered the poor, pale remains, shivered against the icy breeze that licked through the open door and stalked the tall eucalypts that lined the dark valley.

"If the old man gets wind of this," Tony said, punctuating his observation with a short puff of his cigarette, "he'll slam that bank vault shut and Flora here won't get a thing."

She wanted to say she didn't care about the money, that death had never seemed so vast and present and final than in this moment, standing by the remains of a real person who only yesterday breathed and cried. Her lips moved, but no sound emerged.

"What do you want to do, Florrie?" Sweetie asked her.

"No point speaking to her," Tony said, shaking his head in the low light of the hurricane lamp. "She's going to need a few belts of whiskey to snap her out of it. Look, the only thing we're certain about is that people can't know. It must seem to have been an accident. A fall while out walking the bush track."

"In the snow? Will anybody believe that?"

"Ask yourself what this person's reputation has been," he said, and—oh, dear God—he pushed the toe of his patent-leather wing tip gently against the body so that it lifted then sagged back onto the floor. "Not really a solid citizen." Tony seemed to realize Flora was listening and checked himself. "Apologies, Florrie. I'm just being practical. You have to trust us."

Flora nodded, in shock, unable to make sense of the situation.

"How far shall we take it, then?" Sweetie asked.

"As close as we can get to the Falls."

Sweetie nodded and reached down to lift the limp legs in his meaty hands. Flora moved to help, but Tony pushed her away, gently but firmly.

"You wait here. You're no use to us as you are, and it's murderously cold. I don't want two bodies on my hands." He flicked his cigarette butt out the door ahead of him and it arced into the snow, a brief ember soon extinguished.

Flora watched them go. They lumbered into the dark and the cold, until they became small figures at the boundary of the garden, then disappeared down the stone steps that led into the valley. Rain had begun to fall, fat drops from the swirling night sky landing silently on the snow. She stood at the door, her fingers turning numb, and watched for their return.

The rain would wash their heavy footprints out of the snow, along with the possible track of limp, dead arms that dragged between them. But the rain would also wash over the body, a wet shroud, a sodden burial. Flora put her head in her hands and wept, for her shock and her disappointment and her loss and for the horrors that were no doubt to come. *Poor Violet*, she said over and over in her mind. *Poor, poor Violet.*

And poor Sam. Will had been wrong: the withdrawal had killed him after all. If she'd known that was possible, she would never have let things get so bad. Her knees began to shake. She couldn't stand here and wait in the cold. She needed to lie down. Flora took herself up the stairs to Sam's room, closed the door, and lay on Sam's bed, breathing deeply the smell of his hair and skin from his pillow, and sobbed and sobbed and sobbed.

*   *   *

Violet finished the last sandwich on the tray and poured herself another cup of tea. "It's not really enough, is it?" she said. "Sandwiches for dinner." She sat on the unmade bed opposite Clive's. He had returned to bed as she commanded, and she was glad. His cough wasn't any better.

"I'll get the flying fox working tomorrow," he said. "This rain will melt a lot of the snow and soon it will be business as usual. Eggs and fresh milk and bacon up from the valley."

"As much as I love bacon," Violet said, "I don't think you'll be well enough to be out working in the cold tomorrow. Besides, who knows what's happening with the farms below?"

"Perhaps you're right."

"Just wait for Miss Zander to be up and about. She'll restore order. Everyone's reverted to savagery, despite what Lord Powell says. Look at us—dining in your bedroom, no less."

He laughed, then tilted his head and examined her. "You seem very merry tonight, Violet."

"I do feel a certain lightness of mood," she replied.

"It's nice to see you smile. Yesterday, you seemed quite hopeless."

"Where there's life there's hope," she said, lightly. "Here, you relax. I'll take this tray up."

"You should get some rest, too."

"I'm fine. Being busy is good. I don't dwell." She offered him a tight smile, took the tray, and left.

She was up the stairs and almost at the kitchen when she smelled cigarette smoke. It could only be Tony or Sweetie, who had both started smoking in the past two days. She hesitated in the hallway. Why were they in the kitchen? She heard low voices, and inched closer to the door, her shoulder against the wall, to listen.

"Is Flora going to tell people the truth, though?" Sweetie was saying. She recognized his unctuous voice from his recent insults.

"Florrie's a practical lass. If Father finds out Sam died from opium, there will be no money."

Violet's blood chilled.

"You want her money?"

"No. Never have. I want her name. Frankly, that's the only thing about her that interests me. I'd rather it wasn't tainted by the stupid death of a stupid boy who didn't know when to stop."

Violet tried to wrap her mind around what they were saying. Surely they were speaking hypothetically. Sam wasn't dead. Sam was better. She had made him better. She leaned against the wall, unsure whether to march in and demand clarification, or keep listening for the explanation that undid it all, that made sense of the previous frightening conversation.

"So, if they find his body . . ."

"Will they? It's down in the valley somewhere, a long way down. Past all the bush tracks. Nobody's going to find it."

"Oh, God," she murmured. "Oh, God, no." She hadn't got the medicine to him in time. It was Flora's fault! She should have let Violet in! She should have got him help earlier!

"So we've dumped his body and now he just disappears?"

"It's better . . . easier that way. We'll say he went out walking and just didn't come back. Flora will be happier, too, in the long run, though she may not know it yet. She was very fond of the lad. I've never seen her so distressed."

Violet began to shake, unable to control her limbs. The tea tray jumped from her hands and smashed onto the floor. The sound seemed deafening. Hurried footsteps. Tony and Sweetie.

"How much did you hear?" Tony began to shout.

"Is Sam dead?" she asked him. "Please, tell me he's not dead." Hot panic flooded her, made it hard to see or think.

"How much did she hear?" Sweetie said, grabbing her around the waist and half lifting, half dragging her into the kitchen.

Fear kicked at her heart. "I didn't hear anything," she protested. "I don't know what you're talking about."

"Oh for God's sake, she *knows* now, Tony."

"I don't know anything."

Tony had his head in his hands. "What an enormous *inconvenience*."

Sweetie hitched Violet up, over his shoulder. She pounded on his back, frightened of falling forward on her head, but even more terrified of what he might do to her. "I'll take care of it," he said. "You go be with Flora."

"Don't do anything—"

"Just go. I'll take care of it."

Then Violet was bouncing around over Sweetie's shoulder, out the kitchen door and into the cold.

"Do you know how to shut up?" he said to her over his shoulder.

"I swear I won't say anything."

"I doubt that's true. You were in love with him, weren't you?"

"Is he really dead?"

"As a doornail, dollface." Thump, thump, thump, over the snowy ground, while rain misted around them. The light of the hurricane lamp in the kitchen retreated into the distance. She heard a creak of metal on metal, and tried to turn her head to see where they were. He had one burly arm locked over the backs of her knees.

The flying fox. He had the door of the flying fox open and was trying to wrestle her into the tiny space.

"No!" she screamed.

"Shut up!" he shouted back, smacking her across the jaw and gathering her in his arms. He shoved her. Her limbs scraped over the metal edges around the door. She pushed back, but he pushed harder, his meaty arms no match for hers.

"Please!" she cried. "Please don't do this."

"Stay here till we figure out what to do with you."

He thumped the door shut and she heard the rusty latch slam into place. Desperately, she hammered against the door, screaming until her throat was raw. It was a few minutes before she realized he was gone, back to the kitchen—to the end of the pulley.

Slowly, creaking on the frozen cables, the box began to move out over the valley.

"No!" she screamed. "Please, no!"

Then it stopped, swinging slightly in the cold night air.

The door to Sam's room opened a crack, and Flora looked around to see Tony standing there, his face grim in the lamplight.

"I thought I might find you here," he said.

"Go away."

"Florrie . . ."

"You shouldn't have taken him out there."

"It was for the best. Before anyone else saw him dead." He walked over to her, stroked her back gently through her dressing gown. "Come on. Come to your bedroom. It's horrible in here."

She sat up and looked around. He was right. Clothes strewn about, sour odors, a chair upended, objects overturned: the evidence of his last, horrific few days.

Then her eyes lit upon a green wallet, unfolded, near the bed. Flora bent down to peer at it. A medicine bottle. A syringe. "Tony, he took something."

"He did?"

She held the syringe up to the light. "There's blood on it. He took something. That's what killed him."

"What did he take? How did he get it?"

"I don't know." Had Sam killed himself? Had the pain and distress been too much for him?

Tony took the syringe from her, wrapped it with the bottle and other implements in the green pouch. "We'll have to get rid of this, too."

She snapped. "Have you no pity? Is the cover-up all you're interested in?"

She watched Tony fight down his first response, which she imagined was an impatient one. Instead, he lifted her gently to her feet and said, "You need to get out of here now. He's gone, and lying here in his filthy bed won't bring him back."

Flora let him lead her out into the cold hallway, then up the stairs to the ladies' floor. As they passed Violet's door, Flora thought about knocking, to tell Violet the terrible news. At least that way Flora could cry with somebody who loved Sam as much as she did. But Tony seemed to sense her hesitation, and propelled her past the door with firm hands.

"To your room, Florrie," he said. "You need to rest. You've had a horrible shock."

Then she was sitting on her own soft bed, surrounded by her own things. The last time she'd looked at these things—her letter-writing compendium, her inkwell, her shoes, her brolly—Sam had been alive; her life hadn't yet been tipped on its axis.

Tony fished in his pocket for his hip flask and gave it to Flora. "Here. Take a few belts of whiskey."

"I don't want it."

"Just do as you're told," he snapped. "You're no help to anyone, including Sam and his legacy, in this state."

"What do you mean?"

"Drink. Now."

She lifted the flask to her lips and poured some of the scalding liquid into her mouth. Swallowed. Took another sip. Tony indicated with his hand she should keep going. Another gulp. Another. Then her stomach began to burn, and she handed it back to him.

Tony pulled her chair up beside her bed and sat on it, knees apart, hands reaching out to hers. He squeezed her fingers too hard.

"I'm sorry, Florrie. I wish there was something I could do to make it better."

"There is. We need to go out there, as soon as we can, and retrieve his poor body and give him a proper burial."

Tony was already shaking his head before the end of her sentence. "No, we can't."

"He shouldn't be out there in the cold and the rain! He should be properly buried, properly remembered. He's my baby brother. We need his body, and we need to find a doctor who will tell us how he died and—"

"Listen carefully," Tony interrupted. "We can never tell anyone what really happened to Sam."

"But we don't know what happened. That's just it."

"He either died from illegal drugs or his own hand. That's what happened. Either way, if your father finds out, nothing but bad things will come next."

"I don't care," she said. "Do you not see? All that is irrelevant now. I don't care what Father does to me."

"You should."

"Why? We'll have enough money, won't we? Please tell me this isn't about the money."

Tony shook his head. "No."

"Then, what is it?"

He sat silently for what seemed like an age, considering her in the lamplight. Overhead, the rain grew harder. Finally, he said, "It's not my intention to marry into family scandal."

"What?" Confusion made it impossible to follow, but she suspected he was saying something momentous and awful.

"My father will be just as shocked and angry as yours."

"These things are so meaningless as to be laughable. *My brother is dead.*"

"One of the reasons the marriage is so advantageous on our side is the Honeychurch-Black name. My father is one generation out of the working class. You have no idea how much it means to him to be married to that name."

A stone dropped on her heart. "And you? Do you care that much, too?"

He shrugged. "It's not unimportant. Florrie, don't look so shocked. I'm just being practical. You and I, we're both practical, aren't we?"

"I can't believe I'm hearing this." Flora's head seemed filled with the sound of mad birds' wings beating.

"It's just easier this way. We don't have to explain anything to anybody. No criminal activity has to be reported, and Sam dies leaving behind only memories of him being a young, slightly fey but ultimately upstanding man. Your father is happy, my father is happy, life goes on." He paused for effect, then said, "Sam would have wanted it this way."

She snorted derisively. "Sam would have been appalled. He abhorred such snobbery."

"No, he didn't. He was as bad as the rest of us. Rude to the servants, chasing after waitresses. Lord, he's been dead less than an hour and you're already canonizing him."

The effects of whiskey and grief confused her. Was he right? She lived in such a rarefied world of money and privilege, all earned at the cost of individuality and personal freedom. There was no doubt that a death as sordid as Sam's would damage the family's reputation. But how cruel of Tony to bring it up now, to tell her how important a role her name played in his decision to marry her.

"What do you say, Florrie?"

"I don't want to talk about it anymore," she said. "Leave me be. I need to cry and to sleep and to . . . think everything through. Life without Sam." She shook her head. "I can't even imagine it."

"Imagine it sensibly," he said. "You're a sensible girl." He leaned forwards and kissed her cheek. "You know where I am if you need me."

The door closed behind him, and she had a strong urge to shout after him never to come back.

The rain came down.

Violet sat, her knees uncomfortably jammed up under her chin, her back hunched over. Shivering and shivering. The shivers started at her skin, under her uniform and her stockings and her singlet and bloomers, and then spread deeper and deeper inside her. Her blood shivered. Her muscles shivered. Her marrow shivered. Her guts shivered. The rain seeped in through a top corner of the box and trickled out through a bottom corner, after it had run behind her back, leaving a damp patch on her skirt. The box smelled of iron and dirt and blood—a reminder that it had been used many times to transport quartered pig carcasses and sacks of potatoes.

She had screamed for an hour, but her little voice out here over the valley was no match for the rain. With the rain, though, came warmer air. Now and again, a huge gust would spring up, carrying the cold off the snow and howling around her metal prison, but mostly she was able to keep herself from freezing by staying curled in a ball, her head tucked down.

After an hour she stopped screaming and started to pray. She prayed that Clive would wake up in the morning and stubbornly come down to fix the flying fox. That he wouldn't listen to her admonitions to stay in bed. That his sense of duty would win out and he would come and find her and take her to the police, where she could report what had happened to Sam and what Sweetie and Tony had done. She had to get somewhere safe; she had a baby inside her, Sam's baby. If she survived this, and she was determined to survive this, she vowed she would do whatever was in her power to give this child the safest, happiest life possible.

These thoughts turned over and over in her mind as the night wore on. She sometimes dozed on her knees and sometimes she woke and remembered where she was and what had happened and then cried all over again. All the while the shivers continued. Not from cold, nor from fear, but from grief. The remorseless shivers of somebody who has lost the very thing they love most in the world, irrevocably and forever.

CHAPTER TWENTY-SIX

Flora woke with pain stinging every muscle of her body. She looked around groggily. She was lying on top of her bed, still in her robe. The events of the night before came back to her, and she realized what had caused the pain. Sorrow. Her whole body was grieving.

She sat up and checked the clock beside the bed. It was six in the morning, still gray outside the window, with rain falling steadily. She stood and peered out. The snow was melting to dirty gray mush. Today, if they wanted to, they could get out. Go to the village. Perhaps the trains would be running.

What was the point of getting out now, though? Getting out to go where? Home without Sam? Her wedding without Sam? The rest of her life without Sam?

Heavy feet dragged her to the bathroom, heavy limbs pulled on her clothes for the day, then with a heavy heart she set out to do what she knew she must.

Flora knocked softly on Violet's door, tensed against discovery by Tony. There was no answer. She knocked again, a little louder, a little bolder, and said, "Violet? I need to speak with you."

But of course, Violet would be downstairs helping prepare breakfast. The poor girl had barely had a moment off since the snow had come down. Flora went down the stairs, stopping at the bottom to listen. Everything was quiet. So quiet. She headed along the hall and towards the kitchen. Empty. The stove had gone cold.

The first delicate tendril of worry touched her heart. Where was Violet? She supposed Violet might be anywhere in the building, as big and rambling as it was. But she would have to come to make breakfast. So, Flora pulled out a chair and sat down to wait in the cold kitchen. Her stomach growled. How she longed for the days of the bustling dining room, the heaped plates of hot food, the bottomless pots of hot tea.

She longed for the problems she used to have, when Sam was just a man who smoked too much opium, but was still warm and breathing.

Her own breath left her body again, and she had to force it back into her lungs. This wouldn't do. She couldn't keep letting the shock knock her down. He was dead. Now she had to do the right thing, starting with telling the mother of his unborn child.

But Violet didn't come.

At last, she heard footsteps in the hallway and she stood, ready to face Violet. Yearning to share tears with her. But the person who appeared at the door of the kitchen wasn't Violet. It was the handyman who drew the pictures. Mr. Betts.

"Ma'am?" he said, surprised to see her.

"I'm looking for Violet."

"I haven't seen her this morning. I suspect she's still in her room."

"She's not in her room."

He frowned. "She's not?"

"Is she with Miss Zander?"

"I've just come from seeing Miss Zander. She's still too ill to get up. Violet wasn't there."

Flora put her hand over her mouth. Sam was dead, Violet was missing. Had they made some foolish lovers' pact?

"What's wrong, ma'am?"

She took a step towards him, dropped her voice low. "Mr. Betts, what I am going to tell you may alarm you."

"What is it?"

"Last night, my brother died."

His face fell. "Miss Honeychurch-Black, I am so sorry for your loss. Please, sit down. Can I get you tea? Perhaps the snow has melted enough for me to go for the village doctor—"

"Listen. I'm worried about Violet. She and my brother were . . ."

"I know," he said, simply but meaningfully.

"Sam dies, she disappears. I'm worried she's . . . done something foolish."

She sensed the anxiety flexing through his rangy body. "Do you think that's possible?"

"They were young and in love. I don't want her to die, too, Mr. Betts. She has something . . ." She started to cry again, but then stopped herself. "I'm sorry. I'm not myself."

"It's been a terrible shock, ma'am. To happen at a time like this when we can't call outside help is the worst kind of luck. Now, you're not to worry about Violet. I'm sure she's around here some-where, and when I find her, I'll send her to you for the . . . news."

"Would you?"

"In the meantime, let me bring some breakfast up to your room. I'll let Miss Zander know about your brother, and as soon as ever we can, we will fetch the doctor. Take care of your brother. Do what needs to be done to get him back to your family."

His sympathetic words scorched her fragile heart. This man, as low born as she was high, knew the right thing to do better than did her fiancé. "I . . . give me some time. You can't let Miss Zander know. I shouldn't have even told you. Can you forget it?"

"Ma'am?"

She put her hands around her temples, and it was all she could do not to scream. "Mr. Betts . . ."

"Clive," he said. "Please call me Clive."

"Clive, I have never been so unhappy nor so unsure in my life. Could you let me deal with my people, and you deal with yours? I'll take care of what happens to Sam. You find Violet."

"Of course, ma'am."

"Flora," she said. "My name is Flora."

She hurried back along the hallway and up the stairs. Clive was right. She had to talk to Tony, convince him that they needed to go back and retrieve Sam's body. She wouldn't leave him out there like wildlife. She wanted to do as Clive had suggested: tell Miss Zander, call the doctor—Will would come. Will would know what to do.

At the top of the stairs, she paused. She heard voices coming from Sam's room. His door was open. A horrible shudder came over her, as she remembered Sam's hallucinations about the dead man come back to life.

But it was Tony's voice, and Sweetie's. She listened long enough to realize they were clearing evidence from his room.

"All the pipes," Tony said. "The lamp, too. All of it."

No, not Sam's precious things. She steeled herself to march in there and demand they stop, but then she took a moment to consider.

Tony would not stop. Sweetie would not stop. They had no empathy for her or for Sam. They were used to getting their own way, and eventually they would wear her down with their refusals, their combined will. Tony only cared to avoid a scandal, to keep her in her father's good favor. He seemed at once a stranger, a handsome man with no heart who hid his callous nature under a veneer of practicality. Her fiancé? She would expect an enemy to behave as he had, not an ally. Her abject aloneness made her shudder.

There was only one person who would listen to her, who would tell her the right thing to do.

Flora went to her room to dress as warmly as she could for the walk through the snow to Will Dalloway's house.

Violet struggled to keep her mind and her body together. Her backside was numb, her spine ached, and her joints burned from being cramped in the same position for hour upon hour. The dampness that had collected in the bottom of the box had turned icy. Her fingertips were so cold that she had to suck on them to keep them from going numb. Even the thinnest fragment of relief was denied her. The night passed, the rain sheeted down, and she remained locked in her miserable prison with her fear and her sorrow and her hunger, wondering if anyone would ever come for her.

Sometime around dawn, though, she drifted into a half-waking, half-sleeping state, in which strange dreams of haunted corridors drifted through her mind. She had no idea how long this nebulous doze lasted, but she woke with a jolt to the first glimmer of daylight through the cracks in the box. Her mind no longer bent out of shape with tiredness and fear, she began to wonder if she could break out of the box with brute force. The only thing holding the door was a latch on the outside: a simple latch to stop the door falling open as produce was hauled up the mountain. Dead pigs and sacks of potatoes didn't try to escape, so it didn't need to be the strongest latch ever made.

Violet shuffled backwards, so her back was against the metal. Now she was sitting directly in the damp spot, and the icy water penetrated her clothes in moments. It allowed her, though, to unfold her legs a fraction of an inch, relieving the cramping pain in her knees. Then she retracted her legs tightly and kicked out hard against the door.

Bang!

The noise seemed deafening, and the flying fox swung wildly. Violet's heart raced and she sat very still for a few moments while the box came to rest. When she looked, she discovered she had managed to bend the bottom of the door nearly an inch. She could see daylight, and dirty melting snow below, a long way below.

Once again, she coiled her legs up like a spring and—*bang!*

The swinging was more violent, but the corner of the door was now bent out nearly ninety degrees. She shrugged and struggled, catching her clothes on the metal walls, turning herself over so she could put her face close to the gap she'd opened. She was at least thirty feet above the ground. Even if she did break the latch, she wouldn't be able to jump out. Should she just wait? Somebody would come eventually. Clive would come to fix the flying fox.

She put her mouth close to the gap and started shouting with throat-tearing force. "Help! Help me!" This time, instead of her voice being trapped inside the box, she could hear it echoing out over the valley. Surely somebody would hear her.

Violet shouted for as long as her voice could hold out, then she leaned her head on the door and cried helplessly.

After what seemed an age—she couldn't say how long because she'd lost track of time—the box jumped.

She jolted, alert. She hadn't felt a gust of wind. Had somebody heard her? Was it Clive?

The box jumped again, then began a slow, lurching journey back towards the hotel. "Thank you, God, thank you," she said. She needed warmth, the woodstove, hot tea, something substantial to eat.

Slowly, slowly backwards. Then she could see the ground. She could see a man's shoes and the fear boiled up inside her because they weren't Clive's shoes. Clive had never had a pair of shoes that expensive. Time seemed to slow as the man fumbled with the latch.

Everything that happened thereafter happened in a jolting, too-bright rush. The door opened, and it was Sweetie, Tony's thuggish friend. Tony was nowhere to be seen and something about this fact made Violet's stomach turn to water. Tony could at least be reasoned with. This other man, however, had made it clear that he thought of her as something less than human. Before she could scream, he reached in and covered her mouth with his meaty hand, then dragged her kicking and flailing out of the box and dumped her on the ground. The world looked quite different from the night before. The gleaming white mounds of snow had dissolved to dirty slush. He pinned her to the ground with his foot in the center of her back, her mouth pressed against the snow so she could neither breathe nor scream, and tied her hands behind her. Then he lifted her head by her hair and tied a cloth—A tie? A scarf?—between her teeth then around again over her mouth. She tried to shout for help, but all that came out was a guttural gasp.

He lifted her roughly in his arms, facing down. She kicked as hard as she could, but he plowed on, down the steps to the bush paths. Violet flexed her wrists back and forth to work her bonds loose, and he shook her roughly and said, "Stop that if you know what's good for you."

She stopped, her heartbeat deafening in her own ears. She didn't know what he intended and she didn't want to anger him further.

A mound of snow was still piled at the base of the fingerpost. Everywhere else the snow had melted unevenly. She watched Sweetie's feet. Sometimes the snow was above his ankles, but never above his knees. His feet must be sodden by now, and cold. Good. She hoped he was suffering for whatever horror he intended to inflict upon her.

Down the bush path they wound. She could hear the Falls. She thought about the afternoon she had met Sam there, the plunge they had taken under the cascade, nearly naked. It seemed at once both achingly recent and terribly long ago. A more innocent time. Before death and . . . whatever this morning would bring.

If he hadn't gagged her, she would never have been quiet. *What are you going to do with me? I'm pregnant, you mustn't hurt me. I've done nothing to you, let me go.* But most of all, she would have screamed. Any name she could think of. Clive. Flora. Tony. Miss Zander. Because she was afraid of what he intended. She didn't know how far he would go to punish her, to silence her.

What she never imagined was that he intended to kill her.

As they approached the water hole, panic rose through her like a flame. *No, no.*

"I saw you here with him," Sweetie said, gruffly. "You thought nobody was looking, but I was. I saw you. Stripped off like the whore you are. Then you pretended you were too proper, too decorous for me. But I know what you really are."

She bucked her body violently, trying to get out of his arms, but he had her tightly.

"So, when Tony says to me that we need to make sure you shut up, let me say I know how to make you shut up." He waded into the water then threw her in to the deep part of the pool.

Down, down she went, her legs kicking madly but her arms useless behind her back. She struggled against the ties around her wrists, couldn't loosen them. Her heart was frantic, her lungs blocked and desperate. She curled up, sinking farther, and tried to bring her arms under her hips so she could push them in front of her. No use. She kicked against the bottom of the pool, propelling herself up, but the surface was just too far away, and she was running out of breath.

Wildly, she pulled her hands apart, pulling and pulling, hoping she wasn't making the knots tighter. With a slow drag they came free of each other. She speared them through the water ahead of her and swam towards the surface. She could see bubbling, churning water ahead and knew it was where the cascade fell. If she came up behind it, Sweetie might not see her.

Air. She needed air. But she needed to breathe cautiously.

Her face broke the surface, and she tore the tie from around her mouth. She gasped. Water rushed into her mouth, and she went under again. She hadn't seen him. Had he gone already? She rose again, just tilting her face out of the water. She breathed, looking around. Everything was distorted through the screen of the falling water. Sweetie was nowhere to be seen.

Still, she stayed behind the wall of water. The silk cravat he'd used to tie her hands was now hanging limply off one wrist. She waited for her heart to still, but it wouldn't. Now she was wet, freezing, outside. She couldn't return to the hotel—Sweetie would be there, and she couldn't be sure Tony and Flora weren't in on it, too—but if she stayed out here, the cold would certainly kill her. The only negotiable tracks led back to the hotel. Everywhere else was rough ground, layered with snow.

Her body began to shake, such huge shuddering shakes that she feared she would die right here in the water. She had to get out. She had to make for Lovers Cave.

Violet swam to the shallow side of the pool, then stumbled out. Her body felt as though it would shake into pieces. She could hardly walk, and her breathing was still labored. All around, rain still fell. Falling and falling as though the sky couldn't bear to see the horrors being played out below, and wanted to wash them away. Violet needed shelter, and she needed it soon.

She started the ascent up the path. Her feet slid and slipped underneath her in the slushy snow. Her lungs burned. The big muscles in her thighs felt as though they had turned to butter. Her skin was puckered and blue.

Violet started to suspect she wasn't going to make it. She sat down on a rock.

"Sam, Sam," she said. "What do I do?"

Her aching heart dragged her body down. She put her face on her knees and waited to die. But then she focused: it wasn't just her who would die. Sam's child would die along with her.

She pushed breath into her lungs, willing her heart to thump harder and move her blood all the way to her toes and fingers and nose. "Get up," she told herself. "Get up."

She got up. She went a little farther, then pushed herself to go farther again. She stopped and rested, then pushed herself once more.

Then she heard a sound that made her whole body warm. A voice. Not awful Sweetie's voice.

Clive's voice. "Violet? Violet?"

"Here!" she cried, in a voice so weak it frightened her.

Then she heard footsteps, lumbering footsteps as he pounded as fast as he could through the slush and snow. He was there, hands grasping her shoulders. "You're soaked. We need to get you back to the hotel."

"No. Did you see Sweetie on your way down here?"

"I saw nobody. Why?"

"He locked me in the flying fox all night, then this morning he tried to drown me."

"What? I—Violet, we need to get you somewhere warm. You're blue."

"I can't go back to the hotel. I don't know what's happening. Oh, Clive. Sam's dead. And Tony and Sweetie think I know something about it and they're willing to do anything to cover it up."

"The cave," he said.

"That's where I was heading."

He put his arm around her. "Come on, then. Out of this rain."

When she couldn't keep up with him, he lifted her so her feet skimmed across the snow, then put her down for a few steps on her own. She hungrily clung to his side, his body heat. They climbed the last few rocky steps up to the cave, then finally they were out of the rain.

Clive was already shrugging out of his greatcoat, scarf, hat, and gloves. "Take those wet clothes off," he said.

"I can barely move," she replied, her shaking fingers jumping about on her buttons.

He came to her, stopping a few inches in front of her. His face was sad, and she started to cry.

"He's gone, Clive, he's gone."

"I know. I saw his sister this morning." He reached across the space between them, and, as gentle and patient as a parent undressing a child, he undid her buttons one by one. He slipped the dress off her shoulders and it landed at her feet. He left her underwear on her for modesty's sake. "I'm sorry this is awkward," he said, removing his own shirt and trousers so he stood in his long johns, "but you need clothes." He offered them all to her. "Put these on."

She indicated he should turn around, and she struggled out of her wet underwear, stockings, and shoes. Then she wrapped herself in his clothes, fastening his trousers around her waist with the damp tie from her wrist. Then his shirt, his scarf, his coat. Instant relief. He pulled off his Wellington boots, the same ones she had worn on her mercy dash to Malley's, and his socks, and offered them to her.

"You'll be cold."

"I'm not soaking wet. I'll be fine."

She pulled on the boots but refused his socks. Bare feet in this cold were too much to ask of him. She gratefully took his hat and gloves, then collapsed on the floor of the cave. He sat next to her, his shoulder pressed against her.

"You don't mind, do you?" he said, indicating their proximity. "Body heat."

"Of course I don't mind." She leaned into him. Minutes passed. The rain hammered, but they were dry. The shivers began to ease. Her tired brain began to slow.

"We will have to make our way to the village," Clive said. "When the rain stops."

"It seems as though it will never stop."

"You look so tired," he said.

"I didn't sleep. I'm sore and sad and frightened."

"You can sleep now." He pulled her down, shifted so he lay curled behind her, his arms around her. "Sleep. You're warm and safe."

The floor of the cave was cold and rough beneath her, but the weariness that penetrated her bones responded to his kindness, his warmth. "I'll just close my eyes a little while," she said.

"We can keep each other warm," he said.

She lay with her eyes open, Clive's arm over her waist. She watched the rain, falling and falling outside. Her gaze went to the carved heart on the stone, Sam's initials still there. Sam was gone, but the mark of her love would be there long after today, long after her baby was born, long after she died. Something about that thought made her smile, and the haze of sleep descended.

CHAPTER TWENTY-SEVEN

Flora had wrapped up as well as she could, and of course she had taken an umbrella. But she hadn't counted on the rain splashing under it, or the melting snow getting into her boots.

Her heart was glad, though, to see that other people were out in it, that the great isolating snowfall had lost its grip on the world. A man swaddled in layers of warm, waterproof clothing was sweeping snow off the train platform, and a tractor was clearing roads on the other side of the rail line. The rails themselves were clear, so no doubt the trains would come again soon. Probably today. Life had begun again.

But not for Sam.

Flora was sodden and freezing when she climbed Will Dalloway's front steps, and it occurred to her for the first time that he might not be here, that he might have been one of the clever people who evacuated to Sydney before the snowstorm. The thought knocked the breath out of her lungs. She raised her hand wearily and grasped the knocker with her glove. She gave it three hard raps and stood back to wait.

Almost immediately she heard footsteps inside. The door opened, and Will was there.

"Flora," he said, surprised.

"Will, you have to help me."

"Come in. Come in. I have a fire burning in the sitting room. What's happened?"

She followed him inside, in through the door marked PRIVATE. His house was warm and neat. He pulled the wing-backed chair close to the fire and offered it to her.

"Sit down," he said.

"Can I take my shoes off?"

"Of course. I can't believe you came out in this weather. I haven't seen anyone in days."

She unbuttoned her shoes and slipped them off. Her stockings were sodden, but she'd rather they were damp than take them off in front of Will, and he didn't seem to notice. She stretched her feet towards the fire, and the warmth was penetrating and good.

Will pulled an ottoman up beside her and sat on it. "What has brought you here?"

Flora took a deep breath, and the story poured out. Sam's withdrawal, finding his body, being pressured by Tony to let them dispose of it in the wilds, Violet's disappearance. Through it all, he didn't touch her or make a sound. He listened, shocked but silent, his eyes fixed on hers. Her voice seemed to go on forever in the warm, fire-lit room, then finally it wound down and stopped.

"Oh, Flora," he said. "I can't begin to express my sympathy."

"Will you help me?"

"I will do anything in my power. What particularly do you want my help with?"

"How did he die? You said the withdrawal wouldn't kill him."

Will nodded sadly. "The pouch with the syringe that you found," he said. "It sounds as though somebody obtained for him an injectable drug to ease his pain. There's an injectable opiate called heroin that works very quickly. Unfortunately, it's much stronger than he would have been used to. Too much and . . ."

"It killed him?"

"Yes. That's my educated guess."

"But how did he get it? He couldn't leave the hotel. He could barely leave his room—"

Flora froze as the answer became clear. It was Violet. Violet, who would have done anything to relieve Sam's pain. Violet, whom Flora had seen that day with florid cheeks and damp hair, as though she had been roaming outside. Violet, who couldn't know that her actions would kill him. Anger and pity warred in Flora's breast.

"This is a horror," she whispered, gazing at the fire in the grate. "A nightmare." Then she lifted her head to look at Will. "I want to find his body, and I want to take him home and bury him properly. I don't care what Father thinks."

"I can help. Once the rain has eased, once the road is open. Later today, maybe tomorrow. I will go down there myself and look for him."

"Good. Thank you. If Father cuts me off . . . well, then I will survive anyway. And if Tony no longer wants to marry me because my name is muddied, then I no longer want to marry Tony." She paused, listening back to her own words. *I no longer want to marry Tony*. The thought gave her such freedom. "I no longer want to marry Tony," she said again, more emphatically.

"Nor should you if all he's interested in is—"

"No, no. You don't understand. I mean under any circumstances. I don't want him."

Will's eyes were soft. "Don't you love him?"

"I don't know anymore. He's not the man I thought he was. There's something cold in his heart. His friends are awful. They're either sycophants or thugs. Sometimes both." The idea of a life not subject to the opinions of her father or Tony seemed an impossible bliss. "Do I have to marry him?"

Will smiled. "I've never thought you should."

She smiled back, then stopped herself because it felt wrong to smile the day after Sam had died. "First things first. Find Sam."

"First things first. Let me make you food and tea and wait for the rain to ease. Perhaps by this evening I'll be able to take my car out of the garage, and then we can get help from anyone you need: Miss Zander, the police, your family; whoever you think can help. But until then, I will keep you warm and safe, and you aren't to worry. Save your energy for grieving."

Impulsively, she reached for him, grasped his hand in hers, and ran her thumb over his knuckles. He looked from her hand to her face, and she could see the tenderness in his eyes.

"You are a lovely man, Will Dalloway," she said.

He hid a smile, gently extricated his hand. "I'll make tea," he said.

Flora leaned back in the chair, taking deep breaths and watching the fire, letting the tears fall freely down her warm cheeks.

Violet woke to a hacking noise. Disoriented, she blinked rapidly. Shifted. Felt the hard ground under her and remembered where she was.

What was the noise? Where was Clive? She sat up. Clive, dressed only in his long johns, was crouched in front of the stone, the one with the lovers' heart etched into it, and was scratching furiously at it with a sharp rock. But that wasn't the hacking noise.

The noise was his cough.

"What are you doing?" she asked, groggy and sore.

He dropped the rock and looked around guiltily.

"Why would you do that?" she asked.

"Because he caused you nothing but sorrow."

"I loved him," she protested. "He's the man I loved, and he died, and you would do something as . . . petty as that?"

He coughed again, a deep rattling cough in his chest that alarmed her.

"How long have I been asleep?" she asked.

"A few hours," he replied.

She rose, shrugged out of his overcoat. "How long have you been coughing like that?"

"Just the past hour or two. No, you keep the coat."

As she reached for him, she realized his skin was burning. "You have a fever."

He shrugged. "I had it when I left the hotel this morning. It started last night."

"Yet you came out in the cold and the wet and you stripped to your underwear?"

"What was I to do, Violet? Flora was worried that you were in some kind of trouble, and she was right. So, I came looking for you."

She glanced from him to the scratched-up love heart and back again.

His voice grew quiet. "That's what real love is, Violet. It isn't empty promises and drawings on rocks and desire that can't contain itself." He looked pointedly towards her belly. "It's sacrifice and selflessness. Tell me one time that man was selfless, one thing he sacrificed for you."

She couldn't answer him. Wouldn't answer him. "Put your coat back on. I'm dry now. We'll share the clothes."

He slipped the coat on and she pulled off her scarf and tied it firmly around his neck. She heard the wheeze as he breathed in, breathed out, and noted the thin film of perspiration on his upper lip.

"I'm sorry," he said, his eyes going to the love heart. "It was childish of me."

Violet remembered Sam scribbling over Clive's name on her portrait, and it made it easy to forgive him. "You are very ill."

"Don't worry about me."

She touched his forehead. He was burning up.

"We can't do anything now," he said. "We have to wait out the worst of the rain."

So they sat, silent, waiting and waiting. The rain seemed to grow deeper rather than lighter. His cough worsened. An hour passed, two. His decline was rapid, horribly evident, right before her eyes.

Violet could stand it no longer. "We have to go for help."

"But the rain—"

"I'll go."

"That's madness. What if Sweetie or Tony are on the walking paths?"

"I won't take a walking path. I'll find my way up another route. There are houses on the escarpment, on the western side of the hotel. Somebody up there will help."

Clive coughed again, for such a long time that Violet was afraid he would never catch his breath. Then, finally, he said, "We'll both go. I need shelter, a fire. I'll die out here."

They commenced their ascent from the far side of the cave, towards a ledge that led up to a narrow groove, steep but passable. Clive climbed up first then put his hand down to help Violet. They made their way upwards, over tree roots and rocks. The rain soaked them in minutes, soaked them to the bone. When they came to a gap between two bulging boulders, Violet went through first, turning on her side and breathing in. Her hip bones caught then slid through. Clive got stuck, and leaned for a moment on the rock, coughing and coughing.

"Go back if you can't get through."

"I can't go back. We must keep pushing in this direction." With a huge effort, he hauled himself through, calling out in pain as the rocks tore at his clothes and broke his skin. Blood bloomed over his kidneys.

"You're hurt," she said.

"It's a graze, that's all. We have to keep moving."

They found themselves under a huge overhang. No snow had collected here, but the ground was green and slimy with years of no sunshine. They made their way along, crouching as the overhang descended dramatically, then out the other side onto a steep, bushy slope. Rain and snowmelt poured down it, through their shoes.

"Up here," he said.

Violet began to walk, trudging, her heart thudding, hanging on to saplings or rocks, sometimes crawling on her hands and feet. Up and up, behind Clive, who periodically stopped as his body was racked with coughs. Just ten feet up, now, they could see the edge of the escarpment. But that final ten feet was no longer a passable slope. It was a sheer rock face.

Clive stopped. Sat down. His skin was ashen.

"How do we get up there?" she asked.

"We have to climb."

Her eyes searched for handholds: small outcrops, recesses, sturdy plant roots. She was cold and ached with weariness.

She became aware that Clive was sobbing. The failure of his courage frightened her terribly.

"Clive, it will be fine."

"You go. You go. I can't take another step."

"I won't go without you."

"If you go, you'll live."

"You must come with me."

"Do you not see? I can't. I've pushed past my endurance. Go. Go and live your life and be happy."

Violet glanced up at the rock face, plotting a route for them both. Then she reached down for Clive's forearm and hauled him to his feet. "Up!" she commanded. "Clive Betts, if you do this, I promise I will marry you."

He stood, weakly. "Violet, don't play with my heart. Not at a time like this."

"I am perfectly serious. If you climb up there, and we reach the top—together—I will marry you in the spring."

"Why?"

"Because you're a good man with a good heart, and I will have a good life with you."

Clive looked up, then walked along the ridge for a few feet until he found a rock to stand on. Then he started to climb. Violet was right behind him, reaching for handholds, using branches as precarious footholds. Neither of them spoke. The climb was only ten feet, but it may as well have been ten miles as rain and slippery rock conspired to force them back down. The whole time her heart thundered and electricity jumped in her veins. She banged her limbs, overstrained her muscles, but she would not allow herself to feel it all until tomorrow. For now, to ensure her survival, her dear friend's survival, she had to keep going. Keep going.

Keep going they did, finally clambering over the top of the ridge, then up a short slope and into the back of a eucalypt wood.

Clive doubled over, gasping for breath. Violet caught him, fearful that the exertion would finish him off. But then he stood, straightened his back, and pointed to the back of a house in the distance. "There," he said. "Smoke from the chimney. There's somebody home." He stumbled forwards, but stopped again, hands on knees.

"Let me help you," she said, her arm around his waist. He leaned on her, and she nearly collapsed from the weight. But she labored on, one foot after the other, through the sodden wood. The house came into clearer view. Clive's cough shook him violently, but they kept moving. Up the stairs, thundering on the back door.

An elderly woman with snowy hair opened the door, an alarmed expression on her face.

"Please," Violet said. "Please help us."

And Clive pitched forwards, falling to the floor at the old woman's feet, limp and pale.

Flora didn't move for a long time. She was aware of Will going about his day, back and forth to his surgery, carrying books and paperwork about. He stopped by her from time to time to give her tea, buttered toast, or just to touch her shoulder. She was in a kind of stasis, after the terrible past, before the uncertain future; just sitting, breathing, watching the fire while the rain hammered down outside.

The knock at the door roused her. She heard Will's footsteps, then heard him say, "Oh my God."

Flora was out of her chair a second later, moving towards the door, nearly colliding with Will, who had under his wing a shivering, sodden Violet, dressed in ill-fitting men's clothes. Her lips were blue, and her breath was short.

"Violet!" Flora exclaimed. "Bring her in by the fire. Oh, good God, what has happened to you?"

"Clive," the girl managed. "Clive is . . . terribly sick. I ran . . . I ran as fast as I could."

Flora looked up at Will. "Clive Betts is one of the staff at the hotel."

"Is he injured?" Will asked.

"He's . . . coughing. Can't breathe properly. He's been sick. Thought it was just a cold. Much, much worse."

Will met Flora's eye. "Get her warm and dry. I'll go to him."

"Not at the hotel," Violet managed. "The white cottage west of the Evergreen Spa. Mrs. Huntley's place."

"I know it."

"Can you drive on the roads the way they are?" Flora asked.

"I'll drive as far as I can, then I'll run," he said. "Get her warm. She's in shock. Possibly hypothermia. Warm and dry." Then he dashed off.

"Violet, you must get these clothes off," she said. "Do you understand?"

Violet nodded, and started to strip. Her skin was white and puckered. Flora went across the corridor into Will's bathroom—neat, smelling of wood and spices—and fetched a towel. When she returned to the sitting room, Violet was completely naked, her back to Flora. She was a slender thing, with round hips and a tiny waist. Flora came up behind her and covered her with the towel, then turned her around.

"Sit down. I will get rid of these damp clothes and see if I can find you something else to put on. But sit close to the fire and get yourself warm." The girl wore a haunted, agitated expression. "Don't run off anywhere, all right? We have a lot of things we need to talk about."

"I won't."

Flora found Will's bedroom and brought Violet his thick dressing gown and a pair of wool socks. Then she went to the kitchen, where she made a pot of tea and toasted some bread. Just in the other room, sitting in front of the fire, was the person who had killed Sam. Flora fought with her feelings. On the one hand, she wanted to rage and scream at Violet. On the other, she knew it was an awful accident. An accident that, in many ways, had been inevitable.

She arranged the tea and toast on the tray and brought it back to the sitting room. Flora placed it on the floor and sat with Violet, who still shivered beneath the robe. Flora reminded herself that Violet was pregnant—pregnant with Sam's baby. She knew that Violet was no villain; she was a victim. A naive girl who had fallen for the wrong man and paid the highest price for it: her future. Not only would Flora not blame Violet for causing Sam's death, she would never tell her she had caused it.

Flora handed a cup of tea to Violet, who took it, sipped it once, and said, "I know you won't believe me, but Sweetie tried to kill me."

There it was. The uncertain future that Flora had feared. The sweet moment of respite sitting in the wing-backed chair had passed. Now she listened as a nightmarish story unfolded, about how Violet had overheard the talk of Sam's death, how Tony had been keen to silence Violet, and how Sweetie had taken it upon himself to make that silence permanent. And while it was shocking, she wasn't as surprised as she perhaps should have been. Sam had always warned her that Tony was a brute.

Flora let Violet finish, then held her close and let her cry.

After a few minutes, Flora asked, "What is your favorite memory of Sam?"

Violet sat back, looking puzzled.

"Go on," Flora said. "You loved him as much as I did. Tell me your favorite memory. I don't mind what it is."

"He took me into the empty ballroom, very late one night," Violet answered. "We danced by lamplight, no music. It was like . . . magic." She sniffed. "What's yours?"

"When he was nine, he made me a little book. On each page, he'd glued a dried flower and on the facing page he'd written a story about the flower. Some of them were ghastly: the poor daisy had died quite horrifically under the hooves of a draft horse." She laughed, and Violet laughed with her. "But it was such a special gift. He was so artless in his love for me. I still have it somewhere at home." Then she remembered, and smiled. "There was a violet," she said.

"What happened to the violet?"

Flora couldn't remember. It had receded down the dark corridors of her memory. So, she said, "The violet came through bad times, with a strong spirit and joy in her heart."

Violet smiled through tears, her hand dropping to her belly. It occurred to Flora that if they did go out and find Sam, if there was an inquiry into his death with police and doctors, they would likely discover how he'd died, and Violet would be implicated. She knew then that she would go along with the deception—not for Tony or her father, but for Sam's child.

"Violet," she said, "as soon as the trains start again, you need to leave. You need to disappear. I don't know what Tony and Sweetie are capable of, but I'd be happier if you and the baby were far away from the Evergreen Spa."

"I know. But I'll have to wait for Clive. I'm going to marry him."

Flora's eyebrows shot up. "You are?"

"It's the only sensible thing to do."

Flora nodded sympathetically. "Well, I'm going to break off my engagement to Tony."

"Really?"

"Yes," she said. "It's the only sensible thing to do."

Violet paced. Around and around. She wanted to go out there, she wanted to return to Mrs. Huntley's and be with Clive, but Flora wouldn't let her. Will Dalloway had been gone for hours. Hours.

"He's a good doctor," Flora said.

"It matters little how good the doctor is if the patient is dying," Violet responded, more heat in her voice than she had intended. In the wake of Sam's death, she couldn't bear to lose Clive as well.

Then, finally, they heard the key in the door. Violet raced to greet him, but he gently pushed her back inside. He wouldn't speak until they all sat in the sitting room. He looked exhausted and his clothes were damp.

"Violet, Clive will be fine. Mrs. Huntley has agreed to let him stay there until he's fit to be moved. The infection hasn't made it all the way to his lungs, and I've set his ankle fracture."

"Ankle fracture?"

"You didn't realize? He was in severe pain, and he put a lot of pressure on the joint, walking and climbing. It will probably never heal just right, and he'll always have a limp. But as I said, he'll live."

Violet palmed away tears. "He didn't even tell me."

"You both had a lot on your minds. He told me what happened." He turned to Flora. "While I was at Mrs. Huntley's, the alarm was raised. Tony DeLizio, your fiancé—"

"Ex-fiancé," Flora muttered.

"He was out on the bush track. He found a body."

"Sam's body?"

Will shook his head. "Sweetie's. It looked as though he slipped and fell after . . ." He indicated Violet with a soft hand gesture.

Flora put her head down and exhaled loudly. Violet tried not to feel the surge of jubilation in her blood.

"Miss Zander was alerted, and she came next door to the Huntleys' house to see if they had a phone. Of course they don't. We still haven't alerted the authorities."

"Two deaths," Flora said. "Two deaths in two days. I need to get back there. I need to speak to Miss Zander before she speaks to anyone else." Flora stood. "Will you look after Violet? She'll have to stay here until she can catch a train home."

"You're welcome to stay, Violet," the doctor said. "I have a spare room, and I'd like to keep an eye on you until your color comes back. Flora, the road is mostly clear until the train line. Would you like me to drive you back?"

"Thank you." Flora turned to Violet, gave her a quick, awkward hug. "I will see you soon."

They left, and Violet lay down by the fire, thinking. Clive had said he hadn't seen Sweetie on the bush track. Was that because Sweetie had slipped and fallen to his death before Clive had come after her? Or was it because Clive *had* encountered Sweetie? Sweetie was a bully and a braggart. Had he told Clive he'd got rid of Violet, that he'd do the same to Clive? Clive was not a large man, but he was tall, agile. Smart.

Violet smiled. It didn't matter. She would never ask. She and Clive would get away from here, and life could start anew. What had happened before this moment need not matter anymore.

Will dropped Flora near the train station, and offered to walk her to the hotel.

"No," she said. "I need to think. Look after Violet. She's pregnant with Sam's child. She's just about the most important person in the world to me right now."

Will smiled. "I will do that for you, Flora. I would do anything for you."

But they both knew that now wasn't the time for declarations of affection. Flora needed to instruct Miss Zander in how things would unfold.

Two men fatally lost on the bush path in icy weather. It was almost perfect in terms of explaining Sam's death: the story wrote itself. Sweetie and Sam went out for a walk; the conditions were terrible; they both died. One body was found, one body remained undiscovered. But Flora couldn't bear the idea that anyone might think Sam would keep the company of a man like Sweetie. No, she intended to take Sam home with her. Not his body—that was lost in the wilds—but she *would* take him home with her in her heart, and only when the time was right would she announce his death, and arrange a proper funeral. The idea would appeal to her father and mother. They wouldn't want a Honeychurch-Black to disappear off a bush track in a snowstorm. It would put them in the news. Especially if it was alongside that thug.

And as for Tony. Well, she would make him break off with her, under threat of exposing his role in Violet's imprisonment and attempted murder. She could return home nursing a broken heart, and there would be nothing anyone could do.

Without intending it, Sam had set her free.

CHAPTER TWENTY-EIGHT

Six months later

"This will be your room," Violet said, opening the door. "And across here will be the nursery."

Her mother peered into the room with an expression somewhere between bewilderment and suspicion. "And how are you affording this house?"

"That's not for you to worry about."

Mama dropped her voice low. "Is it Clive? Is he secretly wealthy?"

Violet shook her head sadly. Poor Clive, who could barely work now, with the constant pain in his leg. Still, he'd slowly but surely painted the rooms and polished the floorboards. It was a small house, a modest gift, but more than enough to give them a start. The rest was up to Violet, and she intended to work hard—while Mama and Clive looked after the baby—to build on what she had been given. "Mama. I can only say that I have a generous benefactor who would prefer to remain anonymous."

"Well, you're luckier than I ever was," her mother said, indicating Violet's swollen belly. "First, you got the chap to marry you. Now, this."

Clive came up behind them. "What do you think, Mrs. Armstrong? Will you be happy here?"

"I will be happy, to see my daughter happy and my grandchild grow up happy, too," Mama said, dropping her suitcase on the floor of her new bedroom.

"I will do my best to make them happy, then," Clive said, sliding his arms around Violet and gently rubbing her belly.

Mama arched her eyebrows. "In my day, nobody would have behaved like that in decent company."

Violet laughed. "I'll let you settle in." She was halfway down the corridor with Clive when Mama called her back.

"I'm dying to know. You can tell me, and I promise I'll never breathe a word," she said. "Who is he? This benefactor."

"*She*. My benefactor is a she."

The idea of a woman with money made Mama temporarily speechless.

"I can't tell you anything about her. She has her own life. She's getting married next month. To a doctor. I've agreed never to reveal her name. But I can tell you this." Violet smiled. "She is the kindest woman I have ever known."

CHAPTER TWENTY-NINE

2014

"Am I interrupting something?" Tomas said from the doorway. Lizzie and I sat on the couch surrounded by empty teacups and used tissues.

Lizzie struggled to her feet. "I should go. I've taken up enough of your time."

"You don't have to go," I said.

"You don't have to go," Tomas echoed. "Is everything all right?"

Lizzie tried a smile. "I'll let Lauren tell you."

I handed Lizzie the sketch. "Here, you should have this."

"No, no. I don't want it just now. I'm still . . . there's rather a lot for me to comprehend."

"I'll keep it safe for you."

"Thank you, dear." She stroked my hair, tucked it behind my ear. "You are a good girl." Then she left, closing the door behind her.

"What happened?" Tomas asked.

I pointed to the portrait. "Violet. Lizzie's mother."

"No!"

I explained the whole story, though it was hard to capture Lizzie's reaction in words. She'd been at once shocked and excited, sad and delighted. I wished I'd kept my mouth shut for a little longer, until she'd properly recovered from her illness and surgery. But once I'd started, it had all come out.

God help me, I even showed her the copies of the letters. She'd read two lines and handed them back. "I don't want to see that," she said.

"She's fiercely protective of her dad," I explained to Tomas. "Clive—the man who raised her. It was all a bit much for her."

"I can imagine." He took my hand and squeezed it. "You did the right thing, though. You couldn't have kept it from her."

"I hope she'll be okay."

"She's tough." He pulled me into his arms and kissed me. "I have news."

"Good news? Or bad news?" Deep down, perhaps, I thought my relationship with Tomas was too good to be true.

"That depends on how you look at it."

I sat on the couch, wondering if now I would be the one to need the box of tissues that sat nearby. "You'd better tell me, then."

He sat on the coffee table, his knees either side of mine, and leaned forward. "There's been a change of plans at the hotel."

"You mean the redesign?"

"Yes. They're sending me home early."

My heart fell and fell, all the way through the couch. "Oh. How early?"

"Whenever I want to go. Soon, probably. I'll need to find another contract back home."

"And you won't be back until January?"

"February. Or maybe March. But I'll definitely be back. After about nine months."

Nine months without Tomas.

"I need to say something," he said, straightening up, squaring his shoulders. This was it. He was going to break it off with me.

"Make it quick," I said.

He took a deep breath. "I want you to come with me."

I stared at him blankly for a moment, before his words sank in. "Seriously? To Denmark?"

"I know it's soon. And I'm not asking you to marry me or commit to me forever. We don't even have to live together. My sister has a spare room you'd be welcome in. I'm just asking you to seriously consider it. You make great coffee and you'd be sure to get a job and—"

"But I don't speak a word of Danish."

"You'd learn it quickly. I'd love to help you."

Did he think I was mad? To run off to a foreign country with a man I'd spent only a few weeks with? Without any prospects of a job, without any language skills, without any guarantees about Tomas or . . . well, anything?

I started to laugh.

"What's so funny?" he said, smiling cautiously.

"You know what?" I said. "I *am* going to seriously consider it."

I was in the staff bathroom, washing the day's grime off my face and tidying my hair, when Penny walked in.

"Your mother and father," she said.

My heart jolted. "What? Here?"

She nodded. "You weren't expecting them?"

"No. But I should have." Mum hadn't called. I hadn't called her. What I'd thought was a mutual agreement not to speak for a while was actually an opportunity for her to quietly plan a visit to prod me in person. I leaned my back against the sink. "What am I going to do?"

"You have to go out and talk to them. They've come all the way from Tasmania."

"But I'm so angry with them and . . ." I checked my watch. "I'm meeting someone in ten minutes."

"They're your family," she said, and she gave me a gentle punch on the shoulder. "You have to forgive them."

I grumbled and pushed the door open. I could see Mum and Dad outside now, waiting for me. They had their heads bent together in conversation.

Their timing was terrible.

I grabbed my bag and called out a good-bye to Penny, then went outside to meet them.

"Lauren!" Mum exclaimed, and folded me into a tentative hug. "You've lost weight. Have you been eating? What did you do to your eyebrows?"

Dad gave me a kiss, mouthed the word *sorry*.

"You really should have called first," I said.

"Oh, we won't be any trouble," Mum said. "We're staying at a B and B, just here for a night or two until we get things sorted out. Is there somewhere we can sit and talk? Your flat?"

"I'm meeting someone in ten minutes. Up there." I pointed to the viewing platform.

"Ten minutes isn't enough. Is it that boyfriend of yours? Can't you call him and tell him—"

"Lauren has plans," said Dad, interrupting her for perhaps the first time in his life. "If she's willing to give us ten minutes, then that's where we'll start."

"Come on," I said, leading the way up the path.

Mum and Dad sat on the long wooden seat, but I stood with my back on the railing. I checked my watch, wondering if this was a very bad idea, if I should have just sent them back to their B and B and told them I'd talk to them tomorrow.

"Go on," Dad said to Mum.

"Well," Mum said. The afternoon sun caught deep lines around her eyes. Were they new? "Well," she said again, "Lauren. I understand you're angry . . ."

I waited.

"But I want you to know that it was a choice we made . . . well, a choice I made and your father agreed to . . . because we thought Adam would get the best care at home with us and—"

"He was in love, Mum."

"He was too young to be in love. He was just experimenting. That's what we thought. And it would have been the same if he'd thought himself in love with a girl."

I wanted to believe her.

"In any case, it was the wrong thing to do, but we had bigger fish to fry. Our boy had a terminal illness. We made a bad decision, and we're sorry. Really sorry."

"You're saying sorry to the wrong person," I said. "You should be saying sorry to Anton."

Dad interjected, "Maybe you can pass on our apology."

"Maybe you can tell him in person," I said, pointing down towards the end of the road. "Because that's who I'm supposed to be meeting now, and he's right there."

Anton saw us together and hesitated. I knew that this would be hard for him. It might even undermine our newly formed friendship. But this wasn't my business anymore.

Dad stood, squared his shoulders. "I'd be happy to talk to him," he said softly. "I'm not afraid to admit I wronged him terribly."

Mum's mouth turned down, like a child trying not to cry. I felt a pang of pity for her. It was her past coming back to haunt her.

"Talk to him," I said gently. "I'll be waiting by the café."

I walked back towards the hotel. When I turned around, Mum, Dad, and Anton were leaning on the railing together, talking, the slanting sunshine on their backs. Watching Mum from this distance, I thought about how effectively she had commanded every one of us, and it seemed ridiculous. She was barely five feet tall, a little lady with a big bust and a bad perm. I couldn't hear what they were saying, but Mum was talking and Anton was listening. I didn't know how it would end, but if she apologized, and if he accepted her apology, they might be able to make a start.

Mum and Dad came for dinner at my place afterwards. Dad was full of admiration for Anton and his quiet dignity. Mum was more guarded, telling me she didn't want to talk about it. We ate pizza and tried to keep the conversation light, but then Mum came in with her killer blow.

"This place is very small," she said.

"It's big enough for me."

"We've kept your bedroom exactly the same." She smiled. "It's about time you came home, isn't it?"

"Home?" I looked over her head at Dad, who gave me a meaningful stare.

"It's been months now," she said. "I could use your company. I miss you."

I wiped my greasy pizza fingers on a napkin then gently took her hand. "Mum," I said. "I'm not coming home."

She pouted. "Why not?"

"Because," I said, "I'm moving to Denmark."

"Are you all right?"

Lizzie nodded. She hadn't spoken more than half-a-dozen words since Tomas had picked us up that morning to drop us at the train station. Now we were clattering through the suburbs of Sydney, and she was looking distinctly pale.

"You don't have to do this, you know," I said, but I didn't mean it, and she probably knew it. It had taken me weeks to set up this meeting between her and Terri-Anne Dewhurst. Terri-Anne, for her part, was more than keen.

"She's my mother's cousin!" she'd exclaimed. "She's Honeychurch-Black flesh and blood. We will welcome her with open arms. I'll come up there, or if that's too overwhelming for her, I can meet her in Sydney."

But Lizzie had bristled with misgivings. "He wasn't my father. Clive Betts was my father. He raised me. That's what a father does." The letters Sam had sent to Violet were too much for her to bear. They undid the dream of her own past in which her mother and father had loved each other madly. Young love, first love.

"I *do* have to do this," Lizzie said to me now, as the train rocked along. "She's come all this way."

"Just from Goulburn."

"Still." Then she said, "She'd better not think to make me part of her family. I have my own family."

"She just wants to meet you." I pulled the sketch of Violet from my carry bag and handed it to Lizzie.

"What?" she said.

"Go on. Unroll it."

She did, smoothing it out on her lap.

"Your father. Clive. He drew that."

"Somebody else wrote that," she said, stabbing at the *My Violet* at the top of the page.

"Yes, but Sam didn't draw it. Look at it. Really look at it. You can see the love in every line. And her eyes. They're so vulnerable. I think you can tell she loved him, too."

"She didn't carve *Dad's* initials into that rock you found."

"No, but I told you, she scribbled those initials out. Maybe she had a silly, girlish crush on Samuel Honeychurch-Black. But when she found herself in trouble, it was your father she turned to. The man who raised you and loved you as his own, and never let on that you weren't."

Lizzie studied the drawing for a long time. Her eyes grew teary. "I wish I knew what happened."

"We do know what happened. We know that Violet left the Evergreen Spa and went on to have a fulfilling life. Went on to have you. Went on to have a loving relationship with your dad." I tucked her arm under mine. "Come on, Lizzie. Smile."

"I'm too old for this, Lauren. Secret paternity and steamy old love letters. I just want to go back to believing that my mother and father married because they loved each other, that I was planned, wanted . . ." She shook her head. "A normal family."

"I don't think there's any such thing. You know that."

The train slid into the station.

"Ready?" I said.

"As I'll ever be."

I pointed out the window. "Look, there's Terri-Anne. She's brought some people with her."

"I'm not good with names," Lizzie said, sounding very old all of a sudden.

"Just smile and relax. I'm here."

We stepped out of the carriage and onto the platform together, where Lizzie's new family were waiting to welcome the cousin they'd never met.

EPILOGUE

1927

Violet opens her eyes. Sleep recedes. Last night's wonders return to her memory. She smiles and rolls onto her side. There she is: tiny and pink and wrapped tightly in a white knitted blanket, sleeping peacefully in the crib next to Violet's hospital bed. Violet reaches for her daughter, born just hours ago, and touches her sweet, soft hair.

A shadow at the door. She looks up. Clive stands there. He looks happy but uncertain, vulnerable.

"I didn't wake you, did I?" he asks.

"No. I'm too excited to sleep for long."

He pulls up a chair next to her and takes his hand in hers. "That was the most amazing thing I've ever seen," he says.

"Why didn't you leave when they told you to?"

"Because it's not every day a man gets to see his child born."

His child. Violet's eyes well. "You don't mind, do you? That it's Sam's baby."

Clive brings her hand to his mouth and kisses it gently. "This isn't Sam's baby," he says, slowly, definitively. "This is *our* baby. I will love her and cherish her and give her everything I can: my time, my money, my body, my soul. We're a family, Violet. And I love you so passionately."

Passionately. Once she had thought the word described something different. Something fast and hot, like lightning. Now, she realizes, passion is a deep well, ancient and fathomless. It rises slowly, like the tide, but when it does it is mighty and unyielding, and it causes things to happen in the world. Real passion is not content simply to dream. It endures. Clive loves her passionately—a passion that grows day after day and is evident in every word, every caress.

She gazes at his dear face and lets her tears fall. "I have been a fool in my life," she says.

"We are all fools from time to time. You might be a fool again: Who knows? I'll stay with you nonetheless."

"And I'll stay with you," she swears, pressing her hand across her heart. "You are the right one."

"The right one?"

"It isn't always obvious at the start," she says.

The tiny girl wakes, then lets go of an equally tiny cry. Clive scoops her out of the crib, and she quietens immediately. He holds her in his arms, gazing down with wonder written on his face. "As long as I live, I will love you, little dear," he says to the baby, to his daughter. "And when I'm dead, I'll become a star, and I'll love you from heaven."

Violet watches him, and her heart is at peace.

ACKNOWLEDGMENTS

As always, I rely on the goodwill and support of many others while writing a novel. I would like to particularly acknowledge Selwa Anthony, Brian Dennis, Vanessa Radnidge, Heather Gammage, Paula Ellery, and my colleagues at the University of Queensland. I wrote a good portion of this book while staying with Bill and Maria at Whispering Pines Hotel, near Wentworth Falls, and thank them especially. Special mention must be made of my family, who are now well used to me ignoring their needs while I write. Luka, Astrid, Ollie, Mum, and Ian: I love you with all my heart.

Finally, even though she's no longer with us, I thank my grandmother, Stella Vera Spencer, for her lively and detailed memoir, which inspired so many aspects of this book.

ABOUT THE AUTHOR

Kimberley was born in London and her family moved back to Australia when she was three years old. She grew up in Queensland, where she currently lives.

Kimberley has written for as long as she can remember and she is proud to write in many genres. She is an award-winning writer in children's, historical, and speculative fiction under her birth name, Kim Wilkins. She adopted the pen name Kimberley Freeman for her commercial women's fiction novels, *Duet*, *Gold Dust*, *Wildflower Hill*, *Lighthouse Bay*, and *Ember Island*, to honor her maternal grandmother and to try to capture the spirit of the page-turning novels she has always loved to read. Kim has an honors degree, a master's degree, and a PhD from the University of Queensland, where she is also a senior lecturer.

Find out more about Kimberley and her writing by visiting her Web site and Facebook page or by following her on Twitter:

kimberleyfreeman.com
facebook.com/KimberleyFreemanAuthor
twitter.com/KimberleyTweets

EVERGREEN
FALLS

After the tragic death of her older brother, Lauren Beck decides to move from her family home in Tasmania to Evergreen Falls in the Blue Mountains—a place her brother cherished as the site of his last happy memory. In her new life, Lauren begins a relationship with the architect in charge of the refurbishment of the Evergreen Spa Hotel, and together the two discover evidence of a secret love affair from 1926 in the old hotel. In Lauren's quest to piece together the narrative of the star-crossed lovers from long ago, she also uncovers family secrets of her own and begins to understand that love, while not always easy, will always triumph in the end.

DISCUSSION QUESTIONS

1. When Lauren discovers that Tomas has inadvertently left behind his key for the west wing of the hotel—the wing no one has been in for decades—she decides to let herself in, and in so doing, uncovers Sam's letters to Violet. What do you think prompts Lauren to do something so bold, so uncharacteristic? Does this show of bravery hint at the Lauren we come to know by the end of the novel?

2. In many ways, Violet Armstrong is the foil character for Lauren Beck. Discuss the differences between the two women. Ultimately, does one character become more like the other? Which character changes the most as the novel unfolds?

3. Many of the characters in the novel are bound by a sense of duty. As Flora explains on page 51, "since the moment [Sam] had come into the world, Flora had been compelled to look after him—both by her parents, who had little time for children, and by her own heart, which loved him immeasurably and fearfully." Discuss this obligation to others, and consider what it is that motivates each character. Is it love, as Flora says? Consider Flora, Lauren, Clive, and Tomas in your response.

4. When Flora admits to Tony that, had she not been born into her family and position, she would have liked to have been a doctor, Tony laughs and tells Flora she is "being ridiculous" (p. 116). Are Flora and Sam as trapped in their class position as Violet and Clive? Do you think that any of the characters are happy with their lot in life? Why or why not?

5. Why do you think it was so important to Violet to carve Sam's initials into the rock by Lovers Cave? What significance does the permanence of his name in stone have for her? Does it become an epitaph of sorts after Sam's overdose?

6. Discuss the location of the story, both in 1926 and 2014. How does the setting of the Evergreen Spa Hotel influence decisions the characters make? What is it about this location that helps people fall in love and confront tragedy?

7. The character of Miss Zander is based on a real woman who managed a hotel where Kimberley Freeman's grandmother worked in the 1920s. How does her characterization match or differ from your understanding of social attitudes during that time? How does she compare with the other women in the novel? Consider the moment she counsels Violet to live her own life: "Really, I get quite tired of the way girls get carried along on the wills of others so easily" (p. 262).

8. Consider the following description: "Even with the ballroom divided in half and the fire roaring in the grate, the cold seemed close, gathering in the corners of the room and up in the high ceiling" (p. 269). Does the onset of the winter storm parallel the downward spiral of any characters in the story? Is there anyone in the novel who has *not* been altered after the storm passes through?

9. Do you think Flora made the right decision about covering up Sam's death? Do you think she would have been able to financially support Violet and the baby had she not gone along with Tony's plan? Would you have made a similar decision in her place?

10. Revisit the moment Flora discovers Sam's cold body. Do you think deep down Flora is relieved that Sam is "free from the torment of his withdrawal at last" (p. 316)?

11. "Family secrets had such power" (p. 330), Lauren says, and she realizes that she doesn't want to live in denial any longer. Do you think that the weight of family secrets oppresses the characters in the novel? Are the ones who survive the ones who are able to overcome the weight of these secrets?

12. The opening scene in the Prologue gets repeated once Sam's body has been discovered on page 343. Rereading this scene a second time, what has changed? Do you find Tony's and Sweetie's responses to Flora and her deceased brother more callous on a second read? Why do you think the author chose to repeat this scene for us? Does it send a message about the characters?

13. Is the theme of the novel one of the horrors of love, or the triumph of love despite tragedy?

ENHANCE YOUR BOOK CLUB

1. The love between Sam and Violet is forbidden simply because they come from very different worlds. In 1926, it would have been difficult for Sam to have convinced his family that his love for Violet superseded social norms, although such unions were not altogether unheard of. Host a movie night with your book club and watch the popular PBS show *Downton Abbey*. Are the two worlds—the servants' and the Granthams'—so drastically different? As a group, discuss how the employees and the guests at the Evergreen Spa Hotel live lives similar to the characters in *Downton Abbey*. Does the love affair between Sam and Violet have a counterpart in the show?

2. Lauren's discovery of the love letters from 1926 sets in motion the unfolding of Sam and Violet's narrative and the love story between Lauren's brother, Adam, and Anton. The letters in some ways also released Lauren from the hold her mother has over her and allowed her the freedom to fall in love with Tomas. Look through old photographs and items that you have from your parents, grandparents, or even great-grandparents. What stories do these items tell? Have a "show-and-tell" night with your book club. Share the family items and discuss how they tell a story about the people you came from.

3. Sam's death was so tragic in part because it could have been avoided. Opiates still have a strong hold in the world today. Learn more about the effects of these drugs by watching the documentary *Raw Opium* (2010) with your book club. Afterward, discuss why you think Sam was so taken by this drug.

What void did it fill in his life? Do you think he would ever have been able to have a clean, meaningful life with Violet? Why or why not?

4. Author Kimberley Freeman has written other novels that move through time and place like *Evergreen Falls*. Read her previous book, *Ember Island*, with your book club. What do the two books tell you about Kimberley Freeman's prose style? Do the characters in *Ember Island* resemble the characters in *Evergreen Falls*?

A CONVERSATION WITH
KIMBERLEY FREEMAN

As with your last novel, *Ember Island*, you chose to set *Evergreen Falls* at two very different moments in history: 1926 and 2014. How do the two narratives speak to each other in *Evergreen Falls*? Do you think the present informs the past as much as the past informs the present?

I am endlessly fascinated by the idea that the past and the present are not quite so neatly separated as we might think, and that idea comes out time and again in my work. We are all influenced by what has gone before and pass those influences on down the line to our own children. And yes, I do believe that what we choose to think and do in the present can influence how our past is shaped as we talk about it in the future. *Evergreen Falls* was inspired by reading the memoir my grandmother wrote before she died twenty years ago. I had never read it before, but it had fifty very detailed pages about her time as a waitress in posh hotels in Sydney in the 1920s. I learned so much about my grandmother and gained an enormous respect for her and the difficulties she faced. It made me so proud to be her granddaughter, and it also helped me understand my own mother better.

The Examiner **wrote that "the complexities of character and female relationships make [*Ember Island*] very rich and emotional." Were any of the complex characters in *Evergreen Falls* inspired by people in your life?**

I love what Anthony Trollope said: of course he drew characters from life, but you'd "never recognize a pig in a sausage." Like most writers, I am a committed people watcher. I am interested by all kinds of people and their relationships, and I watch them and turn it over in my mind in a kind of detached way that I sometimes worry borders on sociopathic! But as I have said above, I drew a lot from my grandmother's memoir, and some of the characters are directly lifted from it, especially the guests at the hotel. The opera singer, the beauty queen, the brother and sister from the wealthy family. Violet is nothing like Grandma, though, or at least I hope not! One doesn't like to think about the grandparents having an opium-fueled sexy affair!

Tell us about the research that went into the making of this novel. Was it a lot or a little? Describe the project of this novel from conception to completion.

I wanted to set a book in the Blue Mountains, in a place where there was snow, because I had the idea of the hotel snowed in and bad stuff happening: kind of like *The Shining* but without the supernatural. As soon as I mentioned it to people, they started offering me research advice. The first piece of advice was from my agent here in Australia, Selwa Anthony, who suggested I look up the Hydro Majestic Hotel in the Blue Mountains, as it was an old hotel that was being renovated. I drove up the mountains and climbed over the hurricane fence and wandered around the beautiful old crumbling hotel for an hour. The view from the back fence out over the Megalong Valley was incredible, and I knew it hadn't changed for hundreds of years, that many other people had taken in that view before me and many more would in the future. It was incredibly inspiring.

Then when I mentioned the story to my mother, she told me firmly that I needed to read Grandma's memoir, and determinedly unpacked an old box and found a thick wad of typewritten pages. Grandma had worked as a waitress at the Wentworth—Sydney's finest hotel—in the 1920s. The memoir was full of the kind of information I simply wouldn't have gotten anywhere else: the dresses, the dance parties, the attitudes. All of it in such rich language and detail. Every dress Grandma describes in the memoir—hers and the guests'—made it into the manuscript. I had a research assistant to help me with other bits and pieces, but Grandma's memoir was a gift, and I wrote the book very quickly.

I always plot the novels out in advance, which saves a lot of time and allows me to plan for the key turning points. When I wrote the prologue, I already knew it would appear in the novel about two-thirds of the way through, so in a way I was writing toward that terrible scene from the start. It gives the plot such momentum if you know exactly where you're going. But as I do in all my books, I try to give the characters lots of problems to solve. It makes them grow and become more interesting.

Do you agree that a theme of the novel is the burden—and freedom—of love? If not, what would you name as a major theme of the novel?

Yes, it is definitely about the burden and freedom of love. How love makes us responsible for each other in a way, which is perfect, because we do all need each other. But that love with the right person means they take responsibility for you in some ways, too, letting you be free to become all that you can be.

Is *Evergreen Falls* a commentary on social class and position?

Everything I write is! I grew up very poor. My dad was on welfare: he was a drinker, and we never had anything. Even in these days where we aren't supposed to have a class system, I see social inequality everywhere. I suppose I'll never grow out of it.

Who is your favorite character in *Evergreen Falls* and why?

I love Flora because she tries so hard to do the right thing. She's the person who is often overlooked because she's not beautiful nor charming, but she is the person whose heart is true and whose mind is strong. I would like to be more like Flora. I have a horrible feeling I'm more like Violet: a bit flighty and vain.

Do you think any of the characters live happily ever after? Specifically, do Flora and Violet overcome their grief over Sam's death? Is that even possible?

I do think it's possible. I mentioned my father's alcoholism earlier, and he died from it while he was still only in his forties. I adored him, and he was gone by the time I was twenty. But I overcame it and have gone on to live a wonderful life despite his negative influences. Substance abuse really is an awful thing, and there's a sense that when you love somebody who is addicted to something, you always know you will lose them eventually, so you keep a little bit of steel in your heart. It's like Neil Young said, "Every junkie is like a setting sun."

In my mind, Violet and Clive had a good life, and Flora and her doctor were blissfully happy.

There is much overlap in the fear about Adam and his illness and the fear that Sam will never stop smoking opium. Does this type of craft decision imply something bigger about human nature, about our fears of letting people be who they need to be?

I think it's more about how that responsibility to those we love, which I cited earlier, doesn't guarantee us anything. We can't keep people safe just by loving them. In a way, to love somebody is to always fear losing them. This story dramatizes that a little more keenly than most of us have to feel.

Can you tell us anything about your next project?

I am writing a novel (nearly finished) set in the 1950s. It starts in a girls boarding school when a new girl arrives who is wild and fierce and brilliant, and she turns lives upside down. She and her two friends do something terrible, which they have to spend the rest of their lives atoning for. I LOVE it.

What advice do you have for aspiring young writers?

Read a lot, then write a lot, then read and write some more. Writing is like mining: nobody breaks the surface and finds gold. There's a lot of dross that has to be gotten out of the way first.

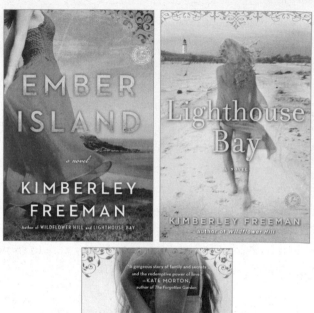